MISS RUFFLES
INHERITS
EVERYTHING

Nancy Martin

St. Martin's Paperbacks

This is a work of fiction. All of the characters, organizations, and events portrayed in this novel are either products of the author's imagination or are used fictitiously.

MISS RUFFLES INHERITS EVERYTHING

Copyright © 2015 by Nancy Martin.

For information address St. Martin's Press, 175 Fifth Avenue, New York, NY 10010.

ISBN: 978-1-250-09655-5

Our books may be purchased in bulk for promotional, educational, or business use. Please contact your local bookseller or the Macmillan Corporate and Premium Sales Department at 1-800-221-7945, ext. 5442, or by e-mail at MacmillanSpecialMarkets@macmillan.com.

Printed in the United States of America

Minotaur hardcover edition / November 2015
St. Martin's Paperbacks edition / September 2016

St. Martin's Paperbacks are published by St. Martin's Press, 175 Fifth Avenue, New York, NY 10010.

10 9 8 7 6 5 4 3 2 1

MISS RUFFLES
INHERITS
EVERYTHING

ALSO BY NANCY MARTIN

Roxy Abruzzo Mysteries

Sticky Fingers

Foxy Roxy

Blackbird Sisters Mysteries

A Little Night Murder

Little Black Book of Murder

No Way to Kill a Lady

Murder Melts in Your Mouth

A Crazy Little Thing Called Death

Have Your Cake and Kill Him Too

Cross Your Heart and Hope to Die

Some Like It Lethal

Dead Girls Don't Wear Diamonds

How to Murder a Millionaire

For Edith Ellen Christopher, Texas born

ACKNOWLEDGMENTS

With many grateful thanks to scientists Kerry Kilburn and Lila Shaara for timely scientific input. To Deborah Coonts, my Texas friend with a writer's keen eye for details. To Tom Christopher, whose book *In Seach of Lost Roses* inspired me years before we became part of the same family. To Deb Dunton, for her double duty as Browning Road's Critter Control and our Madame President. Also to Ramona Long, Meredith Mileti, Kathy Miller Haines, Nicole Peeler, Barbara Aikman, and Cassie Martin Christopher. Couldn't have done it without you! Meg Ruley and Christina Hogrebe are the best in the biz and I'm glad they've got my back. And the Minotaur team—I love you all! Special thanks to Kelley Ragland, Elizabeth Lacks, and India Cooper.

CHAPTER ONE

You may all go to hell, and I will go to Texas.
—DAVID CROCKETT

When I first arrived in the town of Mule Stop, Texas, I developed a theory that Texans are always polite to each other because they figure everybody else is packing a gun. The checkout girl at the Tejas grocery store proudly told me she was descended from Bonnie Parker and carried a replica of the same .38 revolver Bonnie used in her shootout alongside Clyde Barrow—a fact the young lady disclosed at the same moment she handed me a brochure for the Cowboy Church, her place of worship, which was located at a former drive-in theater. Parishioners were invited to bring folding chairs if they didn't want to sit on their horses or tailgates for the worship service.

I felt as if I'd landed from another planet. I still do. Texas has that effect on people.

Honeybelle Hensley's memorial did not take place at the Cowboy Church, but rather at First Methodist, where the leading citizens of Mule Stop came early and packed the pews shoulder to shoulder to send the famously rich Honeybelle off to the Promised Land. When I hauled open the creaky oak door at the back of the sanctuary, every man and woman suddenly craned around with one thought in mind—that maybe it was all a big mistake and Honeybelle was showing up for her own funeral. They probably hoped she might drive that white Lexus convertible of hers right up the steps, tossing rose petals in her wake—or maybe silver dollars. Yes, big, shiny Texas silver dollars were more Honeybelle's style.

But it was only me. Me, Ohio-born Sunny McKillip, hopelessly out of place, holding a rhinestone leash with Miss Ruffles at the end of it.

The sight of Miss Ruffles triggered a collective gasp.

At my side, Miss Ruffles growled deep in her throat. Softly at first, then with growing menace. Her body vibrated with barely suppressed rage. I knew what she was saying— that no puffed-up garden club lady in a hat from Dillard's Easter collection was going to stop her from attending the service of the woman she loved more than anybody.

Posie Hensley marched up the aisle toward us, hat hiding her furrowed brow, but we held our ground.

Posie stopped short and in a hissed whisper, said, "You better not be here to make fools of us with that dog."

"Miss Ruffles belongs here as much as anybody else." My Yankee voice carried farther than I expected in the church, so I lowered it fast. "Maybe more."

Posie blocked our way. She was Honeybelle's very own daughter-in-law, an ex–Miss Texas finalist, thin as a lizard and just about as appealing. Even her peplum skirt had the look of a scorpion's tail.

The whole congregation held their breath and leaned closer to hear her response.

She frowned and considered her social standing. Posie stood the biggest chance of stepping into Honeybelle's role as beloved community leader and power broker—a despot with a drawl who made councilmen tremble—but only if she inherited Honeybelle's considerable charm as well as her money. Aware that several hundred people could hear, she finally uttered the immortal words used in just about any tricky situation south of the Mason-Dixon.

With a sugary tone, she said to me, "Well, bless your heart."

To those seated in the pews, she probably sounded like she was trying to stop a crazy northerner from making a fool of herself. And maybe she was right. The accompanying look in her eye made me think she'd rather boot me out the door and down the steps—with the dog, too.

If she could, Miss Ruffles would have rolled her eyes at such fakery. Instead, she lunged with a ferocious bark that echoed to the rafters. I barely held her back with the leash. To save herself, Posie jumped out of our way.

According to the American Kennel Club committee currently appraising the breed's pending application, Miss Ruffles was a Texas cattle cur—a small but powerful dog with the speed and temperament for driving cows over a cliff, if need be. She stood about knee high, with a tough, brindle gray coat that bristled over her compact body. At one end, her tail was an ugly stub; at the other, her muzzle narrowed to a foxy point. The wide space between her pricked ears—one was floppy, the other constantly erect— made room for a quick, cunning brain. At home in Honeybelle's mansion, she didn't match the Chinese porcelain or the silk-upholstered furniture. In fact, she was often caught chewing the chairs. But Miss Ruffles had a habit of grinning when she panted, and her intelligent eyes conveyed more personality than most people. She liked to have fun, and she didn't care who she annoyed to get it.

Out in the church parking lot, the marching band of the University of the Alamo struck up the first stirring bars of the school's fight song. In farewell to the university's biggest donor, they blared their music loud enough to rattle the church's stained glass windows. To the blasts of their rousing tune, Miss Ruffles yanked me down the center

aisle with the momentum of a marauding rhino. She
headed straight for the only seats left in the whole church—
in the front pew.

No bride could have drawn as much attention as Miss
Ruffles did. No casket carried by a platoon of pallbearers
could have instilled more feelings of doom, either. She had
recently bitten the president of the University of the Alamo, and the whole town knew it. The VIPs sitting on
either side of us visibly edged out of range of Miss Ruffles's
teeth. The garden club ladies—all wearing pastel ensem-
bles with matching yellow corsages—were careful not to
meet the dog's malevolent eye. Their men, in summer suits
with bolo ties and hand-tooled cowboy boots, held still as
terrified deer until we passed them by.

Halfway down the aisle, Miss Ruffles almost wrenched
my arm out of its socket. She dragged me over to a line of
big men squished together with their hats in their hands
and smelling strongly of hickory smoke. They were the
proprietors of Bum Steer Barbecue, Honeybelle's favorite
lunch to serve on football game day. They sat still and
frightened as Miss Ruffles gave them all a thorough sniffing before catching wind of the men sitting across the
aisle—the pitmasters of Low 'N' Slow, the competing barbecue joint that had been the choice of Honeybelle's late
husband, "Hut" Hensley. The pitmasters nervously eyed
Miss Ruffles, so I tugged her away before she decided to
sink her teeth into an innocent someone's brisket-dripped
boots.

Then Miss Ruffles caught sight of the easel at the front
of the sanctuary. She stopped growling and dragged me
forward until we stood before an enlarged, smiling photo
of Honeybelle placed beside an Egyptian-style urn containing her ashes. The display was surrounded by enough
flowers for a royal wedding.

For a long moment, Miss Ruffles stared up at the photo.

Then she snuffled the bottom of the urn as if trying to recognize something of Honeybelle in her remains. I maintained a death grip on the leash—afraid she might seize the urn in her jaws and make a run for it. But she gazed up at Honeybelle's likeness again, still and contemplative.

In the photo, Honeybelle smiled down on us with her distinctively beautiful twinkle. In life, she had been a woman to be noticed, to be passionately loved, to be reckoned with wherever she went. Probably dressed for an afternoon football game, she wore a cocked white Stetson with a yellow satin ribbon hatband, big white pearls, and diamond earrings the size of pinto beans. A corsage of yellow roses bristled on the lapel of her St. John suit. Her coquettishly raised eyebrow assured us all that she had successfully sashayed through the Pearly Gates and was sitting pretty, ready for her champagne cocktail. I was sure she was already holding court in heaven alongside Robert E. Lee, Clark Gable, and Dale Earnhardt. And probably Elvis, too.

I had arrived in Texas several months earlier to become the administrative assistant to the new dean of the local college. I was floored when he was suddenly fired—for falsifying his professional vita—and it just so happened I desperately needed a job at the same time Honeybelle decided she desperately needed a personal secretary. We shook hands on it, and the job morphed into a variety of duties until the next thing I knew I was really a personal secretary to Honeybelle's dog. Honeybelle rarely went anywhere without Miss Ruffles, so one of my tasks was to bring both the dog and Honeybelle's official presidential notebooks to the garden club's annual election meeting in the church's social annex. Which meant I was present at the showdown that broke her spirit.

And maybe killed her.

During the election portion of the meeting, Posie

Hensley—yes, the very same daughter-in-law who appointed herself bouncer at the memorial service—stood up to make her pitch to become president of the club. Nobody took her bid for office seriously until in a clear voice she made a campaign promise to abolish the annual Lady Bird Johnson Bluebonnet Festival.

The club members sucked in a collective breath of shock at such a suggestion. Honeybelle had been sitting on the dais with her ankles neatly crossed and an expression that said her mind was confidently elsewhere, but at that moment, her face froze. Everybody knew the former first lady was Honeybelle's idol. (Lady Bird came first. The late governor Ann Richards was a close second.) For decades Honeybelle had organized a festival in Lady Bird's honor, railroading the whole club into creating bluebonnet centerpieces, giving away bluebonnet nosegays on a downtown street corner in the blazing heat, and showcasing Honeybelle herself in a bluebonnet aromatherapy workshop, public welcome.

After the moment of horrified silence that greeted Posie's proposal, an epic squabble broke out. The longtime club members were Honeybelle's loyal friends, but the younger generation wanted an end to Honeybelle's era of tyranny.

"We want to keep Lady Bird's memory alive!"

"With all this drought, we can hardly allot precious water to wild flowers."

"The bluebonnet *is* Texas!"

Posie raised her voice to be heard above the hubbub. "Of course there's nothing *wrong* with bluebonnets, and we *all* love Lady Bird more than pecan pie. But it's time for a more environmentally friendly event. We should be encouraging our friends and neighbors to plant more ecological gardens instead of old-fashioned flowers that are a waste of water."

"A waste of water!" Honeybelle cried.

"It's not your fault, Honeybelle." Posie hastily tried to cover her unfortunate choice of words. "You've never set foot outside of Texas, so you don't know these things. The world has changed. It's time we all planted succulents and were more responsible about water."

"The bluebonnet is a native plant! Since when does a prickly old cactus look nicer than a pretty bluebonnet?"

The conflict raged for an hour. On the refreshment table, ice in the pitchers of sweet tea melted and the lemon shortbread cookies grew stale, as ladies who had been friends from the cradle or dated each other's brothers or sons insulted each other. Stormy tears were shed, and plenty of shameful abuse hurled. Posie held her ground, though—a brave choice, because even a newcomer like me could see she stood to get herself blackballed if her effort failed.

Finally someone called for a vote, and Honeybelle just caved. She turned pale and sagged into her chair. Even her big blond hair seemed to deflate. For the first time since I'd met her, she looked her age. And while her friends waved smelling salts under Honeybelle's nose, Posie got herself elected president of the club by a narrow margin.

With the gavel in her hand, she settled the dispute with a bang that sounded like an auctioneer dropping the hammer on a final bid.

The Lady Bird Johnson Bluebonnet Festival was canceled.

Honeybelle wavered to her feet. She had recently taken a fall and hurt her knee, and she wobbled on the cane that she had previously used more like a prop than a walking aid. "If you don't have any respect for Lady Bird, it's clear you have no respect for me."

Tearfully, she resigned her membership and walked to the rear of the social hall with her head high and an embroidered lace hankie pressed to her nose. At the door, she paused and looked back as if expecting her friends to follow.

But nobody moved. After all, without the garden club, some of those ladies had no social lives whatsoever—no reason to pull on pantyhose or powder their cheeks except for church and Wednesday night Bible study.

As her sob echoed in the room behind her, Honeybelle made her solitary exit. When she hobbled out of sight, Miss Ruffles let out a howl that shook everyone in the room. Then Miss Ruffles bolted after Honeybelle, me scrambling on the end of her leash as if keelhauled behind a powerboat.

A week later Honeybelle's private nurse, Shelby Ann— who had been hired to help after a previous tripping incident and stayed on for another year—insisted a dejected Honeybelle keep her Friday appointment with Estelle, her longtime beauty operator at the Ambiance Salon. Afterward, Shelby Ann left Honeybelle sitting on the front seat of her Lexus convertible so her hair wouldn't get mussed in the wind while Shelby Ann ran into Pinto's Pharmacy to fill a prescription. When she came back to the car, Shelby Ann said, she found Honeybelle slumped over her handbag, dead and gone. Miss Ruffles was chewing on the leather steering wheel, although Shelby Ann claimed the dog had been trying to blow the horn to call for help.

Shelby Ann, who had been an army nurse before she started working for Honeybelle, checked Honeybelle's pulse, then got behind the wheel and drove the body directly over to Gamble's funeral home, no muss, no fuss.

The news of Honeybelle's sudden death shook the whole town. The university dimmed its lights in sorrow. The town council voted to celebrate Honeybelle Hensley Week as soon as April rolled around. To relieve their guilt for sending Honeybelle to her early grave, the garden club members slapped together a special memorial service for a few days after the family's private funeral. There was a serendipitous opening in the church schedule on Saturday at First United Methodist—before Jessie Lee Markland's wedding to a nice medical resident from Houston—so the club grabbed it. They also planned a light luncheon for afterward, when the members intended to announce a scholarship in Honeybelle's name and to serve Honeybelle's recipe for lime and crushed pineapple congealed salad one last time.

Because my own mother's funeral still felt like an anvil in my heart, I had been glad not to be invited to the family funeral. But then Miss Ruffles stopped eating. After a first burst of enraged energy in which she chewed up the mail and left the bits for me to clean up, she did nothing but mope. The gleam in her gaze turned dull. I couldn't tempt her to chase a ball. Before my eyes, she began slowly fading away.

Before Honeybelle's death, Miss Ruffles had patrolled the house and property to protect Honeybelle from invaders. She traumatized the UPS man, lay in wait for the mailman. In perhaps her most important role, however, Miss Ruffles stood guard against Honeybelle's many gentlemen callers. From the moment potential suitors rang the doorbell at cocktail hour, Miss Ruffles growled and sniffed and bared her teeth and otherwise warned off any overeager man who showed his face. Some never made it up the front steps. Being permitted to step over the threshold was a major milestone for the brave men who came courting the widow Hensley.

Now that Honeybelle was gone, though, Miss Ruffles was bereft. In the morning, she crept downstairs to crouch dejectedly for hours under Honeybelle's desk. I was watching the indefatigable Miss Ruffles pine away. So off we went to the memorial service—probably my last act as personal assistant to Miss Ruffles.

As we stood at the front of the church in front of Honeybelle's urn, Miss Ruffles said her final, silent good-bye. Honeybelle's son, Hut Junior, cleared his throat to get my attention. Sternly, he pointed at the empty end of the front pew to tell us to sit.

Hut Junior was a well-fed Texan in a snug summerweight suit. He looked every inch the new CEO of Hensley Oil and Gas, his mother's lucrative company and now, after her death, presumably his. His boots were shined, his face closely shaved, his crew cut newly trimmed. He bore little resemblance to his vivacious mother, but a lot to his father and Honeybelle's much-loved husband, the late, great college football coach Hut Hensley, who was buried in a massive tomb on the university campus. Hut Junior's bulldog face rarely cracked a smile, not even at his wife as Posie slipped past Miss Ruffles and plunked down beside her husband. She wrapped her arm around his, either staking her claim to the richest man in the church or hanging onto the person who might save her if Miss Ruffles went on a rampage.

The glare Posie sent me could have warned off a rattlesnake.

Their sixteen-year-old son, Trey, slouched on the pew with his nose in a cell phone game. His cowboy hat was tilted down to show a Junior Rodeo patch instead of his face.

Ten-year-old Travis Joe perched on Hut Junior's lap, wearing a bow tie and bouncing as if he'd skipped his morning Ritalin. At the sight of Miss Ruffles, though, Travis Joe let out a cry of dread and tried to climb to the higher safety of his father's shoulder.

With some of her old spunk, Miss Ruffles turned and fastened a hard, predatory stare on the boy.

"Sit down, Miss McKillip," Hut Junior said to me over the band's music as he attempted to subdue his squirming son. "But if that animal becomes a nuisance—"

"I'll take her out, I promise."

Meaning something else, Trey muttered under his breath, "I'll take her out."

Posie slapped her son's arm. "Hush, Trey. Honeybelle loved that dog. Show some respect for your grandmother."

Trey heaved an intolerant sigh.

I tugged the leash, and for once Miss Ruffles obeyed me. I eased down onto the pew, and Miss Ruffles flopped down on the cool floor at my feet, still glaring at Travis Joe.

Miss Ruffles and I both knew there wasn't any use trying to endear ourselves to Hut Junior. I figured he planned on sending me on the first bus back to Chagrin Falls as soon as the service ended. And I'd overheard what fate he had planned for Miss Ruffles.

I had accidentally eavesdropped while scrubbing one of Miss Ruffles's mistakes out of the rug on the second-floor landing when he and Posie came like a couple of carpetbaggers to Honeybelle's mansion two days after her death.

"Can you believe it?" he'd said to his wife while she stretched a tape measure on the marble checkerboard floor at the bottom of the graceful curved staircase. "Mama's nursemaid, Shelby Ann, declined to come to the memorial service because she's already on a world cruise! There's a reason half the town called her Moneybelle. Mama overpaid everybody."

Posie made a noise of agreement. "She's been taking care of that crazy voodoo cook of hers for ages, and that ancient butler, too. They should have been sent away years ago."

"And I can only imagine what salary she gave the glorified dog walker."

Posie shushed her husband and told him to hold the other end of the tape measure. "We have to make sure my grandmother's rug fits here. If it doesn't, we're going to take it to Dallas to get trimmed right away, because I want it here for my baby sister's wedding."

Hut didn't remark upon the wedding, which I knew had been a big bone of contention in the family. Posie wanted her sister's lavish nuptials to be held in Honeybelle's beautiful rose garden and had pushed hard for it. But at the time of her death Honeybelle still refused to give permission. With Honeybelle out of the way, though, I supposed Posie intended to throw a big society wingding, after all.

Sounding strained, Hut Junior said, "We don't have to move in here right away, do we?"

"Why not?" After a pregnant silence, she said, "Oh, sugarpie, don't get all weepy again."

He blew a honk into his hankie. "I have a hard time thinking about her being gone, that's all."

"I know, I know. But your mama has been hiding your light under a bushel for too many years. You're gonna be the big boss now. And you deserve this house. Besides, after her wedding, my sister's going to need a home, and I promised she could have ours. Don't you want to live here? You can smoke all the cigars you want on the terrace, and the boys will love the pool. And the rosebushes! At last I'll get to enjoy the roses. We'll make the place even more beautiful than it is already, you'll see."

Hut didn't respond to that. After a moment, he said more quietly, "If we're going out of town for a rug, we should take that dern dog with us. I hate that dog. We could drop it off at a pound somewhere."

"Get rid of it?"

"Do you want to be the one to start walking that wild animal? She's dangerous. Not to mention obnoxious and . . . and . . . you know it's the reason my mama kept falling. I ought to have insisted she get rid of it a year ago."

"Oh, Hut, don't get upset. Honeybelle loved you more than Miss Ruffles." Posie dropped her voice, too. "I hoped maybe she hired the dogsitter so she'd have more time for you and her grandchildren. Now we'll never know, will we?"

The dogsitter. She meant me.

The prememorial band music came to a climactic close. Reverend Jones appeared like a magician through the hidden door behind the church's altar. Miss Ruffles lifted her nose and gave a growl. The reverend had visited Honeybelle's house regularly, and Miss Ruffles loved to torment him. She nipped at his shoes until he danced on Honeybelle's fine rug. Seeing him appear so suddenly in the church, she sat up and barked. The sound must have carried the length and breadth of the sanctuary, because another frisson of silence passed over the congregation. I grasped her collar, but she fought me—eager to get free and dash up onto the altar to get herself a bite of the reverend's tasty socks. About to speak, Reverend Jones hesitated as if stayed by the cautious hand of God.

Hut Junior and Posie froze me with identical glares.

"I'll take Miss Ruffles outside," I whispered.

"Yes, you've made your point." Posie fanned herself with the memorial program.

Suddenly I didn't care that we were going to miss the service. I could see the trip to the church had already served its purpose. Miss Ruffles looked her old self again, full of vinegar and eager to make trouble. She had said goodbye to Honeybelle and was ready to rumble.

So we made a dash for freedom—not the way we'd come in, but by the side door that put us out on the parking lot side of the church.

As we stepped outside, a whole crowd of people looked up at us from where they hung around their vehicles—pickup trucks and dusty cars that had clearly come from the outlying cotton farms. There were no fancy ladies in department store hats here, no distinguished town leaders.

These were Mule Stop people who had come to pay their respects to Honeybelle but hadn't found places for themselves in the church.

At the sight of Miss Ruffles, the men removed their hats. A few ladies took out their hankies. One couple stepped forward. The woman bent down to pat Miss Ruffles.

The man held his hat to his chest and said to me in a strong voice, "Miss Honeybelle loaned me seven hundred dollars back when we needed it bad. She drove it out to our place in her convertible and pretended like she owed me poker winnings so our kids didn't know the truth. She didn't have to do that, but it saved our family, got us back on our feet. She was a real lady. We're gonna miss her."

His wife said, "We can't believe she's dead. Not our Honeybelle."

"Maybe half the town wanted to bump her off," the man went on. "Her being so bossy and all. But the rest of us loved her."

A quiet line formed behind him, and one by one the silent mourners came forward. A lump rose in my throat as the people came closer to see Miss Ruffles, who never moved a muscle as they touched her. Here were people who had loved Honeybelle, and Miss Ruffles knew it.

As they said their good-byes, I found myself remembering something Honeybelle joked about one afternoon when I helped her balance her personal checkbook.

Flipping through a few ragged checks that had come in the mail, she said to me in her sweetest drawl, "If I die under suspicious circumstances, Sunny, please go to my funeral and decide who among my so-called friends likely killed me. Nobody likes repaying debts, do they? And they hate me for loaning money to them in the first place. So go to my funeral. Take Miss Ruffles with you. See if she can sniff out a murderer."

I had remembered her words the day I heard she died. And I hadn't been able to get them out of my head. The people who lined up to pat Miss Ruffles seemed very grateful indeed. But maybe Honeybelle had been right. Maybe someone had wanted to murder her.

★ ★ ★

CHAPTER TWO

I'm southern. I like big hair and eyeliner.
—CARRIE UNDERWOOD

My mother, who prided herself on being a solid research scientist, always said, "Believe nothing until it can be verified."

It didn't take the psychology professor I once worked for to see that after the loss of my mother, I had probably set out to find another strong, charismatic woman to take her place. Maybe this time someone who didn't run off to distant jungles to study dying insects when I could have used some help writing book reports or choosing a prom dress. Or figuring out what to do with my life.

Not that my mother was a drag. She was a hippie chick, a sometime college professor who studied butterflies and believed in field experience over classrooms. She got me into college courses with no particular goal in mind—whatever interested me at the time—and she didn't care about my grades. She was too busy chasing butterflies in foreign countries. The most diplomatic way of describing her parenting philosophy was benign neglect. She could hack a trail through a jungle or look great on a bar stool to talk someone into donating money for a new expedition. My friends liked her sense of humor. Men liked her off-handed sexuality. She wasn't the motherly type, and eventually I realized the butterflies needed her help more than I did.

As for my father, she never thought it was necessary for me to know who he was. Maybe she wasn't sure herself.

Each summer when she went to save butterflies, I was sent to live with her parents on their dairy farm. But my grandparents tended to look at me as if I were some kind of exotic specimen my mother brought home from an expedition, so I never stayed long. I was happier on a college campus. As an adjunct, my mother wasn't terribly well paid, and it became my job to keep her finances and her academic life on track. I smoothed her frequent dust-ups with whatever dean objected to her travels and organized her scientific data on computer files. It was the kind of work that made me valuable to other professors. So one job came easily after another.

Before she went off to one of the last butterfly mating grounds in Mexico, I had handed her some clean socks to stuff into her duffel. My mother took them with thanks and then looked at me as if suddenly waking up to a research factoid she'd missed. She said, "Nature is strange and wonderful, kiddo. There's something out there for you. Why don't you go find it?"

It stung—her perspective that I didn't have a life.

A month later, a person from the State Department found me to say she'd been killed falling off a cliff while chasing a butterfly—hardly a big finish for someone always in search of adventure.

Honeybelle died with an equal lack of fanfare. But for me, her death felt as if my mom had tumbled off her cliff all over again. It was hard for me to accept they were both gone—both larger-than-life women who should have had more impact on the world before they left it.

After the last humble citizen of Mule Stop said

good-bye to Honeybelle with a pat for her dog outside the
church, Miss Ruffles jumped against my leg. She looked
up at me, eyes perky again, her stub of a tail suddenly
wagging. The next moment, she took off down the steps.

She knew her way home, and she pulled me down Sam
Houston Boulevard, the town's main drag, which ran all
the way east to the interstate and west to where the old rail
station and stockyards used to be, bisecting the college
campus in the middle. The University of the Alamo was a
noisy college that gave an otherwise sleepy town most of
its energy. Students tended to major in agriculture or en-
gineering for the oil industry. Or sports broadcasting,
sports management, or sports medicine. Football provided
the heart of the school.

We passed by the public library, where a kind librarian
often took her smoke break to look after Miss Ruffles
while I checked out books. At a trot, Miss Ruffles led
me past Gamble's funeral home, the stately bank where
Honeybelle served as a director, and the first of many college bars.

The corner was taken up by the Boots 'N' Buckles Em-
porium, which advertised Tony Lama cowboy boots, Stetson hats, fancy belt buckles, and saddle repair. Honeybelle
had often stopped in to ask Joe, the elderly proprietor, to
polish her boots. Barefoot while he made her boots
shine, she tried on hats and teased him. He treated her
like a queen. I remembered his check being among those
from townspeople Honeybelle loaned money to, and I
hoped he could afford to remain in business now that she
was gone.

Everywhere I looked there were things that would never
be the same without Honeybelle—not just the businesses
she patronized, or the small shops she'd financed. She had
recently won a campaign for new street signs and flowers
in window boxes, and triumphed in a fierce battle against

litter and graffiti. Thanks to Honeybelle, Mule Stop looked pretty enough for its own postcard. Not a bad legacy, but not as good as seeing Honeybelle herself motoring down the main street, waving from her convertible as if she owned the whole town.

Gracie Garcia came out of Cowgirl Redux, the clothing resale shop, and grabbed my elbow.

"Is the memorial service over already? Or did they throw you out of church? Or—Lord have mercy, Miss Ruffles didn't bite anybody, did she?"

Gracie was the first person my own age I'd befriended when I came to Mule Stop. It had only taken a couple of days for me to realize my Ohio clothes weren't suited to the searing Texas sun and heat, and Gracie had been a big help.

"You might as well wear a big ol' Yankee sign around your neck," she had said pityingly when I first ventured to the door of her colorful shop. "What are you wearing? Darlin', come inside and we'll find you something real pretty. And bless your heart, you're not wearing near enough makeup."

Today I hauled on the leash to prevent Miss Ruffles from trying to sniff the crotch of Gracie's snug capri slacks. Gracie wore enough mascara to blind a whole cheerleading squad, and her long, glossy black hair curled fetchingly around her plump bare shoulders. She had come to Mule Stop to follow a "no account" boyfriend enrolled at Alamo, but when he dropped out to work on a gulf oil rig, she had stayed and made a place for herself. She ran the resale shop on weekends, and during the week she had a real job as a paralegal in a law office to keep up on her bills.

I said to her, "Nobody threw us out of the memorial service. We said our good-bye to Honeybelle, and that was it. But I think Miss Ruffles really knew what was happening in there. Look, already she's getting her energy back."

Miss Ruffles proved my point by trying to untie the ribbons on Gracie's espadrilles.

Gracie side-stepped to stay out range of the dog's teeth. "Well, I'm glad nobody pitched a fit. Miss Ruffles belonged there just as much as that family of Honeybelle's."

"The family was on relatively good behavior."

"I hear Hut Junior's real broken up. All good southern boys love their mamas, of course. Or else use them for target practice. But what about Posie? Did she throw her hat in the air and dance a jig to celebrate her mother-in-law's passing?"

"Posie wasn't happy—mostly about seeing Miss Ruffles in the church."

"Everybody knows Miss Ruffles bit President Cornfelter. But didn't she take a bite out of Posie's oldest boy once, too, right?"

"Just nipped him," I said quickly. "Tried to herd him into the swimming pool. She wasn't the only one who thought he needed a dunking."

Miss Ruffles continued skittering around Gracie for attention and finally let out a frustrated yip. Laughing, Gracie bent down and took the dog's head in her hands. They gave each other enthusiastic kisses. "You sweet puppy! No wonder Honeybelle loved you so much. Why, you're just cuter than a possum!"

Miss Ruffles panted happily, and I found myself smiling at last. "Already she's cheering up. The memorial service really helped."

"Dogs are sensitive creatures." Gracie gave the dog a pat on her ribs, then straightened to study me through narrowed eyes. "How about you? You still look poorly."

"I'll be okay." I couldn't quite articulate how sad I felt about Honeybelle's passing. Maybe I should have stayed at the memorial service to hear some noble words spoken on her behalf. I still felt swamped by emotion, but seeing

Miss Ruffles cavorting around us improved my spirits. I said, "It made us both feel better to say good-bye. And there were scores of people waiting outside the church. They were all so kind. It was touching to see them."

"Honeybelle did a lot of good things for people. I'm glad some of the grateful ones paid their respects. The rest of 'em are as common as pig tracks for not showing up."

"One thing surprised me. A man said half the town wanted to bump her off."

Gracie grinned. "Why does that surprise you?"

"Because she did so much good."

Gracie had an unladylike snort. "She also had this town by its . . . well, its private parts. Not much business got done here in Mule Stop without Honeybelle's approval. And Hensley Oil and Gas? Employs a lot of people—and she wasn't shy about firing anybody who didn't give her a hard day's work."

"You really think Honeybelle had enemies?"

"Sure as shootin'," Gracie replied.

I was still stewing over Honeybelle's request that I be on the lookout for someone who might have wanted to kill her. She'd been joking at the time, but her words rang in my ears.

I said, "One of Honeybelle's grandsons seemed very upset that she's gone."

"The younger one? Yeah, I heard he was sick when he was a baby. Story goes, Honeybelle read him books every day in the hospital. That was real nice, and they bonded. Not that her daughter-in-law would notice."

"They were always a little cool with each other," I said cautiously.

Gracie had no qualms about gossiping. "I reckon Posie resented how Honeybelle wouldn't let Hut Junior take over the oil company. I mean, he's forty, if he's a day, right? Why he didn't just buy himself a bass boat and go fishing for the rest of his life, I'll never know. So tell me. What did the memorial look like? Did they have some pictures of Honeybelle around?"

"Yes, a big photo. And lots of flowers, of course."

"It's a terrible shame they cremated her. I mean, she just had her hair done! She'd have looked real pretty in a casket."

I couldn't come up with a response to that one.

Gracie must have seen me turn pale. "You want to come in out of the sun and cool off? I got a couple of Coronas in the cooler. Just the thing on a hot day like this."

"No, thanks. They're reading Honeybelle's will at the house this afternoon. It's some kind of party. I need to get back to help out with the refreshments."

"Knowing that family, they'll be splitting her assets while they drink her champagne." Gracie enveloped me in a hug—all bosom and perfume. "Don't get yourself too upset, okay, Sunny? You go on taking care of Miss Ruffles the best you can, for as long as you can. That's what would make Honeybelle happy."

"Thanks, Gracie."

"Swing by for a drink tonight. I close up at seven. We can give Honeybelle our own send-off."

"A farewell party for me, too?"

Gracie gave me a comforting pat. "Tonight we'll brainstorm some ideas for a new job for you. I don't want you to leave town. Maybe we'll meet some cute guys, too. I have my eye on one of the bartenders." She waggled her eyebrows. "You might find somebody worth sticking around for."

I made no promises. I didn't feel like celebrating the loss of a second job in just a few months, and although I'd be needing a paycheck, it felt too soon to start hunting up a new position. Gracie gave me another hug anyway and let herself back into Cowgirl Redux. I usually made friends easily, but the thing about growing up on a college campus is that friends tend to last only four years before moving on. I had hoped Gracie might last longer.

Miss Ruffles jumped at my leg and growled with some of her old pizzazz. She spun in a quick circle and pulled me to get going again.

"Okay, okay, I'm coming," I said to her.

Ahead on the corner of Jim Bowie Avenue, another local character stood in front of an open banjo case, hammering out a tune, eyes closed, communing with her music. Behind her leaned a ratty old backpack stuffed with belongings—a sign I took to mean she was homeless. A few kindhearted souls had dropped crumpled bills into her case. I'd heard someone call her Crazy Mary. Today she wore a dusty, flamboyant Mexican skirt along with a couple of layers of T-shirts and wraparound sunglasses. Her hair was a mess of dirty blond dreadlocks. She ignored the bustle of people around her, seeming to be immersed in her music.

Miss Ruffles darted close and snatched a dollar bill out of the instrument case.

"Miss Ruffles!" I wrestled it out of her mouth and dropped the bill back where it belonged. The musician never stopped playing. I double-wrapped the leash around my hand and pulled. "Let's go."

We had to get back to Honeybelle's for the reading of the will.

★ ★ ★

CHAPTER THREE

We don't dial 911 in Texas.
—PROVERBIAL WISDOM

With her nose tipped up to the wind, Miss Ruffles noticed before I did that the sleepy town of Mule Stop was unusually busy. Today the street was crowded with families, mostly, with children in tow, but students, too, and retirees.

"Here comes the parade!" A young mother tugged her daughter away from Crazy Mary. With ice cream cones in hand, they rushed to the curb and found a spot between other family groups.

Miss Ruffles forgot about licking drips of ice cream from the sidewalk and peered through legs as I peeked over the shoulders of the crowd in front of me to see what the commotion was. Sure enough, it was a parade. Miss Ruffles gave a yip and dragged me for a closer look.

In the lead came a rodeo queen—a smiling teenager in full makeup, riding a palomino and carrying an American flag like an Amazonian spear. Behind her, three men on horseback herded a dozen languid longhorns from the direction of the historic stockyard down toward the campus, probably to drink from the school's spectacular central water fountain. After that, I figured, the cows moseyed the mile back up the boulevard to the stockyard, where they spent the rest of the week eating and dozing and generally living the good life.

When the cows appeared, Miss Ruffles narrowed her eyes. She strained against the leash, and her body began to quiver with long-lost instinct. I held on tight in case she decided to charge into the herd.

The shoes of the horses rang on the asphalt as they moseyed along. The cowboys joked with each other and occasionally whistled or waved their ropes at the cows, although the placid cattle seemed to know the drill. Following the herd rumbled an authentic chuck wagon pulled by mules in harness. A big sign on the wagon advertised a rodeo next week. The driver wore clown makeup, a plaid shirt, red suspenders, and a mashed hat that looked as if it had been stomped by a bucking bull. He tossed candy to the children on the sidewalks and comically waved his elbows as if dancing to Crazy Mary's banjo music.

Before Miss Ruffles could decide to snatch up some candy for herself, I gave a soft whistle. "C'mon. We have to get home."

Miss Ruffles twisted and fought at the end of her leash, but reluctantly let herself be pulled along. Her fierce attention didn't waver from the cattle, though.

One of the cowboys reined his horse closer to the sidewalk. "Need a lift, little lady?"

He was smiling behind sunglasses and under the brim of a dusty black hat. I couldn't see his face except for a long jaw and a grin. He wore a faded pair of Levi's and a checkered shirt probably chosen to make the cattle drive look more authentic. He had a lariat in one hand, reins in the other, but seemed to communicate with the horse with his legs. His saddle looked well used, trimmed with silver medallions. The horse was a muscled Appaloosa that gave the dog an intelligent once-over without breaking stride.

"No, thanks." I kept moving. I was never called "little lady" except as an insult. Barefoot, I stood five ten.

"You look just about broiled."

I was hot, all right, and since coming to town, I seemed to have a perpetual sunburn, but I said, "I'm fine."

"You know why this town is called Mule Stop, right?" he said. "It's a place so hot all the mules died. I'd hate to see you roast to death, too."

I always figured a town had popped up in this particular sun-baked bit of Texas because a wagon wheel broke and some sensible woman declared she wasn't traveling another mile. But his story made sense, too.

Being compared to a mule didn't sound very flattering, though, so I said, "Hit the trail, Roy Rogers."

"Boy, you know how to hurt a guy's feelings. Roy Rogers hung up his spurs a long time ago."

"He knew how to take a hint."

The cowboy didn't get offended but nudged his horse to keep up with us. "How about you, Miss Ruffles? Care to jump up here?" He patted the horn of his saddle.

I slowed on the sidewalk. "How do you know who Miss Ruffles is?"

"Everybody knows Miss Ruffles. She's kind of the town mascot. Tough. Maybe ornery, too. But lovable once you get to know her. Just like Mule Stop. And you're the one takes her running through town every morning."

"You get up early if you see us running."

"You know what they say about the early bird," the cowboy said.

Despite his friendly tone, my radar switched on. Miss Ruffles was my responsibility now that Honeybelle was gone. "We're late," I said to the cowboy, tugging the leash. "And I don't want her getting kicked by a cow."

"That dog knows more about cattle than both of us put

together. Turn her loose." He waved his rope to indicate the cows. "Let's see what she can do."

Miss Ruffles was rarin' to go. With her growl rumbling in the deepness of her chest, she told those slow-moving cattle her low opinion of them.

"Sorry." I used all my body weight to hold her back. "We've got places to be."

"Okay, then. See you around. Come to the rodeo next week, maybe."

"Maybe not," I replied, and he laughed.

I dragged the dog to the corner and turned onto John Wayne Avenue. The cowboy waved good-bye and went back to his cows.

With a resigned sigh, Miss Ruffles stopping fighting the leash and obeyed me. She patrolled alertly for ne'er-do-wells from then on, finally pouncing on a cricket and eating it in one gulp. Half a block later, she choked it up again. She barked at the corpse.

Next she tried to pull me toward the university campus. I knew she had often gone there with Honeybelle to put flowers on the grave of Coach Hut, but today I tugged the dog toward home.

According to Honeybelle, a tornado had blown half of Mule Stop off the map twenty years ago, so most of the residents lived in low, cozy ranch houses that were relatively new. Miss Ruffles took the opportunity to pee on the first yard we reached. Some lawns were grassy and had struggling trees or yucca plants. In other yards, I had been amused to discover, the dirt and weeds were spray-painted green for lack of water. The West Texas scrub was only a quarter mile away and seemed to threaten to take over the town as soon as the well water ran out. The constant breeze tasted gritty, full of dust.

Miss Ruffles perked up as we got closer to the oasis in

the desert that was Honeybelle's place. The air temperature dropped a couple of degrees as soon as we reached its shade trees. The house had tall white columns out front with a glassed-in conservatory on one side and a smaller wing on the other side for the spacious living room perfect for big parties. Half plantation house, half New Orleans–style mansion, it provided an elegant backdrop for the masses of rosebushes Honeybelle had collected. The only house with an underground watering system, Honeybelle's was a southern showplace surrounded by an English garden. In the backyard, a swimming pool shimmered in the middle of another spectacular flower show. The whole property was surrounded by a hedge that required constant trimming by a landscaping crew that turned up every week to manicure the yard.

In other words, the house was ideal for an extravagant wedding. So why hadn't Honeybelle wanted her family to throw one on her property? Had it all been because Honeybelle resented Posie's garden club takeover?

We headed around the side of the house to the garage and the back gate. There, I pulled the mail out of the mailbox and found a big envelope from a travel agency, addressed to Honeybelle. I looked at it, thinking maybe she'd been on the brink of taking a trip, finally. Too bad she never got out of Texas.

Once inside the backyard, I turned Miss Ruffles loose, and with some of her old vitality she made a dash for the terrace, where she drank water noisily from her dish, leaving a big wet splotch on the flagstones. Then she ran for the grassy spot where she'd left one of her tennis balls. For the first time since Honeybelle's death, Miss Ruffles snatched up the ball and raced back to me with it. Wagging her stub, she dropped the ball at my feet and yipped at me, eyes bright.

"This is a big improvement." I marveled at how the me-

morial service had made her feel better. "Did you pick out
a murderer?"

She tilted her head.

"You heard me. Do you think Honeybelle might have
been murdered?"

She yipped again, so I gave up on the question and
threw the ball. Maybe Honeybelle hadn't been serious.
But the man at the church had said that a lot of people
wanted to bump her off. I tried to put my suspicions down
to being a stranger who didn't understand the local ways.
In Texas, were the dead usually rushed off to the grave
as Honeybelle seemed to have been? That seemed weird.

My mother used to talk about the rules of scientific research, and I found many of her so-called rules applied to
life, too. She always said that just because something was
weird didn't mean it should be ruled out. Skepticism should
be paired with open-mindedness.

I decided to be open-minded about Honeybelle's death.

I got myself a cold cherry Popsicle from the fridge in
the outdoor kitchen, and I sucked on it while flinging the
ball for Miss Ruffles to chase.

We played until Mae Mae Bellefontaine came out of the
kitchen door with a spatula in one hand. Honeybelle's cook
was tight-lipped and frowning—as always. She kept her
gray hair raked back from her round face as if cranked by
a vise, and today was no different. Her other hand was
knotted in a fist and propped on her ample hip. Her apron
was starched and immaculate except for the words I'M
GRILLING A WITNESS! Mae Mae loved her cop shows on
television.

She said, "Is that animal ruining Honeybelle's roses?"

I slurped my Popsicle before a drip splotched my dress.
"The roses are in the front yard, Mae Mae. Miss Ruffles
doesn't go there."

"Hmph. Well, something's out here digging." She

pointed beyond the pool to the back of the yard. "Maybe we got prairie dogs back again."

"Prairie dogs?" I stared back into the rolling curves of the garden to catch a glimpse of such a rare beastie. So far, I had seen one armadillo dead along the highway, and a tarantula in a garbage can at a taco truck, but no prairie dogs.

"We had an infestation a couple of years ago. First just one, then two, then dozens. Why can't Miss Ruffles make herself useful and chase them off?" Mae Mae glared out into the yard. "If prairie dogs ruin Honeybelle's roses, she gonna turn over in her grave."

This was more conversation than I'd had with Mae Mae since my arrival. To keep her going, I pulled the Popsicle from my mouth and asked, "Roses aren't native to Texas, are they?"

Mae Mae refused to look at me when she spoke. "How do I know? Honeybelle got hers from abandoned farms and ranches, she said. They're old kinds of roses from Europe, I think, brought here by pioneers. But prairie dogs'll ruin them right quick. We'll have to get Critter Control to come."

I forgot about roses and started thinking about the animals. "Does Critter Control kill the prairie dogs?"

"No," Mae Mae snapped, "he traps them in a satin pillowcase and turns them loose in a hotel with featherbeds. What do you think he does with them? This is Texas, not New York Tree-hugger City."

I had stopped worrying about the way Mae Mae treated me. Maybe she disliked me because I came from Chagrin Falls, a place she'd never heard of, or just on general principle. Or had I done something unintentional that turned her against me?

She finally looked me up and down in a way that registered displeasure with the plain black dress I had worn to the church. "How was the memorial service? Did many people show up?"

"Too many to fit into First Methodist." I pasted a smile on my face and went up the porch steps to her. "And Miss Ruffles did just fine."

"You didn't take that dog to church?" Mae Mae was outraged. "I told you that was the wrong thing to do. Did she chew up anything? Make a mess? Frighten anyone?"

"She was perfect." Well, maybe not perfect, but good enough. I said, "Honeybelle would have liked to see her there. And Miss Ruffles needed some closure."

"Closure? Closure! What kind of fool Yankee idea is that?"

"She's been miserable without Honeybelle. I've tried playing with her to cheer her up, but that didn't work. My mother used to say that if you're studying something and not learning anything new, it's dumb to wait for change. You have to be the one to do the changing. So I took Miss Ruffles to church. And just look at her. Isn't she happier than she's been all week?"

Mae Mae refused to glance at the dog or remark upon my mother's scientific wisdom. "What did Hut Junior say? That poor boy has enough on his plate without you making things worse for him."

"He gave me a seat. Miss Ruffles, too."

At the sound of her name, Miss Ruffles charged nimbly onto the porch and dashed around us, stub wagging, eyes lively.

Mae Mae glared at Miss Ruffles. "Honeybelle never took that animal into church, so why should anybody start now?"

"Well, I did, and no harm done." I was determined not to get into another argument with Mae Mae. I tossed the last of my Popsicle to the dog, and she gulped it in one happy swallow. "What can I do to help you?"

"I don't need no help today," Mae Mae shot back. "When Mr. Hut Junior and his family get here, you just keep that dog away from Miss Posie. I'll be serving punch and sweet tea and some of Honeybelle's favorites before they read her will."

"That sounds nice."

"These are my last refreshments for the Hensleys, and I want to honor Honeybelle's good taste." If her lips trembled for an instant at the imminent loss of her longtime job, she quickly pressed them together to avoid showing me any emotion. "So everything's already ready. Except you forgot to get my silver trays down from the shelf."

"Did I?" I had no memory of being asked, but I followed Mae Mae into the kitchen.

My height made me useful to Mae Mae and Mr. Carver, Honeybelle's butler. They were both elderly and had difficulty reaching high shelves. Not to mention carrying heavy objects. And setting the new security system at night, reading fine print, and working anything electronic. So I often stepped in without being asked. I had sensed they both disapproved of Honeybelle hiring me in the first place. Or maybe they suspected—correctly—that Honeybelle had asked me not just to provide secretarial help and to look after Miss Ruffles but to surreptitiously pitch in around the house. She knew her staff was too old to be doing all the manual labor in her home, but she didn't want to hurt their feelings by bringing in a spry twenty-something to do their jobs.

I agreed to keep her secret.

"These trays?" I asked from the top step of the pantry ladder. Around me, the glass-fronted cupboards glittered with Honeybelle's fine china and glassware. Her silver candlesticks gleamed. Her Waterford crystal sparkled.

"Hand 'em all down to me," Mae Mae said. "I'll go through and pick out the pretty ones."

"I can pick pretty." I held up a large, glinting tray. "What about this one with the engraved flowers?"

"Those aren't just flowers! They're bluebonnets." Again Mae Mae's face tightened again to stop herself from showing emotion. I wondered if she was as heartsick as I was about losing Honeybelle. But she snapped, "Don't you know anything about Texas yet?"

Mr. Carver poked his head into the pantry and peered at us through the round bifocals that magnified his wide, hound-dog eyes to comic proportions. A small man, he looked up the ladder at me and said, "Oh, you're back, Miss McKillip. Making yourself useful, I see."

Pursing her mouth again, Mae Mae gathered the bluebonnet tray to her bosom and marched back into the kitchen. She let the door swing closed behind her.

Softly, I said, "I upset her. She's very sad about Honeybelle, isn't she?"

"Don't pay her no mind," Mr. Carver said on one of his morose sighs. "She's just worried about what she's going to do after losing this job. She's too old to stand all day flipping hamburgers." He had a soft Memphis drawl I had learned to discern from the Texas twang.

Mr. Carver had been my first guide to southern behavior. He'd taught me to say "ma'am" when I spoke to Honeybelle, and that if I answered the door in his absence I should make the guest feel welcome by asking about the weather on their side of town, and when or how hard to shake someone's hand. I was still confused about the complicated handshaking rules when it came to ladies; I was learning, though, and I had Mr. Carver to thank for many lessons.

I climbed down from the ladder. "I feel sorry for her."

"Well, for heaven's sake, don't tell her that or she'll slap you upside the head." Mr. Carver took off his eyeglasses and pulled a white handkerchief from his pocket to polish an invisible speck of dust from the lenses. "She's been with Honeybelle ever since Katrina, you know. When the hurricane destroyed her home, Mae Mae ended up here, and Honeybelle took her in. Never made Mae Mae feel like a refugee, though. Treated her with respect. Oh, they had their disagreements—you know Honeybelle didn't like spicy food much—but Mae Mae was Honeybelle's friend more than an employee."

"You were with Honeybelle even longer."

"Forty-one years," he said promptly. "I had an offer to go work for the governor, but I turned it down. I wanted to finish my career with the family. But . . ."

He began to heave deep breaths, so I said, "Sit down a minute, Mr. Carver."

He used the handkerchief to dab his forehead. "I'm perfectly well. Just . . . every time I think of Miss Honeybelle, I feel . . ."

"I know." I patted him on the shoulder.

He mustered a pathetic excuse for a smile. "She was born in a saloon, did she ever tell you that?"

"No. No, she didn't."

"Well, that's what her mother told me. Her mother was out shopping and didn't feel well and stepped into a bar to call an ambulance, and—that's what happened." He sniffled and took another long breath, finally saying, "We had a disagreement, you know, the morning Honeybelle left us."

"Yes," I said.

Hut Junior had come for breakfast the morning of her death, and I'd overheard them arguing. Hut had stormed out of the house after their fight, and then I'd heard Honeybelle squabbling with Mr. Carver behind closed doors—very unusual. I hadn't overheard the specifics of their discussion, but I had seen Honeybelle afterward and knew that she had been uncharacteristically furious with her longtime butler.

I said, "You shouldn't be upset about that anymore."

Sadly, Carver said, "She didn't want to host that family wedding. I said we'd be happy to do the work, but she didn't want to hear it. She was . . . stubborn."

"Honeybelle was a little petty sometimes, too," I suggested. "She was still mad about the garden club."

Mr. Carver sniffed. "Justifiably so."

"But she shouldn't have taken it out on you."

"We both said some harsh words. I surely regret that now."

Afraid he was going to faint, I caught him by the arm. "Look, if you sit on the rung of this ladder for a second, you could steady it enough for me to reach the silver coffee urn for Mae Mae. It's in a difficult spot, see? I'm afraid the ladder might tip if I stretch that far."

He obeyed me and sat.

I had no idea if Mae Mae wanted the urn or not, but lately I had learned to use any ruse to get Mr. Carver to rest when he got short of breath. He was moving much more slowly than he had when Honeybelle was around to keep him on his toes. Whether it was his sadness or his health that caused this change, I didn't know.

I climbed past him and feigned rearranging items on the top shelf as if to reach for the antique coffee urn. I looked down to see Mr. Carver touch the knob on the nearest door. He gazed dolefully at the glassware arranged behind the glass cabinet doors as if reminiscing. Honeybelle had relied on his steady if somewhat melancholy presence. Now, though, he looked very old.

I lugged the coffee urn down the ladder and plunked it onto the marble counter. "Anything else I can do?"

He stuffed his handkerchief back into his pocket and

got unsteadily to his feet, but efficiently checking his watch. "Everything's in order. I'll encourage the family to take their refreshments at the buffet, then sit in the living room for a few minutes until the lawyer summons them into the library."

"Is the lawyer here yet?"

Mr. Carver's frown returned. "About an hour ago, I had a call from Tennyson and Tennyson. Mr. Max has been called away on another case. I can't imagine what case could be more important than the estate of his most valued client, but there you have it. His son is on vacation, too—bad timing. So he's sending his new associate to break the news—that is, to inform the family."

I risked asking the question that we'd all be thinking. "What do you think Honeybelle's will is going to say?"

Mr. Carver let out a sigh. "No matter what it says, there will be shouting."

Yes, even with a large inheritance, Hut Junior and Posie would be unhappy. That was their nature. Mr. Carver and Mae Mae were another story. I suspected neither one of them could afford to retire. The longtime servants had assumed Honeybelle would support them until the end of their days. Now that Hut Junior and his wife were measuring the rooms for carpets, however, their hope seemed doomed.

Mae Mae stuck her head around the pantry door. "That dog is barking her head off in the backyard again. Go see what's got her riled up."

Mr. Carver snapped, "It's not in your job description to give Miss McKillip royal commands, Mae Mae."

But Mae Mae banged the door shut again without apology.

I patted Carver's arm. "Don't worry on my account."

I used the servants' side entrance just off the pantry and let myself out into the backyard. I heard Miss Ruffles barking somewhere beyond the lush shrubbery. I whistled for her, but she didn't come to me. The pitch of her barking changed, sounding an alarm. I took off running across the lawn.

★ ★ ★

CHAPTER FOUR

If you're not God or George Strait, take your boots off.
—TEXAS WELCOME SIGN

I ran across the lawn and past the umbrella tables by the pool, hung a left turn at the long swath of grass, and followed the sound of her barking. At the back gate, Miss Ruffles had her nose pointed at the driveway, and she barked through the bars of the wrought-iron gate. She bounced on all four feet as if to levitate herself over the gate to the driveway.

"What's going on?" I asked her. "Is it trouble? Or just the mailman?"

Every hair on her neck and shoulders bristled like a porcupine's quills.

Tied to the tree on the other side of the gate was the big Appaloosa I'd seen in the parade. His head was down, nose snuffling the flowers under the tree. He had already cocked one hoof to relax. The lanky cowboy was loosening the saddle girth.

"Hey again, little lady," he said.

"Quiet, Miss Ruffles!"

The cowboy opened his saddlebag and pulled out a khaki sport coat—none too well pressed. He gave it a slap as if to shake off trail dust and put it on, still wearing his cowboy hat and sunglasses. He said, "We haven't been introduced yet. You're Sunny, the dogsitter. Your name suits you. You're sunburnt." He took off his dark sunglasses and tucked them into the breast pocket of his sport coat. "I'm Ten Tennyson, Max's grandson. How do you like Texas so far?"

"What makes you think I'm not from Texas to begin with?"

He laughed. "I see you go running past my office in the mornings. Nobody from Texas goes running outside—nobody from West Texas, that is."

To answer his question, I said, "So far, I think Texas is its own country."

"Experienced anthropologists say the same thing. You look different without your shorts and sneakers. Still nice, but different."

I looked down at my secondhand dress, bought at Gracie's resale shop. Compared to the Texas girls with their big hair and lavish makeup, I probably looked like a duck among the swans—dark ponytail, flat-chested, and of course sunburned. "Have you been spying on me?"

"It's not spying when you run straight through town. What's wrong with your mouth?"

Automatically, I swiped the back of my hand across my lips. "I had a Popsicle. Cherry. Would you . . . ? I can get you one."

"No, thank you, ma'am. Cherry looks better on you than me. Anyway, like most Texans, I'm partial to orange."

Miss Ruffles continued to bark and do her little dance of protective outrage. Come to think of it, this display was the first time she'd felt the need to defend somebody other than Honeybelle. I bent down to soothe her. She wagged her stub at me and jumped up to lick my nose.

When I straightened, rubbing the wet from my nose, the cowboy grinned and put his hand across the gate for me to shake. He said, "I'm pleased to meet you."

I found my hand warmly clasped in his calloused one. I looked up into a lean, outdoorsy face with a narrow, crooked nose and light gray eyes with sunburned crinkles around the edges. He had broad shoulders and a lean, whippy body.

I said, "You're Tennyson and Tennyson."

"Soon to be Tennyson, Tennyson, and one more Tennyson." He released my hand. "The third one's me—that is, if I passed the Texas bar. The results aren't in yet. Anyway, Gramps and Dad chickened out today. They hightailed it out of town and left me to deliver the bad news to the Hensleys. They said if I can handle this, I don't have to buy into the family practice."

"Is it going to be bad news?"

"For some. What do you think? Should we ask Carver to confiscate all shootin' irons at the door?" He reached into one of his coat pockets and pulled out a rumpled, narrow tie. He began lacing it around his shirt collar. "Just kidding. I don't foresee any gunplay. Hut Junior will be mad, but he'll swallow his medicine. Posie's the wild card. She was an Appleby, you know, before she married Hut Junior. Appleby girls are known for their tempers. Her sister Poppy, she's a couple years younger than Posie. They're both easy on the eyes, but unpredictable." His grin said he liked unpredictable. "You know Poppy?"

"I'm not sure." I remembered the day Honeybelle invited several young ladies over to the house for a committee meeting. I happened to be in range when everyone arrived in a flurry of summer dresses and high heels. Most of them wore false eyelashes and talked as if they drank molasses by the spoonful. I added, "I'm below stairs."

His grin turned wry. "Honeybelle always liked that *Masterpiece Theatre* stuff. My mama loves it, too, but we never had help in the house like Honeybelle. I figure you're the governess—Jane Eyre, that's the one. I didn't get to meet you at Honeybelle's Fourth of July picnic this year—I was studying for the bar—but Gramps and Dad said you were real nice. Quiet, but smart as a whip. And tall."

I remembered the Tennysons—two lanky, joshing older men in cowboy hats and string ties. They flirted in a twinkly-eyed, gentlemanly way with me, but they had turned up the heat considerably with Honeybelle, who had flirted right back.

Ten Tennyson was high altitude himself. Maybe six three or four, I guessed, and leanly built, as if he could slip a basketball through any hoop without too much effort. Did they play basketball in Texas? He smiled at me while I absorbed his height. There's a thing about being tall that only tall people really understand. We shared a funny second of measuring each other.

Miss Ruffles ki-yi-yied and broke the moment. She began bouncing around us again.

Ten said, "You know how to fix a tie, Jane Eyre? With no mirror, I'm bound to make a mess of it."

"Sorry," I said to the talkative cowboy. "Ties are not part of my skill set."

He shrugged as he flipped up his shirt collar. "I'll have to manage. You think it's okay to leave Hondo here? He'll probably just take a nap while I go inside, but I don't want to upset Carver. I know he's got a delicate temperament."

"Mr. Carver is busy being upset about other things. Your horse is very handsome."

"I think so, too. I raised him from a colt. That was a while back. He still likes to get out of the barn to run cattle, though, even at his age, so I ride him on Saturdays for the parade."

"Why don't I get him a bucket of water?"

"Thank you kindly, but he just had a drink down at the stockyard. Don't trouble yourself." He finished up his tie, smoothed it on his chest, and then craned his head to assess his appearance. "How do I look?"

I thought about fibbing but remembered his remark about my running shorts. "You look like a lawyer who plays at being a cowboy on weekends."

"I used to be a cowboy full-time, but that can be rough work. I broke my leg and a few other things. So I went to law school while I healed, and look at me now." He spread his long arms wide. "My parents almost gave up on me becoming respectable, but I fooled 'em. How about you?"

Lightly, I said, "I never went to law school."

He gave me a look that acknowledged I was keeping my private business to myself. "What were you out to prove at Honeybelle's memorial service?"

"You were at the church?"

"Nope, I was fixin' to start the parade. News travels real fast in Mule Stop. Word is, you showed up loaded for bear, but ended up leaving without firing a shot."

"I wasn't going to shoot any bears. I just wanted Miss Ruffles to see Honeybelle one last time. To say good-bye. She's been very depressed. I thought she was going to pine herself to death."

He squinted at the dog zipping around us, and then at me. "Did it work?"

"Actually, I think it did."

We both looked down at Miss Ruffles. She danced around me like a dervish, spinning and yipping.

Ten said, "I'll bet you take good care of her." He reached again for his saddlebag and pulled out a polished leather portfolio, which he tucked under one arm. Suddenly he almost seemed like a respectable small-town lawyer, even though the smell of leather and sweaty horse clung to him around the edges.

I said, "You clean up pretty well."

With a grin, he opened the gate and let himself into the

backyard as if he knew his way around the place. Prudently, he didn't bend down to stroke the dog but looked down at her from a safe height. "Hello, Miss Ruffles. You gonna take a bite out of me like you did President Cornfelter?"

Miss Ruffles bowed, her stub up in the air, and she barked again as if daring him to play a game.

To the dog, I said, "Behave yourself."

She yipped at me, smiling with her tongue hanging out.

I said, "She doesn't really bite. She might give a nip to chase someone, but she doesn't hurt anybody."

"Except President Cornfelter."

"Well, yes, except for him. She drew blood that day. She's . . . she was protective of Honeybelle. But she's not vicious. And she's definitely better behaved when she gets some exercise."

Ten looked down at the dog but spoke to me. "So you run with her."

"It seems to help."

"Well, you've made some headway, I see. A few months ago, she'd have chewed my boots—or worse."

"She still chews boots if she gets a chance," I said.

"We'll be careful today. Come on inside. I have to talk to you and the others before the Hensleys get here."

"Why?"

He winked. "Come in and find out."

"Mae Mae and Mr. Carver are already worried about what's going to happen to them. You're not going to make things worse, are you?"

"Depends on your definition of worse. Are those the famous roses?" He pointed at a flower bed.

"No, the famous Honeybelle rose garden is out front. Those are foxgloves."

"I've heard a lot about the roses."

"They're in the front yard. Do you want a tour? I don't know all the varieties, but I can point out the ones Honeybelle thought were the most special."

"Maybe we'll do that later."

He was a man on a mission. Miss Ruffles ran circles around us as we crossed the yard and pool terrace.

On the back porch, Mae Mae opened the kitchen door with a startlingly big grin. "Mister Ten, look at you getting around like nothing ever happened!"

On our stroll across the backyard, I had noticed he had a little hitch in his walk, but he disguised it by turning it into a kind of swagger. He went up the steps nimbly enough and gave Mae Mae a noisy kiss on the cheek. He crowed, "Mae Mae Bellefontaine, best cook in Texas!"

Mae Mae grabbed his cheek with her thumb and forefinger and gave him a shake. "Still a flatterer."

'Yes, ma'am, but only when it's deserved." Ten smiled at me. "When Gramps came here to help Honeybelle through her husband's estate settlement, I tagged along. He always came at three o'clock for coffee and Mae Mae's beignets. I made a nuisance of myself."

"You were no trouble at all."

"That's what I wanted you to think," he shot back. "After I stuffed myself with beignets, I carved my initials on one of Honeybelle's trees."

She laughed. "If I'd known it was you coming today, I'da made beignets."

"I'm a last-minute substitution." Ten took her hand and tucked it into the crook of his arm as if she were a great lady. "Let's go set for a minute. Do you still keep a pot of hot coffee for yourself?"

"I never was the sweet tea type."

He laughed and held the door for us both. "Me neither." Before stepping inside, he glanced around the porch. "Where's your boot jack? I've been out at the barn."

"Those boots are clean enough for me, and I'm the one who washes the floors. You come right on inside."

Miss Ruffles dashed ahead of us, skittering on the linoleum. The kitchen was a throwback to the day when red-and-white checkerboard floors matched the calico curtains and the Aunt Jemima cookie jar on the counter. Recent upgrades were the new stainless appliances and spanking white marble countertops where Mae Mae rolled biscuit and pie dough. But an overlay of less tidy cooking habits gave the kitchen its personality. She kept pots of herbs on the sunny windowsill where I stored the vitamins for Miss Ruffles. Ropes of garlic and a basket of onions hung over the sink alongside a rosary. A special wooden spoon reserved for making roux held a place of honor in its own cup, and Mae Mae's black iron pot sat on the back of the stove at all times, ready at a moment's notice. She made gelatin salads in antique copper molds, but her new rice cooker had been the result of a long and detailed on-line search I'd helped with.

Today, Mae Mae had pretty tea sandwiches and cream puffs arranged on the silver trays. The food waited on the sideboard with plastic wrap on it, ready to be whisked to the buffet at a moment's notice.

Mae Mae pulled out a chair for Ten and bustled to pour him a cup of hot coffee. She swiped a cream puff from the tray and arranged it on a lunch plate with a sprig of mint she pinched from a pot on the windowsill. Proudly, she slid the plate and the cup in front of him.

Like a man accustomed to being waited on by indulgent women—after his remark about having no household help at home, I assumed he had a sweet-tempered mother—Ten sat, took off his hat, and set it on the table. Underneath it, his head was covered with a bristle of fair hair, crew cut. The back of his neck was suntanned, as if he spent more than his Saturdays on a horse.

I went into Honeybelle's private parlor and returned with the stack of mail that had arrived for her since her death. "I guess you're in charge of this now?"

He automatically stood up from the table at my return—the Texas gentleman—making me think he must have a very nice mother indeed. He said, "What is it?"

"Please, sit. Mostly bills. A few checks from people who owe her money."

Studying the top envelope, he sat back down. "Not Hensley Oil and Gas business?"

"No," I said, "that mail goes directly to her office. Over there, she had help from Hut Junior and someone else, a secretary, so I wasn't part of that. This was her private banking and household matters. She kept them separate."

"Good thinking. The Hensley secretary is Angela. I went to high school with her. I met with her already. She and Hut Junior have things under control at the office. But after today, you should send all the personal mail over to me." He flipped through the unopened envelopes to note the return addresses and found one that had been slit open. He showed it to me and raised his eyebrows.

"Honeybelle opened that the morning she died. It's a thank-you note from someone she sold a rosebush to. I put it back in the envelope."

"Honeybelle sold roses?"

"It wasn't a real business. Just something she did now and then. Look, the problem is that the day Honeybelle died, Miss Ruffles got into her office and chewed up some of her mail. There wasn't much left but little tiny pieces of paper. I think she ate some bills or letters or something." I was ashamed of myself for allowing that to happen. But when I'd first heard the news about Honeybelle, I'd been incapable of doing my job for a bit. "I know the electric bill was due to come soon."

Ten used one of the envelopes to tap my shoulder, a

strangely comforting gesture. "Whoever sent the bills will send them again, so don't worry about that. The electric company won't go out of business if Honeybelle's account is a little late."

"But if they were personal letters?"

"She's not here to read them anyway," he said kindly. "Don't let it worry you. Tell me. You helped Honeybelle with her personal finances?"

"I've only been here a couple of months, but yes. I balanced her checkbook once, helped her set up online banking to pay bills, went to the bank to make deposits, that kind of thing. She made small loans to people, and sometimes I delivered those checks. I was hired to be her personal secretary, so I kept her calendar, too, made appointments, took notes sometimes. Mostly, I was taking care of Miss Ruffles, though."

"And you did a fine job with that," Ten said. "Didn't she, Mae Mae?"

Mae Mae didn't answer for a second. "That dog hasn't been such a nuisance lately, no."

He grinned at me over that high praise and asked me to go find Mr. Carver.

The four of us were soon seated at the kitchen table with cups of scalding hot coffee in front of the other three and sweet tea for me. I still didn't understand the Texas preference for hot beverages when the thermometer hit 100. I wanted to grab a handful of ice cubes and tuck them in my bra.

Miss Ruffles frisked around us on the floor, paying particular attention to Ten and his boots. After giving her a swift, businesslike pat, he opened his leather portfolio and removed a sheaf of papers.

"Now, then," Ten said. He had polished off his cream puff and used his thumb to wipe a spot of whipped cream from his upper lip. "I can't seem to put my hand on any death certificate, but the directions in her estate file says the will is to be read a week after her death, so here I am. Before the family comes, I want to talk to y'all about some of Honeybelle's final wishes."

"Oh," said Mae Mae, and she put one hand to her bosom.

Mr. Carver looked more grave than ever. "How soon do we have to leave?"

I said, "Get it over with quick."

Ten shook his head. "Let's not get worked up, everybody. Honeybelle thought kindly of each of you, and she has provided for your futures."

Mae Mae let out a wavering sigh. "Praise the Lord."

"She's been real generous," Ten went on carefully, "but her largesse comes with strings attached. Strings, I'm sorry to say, that a lot of other people are not going to be happy about. Y'all are to receive pensions—considerable money that should ensure comfortable living for the rest of your lives. Miss McKillip, you're included because Honeybelle wanted you to be an important part of her plan."

"How considerable?" Mae Mae asked.

"What plan?" I asked, startled.

Ten said, "The three of you are to remain here at Honeybelle's house for the next year—"

"A year!" Mae Mae cried.

"At least," Ten continued steadily, "maybe longer, depending on what agreement can be reached about Miss Ruffles."

The three of us sat in confusion for a moment before Carver said, "What does Miss Ruffles have to do with anything?"

Having heard her name, the dog wriggled herself between my chair and Ten's. She sat and looked attentively from him to me and back again, head tipped alertly to one side as if to ask for more specifics.

Ten said, "Honeybelle wanted to be sure Miss Ruffles lived a good, long life, so she has tied your pensions to the dog's survival. You're to stay here in this house for one year, at which time you three and the family must reach an agreement about Miss Ruffles and her future. Only after that, when she has a suitably safe and comfortable long-term home where she's happy, will you receive your full pensions. It's your shared responsibility to look after Miss Ruffles now, just as Honeybelle would have done if she were alive."

"Hold your horses." Mae Mae's voice climbed to another scale. "You mean the dog inherits everything?"

"Well, not exactly—"

"Now it's my job to take care of that animal?"

"It's Miss McKillip's job to see to the dog's daily routine. You and Mr. Carver are to keep the house as you always have. Except instead of Honeybelle, you're maintaining the property for Miss Ruffles."

"So she does inherit everything!"

Ten continued as if she hadn't interrupted. "Someone from our office will stop by every week to make sure everything's up to snuff. The house, the yard, the pool—"

"I won't do it!" Mae Mae burst out. "Nobody can force me to stay here and work for a dog! Surely I get something if I pack my suitcase and leave right now?"

"Yes, indeed," Ten said. "You can walk out the door this afternoon, Mae Mae, and I'll write you a check for fifty thousand dollars—the amount Honeybelle listed right here in her will. It's a generous sum."

"But," Mr. Carver said hesitantly, "if we stay for a year? And find Miss Ruffles a good home? How much do we get?"

"If Miss Ruffles is happily settled after a year, you'll get a million dollars each."

"A . . . ?" I was sure I'd heard wrong. Mae Mae's mouth opened, but nothing came out. Mr. Carver looked as if he'd been struck by lightning.

"For the year, you'll continue to receive your current salary, and you'll be allowed to live here in this house as you always have. After a year, you get a million dollars. Each."

Nobody breathed. A million dollars. A *million*.

I was glad to be sitting down. My insides were doing the same thing they had when I was a child and my mother roughly pushed me off onto a jungle zip line. Flying weightless over a bottomless chasm, I was terrified—clutching the harness and panic-stricken to be so alone and out of control, but strangely, wildly ecstatic by the time I landed.

Mr. Carver gave a funny little squeak, and with one glance at his slack face I knew he was ill. I found myself on my feet and gently pressing his head down to his knees. "Steady there, Mr. Carver." I knelt beside him and patted his back. "You okay?"

"A million. A million dollars," he wheezed.

Ten stood up to help me steady Mr. Carver in his chair. In a moment, the old man struggled up, looking stunned. Ten sat back down, but kept a wary eye on Mr. Carver.

We all stayed like that while the news sank in. Mae Mae was breathing like a locomotive. For once, she wasn't angry, just flabbergasted. We had all known Honeybelle was rich. But we hadn't realized exactly how rich until that moment.

Mr. Carver swayed dizzily his chair. And I stayed on the floor so I wouldn't have so far to go if I fell over from the shock.

The stillness was broken by Miss Ruffles herself. She scampered across the kitchen and came back to me. She dropped something on the floor and yipped. Her face was covered with flour, and I saw she had managed to open a cupboard again. It had been one of her favorite tricks while Honeybelle was alive—stealing things from kitchen cupboards. The package on the floor in front of me was a bag of semisweet chocolate chips. She yipped again, then sat down, wagging her stub and smiling as if she'd been in on the joke all along.

With sudden concern for Miss Ruffles, Mr. Carver cried, "Chocolate's poison for dogs! Sunny, grab that away from her!"

Miss Ruffles had already surrendered the chocolate, but I picked it up anyway. "You're going to make this as hard as possible," I said to her, "aren't you?"

Miss Ruffles gave me a panting smile. Her eyes sparkled as if she approved of what Honeybelle had in mind for us. To her, it was all one big, fun shenanigan.

To Ten, I said, "You said something about the death certificate? It's missing?"

"I don't think it's missing. I'm just not experienced enough to find it yet."

"When you find it, will that change anything?"

"Not a thing. Y'all take care of Miss Ruffles, y'all get a million dollars each."

"I don't have to do this," Mae Mae said flatly. "I don't have to look after no dog, no sir. I'll take my share this minute, Ten. You can write me that check right now." She slapped her hand on the table as if she expected the money to materialize on the spot.

"Yes, ma'am. No problem," Ten replied easily. "But a million dollars is a lot to walk away from. If you stick around, you won't have to make any more fancy lunches and tea parties for Honeybelle. Just make your own meals and keep the place tidy. Take it easy for a year, and you'll be a rich woman."

"I've got my dignity," she shot back. "People will laugh at me. Already the man that delivers barbecue from the Bum Steer makes fun of me for working in a kitchen."

"At least your kitchen has a roof over it," Ten said, "and you're not breathing hickory smoke all day. You're tough enough to handle a little ribbing. For a million dollars, you can handle a lot. What about you, Carver?"

Mr. Carver still looked shell-shocked. "I don't know," he said faintly. "This isn't what I expected. I thought if we were lucky Honeybelle would give me enough to maybe move to Austin or Nashville. Somewhere I can listen to music."

"Wait a year," Ten counseled, "and you can have a whole band to yourself, anywhere you want."

"What happens if something goes wrong?" I asked. "What if Miss Ruffles chokes on a bone?"

"Or gets into those pills of hers," Mae Mae said. "There was the day she ate too many of her vitamins and had to go to the vet to get her stomach pumped."

"She was real trouble before Miss McKillip came," Mr. Carver said to Ten. "Once she ran away from Honeybelle and was almost run over by a car. What if that happens again? What if she dies by accident and it's not our fault?"

"Then you all lose everything," Ten said solemnly.

The doorbell chimed in the front of the house. The sound rolled back to the kitchen, and Miss Ruffles let out her threatening bark. She dashed to the swinging door. She scratched it and then began to dig at the floor as if she could excavate her way out of the kitchen. I reached over and grabbed her collar. She fought me as I dragged her back to the table. I held her fast, but she wriggled in my arms.

"That'll be Hut Junior and the family." Mae Mae seemed unable to stand up yet. "Do they know about this? About us?"

"No, ma'am," Ten said. "I figured I'd tell y'all first so you'd be prepared when they hear the news."

"They're not getting anything from Honeybelle?" I asked.

"A little something," Ten said. "A big something, actually, because Honeybelle was a wealthy woman. Wealthier than most of us knew. But they won't get this house, not now, anyway, and not as big a share of her money as they expected. Hut Junior doesn't even get the oil and gas company—not yet. A lot of other people in town will eventually receive bequests or have their loans forgiven. Just not until Miss Ruffles is settled. And some were hoping for their money a lot sooner."

"The university," Mr. Carver guessed. "They want that new stadium something terrible."

Ten nodded. "There's a lot of money at stake for a lot of people, but Honeybelle has tied it all up in Miss Ruffles for the moment. I can't lie. It could get ugly around here. There might even be a lawsuit. Or several. But the three of you don't have to do a thing except look after Miss Ruffles and keep up the house like you've been doing."

He tried to sound soothing, but I could see Mae Mae and Mr. Carver were unsettled—bordering on semihysterical. The doorbell chimed again, prompting Mr. Carver to scramble up from the table. He reached for his blue coat and put it on.

"I'll get the door." He tried to regain his professional composure, but his hands were shaking too hard for him to fasten his buttons, so he gave up. "Mae Mae, put the refreshments out. Sunny, take that dog outside and keep her occupied until the family is gone."

We got busy doing as he said. I pulled the leash from my pocket and made a grab for the dog's collar. Mr. Carver disappeared out of the kitchen, unsteadily heading for the front door. Muttering to herself, Mae Mae lumbered to the refrigerator and pulled out a decorative plate with a bright green molded salad jiggling on it, surrounded by a garnish of grapes and lemon peel. She pushed through the swinging door and carried it out to the dining room.

I snapped the leash on Miss Ruffles and dampened a paper towel at the sink to wipe the flour from her face.

As I bent over the dog, Ten said, "You seem pretty calm about this windfall, Jane Eyre."

"The shock hasn't set in yet," I replied, noting that my hands weren't exactly steady.

"Aren't you surprised? To be getting a million dollars from a woman you barely knew?"

"I'm completely stunned," I admitted, dropping the paper towel into the trash.

"To be honest," Ten drawled, "we're a mite surprised ourselves, down at the office. Tell me, how did you get this job in the first place?"

"I interviewed, and Honeybelle hired me."

He shook his head, not believing. "How come Honeybelle hired you and not one of the local girls who applied for the job? Girls she already knew?"

"Because I was better qualified, I guess. I've worked as an assistant for many people at colleges."

He met my gaze steadily, his face less friendly than before. Probably taking in the cheap thrift-shop dress and the butterfly locket my mother had given me ages ago— nothing valuable, really, but it reminded me of her, and how the wings of a butterfly could be the beginning of a hurricane. Next to the young ladies he had grown up with, I was probably colorless, shapeless. A sunburned nose in the land of beautiful southern belles.

He said, "You came all the way to Texas to be a governess for a dog."

"That's not exactly how it happened. I was already here. I had a job at the university, but my boss was fired. And I was hired to be Honeybelle's personal secretary, not just to look after Miss Ruffles. The job happened to evolve that way. Honeybelle had no complaints about my work while she was alive."

"Here's the thing," Ten said. "If the family decides to sue Mr. Carver or Mae Mae, I can make a good case on their behalf. But you? Your story is mighty suspicious."

Miss Ruffles looked from my face to Ten's and back again, aware of the tension between us. I knew she was wondering if she should bite him. I put my hand on her head to quiet her nerves. She trembled with the effort of holding still.

Miss Ruffles wasn't the only one upset. I struggled to control my voice as I said, "I'm not the only suspicious part of this story. Your father and grandfather—Honeybelle went to their office almost every day for the last two weeks. They were rewriting her will, weren't they?"

"That's none of your—"

"All I'm saying is, if she rewrote it and died almost right away—doesn't that make you wonder what was going on in Honeybelle's life?"

He frowned. "What was going on?"

I felt myself getting emotional. I didn't want to tell him what Honeybelle had said about being murdered. I'd sound silly if I blurted out the idea that maybe she had made quick arrangements about Miss Ruffles because she had seen some kind of threat building against her. But the man's "bumping off" wisecrack after the funeral was suddenly jumbled up in my mind with *a million dollars, a million dollars!* And I was thinking Honeybelle's death hadn't been natural at all. I shoved that thought back down where it belonged and heard myself say instead, "A lot was going on. There was a big feud at the garden club meeting. Honeybelle felt all her friends abandoned her. And the next thing you know, the college president was bleeding on her rug. And then she dies—a perfectly healthy woman has a heart attack out of the blue—and her nurse takes off like . . . like there's a fire somewhere." I saw him bite back a smile and decided not to mention the squabble over a wedding and family members measuring the house to move in practically before the funeral music faded. Maybe this kind of conflict was business as usual in Texas, but it felt like one big dangerous carnival ride to me. Plus *a million dollars, a million dollars!* I tried to get a grip and failed. "Now her new lawyer shows up on a horse! It's just . . . it was very complicated around here."

"Honeybelle was a smart lady. She could handle complicated," Ten said. "But she was a soft touch, too. She kept those two old folks around the house way past their expiration dates just because. A lot of people used that softness for their own profit. Maybe you did, too."

"No," I said firmly, stubbornly. "Not me. I liked and respected Honeybelle. I'd return everything she's already paid me to have her back."

"That's big talk."

"She was a wonderful person." A lot like my mother, I almost said.

He eyed me a while longer, absorbing the tumult of emotions that surely showed on my face. He must have drawn a conclusion, because he finally said, "That's good to hear. Because if you turn out to be a con artist who played a nice lady like a deck of cards, you're going to be in a heap of trouble." All of his earlier pleasantness evaporated, he said, "From now on, a lot of people are going to be watching you. Me included."

★ ★ ★

CHAPTER FIVE

You tell a gelding. Ask a stud. Discuss it with a mare.
And pray to God Almighty if it's a pony.
—HORSEMAN'S ADVICE

My mother used to say that field research was a lot like camping. You could have clean pants or dry pants, but you couldn't have both. That's how I felt as I wrestled Miss Ruffles outside, where she promptly ran away and tried to dig under the gate to get to Ten Tennyson's horse. By the time I reached her, she had a sizable hole started and was covered in dirt. Unimpressed, Hondo dozed. And I could have Honeybelle alive or *a million dollars, a million dollars!* But not both.

I refilled the hole as best I could, glad to have something to do while I thought about Ten's threat.

And a million dollars. *A million.* It was hard to think about anything else with that number whirling around in my head.

Honeybelle had liked me well enough, but I had no idea she thought so highly of me.

A million dollars?

"Your mama was very generous," I said to Miss Ruffles. "But also nuts. Who leaves so much to a dog? And not her family? I can't help it. I think there's something more going on."

Miss Ruffles smiled up at me and yipped with glee.

I hauled her back to the porch to wash the mud off her. The two Hensley boys were on the porch swing by then, clearly having been dismissed from the family meeting. The sullen teenager, Trey, kept his cowboy hat on and his nose pointed at his cell phone, thumbs moving as fast as any teen could manage. The younger boy looked terrified when Miss Ruffles trotted into view.

"Don't let that mean dog get us," Travis Joe said as he stood on the swing's seat and clung to the chain. He looked ready to shimmy up to the ceiling. "She bit my brother once."

"Shut up, wuss," grumbled Trey. "It was just a nip. And I guarantee she won't do it again. You have to show a dog who's boss."

Miss Ruffles put her forepaws up on the swing to get a closer look at Travis Joe's shoelaces, her next favorite treat after boots. He screamed and climbed onto the back of the swing. His brother swatted him.

I dragged Miss Ruffles away and resigned myself to babysitting while Ten broke the news to Hut Junior and his wife. Trey, as unpleasant as he was, would be no problem as long as his phone battery held out. Travis Joe was another story. He was already running back and forth across the seat of the swing, fear forgotten, causing the swing to jangle dangerously on its chains.

I held the dog's collar and turned on the hose to rinse her off. Miss Ruffles snapped at the gush, delighted to be making another mess as the muddy water sluiced onto the grass. By the time my dress was half soaked, she was clean again. I shut off the hose. Miss Ruffles shook herself all over, spraying more water on me, then dashed out into the grass and rolled around with glee.

Travis Joe laughed as I tried to brush off the water. He climbed down from the swing but hung on to the chain just in case he had to make a quick escape. With his bow tie and expensive haircut, the kid looked like he was on his way to Princeton. I wondered if anyone ever tossed a ball with him in the back yard. Was his father the too-busy executive? Was his mother the overprotective kind who didn't want her baby getting messy?

I said, "Want a Popsicle? Either of you?"

Trey snorted, but Travis Joe perked up. "Orange?"

"Sure. You think your mom would be okay with that?"

He said, "I ate a good lunch. Even my carrot sticks."

His brother made a rude noise with his lips.

"Okay," I said to Travis Joe. "There's a box in the little freezer over there."

"I know where they are." He clambered down and scampered into Honeybelle's fancy outdoor kitchen. He bent down to the fridge; then his head popped up again. He had a crafty look on his face. "Can I have two?"

"No, just one."

No whining. He ducked out of sight again and found himself a treat. When he had carefully discarded the wrapper in a hidden trash can, he came back with the Popsicle in his mouth. He watched me wind up the hose.

He pulled out the Popsicle. His tongue was orange already. "How come Miss Ruffles is such a bad dog?"

"Miss Ruffles is nice. You just have to get to know her. Give it a try."

Miss Ruffles scrambled to her feet and bounded over to give the boy a panting grin with all her teeth showing. She wanted his Popsicle.

"No, Miss Ruffles," I said firmly. "Why don't you play nicely with Travis Joe?"

"No, ma'am." Travis Joe shook his head vehemently. "I don't want to play with her, and you can't make me."

"I'll hold her collar, and you can pet her."

"No! I mean, no, ma'am. No way!"

"She likes to have her ears scratched." I demonstrated, and Miss Ruffles quit struggling against me and closed her eyes in bliss.

Travis Joe sucked on his Popsicle, unconvinced. "My mama says she poops all over the yard."

"She's a dog. She has to poop somewhere. Besides, I clean up after her."

Travis Joe smiled. "You said poop."

"So did you."

His smile grew more confident, and he went back to sucking on his treat. "Mama says Miss Ruffles has to go so Aunt Poppy can have her wedding here."

It wasn't my place to tell him the wedding plans might still be in limbo. Or would Posie's wishes outweigh Honeybelle's now? I said, "Aunt Poppy's getting married, huh?"

Travis Joe nodded. "I'm supposed to carry a ring on a pillow. My brother's too old."

From the porch, Trey said, "I'm not too old. I'm just not nerd enough to carry a stupid pillow."

Travis Joe said, "Mama says they're going to have the wedding in Miss Honeybelle's rose garden, then put up a tent behind the swimming pool for a party with barbecue and dancing, but no swimming." He looked longingly at the pool. "I went swimming in that pool on the Fourth of July."

"I remember," I said. Mostly, I remembered how Travis Joe had been ordered to stay in the shallow water, where he repeatedly edged closer to the deep end. His mother shouted at him often to stay where his feet could touch bottom. At the time, I'd thought she was overreacting. Behind Posie's back, Honeybelle had urged Travis Joe to push the limits his mother put down.

Travis Joe said, "I want to go swimming now."

Trey said, "Mom will pitch a fit if you get wet."

"Leave me alone!"

"Bite me."

Travis Joe turned to me, eyes steely. "I want to go swimming."

"Did you bring a suit?" I asked.

"No."

"Then you'll have to swim naked."

His eyes popped wide. "I can't do that! You're a girl!"

"So?"

Without further argument, Travis Joe gave up on the swimming idea. He sucked on his Popsicle for a minute before saying, "Nobody's going to swim at the wedding. Mama wants to have floating candles in the water."

"That sounds pretty."

"Mama says a magazine won't come take pictures of everybody if the wedding's at the country club. The country club's boring. Not pretty enough for a magazine. So she wants the wedding here so they can take pictures of the roses and stuff."

I thought about that and decided Honeybelle had been very proud of her home and her decorating and certainly her rose garden. Had she objected to the magazine coverage? If so, why? I couldn't very well pump Honeybelle's grandson on the subject, though—especially now that Miss Ruffles was back to being intrigued by his shoelaces. If she got her teeth onto those, it would be only seconds before she was chewing on his toes.

Travis Joe finished off his Popsicle and said to me, "How old are you?"

"Twenty-nine," I said.

"My mama says you're too old to be a dogsitter."

I was surprised to be a topic of conversation at Posie's home. I said, "I like taking care of Miss Ruffles. We play together. Want to throw her ball for her to chase?"

Travis Joe shook his head.

"C'mon," I said. "Give it a shot."

I picked up her tennis ball and bounced it once off the terrace before catching it in my hand. Miss Ruffles was instantly on alert, forefeet splayed, stub high. Her excitement almost made Travis Joe chicken out. But I gave him the ball, and after just a moment of hesitation he threw it clumsily. Miss Ruffles took off like a rocket and grabbed the ball on the first ricochet. She brought it back and obediently dropped it at my feet. I handed the ball over to Travis Joe, and he threw it before the dog could jump up on him. It went a little farther this time, and Miss Ruffles had to make a dash around a pool chair to seize it. When she came trotting back, she dropped it in front of Travis Joe and yipped at him to hurry up.

He backed against my leg. "I don't want her to bite me."

"She won't bite." Just in case, though, I positioned myself so I could intervene if Miss Ruffles made a premature lunge for the ball. "She only nips at your feet when she wants you to move. It's her natural instinct. She's a herding dog. So we have to help her to like chasing a ball even more. Don't make it too easy on her. Really give her something to go after."

With a gleam in his eye, Travis Joe threw the ball into the bushes, and Miss Ruffles happily dashed after it.

"Don't throw it into the pool," I said, guessing what his next plan was. "Throw the ball into the grass, as far as you can."

He did, and Miss Ruffles raced off to grab it. Every time she brought the ball back to Travis Joe, she circled him a few times, gradually herding him farther out into the yard. He threw the ball over and over, not realizing he was being outsmarted by the dog.

Honeybelle had asked me to try teaching Miss Ruffles a trick she could perform on the football field. A previous Texas cattle cur had learned to race out onto the field after every kickoff and bring back the kicker's tee. I had tried that, but Miss Ruffles had immediately picked up the tee, chewed it beyond recognition, and buried the remaining parts in a flower bed. I had been thinking I needed a second person to help discourage Miss Ruffles from destroying the important component of the trick. Maybe Travis Joe was my best choice.

But before we got around to it, Posie came out onto the porch.

After the reading of Honeybelle's will, Posie was surprisingly, coldly, in control of herself. She was pale with anger, though. She wore her dark sunglasses.

"Travis Joe, what do you think you're doing?"

"I'm playing ball with Miss Ruffles."

"Get away from that animal before she bites you." She took Travis Joe by his shoulder to turn him away from me as if I were suddenly capable of infecting her children with a virulent species of head lice. "Trey, put that phone in your pocket. We're going home."

"Did I get any money?" Trey asked. "Can I buy myself a truck right away?"

She ignored the question. "Did you hear me? Put the phone away."

"You mean the old lady didn't leave me anything?" Trey's voice rose petulantly. "You're gonna buy me the truck, then, right? I told all the guys I was getting the biggest truck they ever saw."

"Well, you spoke too soon," his mother said tartly. "No son of mine is going to drive a monster truck all over town, showing off and acting above himself. Let's go."

He thought about throwing a tantrum, I could see, but instead he sighed and went back to playing with his phone. "I'm almost done."

"This minute, young man!"

His face turned dark, but he got to his feet and muttered, "Yes, ma'am." He slid the phone into his pocket.

Then, from the nearest flowerpot, he picked up a pebble and hefted it in one hand. Before I could guess what he planned to do, he suddenly hurled it at Miss Ruffles. Not for her to catch, but to hit her.

"Hey!" I said.

Miss Ruffles dodged the stone. She glared at Trey and growled.

"Stupid dog," Trey muttered. "Somebody ought to shoot her."

"Mama." Travis Joe tugged his mother's hand. "I think Miss Ruffles might like me!"

Posie's voice was like an ice pick. "Travis Joe, you keep your distance from that animal, hear?"

"But, Mama—"

Hut Junior came slamming out the back door and stood on the porch with steam practically roaring out of his ears. "I don't believe it! Even now, she doesn't trust me to run her dern company!"

"Hut," Posie warned.

"I have a mind to pack y'all up and move to Dallas. I could get a job running any dern oil company in the state, but that fool woman never thought I was good enough to—"

"*Hut,*" Posie snapped. She snatched off her sunglasses to give her husband a glare. "Not in front of the help."

He blinked and finally noticed me standing there. His jaw slammed shut.

Posie yanked Travis Joe by the hand. "Let's go," she said to her family. "We're obviously not welcome here, even now."

Travis Joe hung back. "Mama, I need to say good-bye to Miss Ruffles."

"You'll do no such thing." Over her shoulder, Posie shot me another dagger of a look. "Your brother's right, Travis

Joe. Soon enough, somebody's going to take a shot at that dog, and I don't want you within range when it happens."

To me, she said, "Keep that animal away from the roses."

With that, she swept them out of Honeybelle's house, and I didn't see her for a week.

CHAPTER SIX

Where flowers bloom, so does hope.
—LADY BIRD JOHNSON

After the garden club election debacle, Honeybelle had asked me to help her take cuttings of some of her roses and rake the mulch to check for fungus. It would be good therapy for her, she said, and I could keep her company. It was an unusual request from her. Normally, except for when I was outside supervising Miss Ruffles, my duties were accomplished indoors.

"Do you know anything about gardening, Sunny?"

"Not much," I admitted. "Not at your level, that's for sure."

"Well, then, come along. Everyone should learn to appreciate fine roses."

My antenna went up, of course. In my experience, employers never took their assistants out of the office to discuss things that were good. I'd had one professor announce she was suing the university and wanted my help gathering intel on a colleague. Another declared he was thinking of leaving his wife. For me. But I agreed to lend a hand in Honeybelle's garden.

Miss Ruffles wasn't usually allowed in the front yard, due to Honeybelle's obsession with her heirloom roses and the many chemicals used to keep the lawn green and free of weeds, so today was a special occasion. The dog raced ahead of us to scout the territory, then circled back, tongue lolling with pleasure. I pushed the wheelbarrow. Honeybelle carried a bound notebook with a matching pen.

"I could hire someone to do this chore." Honeybelle tucked the notebook under her arm and pulled on her gardening gloves. She grasped her cane—not that she needed it much anymore, but I knew she didn't want to risk another fall. "But I do everything for my roses. And I never open my garden for tours. No, sir, my roses are too valuable to have people walking around doing whatever they please. So watch your step."

"Yes, ma'am."

I shaded my eyes and looked up at the flowing river of colors. One bush seemed to crowd into another and another, with some branches climbing up a trellis, others snaking along the ground in a chaotic tangle. But in a moment, the colors sorted themselves out, and I could see the garden was very well organized, with a small bronze marker driven into the earth at the foot of each bush.

"Wow, it's beautiful. How many rosebushes do you have?"

"Seventy-two varieties, all of them quite wonderful."

"Yes, ma'am, I can see that. You planted them all yourself?"

"Of course. I selected every one, chose the ideal spot for it, and dug the hole. Used my own two hands to nurture the plants to perfection."

She opened her notebook and showed me a page. "You see? I keep track of where each rose came from, when I acquired it, where it's planted now, plus whatever research I've completed. And here's a picture. When I got started, I took Polaroids. I miss a Polaroid camera. It was very useful. See? Here's a photo of my grandson, helping me plant a rose. What a darling boy Trey was."

"My mother kept journals like this. She wrote entries every day and reread parts of it all the time. Sometimes she read something she'd written a year earlier and it suddenly made new sense. She said science was like that. You have to keep yourself open to discovery." I leaned close and turned a page to see a picture of another rose, with its accompanying text. A lot of Honeybelle's writing seemed to be in code. "This is a big project."

"One very close to my heart. In some cases, I found the plant and dug it up myself, but we don't talk about that."

I stopped reading over her shoulder. "Why not?"

She snapped her notebook closed and turned as pink as the flowers at her elbow. "Well, you're not supposed to dig up whole bushes, Sunny. You're supposed to ask permission and take little cuttings to propagate, but really, if a rosebush was left behind when a family moved on and a ranch just fell down and blew away—I was doing a public service, wasn't I? Who would ever appreciate a rare rose if it's out in the scrub all by itself?"

"So these flowers came from abandoned ranches?"

She hesitated. "Some of them. Why, one time my dear Hut and I were driving out in the middle of nowhere to meet some young high school football prospect, and I suddenly shouted at him to stop the car because I'd seen just the tiniest speck of red out in the desert. We put on our boots and found the foundation of an old farmhouse—nothing else left, except this beautiful *gallica* rose." She cupped a vivid red flower in her hand and tipped it to better show off its qualities. "I think it originally came from Persia, but somebody dug it up and brought it all the way to Texas—by way of Ireland or England, probably. The British were always taking what they wanted, weren't they? And their empire ruled the world. Now, it would be a terrible thing if this beautiful flower just dried up and died in the desert, wouldn't it? I *rescued* it."

I thought about my mother and her obsession with saving rare butterflies. Here was Honeybelle doing the same kind of thing. I could hardly picture her trading her fancy shoes for hiking boots and leading an expedition into the jungle, but apparently she had done almost that. "Who did the farm belong to?"

"I have no idea," she said briskly. "And I have no intention of finding out."

"But if you knew who owned the farm, maybe you could track down where the rose came from, and—"

"I might also have to give it back," she said.

"Oh, I hadn't thought of that."

"It's mine now," she said firmly. "Possession is nine-tenths of the law. They'd have to prove I took it, anyway. Nobody's going to wrestle it away from me now."

"Still," I said, "you could probably look at property deeds for a name, and then do some ancestry research. Nobody would have to know but you. And the history might be fascinating if you—"

"Thank you, Sunny." She gave me a long, quelling look. "I'm beginning to wonder what I ever did without you."

She didn't sound happy with my suggestions. I buttoned my lip and pushed the wheelbarrow after her as she led the way across her dewy lawn, fresh from its morning sprinkle. Miss Ruffles snuffled the grass and briskly scouted the yard for enemy combatants. Honeybelle used her cane to fend off Miss Ruffles once, but eventually she set it aside and took the rake to turn over some of the mulch around the roses. I read off some of the bronze markers, and she told me what she knew about each plant. She had so much information in her head that I was surprised she needed the notebook at all.

"How about this one?" I pointed at a particularly prickly

bush, laden down with yellow blooms. Each petal had a bright yellow throat, but the color turned creamy at the edges. "Why doesn't it have a marker?"

"It doesn't? Oh." She glanced at the rose and quickly went back to raking. "Yes, that one's a mystery, all right. But it's beautiful, isn't it?"

"Very pretty."

Next she went around and cut bits of stems off a few bushes and dipped them into a jar of granules that coated the little snippets. "Stick this stem in the sterile soil, Sunny. Yes, like that. Be careful of the thorns."

Obediently, I took half a dozen of her cuttings and tucked them into a tray of potting soil.

"Now we'll label these and put them in a sunny spot in my conservatory. In no time, we'll have even more roses."

I glanced around. Her garden already seemed jam-packed. "Where will you put more roses?"

"Oh, I'll find homes for these little wonders."

In a few minutes, Honeybelle took a break and repaired her lipstick from a tube in her pocket. She wore her white slacks with a pink polka-dotted blouse tied fetchingly at her waist. Her enormous straw gardening hat swooped over one eye and fastened under her chin in a large pink bow.

"Did you hear everything Posie said at the meeting?" Honeybelle asked very casually as she replaced the top of her lipstick. "That silly business about saving water knocked me for a loop. It's not as if we're using millions of gallons. And bluebonnets hardly use any because they're a native plant. Don't you think flowers are a perfectly good use of water? I can't imagine a world without flowers, can you?"

"No, I can't."

"I'm perfectly aware that we must conserve, but really, what would life be without green spaces? They're restful, soothing. And who doesn't need soothing these days?" From the wheelbarrow, she pulled a trowel, then got down on her knees on a neatly folded towel. "Posie's tone was very accusatory." She jabbed her trowel into the flower bed. "I don't mind a disagreement behind closed doors, but in public like that . . ."

"She counted on your good manners," I said. "She knew you wouldn't disagree with her in front of other people."

"You're right! Why didn't I think of that?" She sat back to consider my theory for another moment, and then said, "I just wish some of my friends had stood up for me a little bit. Not one of them said a word on my behalf. I know I should be a good Christian and forgive them." Honeybelle began to stab at the roots of one rosebush again. "But I don't mind admitting I'm having trouble forgiving that bunch of biddies who wouldn't defend a friend when the chips were down. I've been good for this town," she went on, her outrage gaining momentum. "I give money to every cause. I've attended so many bridal and baby showers I could scream. I go to those awful jewelry parties, too, even the ones with silly games, and I always buy something, even if it's tacky stuff. And I drove Minnie Longwell to every single one of her doctor appointments for her hammertoe last winter. Nobody could say I wasn't a wonderful friend to her. I've been more than generous."

"Yes, ma'am, you have."

"So why can't I get a little credit once in a while? A little loyalty in return? They're all jealous, that's the bottom line. They're jealous of my life and my position and my roses."

"Your . . . roses?"

She took a pair of shears from the wheelbarrow and snipped a faded bloom. "Well, there have been whispers, you know."

"What kind of whispers?"

Honeybelle suddenly appeared uneasy. She picked up her trowel again and began shoving it into the earth. With a wince and an exclamation, she dropped the trowel. She pulled off her glove and examined her fingernails for breakage. "I have a mind to do something."

"Like what?"

She cut her eyes at me. "Well, I thought I'd ask you."

"Me?"

"You being a Yankee and all, I thought maybe you'd have some ideas. About getting back at people."

I almost laughed. She was talking as if anyone from north of the Mason-Dixon had a forked tail. "It's not as if we're . . . well, anyway, I'm not really a Yankee. I'm from Ohio, which is more midwestern than . . . never mind. I don't know any—"

"You must know a dirty trick or two. Something I could inflict on my former friends."

When I could speak, I said, "Former . . . ? Look—"

"I'd like some revenge. There, I said it. Does that make me a bad person? Or simply human? I'd like to see some of those two-faced old bats get some comeuppance."

I was seeing a side of Honeybelle I hadn't expected. "Such as?"

"I don't know! Something satisfying. A prank, maybe. I'm being serious here, Sunny. I'm angry! And I want to make a point, darn it."

"I don't know how to help you, ma'am. I really don't."

She sighed, disappointed. "Well, maybe I'll ask my grandson. He might have some ideas."

A passing car pulled over to the curb and stopped in front of the hedge. The driver rolled down his window.

"Hey, good-lookin'," he called over the hedge to Honeybelle. He was the owner of the local funeral home, Mr. Gamble. I knew him because he had come to the house a couple of times to sit on Honeybelle's porch and drink gin and tonics. Miss Ruffles had tolerated him. Perhaps because he was completely unthreatening, and Honeybelle seemed to like him. He had brought a case of bottled water the first time—a puzzling attempt at a romantic gesture. But Honeybelle professed to be charmed by it.

This morning Mr. Gamble was looking more like a Las Vegas singer than the local mortician. He had shy, downturned brown eyes with Bambi lashes, a thick head of dark hair complete with long sideburns, and a slow smile. His black funeral suit seemed standard issue, except his white shirt was often unbuttoned to show a startling amount of manly chest hair. I guessed he might be wearing a gold necklace, but I was afraid to look close enough to find out.

He said, "Whatcha doing there, Honeybelle?"

Miss Ruffles dashed to the hedge and began barking madly.

Honeybelle forgot about revenge and scrambled to her feet. She ignored her cane and tucked a stray lock of hair back into her hat, her concerns about her friends forgotten. "Why, Mr. Gamble. How nice to see you this morning. Miss Ruffles, settle yourself." She struck a pose, one fist on a hip, looking far from a lady who needed a cane to sustain her balance. "What brings you out so early, handsome?"

I picked up the rake and pretended to be invisible.

Mr. Gamble leaned out his window and shouted over the barking of the dog. "Just passing by." New to the game of flirtation, he was bashfully awkward, but he tried. "It's against nature for you to outshine those flowers, but you certainly do."

"What a flatterer you are!"

"Did you get that emergency water like I told you to?" He turned serious again. "Or do you want me to bring you a few five-gallon bottles?"

"My storm shelter is well stocked, thank you, Mr. Gamble."

"I'll bring my checklist over, make sure you've got everything."

"That," she said, "would be very nice. You're so thoughtful."

He looked pleased. "Or what about lunch on Saturday? I'm in the mood to take you all the way to Dallas."

She clapped her hands together. "Oh, would you?"

"And I checked into that old ranch you mentioned—the one on the way to Dallas. I did a little looking around on some maps—"

"Dallas sounds just wonderful," Honeybelle cut him off, voice bright with enthusiasm.

"Then it's a date?"

"Call me on Friday." With a beaming smile, she pantomimed a telephone to her ear.

He waved and went on his way. Miss Ruffles came trotting back to us, pleased that she had chased off the interloper.

Honeybelle saw me blinking and said, "I'm helping him. The poor man's wife died in the tornado we had here twenty years ago, poor dear, squished by her own deep freezer. I'm trying to bring him out of his grief-stricken state. Except now he's a nut about emergency shelters."

"Can't blame him," I said.

"I suppose not, but it's getting a little . . . well, he badgered me into creating a shelter in one of my walk-in closets. I thought that would be the end of it, but now Mr. Gamble wants me to dig up some of my roses to make space for an underground room to hide in if another twister comes."

"Every house has a basement in Ohio."

"Did you ever go down into your basement to hide from a tornado?"

"No, but it's there, just in case."

"You sound like Mr. Gamble. 'Just in case' are his favorite words. He's a stickler about keeping food and water ready, too, not to mention a ham radio. Honestly, who listens to ham radios anymore? It would be my luck to get stuck in my storm shelter and end up communicating with a randy teenager in Korea!" She collected herself. "A nice lunch in Dallas might be just the thing to budge him off twisters. Really, what are the chances of a town getting blown off the map twice?"

"Well, if the town is located in a path that's commonly affected by severe weather, my mother would say—"

"I'm sure your mother had many good things to say, Sunny. You know what I mean. Hyperbole is a way of making a point."

"Yes, ma'am. Are you going to dig up some roses?"

"What?" She looked stricken.

I pointed at her garden. "To make room for your storm cellar."

"There's a better chance of a new twister drawing the face of Davy Crockett in my front lawn. No, I'm not digging up my roses, and I'm not building any underground storm cellar, either." She swallowed her exasperation and sighed. "I suppose I should be grateful he's so concerned for my safety. I do like to be taken care of now and then. He rather reminds me of my Hut that way."

"That's nice."

"It's not like there are many eligible men in this town. I've run through most of them already. He's the one who's left, so I feel I should give him a chance."

"He seems very . . . thoughtful"

Honeybelle's enthusiasm began to fade. "He's no Rhett Butler, and really, the idea of seeing a mortician is a little creepy sometimes, but he's really very . . . sweet."

"Clark Gable is dead," I reminded her.

Honeybelle saw my smile and laughed, happiness restored. "True 'dat!"

Within moments, more passing cars began tooting jauntily at Honeybelle, and more pleasantries were called from car windows. Miss Ruffles went into protection mode each time, and I made sure the dog didn't knock over Honeybelle. Finally, a pair of elderly ladies stopped to tentatively call out a gardening question. I recognized two of the garden club turncoats.

Honeybelle was very gracious to them, despite the resentment she'd confided to me. Her reply made them smile—relief showing—and they drove off.

When their car had disappeared around the corner, though, Honeybelle let her infuriation explode. "Oh, I need to get out of this town!"

"That trip to Dallas couldn't come at a better time."

"You said it!"

"You never leave Texas," I said, keeping my head down in case she decided to bite it off. "How come?"

"Oh," she said, finally sounding unhappy. "I love Texas, I really do. Hut and I planned to travel. But after he died, I just never had the courage to go anywhere else. It sounds silly, doesn't it?"

"You seem like the kind of person who'd enjoy traveling."

"Do I?" She sounded pleased.

"Sure. Sophisticated. Worldly."

She looked down at the gloves on her hands. "Sometimes I think it might be nice to visit New York. Or Paris! And those European river cruises all look so pretty, too."

"So why not go to all those places? You can afford it, right?"

"Well, yes." As if arguing with me, she said, "I do go to the beach in Galveston once in a while."

I nodded. "My mother used to say . . . uhm, I mean, there's research that says people are drawn to blue water.

Just being at the ocean causes a drop in our stress hormones."

"The variety in your education makes me breathless sometimes, Sunny." More thoughtfully, though, she said, "I wouldn't want to go on a river cruise alone."

"So ask one of your friends."

"Lady friends, you mean? Do you think I have any left?"

"Then ask Mr. Gamble," I said. "Seems like he'd be tickled to death if you invited him to travel with you."

She looked scandalized. "Oh, I couldn't stay in a hotel room with him! That would be inappropriate! People would think—no, no, no."

"So get separate rooms. Or take one of your grandsons. Or better yet, see who you meet on the trip. My mom always said the best people were always the ones she found on the way to meet somebody else. You should talk to a travel agent. Get some brochures."

"That sounds so impulsive." She smiled a little. "Your mother traveled extensively, didn't she?"

I smiled, too. "She was always going off on adventures. She never made it to Antarctica, but she got everywhere else on her bucket list."

"A bucket list." Suddenly Honeybelle was looking off into the distance as if starting her own list that very moment.

Miss Ruffles sat down on the grass and looked up at Honeybelle, head cocked, ears alert.

"Don't worry," Honeybelle said to her. "I won't leave you alone."

Miss Ruffles wagged her stub.

★ ★ ★

CHAPTER SEVEN

If you hear a Texas woman say, "Oh, hell, no,"
it's already too late.
—SEEN ON A T-SHIRT (IN RHINESTONES)

The day after Ten Tennyson read Honeybelle's will and turned our lives upside down, I took Miss Ruffles for her usual run . . . with a lot more apprehension than when Honeybelle was alive. I was exercising a millionaire dog.

"Is it safe to take her out of the yard?" Mr. Carver asked me as I snapped on the leash by the back gate. He had picked up the newspaper from the driveway where it had been thrown by the delivery boy.

"She needs her exercise," I said. "Otherwise, you know she'll chew the furniture."

Mr. Carver looked anxious. "Are you sure this is a good idea?"

No, I wasn't. But I said, "If we make her a prisoner, her behavior is only going to get worse."

"I see. Just . . . be careful, Sunny."

"I'll do my best. Shall I bring back doughnuts?"

His eyes lit up. Mr. Carver had a sweet tooth that Mae Mae rarely satisfied. "Oh, yes, that would be very nice."

I'd taken Miss Ruffles out every day since moving into Honeybelle's house. It hadn't gotten any easier. We jogged three blocks before Miss Ruffles made a U-turn, tripped me with the leash, and dragged me across a lawn to the edge of someone's driveway where a trash can sat oozing a disgusting liquid onto the ground. I practically had to strangle Miss Ruffles with the leash to prevent her from lapping up whatever the goo was.

On the next block, she spotted the Siamese cat that always sat tauntingly in someone's front window. Miss Ruffles tried to throw herself against the window, but I was ready. I managed to divert her with a Milk-Bone.

We'd gotten as far as the next corner when a black car pulled up beside me. It didn't stop but kept pace with us, and the passenger window rolled down. I was close enough to be hit by a blast of air-conditioning.

A man in dark sunglasses said, "Hey, there, young lady, could you give us some directions?"

I stopped running. The car angled in front of me and braked. The passenger popped his door open, and a heart-beat later the driver's door opened, too. Two men stepped out and adjusted their sunglasses against the intense glare of the early morning sun. They both wore dark business suits—one with a tie, one not—and even without an anthropologist around to confirm my opinion, I knew they were from somewhere other than Mule Stop.

The first thought that popped into my head was *The Blues Brothers go to Texas.*

"Miss McKillip? Sunny McKillip?"

Maybe I should have taken off at a run. But I wasn't thinking about the safety of Miss Ruffles or myself. No, immediately, I flashed back to the day a man came to tell me my mother was dead. I stopped on the sidewalk with Miss Ruffles at my side, and my brain tried to process all the possible bad things that could have happened. Whatever it was, the Blues Brothers must have shown up to break the news, I thought. So I was momentarily struck silent.

The men took up position on either side of me and stepped closer until the moment Miss Ruffles flattened her ears and let out one of her most threatening growls. They stopped dead, giving me a chance for a second impression. They could have been brothers, all right. Besides dressing alike, both were heavyset, with lots of curly dark hair, and both with a certain element of menace in their postures.

"Nice doggie," said the driver, sounding unconvinced. A splotch of his breakfast stained the front of his shirt—something yellow and something red. Probably eggs with salsa, a local favorite.

"Miss McKillip?" said the other. He was buttoned up tight, all business. I could see my reflection in his mirrored sunglasses. He tapped a meaty thumb against his chest. "My name's Costello."

When I could gather my breath, I said, "What's wrong?"

"Hey, nothin's wrong." Costello raised his hands in the universal I-surrender gesture. "Take it easy, there. We're just talkin'."

He wasn't from Texas by any means. I guessed East Coast by his accent. New York or New Jersey, maybe.

"We just want to have a conversation," said his partner. "You're Sunny McKillip, right?"

"R-right."

"Your mom was Rachel McKillip? The lady scientist who died?"

"Yes." I was breathless, wondering what new catastrophe could have occurred.

"We're sorry for your loss. We hear she was a nice lady. Pretty, too. Just like you."

"What's going on?" My sanity was returning, and I felt stronger. It helped to have Miss Ruffles beside me, growling softly, ready to spring if needed. "Who are you?"

Costello came closer, and Miss Ruffles swung on him. He stopped. He said, "We were sent to look you up. Sent by a gentleman who financed one of your mom's, y'know, big science trips to Mexico. Mr. Postlethwaite."

"I don't know him."

"Really? He's very big in waste management. Revolutionized the industry. Made a boatload of money. You really don't know him?"

I knew who he was, of course. Just didn't know him personally. Because how many people really knew an eccentric millionaire who popped up on television and in magazines to trumpet news about the environment and climate change? Trumpeting in a very peculiar voice and using the kind of shouty talk that only turned people against whatever views he espoused? I said, "Sorry, no."

Costello looked surprised and exchanged glances with his partner. "Well, he knows about you."

Miss Ruffles jumped in front of me and let out her sharp warning bark. Both men froze again. I had stopped in a tiny patch of shade from a lone tree, but they were stuck in full sun. The heat was already building to intense.

Costello loosened his tie an iota. "Mr. Postlethwaite, see, he's like a whattayacallit, philatelist. Gives money to good causes. He paid your mom a whole lotta cash, see. He was happy to do it. He loves bugs, 'specially butterflies. You should see his collection—he's got drawers and drawers fulla bugs. And your mom said when she finally grabbed that new butterfly she was chasing, deal was, she'd name it after him."

Uh-oh. I knew all about the elusive butterfly my mother had pursued. For years, she claimed there was an undocumented species out there, and she wanted to find it. She had held out that butterfly like a carrot to many investors.

Miss Ruffles must have sensed a change in the dynamic, because she looked up at my face and tried to read my emotions. I rested my hand on the top of her head.

"Trouble is," Costello continued, "the butterfly don't exist. Turns out, she made it up."

"She just ran out of time," I began.

"That don't make things right," Costello said. "Mr. Postlethwaite, he feels cheated. Which is understandable, know what I'm sayin'? He feels like he poured a lotta dough down a rat hole, is what he feels. Boy, it gets hot around here, doesn't it?"

"What is there to talk about?" I asked, regaining some of my courage. "My mother is dead."

"Yeah, like I said, we're real sorry about that," Costello said. "But Mr. Postlethwaite, he thinks he ought to get some of his money back."

"From whom?" I asked.

"Whom, huh?" Costello had a wide smile, and he shared it with his cohort. "What a smart girl. That could work in your favor. We don't really want to make trouble for you. But Mr. Postlethwaite asked us to come down here and talk to you about his money."

"I don't have it. She spent it," I said. "She always worked under a tight budget, but there was never any profit in—"

"So if she was good with a budget, maybe there's some left over. Maybe you got a tidy little bank account, and you could see your way clear to writing a check back to Mr. Postlethwaite."

My mother's scientific trips were her greatest joy, but the cost for a full-blown expedition included travel by air for herself and grad students, wages for local helpers, and equipment that had to be shipped and maintained, not to mention weeks of stay in a foreign country. She often raised a hundred thousand dollars and much more for such an undertaking. The reason every college had reluctantly let her go was that she ran through research money faster than fraternities consumed beer. At the end of her career, she'd been reduced to being hired on a course-by-course basis and relied on grants from less than kosher sources to fund her trips. I'd been left with barely enough money to bury her and buy a plane ticket to Texas.

"Look," I said, trying not to panic. "I'm sure Mr. Postlethwaite is disappointed. I completely understand. But honestly, I am flat broke. I'm very sorry you came all this way for nothing, but you might as well go back and tell your boss that I'm not able to accommodate him."

"Accommodate. You're real smart, aren't you?"

"Who are you two, exactly?" I wound up the leash, preparing to continue our run. "A couple of wiseguys for hire?"

He smiled, pleased. "Something like that. Look, we heard a rumor about you."

"What kind of rumor?"

"That you just inherited a million bucks."

I had been about to dash off, but I forgot about running and faced the two of them again. "Who told you that?"

"It's all over town. We heard it in the . . . whattaya-callit, the restaurant with the wagon wheel out front. Everybody was talking about you at the ice cream machine, while they were putting chocolate and peanuts on their sundaes. Somebody said they heard about you getting a lot of dough from somebody named Moneybelle."

"Honeybelle," I said automatically.

He smiled broadly. "That's not what they were calling her, and somebody else said you were just the dogsitter, which is when we figured out they were talking about you. It's unusual to have peanuts sitting out like that in a restaurant, you know. Half the kids in the country are allergic to peanuts. My little granddaughter is."

"I'm sorry to hear that."

I was even sorrier to hear that I was the subject of ice cream machine gossip. How did the news get out already that we were inheriting a large amount of money? Who had talked? Surely not Ten. And it seemed unlikely that Posie or Hut Junior was going around telling their friends and neighbors how Honeybelle had thwarted their dreams of an immediate windfall. I doubted Mr. Carver or Mae Mae had said a word either.

Miss Ruffles edged over to sniff him.

"We got to thinking," Costello said, holding his position but eyeing her, "that if you're going to be a millionaire, maybe you could see your way to writing a check to Mr. Postlethwaite."

"I'd like to help you," I said. "But truth is, I won't get a penny beyond my regular paycheck for a year."

"A year? Well, I bet we could work out something with one of those cash advance companies. My brother-in-law is always using those. Maybe—"

"It's all very complicated," I said, "and it's really not anything I care to discuss, not with you."

"Hey, is that any way to talk? We're just having a conversation here."

I tugged at the leash. "I think it's a conversation that's going to end with you threatening me. So we're going to go before that happens." I turned and started to jog again. Miss Ruffles joined me.

Costello called after us, "We're just talking. Hey, come back!"

It didn't occur to me to be frightened until they were both back in their car and driving in the opposite direction from Miss Ruffles and me. That's when my knees turned to jelly, and I wanted to sit down on the sidewalk more than anything. But Miss Ruffles nearly yanked me off my feet by charging after another passing car. She wanted to run it down and eat all the tires. I barely managed to stop her by throwing all my weight against the leash. Then we ran as if chased by demons.

About half a mile later, I stopped on a corner and bent from the waist to catch my breath. I groaned. My mother had been known for cutting corners, playing fast and loose with donations, wheedling money for expeditions that sometimes didn't materialize. I should have guessed one of her shady donors might come looking for repayment someday.

But this possibility, that someone might come looking for cash from me, had never blossomed in my mind. I had nothing to give to anyone—certainly not the kind of money the Blues Brothers wanted for their client.

"What am I supposed to do?" I said.

Miss Ruffles jumped against my knee. Puzzlement shone in her face.

"It's okay," I said to her. "They're after me, not you."

She yipped and pulled on the leash. I got the message. We jogged across the street to the next corner and kept going toward the bakery.

I didn't want to leave Miss Ruffles outside by herself, so I was glad the Heavenly Treats shop had a drive-up window. Most restaurants in Mule Stop had drive-up windows. It was possible to eat three meals a day without leaving your car.

The apple-cheeked lady standing at the window was the owner, who sometimes wore angel wings when she worked the counter. This morning she had tied on an apron that had various colors of frosting dabbed on it. She looked like Mrs. Claus, except messy. She smiled at me as she opened the window. "Can I help you?"

I fished some cash out of the tiny pocket in my running shorts. "I'll take a dozen mixed doughnuts, please."

"You want me to choose for you?"

"That would be great, thanks."

Miss Ruffles jumped up and put her front paws on the takeout window to investigate, and the woman's smile widened. "Why, that's Miss Ruffles, right? Honeybelle's dog?"

"Yes." I put a few bills on the counter in hopes of speeding up the transaction.

But the owner rested one plump elbow on the counter and leaned there for a chat. "We're all real sorry about Honeybelle. She used to drive up here in her convertible every Sunday and buy all our pink sprinkle doughnuts. She took 'em to church, she said. She said it was good for the whole congregation to have pink doughnuts. I'm not sure what that meant, exactly, but it sounded nice."

"She was always very generous."

"You want some pink sprinkles?"

"Sure, that'd be great." Belatedly, I added, "Thank you, ma'am."

"I heard Honeybelle was real generous with you."

I opened my mouth to reply but couldn't think of a response.

She said, "You're sure one lucky young lady."

She had a glint in her eye that didn't quite match her cordial remark, and she smiled as if she'd beaten me at Ping-Pong. I thought for a second about what a smart Texan would say to such a clear goad. It didn't take long to hit on just the right thing.

I said, "Bless your heart, ma'am. Thank you."

Her smile changed, and she said more seriously, "I was real sorry Miss Honeybelle had to die right here in our parking lot we share with the pharmacy. Not that I blame her a bit. She had a big fight with that college man."

"Who? President Cornfelter?"

"The one with the bow tie. They had words right out here." She pointed at the edge of the parking lot, closer to Pinto's drug store. "I don't know what he said to her, but it musta been real mean. It like to have killed her, I guess. I'll go get those doughnuts for you."

She went away, and I stood there thinking about something my mother used to say. *Listen to the thing you're studying. Let it tell you when you're going off track.* Maybe it was time to think about President Cornfelter.

When the proprietor came back, I paid and thanked her again and took the box of doughnuts in my arm.

When Miss Ruffles and I walked past the front window, all the patrons inside the restaurant portion of Heavenly Treats came to watch us go by. I assumed Mrs. Claus had told everybody I was outside and they had run to the window to see the million-dollar dog.

We were the topic of hot gossip already.

Balancing the doughnut box and managing Miss Ruffles turned out to be a challenge, and I gave up trying to run, too. By the time we got back to Honeybelle's, two black cars were idling in the street. None of the windows were rolled down, but I could see the Blues Brothers sitting in the front seat of the lead car, watching. I took Miss Ruffles and the doughnuts through the gate.

In the house, Mr. Carver was very happy to open the Heavenly Treats box.

I said, "The whole town is talking about us."

His hand paused in the act of selecting a pink-frosted doughnut. "What about us?"

"About inheriting a lot of money from Honeybelle. Except they're calling her Moneybelle."

Mr. Carver sat down hard at the kitchen table.

Mae Mae stopped slamming things in the pantry and came out into the kitchen. "Why'd you tell anybody?"

"I didn't say a word. But somebody did."

To Mr. Carver, Mae Mae said, "It sure wasn't me."

Mr. Carver sighed heavily. "Everything Honeybelle did

was news in this town. Why did we expect this would be any different?"

"Because wills are usually kept secret," I said. "Unless the Tennysons told someone—"

"Mr. Ten wouldn't say a word," Mae Mae shot back. "He's no gossip."

"Well, then, it had to have been one of the Hensleys."

Mr. Carver spoke up. "Hut Junior wouldn't be caught dead spreading family business around town."

"Posie?" I asked.

"She's a lady," Mr. Carver objected.

"She's no lady," Mae Mae said. "You know as much as anybody, that girl came from trash."

"Don't talk like that." Mr. Carver puffed up. "Honeybelle never said that word, and you won't either. Not while I'm in charge of this house."

Mae Mae sniffed. "Maybe Posie went to college, and maybe she got herself into that pageant and made something of herself by marrying the right man, but she's still an Appleby, and there's no telling what any of those people will do."

"They're an old Mule Stop family," Mr. Carver said to me. "And a big one. There are bound to be a few twisted branches on a family tree like theirs. But Miss Posie is a perfectly nice woman, a good mother, a considerate wife."

Mae Mae snorted and went back into the pantry.

"Our job," Mr. Carver said solemnly to me, "is not to fuel any more gossip. We'll keep to ourselves, and say as little as possible."

"The cat's out of the bag, Mr. Carver. We could lock ourselves in this house for the next year, but that's only going to make people talk even more."

"She's right," Mae Mae said from the pantry.

"We'll do our jobs," Mr. Carver said stubbornly. "That's all we can do. It's what Honeybelle would want us to do."

As I hung up the leash, it hit me then that Honeybelle would have enjoyed knowing that she had triggered exciting town gossip. It was just the kind of thing that made her laugh. I only hoped she didn't have any more surprises stored up for us.

★ ★ ★

CHAPTER EIGHT

All spring and summer she was a classy southern lady.
And then football season started.
—TEXAS TRADITION

I continued to take Miss Ruffles for her morning runs. And every morning—no matter how early I started—the black car was sitting outside the gate. Sometimes a second car sat with the first. Sometimes one of the cars followed us.

"Have any thoughts about paying Mr. Postlethwaite?" Mr. Costello asked one morning after rolling down the car window, keeping pace with us on the street.

"Not today!" I replied with a friendly wave before cutting across a playground.

They didn't get out of their car to approach me. Maybe the Texas heat was too much for them. But they still made me nervous.

The following Saturday, I was scheduled to take Miss Ruffles to the first Alamo football game of the season. Honeybelle had told me Miss Ruffles was an unofficial mascot of the University of the Alamo football team. Coach Hut Hensley had always had a Texas cattle cur on the sideline when he coached, and it was tradition to continue to have a cattle cur at the games. Honeybelle had agreed to honor that tradition by providing the dog. She handed over chaperoning duties to me, citing her sore knee. The last thing she wanted was to break a hip, so I took Miss Ruffles to the game two weeks after her death.

My first mistake was showing up at the alumni office in the wrong clothes.

"Oh, sugar, you can't wear a yellow shirt in the stadium on the first game day of the season. Or any game day!" The secretary looked horrified. The name plate on her desk said TAMMY JAYE and was decorated with Texas stars. She said, "Alamo colors are red and white."

"Sorry."

"No worries!" She leaped up and unlocked a closet with a key, which she tucked into her bra when she was finished with it. "My favorite part of this job is helping outfit Alamo fans. I have to keep all these clothes locked up, though, or they just walk off by themselves. Here's a hat—perfect." She handed over a large white cowboy hat with a sequined red hatband and a silver star so big it was a cartoon. "And this belt is so cute! I've been waiting for just the right person to come along for this. Oh, and I can give you this vest, too—red and white with silver, see?"

I took the giant white hat and the sequined silver belt, but looked at the spangled red vest with doubt. It had silver tassels. "That's going to look funny over my yellow shirt."

"Well," Tammy Jaye said, and stopped. She bit her lip. She had an impressively large hairdo and a red and white dress that said she'd been to Victoria's Secret for her underwear. She waited for me to catch on.

It took half a minute for me to realize she meant for me to remove my shirt and wear the vest alone. I shook my head. "I have not lived in Texas long enough to walk into a stadium wearing tassels."

She understood. "Okay, how about a nice, simple T-shirt?"

She handed over a sleeveless red and white University

of Alamo T-shirt with sequins surrounding a picture of the
Alamo cowgirl. "Gaudy" wasn't a word that began to de-
scribe it. I was grateful that at least the outfit didn't have a
battery pack and lights. When I went into the bathroom to
wrestle it on, I discovered it was too small—more like a
size Miss Ruffles could fit into. If I'd had another cup size
or two, I'd have passed for a stripper. When I looked at
myself in the mirror over the sink, I caught Miss Ruffles
looking as if she didn't recognize me anymore.

When we came out of the bathroom, I nearly ran smack
into President Cornfelter, who was standing in front of the
closet, pulling out Alamo hats, shirts, and sweaters as if
to save them from a fire. Tammy Jaye had sucked in a dismayed breath to see her supply being ravaged.

Cornfelter swung around and caught sight of me. And
Miss Ruffles. He dropped his armload of booty.

The first time I'd seen President Cornfelter, he'd been
pulling the cork on a bottle of Honeybelle's favorite char-
donnay in her pastel living room. In that room she sometimes closed the pocket doors for privacy so the household
couldn't hear what was going on. Whether holding a social occasion or a business meeting, Honeybelle preferred
to keep some secrets. That day, the doors were open just
an inch.

At the time of his visit, I'd been outside with Miss Ruffles, throwing the ball for her in the yard. Not knowing
Honeybelle was entertaining, I'd let the dog into the house,
and Miss Ruffles had gone barreling through the rooms
in search of her mistress. She nosed open the pocket doors
and dashed into the room. With a happy yip, she took a
flying leap into the tufted silk cushions of the sofa and nuzzled Honeybelle with affectionate whines.

Honeybelle had gathered Miss Ruffles close to her bosom, cooing to the dog and smiling up at her guest through
her eyelashes. "Don't you just love her zest for life?"

She made the question sound naughty. But some instinct told me she had said it to defuse an argument.

At that inopportune moment, they realized I was in the doorway. President Cornfelter must have assumed he was alone in the house with Honeybelle. He turned brick red at the sight of me. If he could have magically made his wedding ring disappear, he'd have done it. But he was caught—a married man smelling of aftershave while standing over a woman whose rose-colored lipstick exactly matched the big lingering smooch mark next to his mouth. On the glass-topped table in front of the sofa stood a vase of flowers that I guessed he had brought for her. Daisies and carnations—a humble bouquet Honeybelle normally would have turned up her nose at, but today she had given them a place of honor. It was a signal that he was either a potential new boyfriend or a man who had come prepared to ask for a big favor. Which probably involved money. And yet there was tension between them.

"Hannibal," Honeybelle said cordially, "this is my assistant, Sunny McKillip. Sunny, this handsome specimen is President Cornfelter, from the university. Sunny's from Ohio, Han. Would you like to repeat what you just said to me? So she could hear it?"

He made a choking sound, and after a split second of married-man mortification, he handed Honeybelle a glass of wine.

For no reason whatsoever, Miss Ruffles leaped up from Honeybelle's lap and sank her teeth into the university president's hand. Maybe she had heard what he said to Honeybelle.

He screamed, and Miss Ruffles let go, but not before there was blood dripping on the carpet and smearing on the cuff of his white linen suit. Cornfelter shrieked at the horror of his own blood loss. Honeybelle jumped up and began alternately soothing both her visitor and her barking dog.

I got a wet towel to blot the carpet and called for paramedics.

Thing is, although Honeybelle and Cornfelter had been sweet as pie to each other while I was in the room, I sensed I had interrupted something less than friendly. Honeybelle's flirtatious tone hadn't matched the hard light in her eyes. And Cornfelter had been courtly, but I had the impression that was behavior he could put on as easily as a bow tie. I think Miss Ruffles knew something else besides romance was going on between them.

At the alumni office, Miss Ruffles bared her teeth again at President Cornfelter.

He backed up into the closet as if he hoped to climb inside and slam the door. "Keep that animal away from me!"

I had a good grip on the leash. "I've got her. Don't worry."

"Don't worry! I could have had nerve damage, you know. She did real damage to my hand." He held out his injured part. A pathetically small Band-Aid covered what was left of his wound. "Well, the first bandage was much larger."

I said, "Miss Ruffles has had all her shots."

"I had to get a tetanus booster. It was very painful." More to himself, he said, "I should have asked Honeybelle to pay for it."

"You could talk to her lawyer now," I suggested. "He's taking care of her finances. He might write you a check."

Cornfelter scrambled out of the closet and stepped to a safe distance. He must have become aware of how ridiculous he was looking to Tammy Jaye. He straightened his Alamo tie. "All that's water over the dam. I'm devastated that dear Honeybelle is no longer with us."

"I'm sorry you couldn't attend the memorial service."

"Yes, well, I had a scheduled meeting I couldn't cancel."

"When did you see Honeybelle last?" I asked while he was still shaken.

He put on a mournful face. "I may have been the last person to see her alive."

"I heard you saw her the morning she died."

He came clean. "Yes, I . . . I was buying a box of pastries to bring to my special fundraising committee that morning. I came out of the bakery, and there she was, looking beautiful in her car. I offered her a doughnut."

"Did she accept it?"

He stared at me, finally noticing I was asking strange questions. "Why would you want to know . . . ? Look here, I'm very sorry about Honeybelle, but life goes on. I've got to get out to the donors. Tammy Jaye, why don't you just bring an assortment of shirts and hats to my private box? I'll distribute them myself. Before the game starts, please."

"Of course, sir."

He bolted out of the office.

Tammy Jaye picked up the items he'd left on the floor, shaking her head. "He'd clean out my whole supply if he could carry it all. They call him Hannibal the Animal, you know—always taking more than his fair share." She caught herself being disloyal. "But you look adorable! Now, how about a new collar for Miss Ruffles? Red and white, of course."

Of course. Suitably decked out, the two of us were ushered into a golf cart driven by a young man named Cody, who had dimples and a ready smile. He wore a red and white Alamo rodeo-style shirt with white jeans and cowboy boots. The closest he ever got to a horse, I suspected, was the polo player that galloped discreetly across his clothing. He drove our golf cart around the perimeter of the stadium parking lot where the tailgate parties sprawled out.

At other colleges, I had seen plenty of game-day tail-gating, but the Texans took this particular American form of entertaining to a totally new level. They had tents and RVs set up with smoking barbecue grills and tables laid with baked beans and cole slaw and plenty of beer in cool-ers. Plates were piled with chili dogs and red hots and sausages, nachos and tacos, plus ribs people gnawed on with pregame enthusiasm. And did I mention the beer? I discovered an invention I had never heard of before—the Kegerator, which kept multiple kegs of cold beer on tap for drinking, but also for squirting at people. Each party blared country-western music, and the cacophony was impressive.

There were other mascots besides Miss Ruffles, I dis-covered. Only in Texas would a school feel the need to have three. One was a bespangled cowgirl on an excitable black horse. The other was a boy in a cowboy suit with a huge head and a Texas-sized cowboy hat. He wore a pair of pretend six-shooters that he pulled on unsuspecting fans in the tailgate section of the parking lot.

On the front seat of the golf cart beside Cody, I tried to look inconspicuous, while Miss Ruffles sat on the raised backseat like the homecoming queen. She knew just what to do. When she yipped at the beer-drinking tailgaters, they tossed her bits of meat still hot from the grills. A few students rushed over to pat her, and she panted happily.

We weren't outside for ten minutes before I began to worry about her safety. Was Miss Ruffles going to choke? Be poisoned? Or what if someone in the crowd got too close and grabbed her? Could I chase a drunk student around the whole parking lot to save her? Now that half the town knew she was the heiress to Honeybelle's fortune, she was worth a lot of money. Could I protect her?

Unaware of my growing concern, Cody happily made

conversation. The only downside was that he kept calling me "ma'am," when I couldn't be any more than two or three years older than he was.

"With all this food, ma'am, I used to be afraid Miss Ruffles would get sick in the golf cart. But she has an iron stomach, doesn't she?"

"Just about everything of Miss Ruffles is made of iron."

"Yes, ma'am, I know. I heard she took a chunk out of President Cornfelter. Were you around for that?"

I was the one who called 911 to summon the ambulance, which was overkill in my view, but Honeybelle had gone all southern belle and made a fuss of President Cornfelter's wound. Instead of answering Cody's question, I said, "Are people allowed to carry beer into the game?"

"Technically, no, ma'am. They're not allowed to carry firearms, either. The administration keeps threatening to start checking for those, too, but you know how it is."

The marching band led the fans into the stadium, where ponytailed cheerleaders whisked and fluttered their pompoms. The huge crowd already assembled in the stadium seats roared with approval. When our golf cart reached the field, all the players wanted to rub Miss Ruffles on her head before the game. I was surprised that she put up with their affectionate manhandling. Maybe the enormous players reminded her of the cattle she was intended to herd.

On the sidelines, we stayed in the golf cart listening to the steady noise of the crowd while the teams played their game. Miss Ruffles barked at touchdowns no matter who scored. The cowgirl on the black horse took a celebratory gallop up and down the field when Alamo finally kicked a field goal. The pistol-packing cowboy pretended to have showdown gun battles with the opposing team's mascot—some kind of pig.

At halftime when the band took the field, I led Miss Ruffles to the fifty-yard line, as instructed. She barked at the musicians while they played the theme from *Star Wars* and some Michael Jackson tunes and made formations on the turf. She strained at the leash as if she wanted to slip her collar and chase the musicians around until they were herded into a nice, manageable group.

At the end of the halftime show, I took Miss Ruffles back to the golf cart, and the young man from the alumni office said, "Ma'am, when Coach Hensley was alive, they had a Texas cattle cur that chased a Frisbee out on the field during halftime. It did tricks and ran around the band. You seem to have a way with Miss Ruffles. Any chance she could learn to do that?"

Chasing a ball in the fenced backyard was one thing, but turning Miss Ruffles loose in a stadium full of drunk football fans sounded like a catastrophe in the making. But I said, "I'll work on it."

"Mrs. Hensley always wanted Miss Ruffles to do the Frisbee act, but she couldn't teach her."

"Miss Ruffles is headstrong."

"Yes, ma'am," Cody said. Then, "It's too bad Honeybelle passed before she got the stadium thing done."

"The stadium thing?" I said.

"Yeah, she wanted the university to name the stadium after her husband, Coach Hut. Hut Hensley Stadium. I drove her around all last year, and I got the idea she was working on talking the board into it. All it took was money—that's what she said."

"Why didn't they name it for him?"

"President Cornfelter said we need a whole new stadium. This one's getting too old. Honeybelle didn't want to pay for a new one, though, just to fix this one up. So they were working out a deal, I guess."

"Who's they?" I asked, thinking of the scene I had interrupted in Honeybelle's house. "President Cornfelter and Honeybelle?"

"Well, them and others. When she rode around with me last year, Honeybelle talked about the naming rights with a bunch of people. Board members. Alumni donors. But they were on Cornfelter's side, all trying to sweet-talk her into building a new one. She wasn't backing down, though. She was one tough customer."

"Yes, she was." I thought to myself that although she hadn't backed down, she hadn't won the battle either. Lately, she had been suffering a lot of setbacks. The stadium issue, the garden club debacle, the biting incident, the family squabble about the wedding Posie wanted to throw.

Cody sighed. "It's a darn shame she passed before it came together."

I wondered if Honeybelle's will had anything to say about a new stadium. All I knew for sure was that nothing could happen for the year we were supposed to take care of Miss Ruffles.

Judging by the first half of the game, it looked as if Alamo was going to lose their opener by an embarrassing margin.

I said to my escort, "Do Miss Ruffles and I need to stay until the end of the game? I mean, what's the crowd like when the game's over?" Worrying about her safety had started to wear on me.

Cody scanned the stadium with the eye of an expert. "It's not a bad idea for you to get out of here before Hades breaks loose."

I decided to take Cody's advice. Miss Ruffles and I slipped out through the team entrance and headed for home. I was greatly relieved to have her safely out of there.

We passed Crazy Mary on the corner outside the stadium. The street musician had a violin today, and she whipped her bow in a lively fiddle tune. She played even though nobody was around to listen.

Miss Ruffles yipped at the music, but we kept going.

Trouble was, the afternoon had turned very hot, and even the shortcut across campus and through the sacred burial site of Coach Hut Hensley wasn't going to be a pleasant walk. We lingered in the shade of the trees by his tomb, and I noted there were red and white roses planted around the giant monument. Honeybelle had obviously put them there, under the stone that had been cut to the approximate shape of Coach Hensley's gruff face. Miss Ruffles rooted around in the bushes but was amenable when I urged her to walk again. I could feel the freckles popping on my arms and sighed at the thought of another sunburn. I should have arranged for a ride home, I realized.

Although I was wilting, Miss Ruffles looked perfectly fine in the heat. I knew she was thirsty, though. We took a break at a Jiffy Stop, and I bought a bottle of water for Miss Ruffles and a blueberry slushie for me. She slurped the water from a paper cup. I ate the slushie with a plastic spoon while we walked, then pitched the cup into a trash can at the Valero station.

On a side street, a dusty, noisy Jeep with no doors caught up with me. A set of Jurassic cow horns decorated the Jeep's hood, and the radio was blaring something twangy. Ten Tennyson was behind the wheel. He pulled over to the sidewalk and slowed to a crawl. He turned down the radio but kept his aviator sunglasses on.

His friendly grin was long gone. "Nice hat."

I continued to walk. The floppy brim of the Alamo hat provided a little shade, but not enough. "They gave it to me for the football game. I feel like I'm supposed to sell used cars."

He kept pace with me. "You gotta wear it like you mean it."

"I feel silly."

"It shows." He tilted down his sunglasses and squinted. "Is your mouth blue?"

"No," I snapped with more force than I intended. But he thought I'd conned Honeybelle somehow, an opinion that offended me. "Where's your horse?"

"Back at the barn. We did our Saturday cattle drive, and he'd had enough. I missed the game, taking him home. What's the score?"

"You don't want to know."

He could have driven off then. But he hesitated, then said, "Before you self-combust, I'd better take you to Honeybelle's. I was just on my way to pay a visit anyway. Hop in."

I wanted to refuse the ride. But the heat was intense, and despite my enormous hat, the glare of the sun already had me wincing.

Miss Ruffles didn't wait for me to accept Ten's offer. When he stepped on the brake, she leaped into the passenger seat and nuzzled him with garbled but excited whines. He laughed and roughed her up. When she'd had enough, she braced her front paws on the dashboard to look out over the hood. She looked like the heroic figurehead on a sailing ship. I pushed her over so I could share the seat and buckled in.

Ten threw the Jeep into gear and pulled away from the curb with a neck-snapping jerk of the clutch. He wasn't wearing a seat belt. After a minute, he must have decided to make cordial conversation. "So what happened at the game?"

I held on to the dashboard with one hand, Miss Ruffles with the other. "Alamo has no defense, and the quarterback wants to be a hero on every play. He's not the strategic genius he thinks he is. If not for the kicker, they wouldn't have any points on the board at all. They were down by twenty at the half."

He glanced at me with surprise. "Football fan?"

"Texas isn't the only place where football is a universal

language." As we took the corner, I held on tight. "Are you coming to inspect the house? White gloves to check for dust? Or are you going to take my fingerprints?"

"Fingerprints might be a good idea. Thanks for the suggestion." He shifted gears with another lurch, and we roared past the university. "I'm supposed to take a look around the place every week. Anything out of order yet? Mae Mae and Mr. Carver—are they keeping up their end?"

"Of course they are. The house is immaculate." Deciding to be honest, I said, "Trouble is, Mr. Carver can only dust the picture frames so many times a day. And now that Mae Mae doesn't have to stick to Honeybelle's menus, she's started experimenting with old family recipes. If you're lucky, she'll have something for you on the stove. But Mr. Carver has heartburn."

"I was counting on some good cooking." He finally grinned. "Mae Mae grew up in New Orleans, you know. Honeybelle kinda adopted her after Katrina."

"I heard that. She really likes you. What's your secret?"

"You feeling ignored?"

"If she ignored me, it might be easier. No, she took an instant dislike to me."

"Mae Mae liked being Honeybelle's confidante. It must have been hard enough sharing Honeybelle with Shelby Ann. When you came along, you probably took Mae Mae's place in line."

That possibility hadn't occurred to me. "It wasn't a competition. And anyway, that doesn't explain why she still hates me now that Honeybelle is gone."

"Give her time. Mae Mae could surprise you."

The only way Mae Mae could surprise me was by swearing to be my friend for the ages.

Ten glanced my way. "Y'all getting on each other's nerves already?"

"We're okay." With care, I said. "Maybe Honeybelle intended this arrangement to ease Mae Mae and Mr. Carver into retirement, but neither one of them can quit working."

"That could change. My grandfather announced his retirement as soon as I finished law school. Hadn't skipped a day at the office until Honeybelle died, and now he's made himself scarce." Half to himself, he said, "They both have, actually. My father, too. They worked like crazy on rewriting Honeybelle's will for her, and the next thing you know, she's dead and they've mysteriously gone on vacations. As far as I know, they've never missed an Alamo football game until today. And I haven't heard a word from my mama either. That's mighty suspicious, too."

"Too?" I said.

Ten shook his head as if to discard an irritating thought. "There are a few things that don't add up. I'm trying to get Honeybelle's estate paperwork organized for when my so-called partners get back, but I . . . well, I'm still having trouble tracking down the death certificate."

"You mentioned that. When my mother died while she was traveling, I got copies of her death certificate from the Department of State Health Services, but usually you get them from the funeral home."

He glanced over at me. "When did your mother die?"

"In April."

"I'm sorry. Did she . . . was it sudden?"

"Yes, she was killed in an accident while out of the country." I made an effort to remain calm, but it was hard. There were days when the realization that she was gone still hit me like a punch in the stomach. Honeybelle's death had brought my own loss back with almost as much heartache as when it first happened. I turned my face away, pretending to look at the houses we passed.

"I'm very sorry," Ten said, sounding genuine.

"Me, too. She was an entomologist. A lepidopterist, actually—she studied butterflies and moths. She was a scientist first, a mother definitely second. But I miss her. I miss knowing she's in the world."

"You've had a lot of changes in the last few months."

I was trying to be resilient, but I didn't always feel that way. Especially when I got unexpected sympathy, I tended to tear up. I suppressed that urge and spoke only when I had myself pulled together. "Have you asked the funeral home about the death certificate?"

"Yeah, but the funeral guy put me off. It's Mr. Gamble's nephew, so he's not familiar with all the ins and outs. I should ask him to try again."

"Where's Mr. Gamble?"

"Out of town, so I'm told. His nephew's in charge."

I figured Mr. Gamble was probably upset that his would-be girlfriend was as dead as his wife. A moment passed, and I asked, "How's everything else going for you without your dad and grandfather around?"

"It's like I've been thrown into the pond to learn to swim. Since I'm not licensed yet, I'm just supposed to keep the office open, so it's not too hard. Mostly I run errands."

"Like this one."

"Yes, ma'am. My dad said I should be concentrating on the wedding right now, but—hell, how much attention does that require? I don't like fritterin' time away."

"Frittering?" I said, amused. Then, thinking of Travis Joe Hensley in his role of ring bearer at his Aunt Poppy's wedding, I asked, "Whose wedding?"

He glanced at me with surprise. "I thought you knew all the family business."

"Which family?"

"Honeybelle's. Well, her daughter-in-law's family. Posie's a frustrated wedding planner, so she's starting with us. It's my wedding. I'm marrying Poppy Appleby, Posie's sister. In Honeybelle's rose garden."

★ ★ ★

CHAPTER NINE

Cowgirl up. Or go sit in the truck.
—FEMINIST ADMONITION

I don't know why I was so surprised. Why shouldn't Ten Tennyson get married? But I was struck silent by the idea of him marrying the sister of the garden club lizard. It was half a minute before I thought to congratulate him.

"Thanks," he said, concentrating on roaring the Jeep around the next corner. "I didn't think I'd get sucked into a lot of wedding nonsense when I asked her, but I guess that's the way it is these days. At least we're not releasing doves like Posie first wanted. Throw some doves up in the air around here, that's just asking for my rod and gun club buddies to start shootin'."

I wanted to ask if the location of the wedding had been officially decided. Had Posie won the right to hold the nuptials among Honeybelle's roses? Or did Honeybelle's will somehow prevent that from happening?

But I said, "What did Posie do before she started planning weddings?"

"One wedding," Ten corrected. "Her own. She didn't have any job before she got married, which was right after the Miss Texas pageant she finaled in. Hut Junior proposed, and she's been busy raising Trey and Travis Joe ever

since. Her husband said she needed a career now that her
boys are in school. It makes Hut Junior nuts that she can't
let those boys out of her sight. So she thought she'd start
planning events. Like weddings."

"And you're the lucky recipient of her attention."

"Hey, it's no problem for me. Poppy and Posie are having fun with it. They're into the rose theme. Lots of roses."

"Honeybelle's house is certainly a rose paradise."

"So I hear. I've only been in Honeybelle's backyard
where the pool is. I wasn't shown the roses. I can go along
with just about anything Poppy and Posie want."

"Except the doves."

He grinned. "Somebody's got to think about public
safety."

When we arrived at Honeybelle's garage, Miss Ruffles
jumped down from the Jeep and ran around me until I was
too tangled up in the leash to open the gate. Ten did the
honors, and when I unclipped Miss Ruffles, she zoomed
off like a rocket to find something to destroy. Her bark said
she'd behaved herself long enough and now it was time to
cut loose.

Lingering at the gate, I took off my silly hat and tried
to smooth my hair back into its usual ponytail.

"Listen," I said to Ten, not quite able to meet his eye,
"about the football games."

"Yes, ma'am?"

"I'm not . . . I don't think it's a great place for Miss
Ruffles."

Ten leaned his elbow on the gate. He was wearing a
crisp white shirt with the sleeves rolled over tanned forearms, tucked into jeans. A belt buckle the size of a teacup
saucer gleamed on his belt. He didn't smell horsey, so I
guessed he must have cleaned up after the parade. He
said, "You're trying hard to be the dependable governess,
aren't you?"

Determined not to think about how nice he smelled and to keep going with the subject I'd opened, I said, "I don't think the stadium is a safe place for her. It's huge and full of drunks and . . . and there are too many bad things that could happen."

"Bad things? Like what?"

"I don't know. Like somebody throwing her a poisoned hot dog, maybe."

"Nobody's going to feed her a poison hot dog. People around here love Miss Ruffles. She's been going to the games for years. Well—at least one year." Ten frowned to himself. "Maybe more. While I was laid up, I fell out of touch with what was going on here in Mule Stop, but—"

"There are thousands of people in that stadium. And some of them are carrying guns, I hear. From what you said about Honeybelle's will—about people in town wanting their bequests now, not in a year—I get the feeling they're only going to get what they want when Miss Ruffles . . . when she dies."

Ten laughed at me. "You think Honeybelle's will has given everybody in town a motive to kill a dog? You've been watching too much TV, Jane Eyre. Anyway, Miss Ruffles is indestructible. It's her job to attend the games, so she has to keep going. Relax. She'll be fine."

"I hope so," I murmured, unable to hide a frown.

I wanted to bring up something else. I was back to thinking about Honeybelle's request that I attend her memorial service to see if I could spot her murderer. That joke—had it been a joke?—was back to buzzing around in my head like an insistent bee. There were many other strange things that bugged me, too. Shelby Ann, her nurse, had disappeared into thin air before Honeybelle was cremated. So, it seemed, had both of Honeybelle's lawyers. Mr. Gamble, too. And there was something totally weird about President Cornfelter and his stupid stadium.

While I figured out how to bring up my concerns, Ten let a moment go by, then asked, "What does your mouth look like when it's not some outrageous color?"

I don't know why that remark hit me wrong, but it did.

"It's a normal mouth," I snapped.

I did a fast about-face and went inside to change out of my too-tight Alamo T-shirt and sparkly belt. I spent the afternoon helping Mr. Carver fold up household laundry and delivering the sheets and towels to their appropriate closets. I washed a couple of loads of my own clothes while I was at it, avoiding Ten as he talked with Mae Mae while she fixed him coffee and beignets, and later when he took a look around the house with Mr. Carver. I stayed out of their way, but I could hear them talking. They all sounded friendly.

Finally, I retreated to my room. I had a bedroom with a bath on the third floor at the front of the house. My windows offered the best view of the rose garden. The modest suite had been built for Hut Junior's governess, Honeybelle told me, so it was private without being totally out of the family orbit. I had shared the attic with Shelby Ann, Honeybelle's companion, who had a similarly small suite of rooms across the hall, but who had packed up and left the day after Honeybelle's death, locking her room behind her and presumably heading off on her world cruise. Ten did not come upstairs to inspect my room. I stayed there, though, reading until I heard the Jeep depart.

Not long after that, Mr. Carver took off in Honeybelle's minivan, the vehicle he used to pick up groceries and haul flowers from the nursery. He said he was having dinner with friends. He left every Saturday evening and was very closed-mouthed about where he went. His disappearances were a mystery that had intrigued me, and I wondered who his friends were, but I hadn't dared ask Mr. Carver or Honeybelle, who seemed to treat her butler's social life as none of her business. I couldn't help thinking he had a lady friend somewhere. For a man his age, I thought, good for him.

To Miss Ruffles, who commandeered my bed now that Honeybelle was gone, I said, "Or maybe he goes to church."

She gave me a long, pitying look. Nobody went to church for six or eight hours on a Saturday night, not even in Texas.

"It's better when he's here," I said to Miss Ruffles. "I'm scared to be alone with Mae Mae."

Miss Ruffles greeted this confession by plunking her butt on the bed and using one hind leg to scratch her ear.

Not happily, I went downstairs for my weekly uncomfortable dinner alone with Mae Mae. Tonight she had made a spicy chicken dish that would have sent Mr. Carver reaching for the Rolaids. A man had shown up at the back gate with the whole plucked chicken, saying he owed Honeybelle something nice after she gave him a lift out of town one day. Even though she was gone, he wanted to return the kindness, so Mae Mae accepted it. While I ate the chicken, she watched me from the corners of her eyes, maybe hoping I'd complain about the hot pepper.

"It's delicious," I told Mae Mae. "It reminds me of the stews in Colombia. My mom took me there once. They cook with okra, too."

Impervious to my conversation starter, she hmphed and served me a dish of melon slices—her usual dessert for Mr. Carver.

While I ate the melon, I thought about that trip to Colombia—one of the few occasions my mother lugged me along on one of her adventures. I was maybe thirteen, and I'd been terrified most of the time. The woman who had made the stew calmly killed a snake that slithered into her kitchen, and I'd had hysterics that made my mother disgusted with me. I had disappointed her then. I wondered if I continued to disappoint her for the rest of her life. Thinking about it made me low.

Mae Mae cleared the table. She snapped on the television and turned up the volume to hear the dialogue on a rerun of a forensic cop show, her obsession. I kept my thoughts to myself as I took out the trash. When Mae Mae poured herself a last cup of coffee and went up to her apartment over the kitchen—without so much as a "good night"—I made Miss Ruffles her nightly bowl of kibble. When I rattled the scoop in the tub of food, she usually came running.

Tonight, she didn't.

I went to the back door, held it open, and whistled, but she didn't show herself.

I went outside to look for Miss Ruffles. She wasn't digging up flowers or patrolling for invading UPS men. Nor was she snoozing under the lavender bush. She didn't come when I whistled again. She didn't yip when I called her name.

With a pang of horror, I rushed around to the front yard to check the rose garden. I pushed open the gate and found it beautifully silent, thank heaven—no sign of Miss Ruffles. I ran into the backyard to check the pool, suddenly dreading I might find her body floating in the pristine water. But no. I sagged with relief against the aluminum pool ladder. After that, I made a complete search of the big backyard. There were no telltale holes dug under the fence, no signs that Miss Ruffles had somehow scrambled over the six-foot stone wall by the garage or the hedge that ran around the rest of the property. She had never escaped before—not for lack of trying.

With concern rising in my throat, I stood in the middle of the large expanse of green grass and scanned the yard, trying to imagine where she'd gone. Down a prairie dog hole? Up a drainpipe?

I went out the back gate and stood on the driveway for a long moment, trying to quell the slam of my heart long enough to hear the snick-snack of her nails on the pavement as she trotted home. But the street was silent. Ten's Jeep was long gone, tire tracks obvious in the slight coating of dust on the asphalt. The Blues Brothers sat in their black car. One of them waved at me through the windshield.

No sign of the dog.

I stumbled back inside the gate. Miss Ruffles had run away. The realization hit me like a body blow. That's when I saw a slip of paper stuck between the slats of the gate.

I snatched it out and automatically unfolded it—a sheet of lined paper that had been hastily ripped from a ringbound notebook. The ragged edge fluttered in my hand.

Block letters, printed in plain blue ink.

MISS RUFFELS IS SAFE BUT NOT FOR LONG. FOLLOW DIRECIONS AND SHE WILL BE RETURN TO YOU. YOU WILL GET ANOTHER NOTE ON MONDAY. DON'T TELL POLLICE OR ANYONE OR ELSE SHE WILL <u>DIE.</u>

I read the note twice before the message sank in. The paper slipped from my fingers and fell to my feet. Instinctively I stepped back from it. Then my brain kicked in, and I bent to snatch it up with trembling fingers to read again, hoping I'd been wrong the first time.

When the news came that my mother had died, I felt for a split second as if I were in the midst of a plane crash—as if time slowed down, postponing the inevitable blunt force trauma of impact coming, coming, but not here yet. I was not yet hurled against the ground, not yet changed. One moment she was alive, and the next she was dead—but it took forever for that moment to arrive. When it came, her gone-ness hit me as if the power and momentum of the plunging plane had thrown me into solid earth.

It felt the same way as I read the words printed on the note.

Miss Ruffles had been taken. She was gone.

I cried out and clapped my hand over my mouth.

Then I noticed the blood on the paper. Blood from Miss Ruffles?

No, I thought instantly. Miss Ruffles had bitten her abductor. My heart twitched to life again. *Good for you, Miss Ruffles.* The blood made me think maybe she had escaped her captor. Maybe she had gotten free and was running loose in the neighborhood.

I jammed the note into my pocket to hide it. I ran back through the gate and across the yard and went in the side entrance of the house to grab a leash. In the kitchen, I filled my pockets with Milk-Bone biscuits, her favorite treat. As I moved to let myself out the kitchen door again, Mae Mae caught me. She was in her bathrobe, coming out of the pantry with a bag of microwave popcorn in hand. Her Saturday night ritual was eating popcorn in bed while watching reruns of *CSI* programs.

"Where are you going?" she snapped.

"I'll be back in a few minutes," I said over my shoulder.

"But—"

I didn't wait to explain or hear more. I ran across the backyard and let myself into the driveway by the gate. Out on the street, I whistled once, then bit my lip. I shouldn't be advertising Miss Ruffles was missing.

The black car was still there. As I marched over, the driver's window rolled down. Mr. Costello was reading a newspaper in the passenger seat, but he leaned over to speak to me.

"Hello, there, Stretch. How you doing tonight?"

"Where's my dog? Where is Miss Ruffles?"

"Huh?"

"You grabbed her!"

"The cute dog? No, we didn't grab her. We're staying over at the Fairfield Inn. They don't take dogs. Did she run off?"

"Did you see anybody in the street?" I demanded. "Did anybody stop by the gate?"

Both of the Blues Brothers craned around to look at the back gate, as if someone might be standing there right that minute.

Costello said, "No, we didn't see nobody."

"We took a drive over to the convenience store," his partner said. "Gotta use the toilet sometimes."

Costello poked him. "She's a nice girl. Don't talk to her like that."

I said, "Are you sure you didn't see anybody with Miss Ruffles?"

Costello lifted one large paw. "Right hand up to God. Want us to drive you around a little? We could talk about the money for Mr. Postle—"

"No," I said firmly.

"Hey, wait up. We'll follow you and—"

I didn't stick around to listen what their plan might be. I cut across the lawns of several neighbors and lost them quickly.

I hiked the nearest blocks of the residential neighborhood, hoping Miss Ruffles was loose, had escaped, was still somewhere nearby. When I ran with her in the mornings, we zigzagged through all the neighborhoods, so I prayed she was roaming around the territory we often traveled together, maybe finally getting to knock over the trash cans that always tempted her. I looked between houses, under bushes, behind trash cans and fence gates—I saw no glimpse of her brindle coat. I stopped on a corner and held my breath, listening for her yip, or maybe the telltale yowl of a cat being chased. Nothing. No sign, no sound of Miss Ruffles.

I couldn't believe she'd been kidnapped. I pulled the note from my pocket and read it again to be sure.

It was true. She was gone.

It was a human instinct to find someone to help me. Mae Mae and Mr. Carver would be no use, though, and I didn't want to panic them. The police were out of the question—the note had said as much. I found myself jogging into town.

My mother used to say that scientific research started by knowing your organism. By that, I thought she meant knowing the environment or the community or whatever place your subject lived in. For her, it was the butterfly jungle. For me, it was the town of Mule Stop, and I was very glad I had spent so much time running its streets and learning about its inhabitants. Not just the place, but the people.

The football game was long over, and students thronged on the streets. Small, noisy groups hung out on the sidewalks as well as in doorways of the bars. Students held red plastic cups of beer and laughed with each other over the fiddle music of Crazy Mary.

I pushed my way past the students and barged through the door of Cowgirl Redux. My friend Gracie was leaning on one elbow on the counter. Her hair was in hot rollers. In front of her sat a cupcake with a burning candle stuck in it. The chocolate cupcake was positioned on a pink paper napkin. Gracie's eyes were squeezed shut tight as if she were making a wish.

"Gracie?"

She opened her eyes and smiled. "Hey, Sunny. It's my birthday. I got myself a cake."

"Happy birthday," I said automatically, catching my balance on the counter.

"Actually, I got myself a half-dozen cupcakes. Since I don't have a date, I'm going to drown myself in buttercream frosting. You want one?"

"No, thanks. But Gracie—"

"Just let me finish wishing I could drown myself in Rico Vega instead. The bartender around the corner. He's gorgeous, and I can't get him to notice I'm alive." She took a deep breath, shut her eyes again, and blew hard on the candle.

Instead of going out, the candle tipped over and fell out of the thick frosting. It landed on the napkin, and a small flame sputtered up. A second later, the tiny fire leaped from the napkin to a bundle of receipts. Gracie yelped and grabbed the first thing she could reach—a polyester scarf—to put out the flame.

I blocked her arm and reached for the nearest display rack and a denim jacket decorated with a garish, hand-drawn skull—very ugly. I used the jacket to beat down the flames.

"Wow," Gracie said. "You're quick."

With the fire was out, I handed the jacket over to Gracie. A plume of smoke wafted in the air around us. "You okay?"

"Yeah. But—dang." Gracie waved the jacket to dispel the smoke. "I just lost my chance to meet some firemen for my birthday, didn't I?"

"Sorry."

"Hey, this jacket looks even more badass with the burn marks." She examined the blackened edges of the fabric. "Cool."

For her day job at the law firm, Gracie wore sensible suits, but when she hung out at the shop, she favored either cowgirl skirts with fringes or ruffled Mexican blouses overflowing with a feminine display that turned heads, although maybe not in the way she wanted. Deep down,

Gracie wanted champagne and a handsome prince, but the message she was sending was all about margaritas and cheap motels. Tonight the blouse made her look like she was advertising cantaloupes.

Belatedly, the smoke alarm began to shriek, and it nearly gave me a heart attack.

I fell into the canvas chair in front of the big mirror.

Gracie waved the jacket at the smoke alarm until it stopped. Finally, she noticed the look on my face and the leash in my hand. "You okay, darlin'? What's wrong? Where's your pooch?"

"Gracie, you can't tell." I felt a clog rise in my throat, and my voice cracked. "You can't tell a soul, but Miss Ruffles—she's gone."

Gracie dropped the jacket on the counter and came out from behind it to squeeze my quaking shoulder. "Catch your breath. It can't be this bad. She probably went looking for love, that's all."

I could hardly breathe, and it wasn't from the smoke. All my fears were suddenly boiling. I shook my head. "She's in real danger. She's been taken."

"What? Taken? What do you mean? Why?"

"I don't know. I don't know what to do. Here." I handed over the note.

Gracie skimmed it, growing more alarmed as she read each terse, misspelled sentence. "Wow! This is . . . it's crazy! No, look, calm down. I'll help you. Just . . . get a grip first. You need a drink? I've got some bourbon in the back."

I realized I was rocking in the chair, hugging myself. My adrenaline was all used up. I wiped my eyes and shook my head. "No, thanks. I'm just . . . I'm scared for her."

"I get that. But this note says she's okay for now. That's good, right?" Gracie went back behind the counter and returned to press a cold bottle of water into my shaking hand. "Tell me how this happened."

I took a slug of water and blurted out the words. "She was out in the yard—nothing unusual. I was in the house. The gate is always closed. But someone just took her."

"Why? No offense, but she's not exactly cuddly with strangers, right?"

"Somebody stole her." I couldn't say the word "kidnap." And I didn't have time to explain it all—how if Miss Ruffles was truly gone, Mr. Carver and Mae Mae would lose their chance at comfortable retirements. It had taken me only a week to lose the dog and ruin their futures. I began to tremble all over again. "Whoever took her will ask for money. Gracie, I don't have any money!"

Sensibly, Gracie said, "Maybe it's a joke. When all the students left the football game, they came straight into town to drown their sorrows. Maybe on their way here, someone saw her and grabbed her. You know how college kids get when they're drunk."

"I hadn't thought of that." A fraternity prank. Hope dawned inside me. A freshman stunt, maybe.

"Let's go ask around." She checked her watch and began pulling the hot rollers from her hair. "Just give me a sec."

I grabbed her arm. "We can't tell anybody she's gone. We have to keep this a secret."

"We'll just see if anybody's talking about her." She found a hairbrush and fixed her hair in a mirror, then lacquered it with spray. She muttered, "If I had better hair, I bet Rico would notice me. My problem is, it's always older guys who like what they see."

She locked the shop and took me around the corner to a college bar called the Last Chance Saloon. Inside, the jukebox was playing a country song by a singer who yodeled. Maybe a hundred students jammed close to the bar— all in shorts and Alamo T-shirts and yodeling along, their football team's humiliating loss forgotten already.

Gracie dragged me through the mob.

"Hey, Rico!" She planted her bosom on the bar to get the bartender's attention.

Rico Vega glanced her way, but kept his face neutral as he finished filling a pitcher from the tap. So much for good hair and cantaloupes. He plunked the pitcher on a damp tray before pushing it across the bar to the waitress, then wiped his hands on a bar towel and finally headed over to us. Rico had thick, strong shoulders and black curly hair. His face was secretive—dark brows, pug nose, square jaw, hooded eyes. An earring glittered in one lobe.

Gracie smiled brightly. "Anyone mention seeing a loose dog around?"

Rico snapped to attention and turned to me. "You mean Miss Ruffles? She ran off?"

So much for keeping secrets. I reached to shake his hand. "Hi, I'm Sunny. Don't spread it around, okay? Have you seen her? Or heard anybody talking about her?"

"I'm Rico. I've seen you running with Miss Ruffles." He shook his head, his gaze on mine. "Believe me, if she was running around loose, she'd be the hot topic around here. Everybody knows she bit President Cornfelter."

Gracie was adjusting her long hair to better showcase her cleavage. "Sunny's afraid she might be—"

I cut Gracie off before she revealed too much more. "I'm just worried she might get injured."

Rico nodded. "My grandpa had a cattle cur once. It ran off all the time. What's your cell number? If I hear anything, I can call you." He passed a cocktail napkin and his ballpoint across the bar.

I quickly wrote my number on the napkin. "Thanks. Thanks very much."

"Sure."

Gracie grabbed the napkin and scribbled. "Here's mine, too. You know, in case you can't reach Sunny."

"Yeah, okay." Rico took the napkin and stuffed it into his shirt pocket. "Good luck."

A minute later, Gracie and I were out on the sidewalk again, just in time to see a big car stop at the light on the corner. Not the Blues Brothers car, but a red sedan. A group of students eddied around the car, chanting a football cheer that suggested the worst thing an opponent could be was a native of Alabama.

The driver of the red sedan glanced our way, and through the crowd of students, I found myself making eye contact with Posie Hensley behind the wheel. Posie, the lizard.

Posie's gaze widened on mine. A second later, she floored the accelerator, sending students scrambling. Her car screeched around the corner and disappeared in a hurry. The students shouted after her, but she didn't stop.

I realized I was shaking again. My adrenaline was back. Fight or flight.

"Wow." Gracie stared after the car. "Wasn't that Posie Hensley? She got out of here in a hurry. Does she have an emergency sorority meeting or something?"

I swung on her. "You know Posie? Is she a customer?"

"Her, buy secondhand clothes? No, but she comes to our office now and then. Old Mr. Tennyson is big into fund-raising for the university, so he has committee meetings at the office. She's always standing by my desk to make calls to her kids. She hardly lets them ride a bike for fear they'll break their fingernails."

For no reason, I said, "She doesn't like me much."

"How come?"

I didn't know why, and I didn't know why I'd brought it up. I could feel my brain starting to dissolve again. I tried to gather my wits. "Gracie, could you take a walk down the street and look for Miss Ruffles for me? I'll go around the corner and look for her on the next couple of blocks. Meet you back here in fifteen minutes? I want to be sure she's not just running free."

Gracie hesitated. In her face, I could see her concern for me, but she checked her watch before making a decision. "Sure, can't hurt. Make it twenty minutes, okay? I have to turn off the lights in the shop first. I may not have much inventory, but it would be just my luck for a bunch of drunk students to bust in when my back is turned."

"I'm sorry," I said with all sincerity. "I shouldn't have bothered you. Especially not on your birthday—"

"Of course you should have. I always wanted to be part of a posse."

We split up, and I hurried up the street in the gathering darkness.

★ ★ ★

CHAPTER TEN

Don't piss on my leg and tell me it's rainin'.
—SOUTHERN WARNING

I left behind the busy bars full of students and the cacophony of music. This end of town was quieter. I looked under parked cars and into shrubbery, softly calling Miss Ruffles in the faint hope that she'd escaped. Or been taken by students who maybe tied her to a tree somewhere once they sobered up.

I passed the old Victorian house that had been refurbished into law offices. The lighted sign in the front yard said TENNYSON AND TENNYSON, ATTORNEYS AT LAW. As I passed by, a light suddenly flashed on in an upstairs window, telling me someone had just come to work on a Saturday evening. Since the senior partners were on vacation, I could guess who. I hurried past the house.

Next to the law office, the Baptist church was blazing with light. From inside I could hear choir practice. I circled behind the church and went through its small picnic grove—a cool, shady place where Miss Ruffles and I had rested on a few of our walks. Maybe she had escaped her captors and come here? But no. Someone had left a beer bottle and a crumpled pack of cigarettes on one of the tables, but there were no other signs that anyone had been here recently. I kept going and soon found myself in the back parking lot of Gamble's funeral home.

The lot was lit by a pair of elegant gas lamps. A bunch of yucca plants ran around the perimeter, so I went poking through them, whispering for the dog.

A few minutes into my search, I heard one of the funeral home's doors open. Instinctively, I faded back to the bushes. That's when I noticed a silver Cadillac parked in the building's portico. It was the same vehicle I had seen Mr. Gamble driving the day he'd stopped to invite Honeybelle to lunch in Dallas. Tonight the car was empty.

I saw a male figure step out of the doorway and move toward the Cadillac. He was lugging something bulky in one hand. With the chirp of a key fob, the Cadillac's trunk popped open, and a light glowed from inside.

The man hoisted his load into the trunk, and I saw it was a suitcase. He raised his hand to close the lid, but first glanced furtively around. A bank robber couldn't have looked more guilty. He almost missed seeing me, but his head swiveled back, and he froze against the side of his car.

It was Mr. Gamble himself. Not on vacation at all, but here in Mule Stop. He spotted me in the shadows. I couldn't pretend I didn't see him.

At my approach, he jumped in fright. Only when he caught sight of the empty leash in my hand did he stop himself from running back into the funeral home for safety. He sagged with relief and managed a smile for me. "Miss McKillip! For a second, I thought you had Miss Ruffles with you." He made his voice sound friendly.

"I'm so sorry to have startled you," I said. "Miss Ruffles is . . . well, you're safe."

"She makes me a little nervous. I could have been the one she bit, you know."

"She likes you. Well, tolerates you." I took a careful

look at his suitcase and decided Miss Ruffles couldn't fit inside. It was a garment bag, too thin to hold a dog.

Mr. Gamble had a penguinlike but surprisingly graceful figure that gave him the air of an aging ballroom dance instructor. I was surprised to see him wearing an improbable Hawaiian shirt printed with surfer girls and palm trees. His shorts showed bandy legs and hiking sandals.

Seeing my glance, he self-consciously touched his shirt with one hand, and his fingers wandered nervously upward as if to check that all the buttons were fastened. "Uh, I'm going out of town for a few days. I need to get away. After Honeybelle, you see . . ."

"It's been a shock for everyone," I agreed.

"Yes, a shock. My nephew has come up from Amarillo to take over the business for a while. I'm going . . . I'm headed to a convention. About disaster preparation."

"Honeybelle mentioned you helped her with her storm shelter."

"She should keep more water," he said, then corrected himself. "Should have kept more water. There's nothing more important than having a substantial water supply in an emergency."

I should have been worried about Miss Ruffles. But here was the man who could answer the questions that had bothered me ever since Honeybelle passed away. "I'm puzzled about some things, Mr. Gamble."

"About emergency preparation?"

"No, about Honeybelle's death. It seems—I don't know—odd that she died so suddenly of a heart attack. She seemed very healthy. She never mentioned any heart problem."

"Heart attacks can come out of nowhere," he said, assuming his professional demeanor.

"Well, yes, but she was simply sitting in the car, not chopping wood or running a marathon. It just doesn't seem possible . . . I mean, I wonder if she might have been poisoned, and it just looked like a heart attack."

"I did not perform an autopsy, if that's what you're asking. That's not my job. If something looks suspicious, I telephone the hospital in Lubbock, and they send an ambulance to transport her for a thorough autopsy. But Honeybelle's passing was perfectly ordinary. She died of natural causes. We should all hope to go as quickly as Honeybelle. No suffering, just a quick end." He seemed to realize he was babbling. "It was tragic, that's all."

"Yes, but . . . Look, is there a chance she could have been—I mean, could there have been foul play?"

"Foul play?' He was astonished.

"Could she have been . . . murdered?"

"Murdered! Why would you say such a thing? What a terrible idea."

"I know it sounds crazy, but—"

"Not just crazy. Impossible. She . . . she had a simple, run-of-the-mill, everyday heart attack."

"Could she have been poisoned? Or given some kind of drug that caused that sudden heart attack?"

"Of course not!"

"She was cremated so quickly. Maybe too quickly. It seems—"

"What are you suggesting?" He stiffened with increasing anger. "Are you doubting my professional judgment?"

"No, no." I was too upset to realize my mistake until it was too late. I backpedaled as fast as I could. "You're the only person I could think to ask, that's all. I'm sorry. I didn't mean to be insulting."

"Well," he said, agitated and sweating profusely. "Well. I have to be going."

"Sorry. I didn't mean to keep you. I just—"

He closed the trunk. "Good night, Miss McKillip."

"All right, yes. Enjoy your trip." I stood back and

watched Mr. Gamble climb into his car and start the engine.

People are always getting warned about unscrupulous funeral directors who might try to coerce the grieving into spending extra money on a big casket. Mr. Gamble didn't seem like the shady kind.

Until tonight. As soon as he'd seen me, he'd broken into a sweat. And as Mr. Gamble drove out of his own parking lot—a parking lot he'd been exiting for decades—his front tire hit the curb and jumped onto the sidewalk. He accelerated with a squeal of tires.

I had shaken him up with my questions about Honeybelle. And it wasn't just a matter of doubting his professional opinion. Suddenly I wondered if he had owed money to Honeybelle like so many other local businesses. I didn't remember seeing his name among the checks that came in the mail, but maybe Honeybelle had taken care of those herself.

Tonight, Mr. Gamble sure looked like a man trying to get out of town fast.

★ ★ ★

CHAPTER ELEVEN

Speak your mind, but ride a fast horse.
—COWBOY STRATEGY

My fear for Miss Ruffles doubling, I retraced my steps through the grove and past the church, just as a warbling tenor hit a sour note in praise of the spangled heavens. I reached the dark patch of sidewalk in front of the Tennyson and Tennyson office. The front door slammed, and I cursed myself for coming this direction. I was caught under the streetlamp.

But it wasn't Ten who came striding toward me on the sidewalk. Instead, I recognized Hannibal Cornfelter. He spotted me, and his confident step faltered.

Then he put on his most professional smile and kept coming up the sidewalk. When he spotted the leash knotted up in my hand, he caught his toe on the walk.

The manila folder he'd been carrying went flying and landed at my feet, its contents halfway spilling out onto the sidewalk.

Instinctively, I bent to pick up the folder. It was full of legal-looking documents. The top of one sheet read: "How to fill out a *Divorce Petition*."

Without a word, Cornfelter snatched the folder out of my hands and stuffed the papers back inside.

I said, "Nice to see you, President Cornfelter."

"Good evening, Miss . . . ?"

"McKillip."

"Yes." He manufactured some camaraderie. "Another stranger wandering in a strange land. You're from Chicago, as I recall?"

"Ohio."

Same difference to him. He didn't try to shake my hand but suddenly gathered the folder to his chest as if it were a treasure map he wanted to keep to himself.

He was an attractive man if you went for the college professor type who maybe sang in a men's chorus. Honeybelle told me he sometimes sang with a local barbershop group. He had wavy, Kennedy-esque brown hair and a patrician face that could quickly switch from a cool, intellectual smile to a big country-boy grin that played well in Mule Stop. I first thought Honeybelle liked him because he had more polish than most of her gentleman callers. But now I wondered.

He was smart and knew how to play the politics of college fund-raising. But my personal opinion was that if his life depended on it, President Cornfelter probably couldn't change a tire.

He went on the offensive. "I hear congratulations are in order."

"For?"

"Honeybelle's bequest. A million dollars is a lot of money for a young woman such as yourself."

I had assumed the details of Honeybelle's will were confidential, but obviously the bulletin had gone around town faster than the Pony Express. The fact that even Cornfelter knew about the will made my heart thunk in my chest. Everybody else must know, too. But the "such as yourself" line irked me.

He must have thought he had bested me, because he

went on, "I don't know what Honeybelle was thinking. A woman of her means and values might have established an important scholarship or academic endowment. I suppose you're going to buy yourself a shiny new car or whatever young people waste their money on these days. Exactly what did you do to convince Honeybelle you deserve the kind of cash she left to you?"

Maybe I was too accustomed to the petty bickering that went on among snooty academics who had little common sense to be shaken by his quick attack. Calmly, I said, "I was more surprised than anyone by her gift."

"Were you?" He positively had a sneer on his face. "She was a delightfully unpredictable woman." His tone insinuated something unpleasant.

"Also thoughtful and generous."

He said, "Perhaps you didn't know her long enough to understand her personality completely. Honeybelle was a strong woman. But she was easily flattered away from the most logical decisions. She made emotional choices that didn't always make good long-term business sense."

"Depends on your business," I said, giving him a taste of his own childish faculty-room behavior.

I might as well have swatted him in the face with a rolled-up newspaper. He blinked and said, "What's that supposed to mean?"

"You must be disappointed about your stadium." Suddenly I was reckless. "I know how much a football program means to the reputation of a university. If you don't have football, students will choose to go elsewhere, and pretty soon the University of the Alamo dries up and blows away into the desert. Well, you may eventually get your stadium from Honeybelle, but can you wait that long?"

His face turned ugly. "Long enough for a dog to die?"

Shaken at last, I demanded, "Have you done something with Miss Ruffles?"

"I reported that animal to the town police." He lifted his head nobly, as if he'd committed an act of bravery. "I was lucky I didn't contract an infection."

"Maybe we should get Miss Ruffles tested."

His eyes narrowed. "If she bit me, there's no telling how quickly she might attack someone else—maybe even a child. She's dangerous."

"She was dangerous only to people who threatened Honeybelle."

"You think I . . . ?" He remembered himself, straightened his shoulders and gathered his composure. "Honeybelle's death was a terrible loss. But I had nothing to do with what happened to her. She went far too young. It's all very tragic."

"Yes," I said. "I miss her."

I had the last word. I left President Cornfelter and hurried toward the busy part of town again. I had a black feeling of dread for Miss Ruffles as I jogged into town to find Gracie.

At the corner, I encountered Crazy Mary, the street musician.

She was carrying her violin in one hand, the battered guitar case in the other. Her backpack hung from a strap on one shoulder, and the full bag thumped against her side. Everything about her posture said she was tired.

If anyone might have seen Miss Ruffles, it was the one person who had been out on the street all day long. A ray of hope penetrated my low spirits, and I planted myself in her path. I felt like a jerk for not speaking to Crazy Mary before this, but I brushed aside that regret. I was too worried for Miss Ruffles to care about social propriety now.

"Mary? Hi, I'm Sunny."

She said, "I don't give lessons anymore."

"I'm not—"

"If you want to play the guitar, I can recommend

someone who won't rob you blind, but if you want violin lessons around here, it's going to cost you. Banjo and mandolin, there are guys at the university who can help you." She spoke quickly, by rote, as if she were asked the same questions over and over. "Nobody teaches rock and roll, so if that's what you want, you'll have to go to Austin."

"Actually, I'm not the least bit musical. I don't suppose you've seen a dog tonight?"

She eyed me. Now that I was standing close enough to notice, I realized that her blond dreadlocks were actually quite artistic. Her earrings were dangling bits of silver twisted into the shapes of musical notes and adorned with small stones. Her long skirt had been knotted up on one side to show off a delicate petticoat, and her blouse— with several layers of subtly colored tank tops beneath— was intricately embroidered. From a distance, she looked scruffy, but up close, she had a real artistic flair.

Her face was expressionless. Or maybe slightly hostile, which I deserved. I could see nothing behind her granny-style sunglasses.

"I'm looking for a dog." I put my hand down to my knee. "She's about this high. Mostly gray. With a spot over one eye that kinda looks like an eyebrow—"

"You mean Miss Ruffles?" Crazy Mary's voice was quiet but perfectly clear. Her accent was southernish, but not Texan. I recognized from her vowels that she wasn't a Mule Stop native.

"Yes," I said eagerly. "Yes, Miss Ruffles. Have you seen her?"

"No," said Mary in a flat voice.

She might as well have deflated me with a pin. "Oh."

"I'm pretty sure I heard her, though," Mary said. "She was in a car. About an hour ago. She was yipping. She has a distinctive yip."

My heart leaped. "You heard her?" I almost seized Mary in a crushing hug.

"I have a good ear. I hear things."

"What kind of car? What color? Did you see the license plate? Or—"

"I don't know what kind of car it was. I didn't notice the color either. A woman was driving. Mrs. Hensley."

"Posie? You mean Posie Hensley?"

"She drove by a while ago, that's all, and I heard the dog yelping."

I sagged against a parking meter while the truth sank in. I had seen Posie in her car myself. But I hadn't heard Miss Ruffles.

"Miss Ruffles is missing?"

"Y-yes. I have to get her back."

"Do you have a gun?"

I jumped. "Of course not."

She shrugged. "If you can't take care of business yourself, go to the police."

"I . . . I can't do that either."

"So you're stuck between a rock and a hard place."

My mother had preached peace and harmony and doing unto others. Maybe she had the wrong idea.

I became aware of Mary watching me think, and I said, "I'll figure out something."

"Good luck." Mary squared her shoulders to redistribute the weight of her backpack, then cut around me to go on her way. She was a dozen steps away before she said over her shoulder, "You know, my name's not Mary."

I should have chased her down to find out her real name at least, but instead I stood there and tried to make my whirling brain settle down to think.

Miss Ruffles had definitely been kidnapped. It wasn't a prank anymore. Not a mistake. Someone had taken her in a car. And not just anybody.

Posie Hensley, the lizard.

I needed to figure out how to get Miss Ruffles back, but my brain wasn't functioning. Stumbling with dread, I put one foot in front of the other. I finally found Gracie on the next block over. She was out of breath and looked disheveled. I had just enough room in my heart to feel guilty for making her run all over town.

"Sorry," she said as we almost collided in front of the art gallery. "No sign of Miss Ruffles anywhere."

I couldn't do anything more than moan.

Two police cars sat in the middle of the street, the officers talking to each other through their open windows. Their presence had chased most of the students into the bars. The cops stopped talking and instead began to watch us.

Gracie didn't notice. She tried to rake her hair back into order. "I don't know what to tell you, Sunny. She's not around here."

I managed to speak. "I think Posie Hensley has her. Mary heard a dog yipping in Posie's car."

Gracie stared at me. "You sure? But—that's good, right?"

"Not really, no. Last I heard, Posie wanted to get rid of Miss Ruffles. She wanted to dump her at an animal shelter in Dallas."

"Well, unless she drives half the night, she's not going to get rid of Miss Ruffles right away. And if I know Posie, she won't leave her kids that long."

"I've got to go get Miss Ruffles from her."

"Do you need backup? Do you know where Posie lives?"

"Yes, I helped Honeybelle deliver some flowers for a dinner party last month. I think I can find the house. It's out by the interstate, in that new subdivision. I'll go myself. It'll be safer."

"Wait." Gracie caught my arm as I turned to leave. "You're going over there now? And do what? Knock on the door and confront Posie about kidnapping a dog?"

"What else?" I asked. "Let something terrible happen to Miss Ruffles?"

"What about talking to the cops first?"

We both looked at the officers in the middle of the street. They looked back at us.

The ransom note had been clear about not contacting the police. I said, "I can't run that risk. Besides, I don't want to get Posie into any trouble."

Gracie laughed in disbelief. "You're kidding, right? She snatched your dog! I say we saddle up and get in her face."

"Miss Ruffles isn't my dog. She's not her dog, either, of course, but Posie's part of Honeybelle's family. If I start throwing accusations around or bringing the police, there's just going to be a big uproar."

"You need somebody. If not me, somebody who has some clout with Posie."

Ten Tennyson, I thought. Or his father or grandfather. One of the family lawyers who was supposed to help keep Miss Ruffles safe. But Ten Tennyson was marrying Posie's sister, I reminded myself, so that hardly made him a good candidate for confronting Posie. With every passing minute, my panic for Miss Ruffles grew. I felt dizzy as my fear for her safety doubled.

"Listen," Gracie said, guessing where my runaway thoughts were going. "Posie looked kind of crazed when she drove by. Maybe this whole thing is a mistake. Give Posie a chance to bring the dog back all by herself."

I gave her an impulsive hug. "Thanks, Gracie. You've been great. I mean it—thank you. Go celebrate your birthday. Maybe Rico will give you a free drink."

She brightened. "Hey, it can't hurt to ask. You want to come along?"

"No, I'm going back to Honeybelle's."

Gracie bit her lip, clearly uncertain about leaving me on my own. "If you decide you want somebody to ride shotgun, just holler."

"Yes, of course. Happy birthday."

Behind me, one of the police cars followed.

★ ★ ★

CHAPTER TWELVE

When in doubt, fry it or add cheese.
—MIRANDA LAMBERT

The cop tailed me for several blocks. Then he turned onto one of the residential side streets and disappeared. But as I walked, I could see between the houses to the parallel street. There, the cruiser continued to sneak along, and I knew the officer was keeping an eye on me. I couldn't imagine why, and it made me even more nervous than I already felt. When I turned into Honeybelle's driveway, the police car reappeared. The cop watched me let myself through the back gate and into the yard.

Why were they watching me? My heart was pounding hard. I was too frightened to walk out into the street and ask. Talking to them might endanger Miss Ruffles.

The minivan hadn't returned, I noticed, so Mr. Carver was still out on his mysterious Saturday night mission. I could have waited for him in the garage and told him everything. Part of me wanted an ally. The more I thought about it, though, the more I feared the news might give poor Mr. Carver a fatal heart attack.

At the back of the house on the second floor, the blue light of a television screen told me Mae Mae was tucked in for the night with her bowl of popcorn. She was probably watching another grisly crime show. I was afraid to tell her, too—afraid for my own safety. Mae Mae's probable fury prevented me from climbing the stairs to confide in her. Besides, what kind of help could she be? I couldn't imagine her threatening to bonk Posie over the head with her iron skillet.

I let myself into the house and set the alarm for the night before creeping upstairs.

From my third-floor bedroom window, I could see both police cruisers sitting in the street in front of the house. The officers were talking with each other through their open windows again. About what? One soon departed, but the other remained at the corner, where he could monitor the front door of Honeybelle's house as well as the gate by the garage. There was no way I could leave the house again without being seen. I'd just have to wait them out.

I pulled the coverlet from my bed and tiptoed downstairs. I made sure the front door was locked, At the security keypad, I let myself out onto the back porch. The evening air was already getting chilly. The scent of Honeybelle's rose garden floated over the lawn—normally a welcoming fragrance. Tonight, though, the smell almost turned my unsteady stomach. I wrapped myself in the coverlet and stretched out on one of the pool chairs, prepared to stay awake until the police cars departed. Then, I told myself, I'd go to Posie's house.

My mother used to say that the primary quality a scientist needed was the ability to observe. As I sat under the stars, I forced myself to think about what I had observed—more clearly, with diminishing panic. I reviewed Posie's every interaction with Miss Ruffles. And every word President Cornfelter had said about Honeybelle. And the things Honeybelle herself had said and done when she spoke over the hedge with Mr. Gamble.

If Posie had taken Miss Ruffles, why had she bothered

with a ransom note? And why bother making the ransom note so illiterate? Why not dump Miss Ruffles in a shelter somewhere—or worse, kill her—and simply take the inheritance that was coming to her?

Had Crazy Mary been wrong about hearing Miss Ruffles in a car? Had Mary and I jumped to the wrong conclusion when we thought it might have been Posie's?

And what about President Cornfelter? He admitted he'd been in conflict with Honeybelle over the football stadium. He was angry that she hadn't created a legacy for herself by paying for the stadium, but I had a feeling he was more furious that she had denied him his own legacy as a successful president of the university.

I heard a noise and was instantly on my feet, ears straining. The electric garage door opener rumbled. When the door was up, Mr. Carver pulled into the garage and shut off the minivan. I heard him get out and saw him stand for a minute in front of the garage, looking down the street at the police car—no doubt wondering what the cruiser was doing in our neighborhood. He must have decided there was nothing amiss, because he slowly made his way to the outdoor staircase to his apartment over the garage. I could see his stooped, skinny figure from the shadows. He looked quite fragile as he gripped the handrail. Wherever he had been, he was very tired now.

I faded back against the wisteria bush, unable to bring myself to approach him. Instead, I watched him go into his apartment. He turned on the lights.

A moment later, another car pulled up at Honeybelle's garage. The driver got out, leaving the engine running. I stood very still in the leafy shadows. It was Hut Junior.

Tonight, he wore a large cowboy hat, jeans, and a long-sleeved shirt. He was smoking a cigar.

Upstairs, Mr. Carver came out of his apartment carrying a long, thin box. Too large for a briefcase, not shaped like a suitcase. Too small for a dog to fit inside. Mr. Carver came slowly down the stairs and met Hut Junior in front of the garage.

They had a short conversation, and Hut took the container. With his cigar in his mouth, he shook Mr. Carver's hand, and they shared a laugh. Then Mr. Carver went back upstairs while Hut Junior stowed the box in the trunk of his car.

When he closed the trunk, he glanced down the street at the police cruiser. He raised his hand in a wave. I couldn't see the police car from where I was, but I assumed the cop waved back. Hut got into his car and drove away.

Upstairs in his apartment, Mr. Carver locked the door behind himself and turned on some music—guitars and a voice, Texas swing. I could hear the water running in his bathroom. Eventually, his light went out and the music faded away.

What was that all about? I couldn't imagine.

Except that Hut Junior and Mr. Carver were in some kind of partnership.

My mother used to say that a scientist had to be open to the possibility of surprise. The relationship between Hut Junior and Mr. Carver was definitely a surprise to me. Dizzy all over again, I tottered back to the pool chair and sat down.

My thoughts went into overdrive. If Hut Junior wanted his lion's share of Honeybelle's fortune right away, he only had to collude with someone like Mr. Carver to get Miss Ruffles out of the way. He could pay off Mr. Carver with more than the million Honeybelle's will already promised, and they'd all be happy.

Poor Miss Ruffles. My throat closed up tight. The thought of that high-spirited little dog in mortal danger crushed me. Where was she? Was she cold? Hungry? Frightened?

I had failed to protect the animal entrusted to me, so my job was over. All I could do was go back upstairs and pack my belongings. I could be back in Ohio very soon—broke and jobless, maybe, but with the whole horrible mess behind me.

But then I thought of my mother and how relentless she was about butterflies. She used to get a fire in her eyes when she heard a report about migration problems, or the destruction of feeding grounds by the encroachment of farming. She never gave up—not even on a species that was surely doomed. How many times had she packed her duffel and headed off to protest a chemical plant or help count the number of insects that turned up at a tropical destination? She could have stopped fighting. She could have spent her time in warm classrooms, lecturing sleepy students who didn't care about the battle she was waging.

I knew what my mom would say.

Miss Ruffles had only one person on her side—me.

The hour grew very late. The temperature dropped, and the stars sharpened overhead. I was back to thinking Posie had Miss Ruffles. A plan for confronting her swirled in my mind. I thought of various things I could say to her. I waited for the police car to leave. I waited and waited.

Eventually, though, I must have dozed off, wrapped warmly against the cold air. I started awake when I heard Mae Mae banging plates as she unloaded the dishwasher. I could smell her coffee brewing, too. I was stiff and sore as I pulled myself to my feet. If Mae Mae caught me, I'd have a hard time explaining myself.

I grabbed my coverlet and wrapped it up. I peeked over the hedge to see if the police car was still parked nearby. It was.

I went back to the porch and steeled myself to go inside.

But I heard Mae Mae's voice. From her tone, I realized she was speaking on the telephone. I hesitated, listening.

"My gracious, that does sound exciting, cher! Your first day of school, and already you know half your numbers! Why, you must be the smartest little girl in class!"

I shouldn't have eavesdropped, but the astonishing note of love in Mae Mae's voice rooted me to my spot.

"You bet I'm proud," she said with obvious affection. "I'm the proudest great-gramma in the whole world."

The idea that Mae Mae could have a family—let alone one she loved so clearly—astonished me. From all the details I had gleaned, I assumed Mae Mae left New Orleans and never looked back.

She said, "Okay, sweetness, you have another great week at school, and we'll talk again next Sunday. Let me talk to your mama now, okay, cher?" A moment later, she said in a more businesslike but no less tender voice, "Don't you worry, now, Dasha. I sent the check just yesterday, so you'll have that tuition money, no problem. Sure, sure, I'm happy to do it. Happy I can do something good for all y'all, so don't fuss. I know, honey. I love you, too. Bye-bye, now."

She hung up and began to hum a tune.

I stood, quiet and thinking. Mae Mae had more than herself to support.

There was no question now. I had to stay and fight for Miss Ruffles. Mae Mae needed the money Honeybelle left her.

To avoid talking to Mae Mae just yet, I went around the house and let myself in the side door. I went upstairs and cleaned up, dressed again, and screwed up my courage in front of the bathroom mirror. It took a while before I was brave enough to go downstairs to the kitchen.

"Good morning, Mae Mae."

"What's so good about it?" She was busy at the stove, flipping little puffs of crispy dough from the hot grease in an iron skillet and onto a wire rack on the counter. Glowering, she sprinkled each with powdered sugar.

I chickened out. Telling her about Miss Ruffles wasn't going to help me. She'd probably drown me in the boiling grease.

Mr. Carver arrived silently. He poured himself a cup of coffee and drank it scalding hot. Then a second. He sat at the table and waited for his breakfast in silence, looking sick. I actually wondered if he was hungover. He was in no shape to help me either.

Breakfast turned out to be grits and grillades—a far cry from Honeybelle's daily request for fruit and cottage cheese. I thought I would hardly be able to taste anything, but suddenly I was famished. I ate everything, even sopped up the gravy with my toast before I dashed out the back door to pretend to take care of Miss Ruffles.

After breakfast, Mae Mae chopped an onion and started a roux on the stove before going upstairs to get ready for church.

The house already smelled like gumbo when she shuffled out to the car on Mr. Carver's arm. Her hat, an enormous confection of pink swoops and feathers, looked like an exotic bird on her head. Beside her, Mr. Carver looked frail.

So far, neither of them had noticed Miss Ruffles was missing, but that wouldn't last much longer.

The couple of hours they attended church was the only time during the entire week that I had Honeybelle's house to myself. As soon as they were out of sight, I dashed into the kitchen and turned on the water faucet. Wasting water felt like a sin, but if Mae Mae or Mr. Carver came back unexpectedly, they'd shut off the faucet first thing. I'd hear the water stop and be warned of their return.

That done, I slipped into the little parlor Honeybelle used as an office, and I sat in her chair. The last time I'd been in that chair was when I'd cleaned up the mess of shredded paper Miss Ruffles had made when she chewed up Honeybelle's mail.

If I was going to confront Posie about Miss Ruffles, I needed information. I wanted to know the root of the conflict between Posie and Honeybelle.

Before me, Honeybelle's desk was polished and dusted. In her absence, Mr. Carver had arranged a neat fan of Honeybelle's favorite magazines beside the framed photographs of her husband and the little boy with the guitar, whom I assumed to be Hut Junior. Instead of her usual vase of roses, a glass dish of Honeybelle's favorite candies sat within easy reach. From the dish, I selected a mini lollipop and unwrapped it. Savoring the sweetness, I kicked off my shoes and cautiously opened the top drawer.

The drawer was full of monogrammed writing paper, a selection of beautiful greeting cards, two fountain pens, and tape and ribbons for decorating gift packages—a glimpse into how much of Honeybelle's life was dedicated to other people. I flipped through her address book, bound in chintz and crammed full of names and Texas addresses. The drawer to the right contained fancy wrapping papers. Nothing that would help me.

The left-hand drawers were more useful. I walked my fingertips across a dozen file folders packed with papers and pulled them out one by one.

I had done a lot of financial work for various college professors, but Honeybelle's money matters were much more complex than simple budgets and retirement plans. I could make no sense of her investment statements except to note that she had invested with more than one broker—two located in Dallas, one in New York—and the numbers were very big. Several other folders contained information about Hensley Oil and Gas. More big numbers, but I guessed most of the company secrets were held at the office across town.

I saw Hut Junior's signature on many pages. Perhaps he wasn't running the company, but he clearly played a big role in its management. Looking at all the papers he signed, it hardly seemed that Honeybelle had distrusted her own son. He had his hands on many aspects of the business. I thought about his anger at not being named the CEO after Honeybelle's death. Posie had sympathized with his disappointment. Was that the crux of the problem between Honeybelle and her daughter-in-law? Honeybelle's unwillingness to relinquish control of the lucrative company to her obviously capable son?

Possibly. I stowed those folders away. Family dysfunction took many twists and turns.

A folder marked MISS RUFFLES contained health records from the vet who gave the dog her regular checkups. It also held some old photos of other dogs—presumably the other Texas cattle curs Honeybelle and her husband had owned years ago. Nothing that might interest Posie.

A folder concerning the rose garden contained a detailed map of the roses she had planted, with a code of letters and numbers by the name of each rose. Behind me on the credenza sat the notebook she had taken outside with us the day we had worked in the garden. I made a mental note to take a longer look at that later. If need be, I could steal it out of the parlor and take it upstairs to my room that night and return it the next morning before Mr. Carver started his rounds.

I sat for a long time reading through her folder containing garden club information. It was all cut-and-dried, though—nothing about Posie except the date when she joined the garden club eleven years earlier. I found myself thinking eleven years was a long time to try to win her mother-in-law's approval and not get it.

I opened the folder marked ALAMO BD MINS and found myself looking at the secretary's typed notes of the university's board meetings. This was the kind of thing I understood. Committee and department notes were my specialty after a particularly disorganized English Department chair gratefully handed over many details so he could study some newly discovered e. e. cummings letters.

I put my bare feet up on the desk and flipped through the university board minutes. Someone had doodled little dog drawings in the margins—Honeybelle, bored and sketching little cartoons of Miss Ruffles. She even had caught the mischievous gleam in her dog's eyes.

I felt the prick of tears as I looked at those cartoons. Miss Ruffles looked so alive in them.

The treasurer's report came first. I felt a glow of triumph when I saw the numbers that indicated exactly what I had guessed: Alamo's enrollment was down, and the university was bleeding money. No wonder President Cornfelter wanted a new stadium. He needed something—a lot of somethings—to keep the student body growing. I wondered how close he was to losing his job. Surely the university needed a president who could get good results, and fast.

Halfway down the next page I was intrigued by a paragraph about the naming rights for the new stadium. Honeybelle had drawn a picture of Miss Ruffles angrily chewing on the words "President Cornfelter proposes a committee to study the possibility of building a new stadium. Discussion ensued."

I'll bet a discussion ensued. No doubt some board members wanted the stadium, while others saw insanity in the idea of such a huge expenditure. The date of the meeting was only a month ago. Also in the margin, Honeybelle had written a note to herself. In her handwriting, she said, "Change my will."

I sat up. "Change it how? Were you going to pay for the new stadium?"

Judging by her drawing of Miss Ruffles, I doubted it.

Had the new stadium been the topic of conversation when I interrupted Cornfelter and Honeybelle? Had he come with wine and flowers to seduce her? Not in the bedroom sense, but in order to get sufficient money to build a football stadium in her beloved husband's memory? And if so, why had Miss Ruffles bitten the man? Had she sensed how much Honeybelle disliked him, despite her flirtatious behavior? Or was I mistaken and Honeybelle had a mad crush on the university president? Frowning to myself, I put the folder back in the drawer.

In another folder, I found a list of local businesses. This was a folder I had already seen when I helped her with her checkbook. In an adjacent column, Honeybelle had noted amounts of money. These were the people who had waited behind the church during her memorial service, I guessed, and some of them owed substantial amounts. I paid closer attention to the names on the list. The art gallery owner had received tens of thousands. The local veterinarian had gotten a similar amount to expand his clinic. A grad student at the university had been given money to continue her independent study of Appalachian folk music. Beneath the top sheet of paper came a stack of written agreements, all signed.

Now that Honeybelle was dead, were those loans forgiven? Or were the borrowers all expected to repay their loans to Honeybelle's family?

I said, "I'll bet at least one of these people is happy that Honeybelle's dead."

The idea made me search for a folder that might contain Honeybelle's health records. I thought I might find proof that she'd been treated for a heart problem. But no such folder was in the drawer.

I reached for the ON switch of her computer. Maybe there was more information to be found there.

But just then the doorbell rang, and I nearly fell out of the chair. I dumped everything back into Honeybelle's desk and grabbed my shoes. I ran to the kitchen to shut off the faucet. Then I hopped to the front door while trying to slip on my shoes. When I yanked the door open, a young uniformed police officer stood on the front porch.

"Miss McKillip?" He spoke through the glass door. He was a broad-chested figure in a navy blue short-sleeved shirt with a MULE STOP POLICE patch on one bulky shoulder. His pants rode low on slim hips, and a thick belt was weighed down with an assortment of items, including a gun. But the most apparent characteristic of this cowboy cop was that he was incredibly handsome. He could have starred on a soap opera or appeared on a ten-story billboard advertising men's undies.

The overwhelming fragrance of Honeybelle's roses heightened my first impression that he was a storybook prince who'd just hacked his way through Sleeping Beauty's thorny prison.

His dark sunglasses reflected my astonished expression. The metal name badge clipped to his chest read APPLEBY.

Too late, I realized I still had the lollipop in my mouth. I pulled it out and opened the door, then stepped out onto the porch. "Yes, that's me."

"Miss McKillip, I'm Assistant Deputy Appleby, and it's my duty to serve you with this here temporary protective order."

"This what?" I was still stunned by how gorgeous he was. Chiseled jaw, perfect hair, a mouth like a movie star puckering up to kiss Angelina Jolie.

"Ma'am," he said in a very deep voice for a man so young, "by order of the court, y'all are forbidden to have any contact with the family of Henry Junior and Posie

Hensley." Seeing my blank expression, he said, "It's a restraining order."

"What for?" I demanded, my brain finally kicking in.

"Plain speaking, ma'am, the Hensley family says you are harassing their children, and we can't have that in a nice town like this, can we? You are to stay away from them, hear, and keep Miss Ruffles away, or we'll have the right to arrest you, see, and then you go to jail."

I realized my mouth was slack with astonishment. "What does Miss Ruffles have to do with anything?"

"Well, now, I talked to Posie when she came in to request this order. It's the dog she wants kept away from her kids, but if we got Animal Control involved, they'd have to take Miss Ruffles, and Posie didn't want that, so we came up with this solution." He eased the paperwork into my hand and said more kindly, "You can make this easier on everybody by keeping your distance from those children from now on. You *and* the dog."

"Do you—I mean, are you related to Posie somehow, Deputy Appleby?"

"Assistant Deputy. Yes, ma'am, she's my big sister."

I let that bit of information settle into my head for a moment. Going to the police for any help whatsoever meant Posie would know everything as soon as she sat down to a family dinner.

I said, "But we only saw them in church last week. At Honeybelle's memorial service. And after that, here at this house, on the back porch—"

The deputy didn't even try to be stern. He said quite conversationally, "Well, there's to be no more of that, ma'am. You and Miss Ruffles keep your distance or I'll have to come back and arrest you. Read the letter."

There was nothing to be done with the lollipop but put it back in my mouth. Both hands free again, I opened the envelope and unfolded an official-looking document to try

to make sense of it. The handsome young officer kept talking. I read the scrawled signatures on the paper and the
stamp in one corner and the words "addressed to the adverse party." That was me. The "adverse party."

Assistant Deputy Appleby was saying, "We had to wait
until this morning to get Marcy to open the clerk's office
to make up the order, and then we had to get all the right
signatures, which is hard to do on a weekend, especially
with our bosses out of town at a big convention—"

"That's why you spent the night outside this house?" I
asked. "To make sure I didn't go over to Posie's house to
bother her kids?"

He stopped talking about his own problems and took
off his sunglasses at last. His eyes were more melty-brown
than chocolate in a fondue pot. "You have to report to the
courthouse in two weeks for a hearing. It's all there in the
paperwork."

A hearing. Now I was the kind of person who was summoned to a hearing.

"Would you like to sit down for a minute, ma'am?"

I wasn't feeling too good. And my plan to confront
Posie about Miss Ruffles was blown to bits.

★ ★ ★

CHAPTER THIRTEEN

He was sweating like a sinner in church.
—TEXAS METAPHOR

One thing about Texas is that it tends to look the same all the time—hot and sunny—but wait five minutes and something unusual happens. Like a herd of cattle moseys through town or a scary policemen turns out to be a handsome, sweet-talking boy. I couldn't think of anything my mother might have said that would make it all make sense.

Little black spots danced in front of my eyes. The two rocking chairs Honeybelle kept for show on her front porch looked like a great idea right then, and I allowed Assistant Deputy Appleby to help me totter over to sit in the first one. Once I was down, the black spots evaporated, but I was surprised to find my knees were trembling.

"May I?" Posie's little brother asked.

I must have nodded, because he sat down in the other chair, leaning toward me with concern. It was a little like having a movie star focus all his cinematic attention on me. It took my breath away and made me dizzy all over again.

He said, "You okay, ma'am?"

I sat back in the chair and pulled out the lollipop again. "Surprised, that's all. I hardly know Posie's kids."

"Well, she must have gone to all this trouble for a good reason," he said.

While he waited for me to explain myself, I thought about Miss Ruffles and whether or not I should risk mentioning to the police that she was missing.

It had been awfully smart of Posie to get a restraining order. It prevented me from knocking on her door to look for Honeybelle's dog.

I fanned myself with the envelope.

My handsome prince said, "You're not going to faint, are you, ma'am? I have one of those little smelling salts things in the cruiser. They always used to work on my grandma when she was alive."

Being compared to his dead grandmother snapped me back to reality, and I sat up straight. "I'm fine."

On the street in front of the house, a familiar dusty Jeep rolled up behind the police cruiser and stopped. Behind the wheel was Ten Tennyson in his cowboy hat. Beside him in the passenger seat sat a slender young woman in a sunny yellow dress with a matching wide-brimmed hat, which she pinned to her head with one hand. Even from the front porch, I could see the diamond flashing on her finger. With a stone that size, she could send Morse code messages to the moon.

Ten got down from the Jeep and sauntered around to the other side to help his passenger to the sidewalk. She had to be Poppy, Posie Hensley's sister, Ten's bride-to-be. Her yellow dress was square cut around her collarbones, showing lightly tanned bare shoulders. Her lipstick was pink, her eyes cornflower blue. If Appleby was the handsome prince in this Texas fairy tale, here was his princess sister. Her smile was wide enough to drive a tractor through.

She tucked her hand into Ten's elbow and bumped her cheek against his shoulder.

Seeing her do that suddenly made me want to be the one to drive a tractor through her big, shiny teeth.

Appleby and I stood up. I pulled out the lollipop and held it behind my back.

"Why, Little Bubba," she said when they approached the porch. Her honeyed drawl was playful. "Look how sweet you look in your new uniform."

"Hey, Poppy." The assistant deputy's face morphed into an adoring-little-brother smile. "You're looking real pretty. Y'all just come from church?"

"Why, thank you. Yes, Ten took me out to the Cowboy Church this morning, and the service was real nice. Lots of singing. I just love big, tough cowboys singing about Jesus. They're so sweet. But look at you in your uniform! I guess the town council decided to forget about you shooting the windows out of the Dairy Queen?"

He blushed adorably. "Well, you know I was just eleven at the time, so that didn't stick on my record."

She went on teasing him. "It was all over town your first arrest was Granddaddy. How did that go?"

His grin turned silly. "I called for backup first. Is the TV station still treating you right?"

"I love it more than strawberry ice cream."

Ten shook Appleby's hand. "Hey, Bubba. Congratulations on passing your exam."

"Yeah, it only took four times, but I finally managed."

Poppy said, "What's that you're carrying on your hip? An old-fashioned revolver? Didn't Wyatt Earp carry one of those antiques?"

He blushed all over again. "Well, it's standard issue for rookie deputies in Mule Stop. Nothing fancy. The taxpayers keep a tight lid on the budget."

Poppy opened her purse. "You know, I still carry Grandma's old-fashioned peashooter myself. See?"

She waved a tiny pistol around, and I ducked instinctively behind Appleby.

The three of them looked at me as if I'd grown another head.

"Sorry." I straightened up again. "Sometimes I feel like I'm in a different world."

Ten nodded in sympathy. "I know what you mean. Poppy and I went to New York City in the spring."

"All that noise," Poppy said. "And everybody in such a rush. But *Phantom of the Opera* was really exciting." She tucked her peashooter back into her purse and turned expectantly to me, smile still bright, waiting for an introduction.

Ten had begun to frown at me from beneath the brim of his hat, clearly sensing there was something fishy going on between me and the small-town cop, especially with me holding a large, official-looking envelope. But his good manners kicked in. "Poppy, this is Sunny McKillip. Sunny worked for Honeybelle before she passed. Sunny, this is Poppy Appleby."

If Poppy had heard anything negative about me from her sister, she was a very good actress. She fixed me with her complete attention and put out her slim hand for me to shake. On her wrist she wore several thin gold bracelets and a slender, expensive watch. "Why, hello. You must still be new in town. I haven't met you yet. What an interesting name, McKillip. Are you from Austin? I had a sorority sister from Austin who—no, come to think of it, her name was McKellan. What an interesting shade of lipstick."

I tried answering most of her questions. "No. Thank you. I'm from Ohio."

"What a shame you made such a big life change for nothing. We're all heartbroken by Honeybelle's passing. I was going to ask her to host a show. I'm trying to be a producer at KTXX, after working on-air in Oklahoma City. Honeybelle would have been perfect."

"What kind of show?" I asked, making conversation just to get the impenetrable expression off Ten's face.

"I hadn't decided yet. Home decorating or entertaining, something that highlighted her personality. I wish she had been a cook, since cooking shows are always a hit. Her lifestyle was fabulous, though, wasn't it? Her charity work, community spirit, and gardening, of course. She was a winning combination. And she was so photogenic, even at her age. I'm simply heartbroken," Poppy said again.

"You should do a show yourself, Pop." Appleby was still wearing that goofy smile. To me, he said, "Nobody's more photogenic than our Poppy."

Playfully, she slapped his arm. "Well, I do the weather now, but I want to build a career that will last longer than my looks. I may take off a few years to raise a family." She sent a warm smile up at Ten. "But I'll want to come back to work someday, and producing is just the thing."

Appleby complimented his sister again, but I stopped listening to them. So did Ten. He gave me a raised eyebrow that asked what was going on, and I returned his look with a quick shake of my head, which only intensified his glare. This morning, he wore another of his yoked Western shirts with clean jeans and what I had come to recognize as "dress" cowboy boots made of polished, tooled leather that had not seen a stirrup but looked capable of kicking me in the butt for being annoying. Today's belt buckle was the size of a paperback book.

Poppy turned on me again. "Honeybelle had such an eye for beautiful things, didn't she? Gardens, art, decorating—everything. When my sister thought of having our wedding here, I was over the moon! All of us Appleby girls are named after flowers, see. Posie and I have a cousin Heather and a Daisy and a Ginger—she's the barrel racer—and Ivy."

"And Lily," Bubba added. "Don't forget cousin Lily."

"Well, sometimes we do," Poppy said with a roll of her eyes. "She moved to London, and now she talks like one of the Beatles."

To Bubba, I said, "What's your given name?"

Another blush, this one all the way to the tips of his ears. "Well, ma'am, I was going to be named Achillea, but our daddy put his foot down, thank the good Lord, and they settled on Allium. Our parents thought I could be called Al for short, but that didn't take, so now I'm just Bubba. Daddy says every family in Texas needs a Bubba."

"Anyway," Poppy said to me, "as you can tell, flowers are a big thing in our family. Why, if Ten and I exchanged our vows by Honeybelle's roses, we'd be charmed for life. Her rose collection is practically a national treasure." With a sigh of pleasure, she gazed at the pastel swells and rolls of Honeybelle's garden. "I've never seen it before. Why, it's just magnificent!"

I said, "I'm surprised you haven't had a tour."

"Honeybelle was such a perfectionist, she probably wanted to make her flowers perfect before showing them off. Although all these bushes certainly look perfect to me. The family rumor is she has one from my great-grandma Appleby. A real pretty yellow one that came all the way from England on a boat in 1799, and—"

Ten said, "Let's not get started on that yellow rose again. Seems it starts a big fight every time it comes up."

"Well," Poppy continued, "then I heard there's also a gazebo out back that's real pretty. So Ten said we could drop by after church to take a peek before we decide."

"So you're having the wedding here after all?" I asked.

"Why not?" Her voice sounded like sweet tea, but something in her gaze changed as she met mine—a quick hardening of her eyes, maybe—that told me I had no business exchanging glances of any kind with her fiancé. I had mistaken her for an empty-headed piece of fluff, but I suddenly realized Poppy might be every bit the barracuda her sister was.

Ten said, "Why don't you go have a look at the gazebo out back, Pop?"

She curled her hand around his arm again. "Come on. Your opinion counts, too."

He disengaged her hand. "I need to talk to Bubba for a minute. Business."

She sighed. "Okay, but you can't complain if the wedding isn't what you wanted."

"I won't complain," he promised with a smile.

She stood up on tiptoe and gave him a kiss. "I love you a bushel and a peck."

He smiled. "Run along."

I opened the front door of Honeybelle's house. "Nobody's home but me. Go straight through to the kitchen to the back door." I pointed down the marble foyer. "Maybe you'll like what you smell. Mae Mae is the kind of cook you need for your show."

Poppy blinked at me. "Mae Mae can cook? I thought she only made old-lady finger sandwiches."

Ten gave her a gentle push. "Check it out, Miss Producer."

The tantalizing scent of the gumbo Mae Mae had left simmering wafted out to us, so Poppy followed her nose. As she stepped over the threshold, though, her cell phone rang, and she pulled it out of the handbag on her arm. "Poppy Appleby speaking!" Her voice was friendly but instantly businesslike. We heard her heels click on the marble floor as she walked away.

When she was out of earshot, Ten turned back to me and said, "So what's going on here, Bubba?"

"Sorry, Ten. I shouldn't say without—"

"You can say whatever you like," I said, wrapping up my lollipop. "Mr. Tennyson is my lawyer."

"You need a lawyer now?" Ten asked. "What for?"

"A restraining order." I showed him the papers, which he skimmed. "I have to show up for a hearing in two weeks."

Ten handed the paper back to me. "What's with this?" He directed his question to Assistant Deputy Appleby. "Your sister Posie's afraid of Miss Ruffles? Or . . . ?"

Appleby gave up trying to be a cop "Aw, you know how Posie gets, Ten. Nobody can work up a head of steam like her. Why, the whole department still talks about the day she found those old barrels of toxic stuff near their new house. She practically wanted the National Guard mobilized. Well, now she's got a bee in her bonnet that Miss Ruffles is dangerous. At least, that was my take on it when she came in last night."

"What time last night?" I asked. "After the football game? Before seven?"

With a frown, Bubba said, "It was around eight, I guess."

After Miss Ruffles had been abducted, I thought. While I was looking for her.

Ten asked, "Why do you want to know?"

I tried to wipe all suspicion off my face. "Just curious."

Ten accepted that answer after a second's hesitation. "All right, well, let me consult with my client, Bubba, and we'll see you in two weeks."

"Thanks, Ten. Bye, Miss McKillip. Nice meeting you." Bubba smiled with a sweet, lingering twinkle. He tipped his hat to me before returning to his cruiser. As he strolled away, the rear view of the handsome prince was just as breathtaking as the front. Broad shoulders, narrow waist, tight behind. A manful stride. At the gate, he turned and waved at me one more time. The sunshine glinted off his perfect teeth.

Standing beside me, Ten said, "You've turned his head."

"What does that mean?"

As if English were my second language, Ten looked down at me and said clearly, "He likes you."

"He thinks I'm a criminal!"

"That'll pass." Ten was still grouchy. "You be nice to him, hear? He's the sensitive type."

"Is that why he failed his police exam so many times? His sensitivity?"

"He's also not too bright," Ten admitted, "which I don't want to say in front of his sisters, but that's how it is. He's not exactly your type."

"What's my type?" I demanded, ready to be offended again.

"Somebody who doesn't flunk tests."

Gruffly, I said, "Well, he's very cute."

"Right. Don't tell his sisters, but he falls hard and gets himself lured into bed too soon, and then he gets dumped because he's . . . well, I guess once you put your clothes back on he's not exactly scintillating company."

On a laugh, I asked, "What man gets himself lured into bed these days?"

"I'm serious. That's exactly what happens. So watch yourself with him."

"Get your mind out of the bedroom, please. I'm not taking off my clothes for anybody," I said, feeling prickly. "Certainly not for the cop who just served me with a restraining order."

"He's all right. We all went to high school together. Bubba and I rodeoed, and Poppy probably helped him pass remedial math."

"He obviously loves his sister Poppy."

"Everybody loves Poppy."

"Let me guess. Homecoming queen?"

"And president of the Honor Society," Ten shot back, "not to mention most every other club she belonged to, so don't let your prejudices run away with you. She might talk slow and smile a lot, but she's every bit as smart as you."

"Sorry. I didn't mean to insult your future wife. She seems . . . very nice. I hope you'll be very happy together."

Ten was glaring at me again. "How come when I see you your mouth is always some unnatural color?"

"It has nothing to do with you. I was having a lollipop." I poked out my tongue. "See?"

"I do see. The whole town can see." He switched back to being a lawyer again and indicated my envelope. "You going to tell me what happened?"

I knew what he meant. "With Posie Hensley? Nothing happened. This is out of the blue. Last I spoke with her was after you read the will. She came outside and got her kids and left. I haven't seen her since. Except in traffic last night when she . . . Look, I don't know what Posie's problem is, but Miss Ruffles wouldn't hurt her children."

"You sure about that?"

I hesitated. "Pretty sure."

Ten grabbed the front door. "Is Miss Ruffles out back? Is she going to frighten Poppy?"

I didn't think Poppy could be frightened by much of anything. And although this was my chance to tell Ten the truth, I decided to lie because he was soon marrying the dognapper's sister.

"No. Miss Ruffles is . . . she's not in the yard." Before he went into the house, I said, "Listen, thanks for agreeing to be my lawyer. That was very nice of you. Unfortunately, I can't afford to pay for your services."

"Well, you'll get exactly what you pay for because I'm

not really a lawyer until I get my bar exam results. C'mon. Let's go find Poppy."

We walked through the quiet house, and Ten appreciatively breathed the aroma of Mae Mae's cooking. When we got to the kitchen, we could hear Poppy speaking authoritatively on her cell phone out on the patio.

Neither one of us felt like interrupting her—at least, I certainly didn't—so we hung around the kitchen for a minute. I could only hear snatches of her conversation. She was giving orders with military precision.

I said, "She sounds like she's already organizing a television program."

"She'll be running that station in a few years."

I stepped on the trash can pedal and dropped my lollipop into the can. "She's obviously a catch."

Ten lingered by the stove and lifted the lid on Mae Mae's pot. He sniffed and sighed. "If only she could cook like Mae Mae."

"You could learn to cook yourself, you know. That's how it's done these days."

"Yeah, maybe." He set the lid back down and turned to me.

We looked at each other through the spicy steam, and Poppy's voice faded as she walked away across the patio. Whatever I was going to say next evaporated out of my head, and we shared a moment there in the cozy kitchen, the two of us alone. An expression came over his face, and I knew he was thinking about my lollipop mouth, and I started thinking about his mouth, too, and wondering what it might taste like, and for a few unsteady heartbeats, we almost gave in to a temptation that was clear and strong in both our minds, but wrong, wrong, wrong.

I turned away first.

I opened the nearest drawer. "There's a tape measure around here somewhere if you want to measure the gazebo for a dance floor or an altar, or whatever you've got planned for your wedding."

He didn't have time to answer, because outside on the patio Poppy let out a bloodcurdling scream. And a gunshot went off.

★ ★ ★

CHAPTER FOURTEEN

Texas girls have an amazing sense of purpose when
they lose it. They're the best girls in the world.
They're loyal and fun. But when they get
mad, they'll try to kill you.
—JOHN CUSACK

Ten and I jumbled out the back door onto the porch like a couple of stooges, and Ten nearly fell over one of Honeybelle's big flowerpots. I caught him by the arm, and we both rocked to a stop on the steps, hanging on to each other for balance.

Poppy was standing on top of one of the patio tables, holding on to the umbrella pole and shrieking. "It's a rat! A rat! I saw a rat!" She pointed a shaking finger. "And dammit, I *missed* him!"

It wasn't a rat. A frightened prairie dog scampered across the pool terrace, heading for the back fence, making his escape. He ran as if his tail were on fire.

Poppy's little gun lay on the pool terrace, still spinning from the momentum of having been thrown after her departing target. She had lost one of her shoes, too, and I could see her cell phone sinking into the deep end of the pool, where she must have thrown it when she pulled her gun.

Ten ran clumsily down the steps and over to the table. "It's gone now, honey, but I think you might've winged him." He helped her down.

"I hate rodents! Rats, squirrels, prairie dogs—they're all the same! Posie had a guinea pig once, and the little bastard bit me!" She hit Ten in the chest with her open hand.

He was laughing. "Calm down, now, Poppy. You're cussin'."

She started to laugh, too, but shakily. "He surprised me, that's all. I'm no ninny."

"I know you're not." He pulled her close. Her hands slid around his shoulders. They had a moment, still laughing, but gentle with each other.

There wasn't anything for me to do except to kick off my shoes and go into the pool after her cell phone. I dove down and found it on the bottom, gently sliding toward the drain. I grabbed it and took my time getting to the surface, not in any rush to see them in each other's arms. In the sunshine again, I ducked under the water one last time to skim my hair off my face, and then I waded into the shallow end. By the time I climbed out, gushing pool water from my clothes, Poppy had pulled herself together and wore both shoes again.

Ten handed her the peashooter, and she put it into her purse.

To me, she said, "Did I scare you?"

"I'm not used to guns," I admitted.

"Sorry." Her smile was big again. "I have a tendency to shoot first, ask questions later."

I twisted the tail of my T-shirt to get rid of the excess water, but it still clung to me like a second skin. My shorts sagged on my hips, dripping. I was never going to win a wet T-shirt contest, but I plucked the shirt away from my chest anyway. Feeling bedraggled and silly, I gave the wet phone to her.

She thanked me as she shook it in a vain attempt to get rid of the water. To Ten, she said, "I don't want to have our wedding here if there are prairie dogs. I don't care how pretty that rose garden is."

Ten grinned. "The groomsmen could run a little target practice before the ceremony."

"We're going to get rid of them very soon," I said, not completely sure he was joking. "Critter Control is coming."

Ten said, "Why doesn't Miss Ruffles chase them off?"

"I don't know. Maybe they're her kindred spirits or something." I smiled. "You know how she likes to cause trouble."

Maybe Poppy didn't like that I shared anything whatsoever with Ten. She forgot about her phone and glared openly at me.

"Sorry," I said, feeling wet and foolish. "I don't mean to . . . that is, prairie dogs are a kind of squirrel, actually. And they're herbivores, although they do eat some insects. Anyway, they're harmless. More afraid of you than—"

"I'm not afraid, Miss Know It All," Poppy snapped. "I was startled, that's all."

"Poppy, maybe we ought to get a move on." Ten's voice was still indulgent. "We don't want to be late for Sunday supper with your sister, now, do we? Your phone's going to be good as new, right?"

I said, "Put it in a box of kitty litter. In a few hours it'll be—" I saw his expression and stopped. Miss Know It All, indeed.

"Thanks for letting us have a look around," he said, one hand already on Poppy's back to propel her away. "We'll be in touch."

I stripped off most of my sodden clothes in the kitchen and left them in the sink. In my undies, I went upstairs to take a shower. I took one look at my lollipop mouth in the mirror and brushed my teeth with whitening toothpaste.

Dressed again, I cleaned up the kitchen and tried to

think about how to get around a restraining order. When Mr. Carver and Mae Mae returned, I met them in the garage. I went to help a windblown Mae Mae out of the convertible's passenger seat while Mr. Carver made a fussy business of shutting off the car and running his handkerchief over the dashboard to remove any hint of dust.

"Who's that parked across the street?" Mae Mae asked. "There's two black cars over there."

"Somebody visiting the neighbors, I guess. How was church?" I held Mae Mae's stout arm and pulled.

"It wouldn't do you any harm to find that out for yourself," she said. "What have you been doing all morning?"

"Keeping Miss Ruffles out of trouble."

Mae Mae glanced around, as if expecting Miss Ruffles to come charging out from under the bushes. "Where's that animal now?"

Keeping the dog's whereabouts a secret was definitely going to be a problem. "She's probably hunting for prairie dogs. Poppy Appleby and Ten Tennyson were here, looking at the backyard for their wedding. They were grossed out by the prairie dogs."

Mr. Carver said, "Critter Control is coming on Tuesday."

"Good to know. Mr. Carver, I was wondering if I could borrow Honeybelle's car this afternoon."

"For what purpose?" he asked, frowning as he came around the trunk of the car.

I had my lie ready. "To take Miss Ruffles over to the football field to practice with a Frisbee."

"Is it safe for her over there?"

"It will be empty today. I'm supposed to teach her tricks for the football games. I don't want to risk breaking any windows here."

That convinced Mr. Carver right away. "You may take

the car." He handed over the keys. "Put a towel on the seat so Miss Ruffles doesn't dirty the upholstery."

I hung around the garage while they shuffled into the house for lunch, and then I got into Honeybelle's car. I put the convertible top up, hoping to drive past the Blues Brothers without alerting them to my departure. They weren't used to seeing me driving a car. Luck was finally with me, because they remained parked by the curb as I drove by.

I had spent the last hour trying to come up with various ways to get Miss Ruffles back from Posie. First I needed to do some reconnaissance.

I knew the way to the housing development out by the interstate where the Hensleys lived. Big brick pillars flanked the turn-in. Posie's house must have been some designer's idea of a French country gentleman's estate, except with a vinyl fence around it. I had delivered some flowers there for Honeybelle. On the inside, it had been elaborately decorated with big, plush family furniture. On the outside, someone had planted cactus around piles of rocks.

I parked behind a small rise where a water tower stood, got out, and crept up to the top. Standing in the water tower's shade, I peered across the curving arrangement of huge houses, all with air conditioners humming outside. A couple of cars were moving slowly along the serpentine streets—one headed out of the neighborhood, the other probably delivering a family home from church. Some of the houses had big yards with green grass, obviously sustained with water sprinklers. The majority of homes had dry yards with desert plants to perk them up.

Posie's house had the largest piece of property and the most plantings—none of which required additional water. Honeybelle had sniffed at Posie's lack of flowers. But

standing under the huge water tank with the West Texas
scrub spreading endlessly in all directions, I wondered
if Posie had the right idea. Mule Stop was a place that
couldn't afford to waste any of its precious water supply. I
felt a pang of guilt for running the water in Mae Mae's
kitchen sink.

Beside a big cactus, I could see Ten's Jeep parked in the
driveway. He and Poppy had gone to Posie's home for Sunday supper.

I don't know what I hoped to see while standing under
the water tower. Maybe Miss Ruffles cavorting in the backyard, safe and happy.

I spotted a backyard shed and stood looking at it for a
long time. It was the kind of shed where homeowners
stored lawn mowers and bicycles. Might Posie have concealed Miss Ruffles there?

I couldn't very well march down and search the house
or the shed. Not with a restraining order in place. Feeling
very disappointed, I went back to the car and headed
into town.

I had driven past the local animal shelter on my way to
Posie's house. It was a long, low building the same color
of the scrubland around it. As if drawn by a magnet, I im-
pulsively pulled into the pitted gravel driveway. The shelter's front doors were propped wide, and the noise of
yelping dogs could be heard from the parking lot.

Maybe Posie had dumped Miss Ruffles at the shelter.
A tiny part of me still held out hope that Miss Ruffles es-
caped on her own. Or maybe she had found her way here.
It was a long shot, but it couldn't hurt to check.

A woman with her long hair pinned up to stay cool was
sweeping the floor behind the check-in counter. She wore
a long skirt and a faded T-shirt. A mischievous black cat
with a lashing tail sat on the counter watching her work.
Behind the woman was a wall of cages, each with a me-

owing cat in it. Tabby cats, calico cats, gray cats, white cats, black cats, dozens of ordinary cats.

The woman didn't look up from her task. "Can I help you?"

In the car, I had decided on a plausible story that didn't make me look like a bad pet owner who carelessly let her dog run away. I said, "I'm here to see if you have any Texas cattle curs."

She looked around at last, and I realized she was none other than Crazy Mary.

"Hi," I said uncertainly. "Remember me? I'm Sunny."

"I know who you are." Without her banjo or violin, she pulled the broom handle close as if for protection.

I said the first thing that came into my head. "I'm surprised to see you here."

She shrugged. "I volunteer on Sundays. It's hard to get people to work on Sundays. Everybody else goes to church."

"That's . . . nice of you to volunteer."

"Did you find Miss Ruffles?"

"Uh, not yet. Are you . . . Did you really hear her bark last night?"

"I heard Miss Ruffles yip, yes. She was in a car. What do you want with another Texas cattle cur?"

I was caught flat-footed. I wasn't a good liar, and I couldn't come up with anything that sounded remotely plausible.

Her gaze sharpened.

I swallowed hard. "Look, I know it's wrong to ask you to be quiet about this, but I need to keep it a secret. To tell the truth, Miss Ruffles is still missing. I was hoping maybe somebody found her and turned her in."

That information was enough. She jerked her head toward another door. "Take a look at the inventory. Some curs might have come in this week."

I thanked her and fled through the door. On the other side was a chain-link gate, and I let myself through that and refastened it behind me. I found myself in a hot concrete shed with dog kennels on both sides of an aisle that was damp underfoot as if it had been hosed down. The thought of Miss Ruffles stuck in such a place made me feel like crying.

As soon as I appeared, dozens of barking dogs suddenly tripled their noise and began flinging themselves at their chain-link prisons. There were more large dogs than small dogs—mostly pit bulls and shepherd mixes, but several cages with multiple Chihuahuas, too. The Chihuahuas ran around in circles and took turns jumping against their gates. Some of them huddled together and trembled. The barking and yelping was deafening.

At the last kennel, my heart leaped. For a second, I thought I had found her, but as soon as the snoozing dog lifted its head, I could see it was not Miss Ruffles but another Texas cattle cur—this one older than Miss Ruffles. His muzzle was almost completely gray. He didn't have her distinctive eyebrow, either. And he certainly didn't have her energy. But the brindle coat was similar, and he was only a little larger than Miss Ruffles.

There was a big red sticker attached to the front of his kennel. I put my fingers through the chain link, but the dog didn't have the energy to get up to sniff me.

Crazy Mary appeared behind me. "I forgot about that one. His name is Fred. He came in a couple of weeks ago. Somebody found him out in the middle of nowhere, half-starved and sick. People from all over just dump their dogs out there—especially old ones like this. They can't afford to have a sick dog put down, so they leave them. We named him after Fred, our accountant, because he sleeps all the time."

"He looks depressed."

"Well, this place upsets most dogs. After a while, some of them just shut down."

"How sick is he?"

"Our vet says he doesn't have much longer."

Fred put his head back on his paws and heaved a sigh that sounded hopeless.

Mary said, "The red card means he's scheduled to be put down this week."

A plan sprouted in my head. Perhaps I'd have Miss Ruffles safe at home after tomorrow night's meeting with the dognapper. But until I got Miss Ruffles back, I was going to be spending a lot of time convincing Mr. Carver and Mae Mae that Miss Ruffles was just outside digging for prairie dogs. Maybe I needed a stand-in.

And if Fred only had a short time to live, I could make his final days a heck of a lot more comfortable than the shelter could.

Over my shoulder to Crazy Mary, I said, "What would it take to adopt Fred?"

"Why would you want him?"

"He's been through a lot. I can feed him, give him a nice place to sleep. There's lots of room at Honeybelle's house."

"There's a strict adoption policy. Lots of forms. And technically, he's supposed to be neutered before he leaves the shelter."

"At his age, and the shape he's in, I don't think we have to worry about him making puppies."

Crazy Mary continued to frown. "Probably not."

"I can make him happy."

I must have sounded genuine enough. After a thoughtful minute, she sighed. "If you have all the right information and the adoption fee, I don't see why you couldn't take him home today. I hate seeing him so miserable."

When Miss Ruffles came back to Honeybelle's house, she might be delighted to have a companion, I thought. And maybe Fred's calm temperament would rub off on her a little, too.

Firmly, I said, "I'd like to adopt him."

She shrugged. "Okay. This way."

She made me fill out multiple forms that promised I had a fenced yard and a relationship with a trustworthy veterinarian. I was glad I'd looked in Honeybelle's file and seen the name of the vet who took care of Miss Ruffles. I showed Crazy Mary all the ID I carried in my wallet, and out of my meager pocket money I paid the small adoption fee. I signed a paper that said I'd get Fred a checkup within a month. I bought the required leash and collar from the display by the front desk. I was starting to think I'd have to give up my firstborn when Crazy Mary finally brought Fred out and turned him over to me.

"He's kind of a runt for a Texas Cattle cur," she said.

"He's small for a male," I agreed, thinking he might even pass for a girl dog at a distance. He had the little bristle of longish feathering on his hind legs, too. If Mae Mae and Mr. Carver didn't look too closely, I might pull off the ruse long enough to get Miss Ruffles back safe and sound. I knelt down and exchanged the length of rope around his neck with the new collar and leash.

"It's none of my business." Crazy Mary watched me work. "But are you sure this is a good idea?"

I patted Fred. "I'll make sure his last days are happy ones."

She met my gaze calmly. "That's not what I mean. You're going to try to pass Fred off as Miss Ruffles, right?"

"I . . . well . . ."

"Don't worry. I'll keep your secret. Nobody talks to me

anyway. I just wonder if you're doing the right thing. Do you think Miss Ruffles is dead?"

I gulped and tried to control my expression. The shock of seeing the conditions in the kennel had heightened my concern for Miss Ruffles. I could hardly get my voice to work. "I hope not."

Mary nodded. "Honeybelle really loved that dog."

"Did you know Honeybelle?"

"Sure. She gave money to a lot of people—anybody who asked, really. She paid my tuition."

The grad student who was studying Appalachian music. I said, "Your banjo and violin. You're studying folk music."

"How'd you know that?"

"I read it in . . . never mind. I get it now. You're always playing on the sidewalks."

Crazy Mary turned slightly pink. "Honeybelle paid for my tuition, but I have living expenses. I used to give lessons, but the parents are a pain. So I thought I'd try being a busker, a street performer. It's not bad money. People give me cash when I play. I play in a band a couple nights a week, but there are a bunch of us, so when the kitty gets split up, I don't get much."

"I've seen you play. You're really good."

"Thanks. I'm working on recording and writing a book, too. I really plan to pay Honeybelle back. Even now that she's gone."

"Was that part of the deal?" I asked. "I wondered if her will might have forgiven you the debt."

"Honeybelle was really strict about the loan. I assume I'm still supposed to pay her back. I haven't been told otherwise. Is somebody in charge of her estate?"

"Her lawyers are on vacation."

Hearing that information, Crazy Mary lost interest in

our conversation. We said good-bye. Fred was so sleepy that I ended up carrying him to the car. I put him on the passenger seat, where he promptly began to snore and drool onto the carpet.

"This might be a crazy idea, and you're no Miss Ruffles," I said to him. "But you'll have to do."

CHAPTER FIFTEEN

Don't accept your dog's admiration as conclusive evidence that you are wonderful.
—ANN LANDERS

First thing I did when we got back to Honeybelle's house was to give Fred a bath. He smelled like every dog that had ever done time in a kennel—more like dried poop than anything else. I lathered him up twice with the shampoo I used on Miss Ruffles. He stood still for the indignity of being squirted with the hose, his eyes full of sorrow. After the final rinse when I bundled him into a towel, his stumpy tail gave a disinterested wag.

I gave him some kibble, which he ate with care, as though his teeth hurt. Afterward, he wandered out onto the lawn and went to sleep in a patch of sunlight. I heard him sigh.

To stay out of range of interrogation by Mae Mae and Mr. Carver, I spent the afternoon cleaning the pool with the long-handled hose, trying to plan a way to confront Posie without breaking the law.

I kept an eye on Fred, too. I worried his low energy might attract notice. To me, he was obviously not Miss Ruffles. But that evening at dinner, Mr. Carver and Mae Mae paid no attention to him. He slept in the hot grass through our meal, and only perked up when I fed him more kibble in the evening.

That night I discovered Fred didn't like to be left alone. At first I closed him in Honeybelle's room to keep up the charade that Miss Ruffles was still in the house. But as soon as I scampered up to my room, he had enough energy to let out a mournful howl. I hustled back down to him before he woke Mae Mae with his lament.

"*Shh!* You can stay in my room if you're quiet," I told him. I made a bed for him out of some towels on the floor. But just after I drifted off to sleep, he jumped up onto my bed and scared the bejesus out of me.

"You can't be on your last legs if you can jump up here." I shooed him off and put him back on the towels, but he was determined. Every time I zonked out, Fred jumped up again, until I finally surrendered and let him sleep on the coverlet. Within an hour, he was under the coverlet. He put his cold nose against my foot and made me yelp.

Once he was in bed with me, I discovered he had the noisy digestive issues of a dyspeptic grandfather. I got up and opened the window and made sure his rear end was pointed away from me.

"You're sweet," I said, climbing back into bed, "but you're disgusting."

In the morning, Fred wasn't in any hurry to get out of bed. His eyes were open, but when I tried to lure him down to the floor, he only wagged his tail slightly and stayed put.

I said, "Miss Ruffles would be doing laps around the backyard by now."

The mention of Miss Ruffles gave me a twist in my stomach. Was she okay? If my current plan worked, I'd know in a few hours. I wondered if my nerves would hold out that long.

I pulled out some of my little-used cosmetics and sat on the floor in front of Fred. With a brush, I touched up the white hair on his muzzle. He did look a little more like Miss Ruffles. Fred politely held still for his makeover.

When I tried drawing her distinctive eyebrow over one eye, though, he sighed.

"Don't make me feel any more guilty than I already do," I said to him, touching up the eyebrow.

Fred's stub fluttered.

"Ready to go downstairs now? How about some breakfast?"

Fred allowed himself to be carried downstairs.

My biggest problem on Monday morning was keeping Mr. Carver and Mae Mae in the dark.

I had already decided I needed a diversion. I tackled Mae Mae first. After feeding Fred and installing him on the patio for a nap, I found her in the kitchen making a pot of ultrastrong coffee before preparing breakfast. A carton of eggs sat on the counter alongside an onion and some mushrooms and a whole stick of butter. The iron skillet was warming up on the stove. It looked as if Mae Mae was once again making a meal that Honeybelle would have disapproved of. I opened the refrigerator and reached for the orange juice.

"Mae Mae, have you ever typed up your collection of recipes?"

"I don't type." She frowned as she poured coffee beans into the grinder. "What would I do that for?"

"I was talking to Poppy Appleby yesterday. She's interested in doing a cooking show."

Mae Mae kept her face averted as she worked. "What kind of cooking show?"

"She wants to produce a show for the TV station. You know, recipes and cooking and talking. Since she's doing research, I bet she'd be interested in your wonderful recipes. And you."

Mae Mae punched a button with her blunt finger, and the coffee grinder snarled to life. "I never write down anything."

I had seen Mae Mae cook. She knew instinctively what ingredients went into each of her dishes. I poured juice into a short glass. "Oh, that's too bad. I told Poppy about your cooking. And when Ten praised your food to the sky, she really got interested."

Mae Mae didn't care about my opinion, but she perked up at the mention of Ten. "There's nobody who cooks like I do in this town."

"I know. All the more shame that your recipes aren't written down."

She jutted her jaw as she poured the ground beans into the coffeemaker and added water to the reservoir. "If I write them down, somebody's going to steal 'em."

"Not if you get them copyrighted."

"Copyrighted." From her tone, it sounded as if she didn't know what the word meant, but she wasn't planning on admitting it.

"I'll bet Ten would help you with that part. It would be easy for him to do—wouldn't cost you a penny. You might have to make him dinner once in a while, that's all. He loves your cooking." I drained my juice and rinsed the glass under the tap and put it into the dishwasher. "Too bad you're too busy to write them down. Well, I guess Poppy will have to look for recipes somewhere else."

Mae Mae was silent, thinking while her coffee brewed.

I grabbed the dog leash off the peg by the back door. "Miss Ruffles needs her walk. Need anything from town?"

She had never asked me to run any errands before, but she suddenly said, "Stop at the Tejas and go to the butcher. He keeps a special sausage for me. Get two pounds."

"Of special sausage," I said.

"Tell him it's for me. He'll know what you mean. Did you give that dog her pills this morning?"

"I . . . No, I guess I forgot." I grabbed the bottle of canine vitamins off the windowsill and shook one into my palm. "Thanks for reminding me. See you later, Mae Mae."

She grunted, but out of the corner of my eye I saw her reach for the drawer where she kept a large notepad. With luck, she'd be busy for the whole morning.

I tucked the vitamin into my pocket for Fred—he looked as if he could use vitamins—and went outside to check the back gate. I assumed the dognapper planned to leave me another note there, but I saw no signs of an envelope or paper yet. The Blues Brothers hadn't arrived this morning either. They were probably having their own breakfast somewhere in town.

When Honeybelle was alive, Mr. Carver always got up early to open the house, adjust the air-conditioning, and tidy up anything that Honeybelle had left out overnight. That done, he usually waited for his breakfast in the conservatory while reading the local newspaper.

Now that Honeybelle was gone, though, Mr. Carver waited in his apartment to be summoned for breakfast. Sometimes Mae Mae went out onto the back porch and bellowed for him. On the days she was feeling kinder, she sent me to bring him down from his apartment.

I climbed the outdoor staircase alongside the garage and tapped lightly on Mr. Carver's door. It was a little earlier than usual.

He opened the door promptly and stood before me in his usual trousers and white dress shirt. With an enormous guitar slung around his shoulders by a strap.

I tried not to stare at the guitar. "Miss Ruffles and I are going for our morning run now, Mr. Carver, and to run an errand for Mae Mae. I was hoping to take Miss Ruffles over to the football field again later. Mind if I borrow the car?"

"Go ahead. In fact, I should just give you the keys. I trust you with the car. Except for church, I use the van if I need transportation." From a hook near the door, he lifted a set of car keys and handed them over. Then he glanced around me. "Is Miss Ruffles making any progress with her training?"

"We're making a little progress, but it's slow." I hated lying to him, but I figured it was better for his heart if I kept the truth to myself. "Thanks for the keys. I'll take good care of the car, I promise."

Formally, he said, "Thank you for taking such good care of Miss Ruffles. I haven't said that before, but it . . . well, it's important now. Thank you, Sunny."

I couldn't respond to that. All our futures depended on me taking care of Miss Ruffles, and I had failed miserably.

I eyed the guitar. "Do you need some help?"

"No, no. Just doing a little . . . uh, rehearsing."

Rehearsing? I peered around him.

After a moment's hesitation, he stood back from the door to let me see into his apartment for the first time.

I was expected a tidy living space, I guess, with an English tea spread out on an antique table perhaps, or an ironing board standing ready for Mr. Carver to press his always immaculate clothes into their usual perfection.

Instead I saw what looked more like a music recording studio.

An upright piano stood in the middle of the room with sheet music arranged on it. Beside it was another guitar on a stand, plus a small instrument about the size of a violin but differently shaped. The furniture was pushed to the edges of the room.

"May I come in?" I asked, unable to tear my curious gaze from the instruments. "What's going on?"

"You can't tell Mae Mae," he said shyly. "Only Honeybelle knew about this."

He closed the door quietly behind me, and I advanced

into the room. The rest of the apartment was as clean as I might have expected from Mr. Carver, with simple, worn furniture that might have been Honeybelle's castoffs pressed into service as the furnishings of a modest bachelor pad. But half of the space was taken up by musical instruments of various kinds.

I touched a piano key, and the note rose softly in the air. "I've heard you playing late at night. I thought it was the radio."

I turned to him and found the old man smiling uncertainly at me. "Are you surprised?"

"Yes, of course. You say Honeybelle knew about this?"

"Yes, she encouraged me. But . . . er . . . I don't tell Mae Mae about my music."

"Why not?"

"You know how she gets."

I did. If Mae Mae disapproved of something, she could make Mr. Carver's life miserable. "What kind of music do you play?"

"All kinds. Jazz, mostly, and blues. My mother was a singer in St. Louis. My father was a studio musician in Memphis, back in the day." He couldn't stop himself from smiling at his memories. "It's just a hobby for me. I like to make new arrangements of old songs."

"That's fascinating. I'd love to hear you play. Or am I interrupting?"

"I have a little more work to do on this piece."

"I hope to hear it when you're finished."

"We'll see," he said.

"Breakfast isn't quite ready. You should stay up here and work on your music." Before he caught on that I wanted to know he was out of my way for the day, I said, "I mean— there's nothing that needs to be done in the house, right? So you might as well stay up here."

"There really isn't much household work to do anymore,"

he said sadly. "Without Honeybelle, the house certainly feels empty."

"If Posie were allowed to throw her sister's wedding here," I said on the spur of the moment, "we'd at least have something to keep us busy. Do you know if they'll go ahead with that plan now that Honeybelle is gone?"

"That's up to the family to decide. The more I think about it, the more it seems wrong to go against Honeybelle's wishes."

Now that the door was open, I tried pushing it a little wider. "Why do you think she didn't want to throw the wedding here? She was usually so generous. Why the argument?"

Mr. Carver shook his head. "Honeybelle was a wonderful lady. But she and Miss Posie never did hit it off—and their disagreement went clear back to Miss Posie's mama and daddy."

"How did Hut Junior and Posie get together, if Honeybelle had such a long feud going with the Appleby family?"

Mr. Carver smiled with the affection he always showed when Hut Junior's name came up. "Oh, you know how it is with young fellas and their mamas. Sometimes bringing around the wrong girl can make things right."

"Did that work for Hut Junior?" I asked. "Did he make things right with his mother?"

Mr. Carver lost his smile. "Not really, no."

"So what was the big argument between Posie and her mother-in-law?"

My informant's face went blank, and he clammed up. "I never thought it was any of my business, and it's none of yours either."

I thought of something Poppy had said. "I thought it was over the wedding. But maybe was it roses instead? A yellow rose Honeybelle got from Posie's family?"

With a snap in his voice, Mr. Carver said, "Honeybelle

got that yellow rose fair and square. If the Applebys are still mad about it, they ought to remember she paid them what they asked. Maybe it was worth more than that, but it was a fair deal at the time, no matter what that family says. Now, that's enough questions, young lady. Get on with your work."

I had more questions to ask—I wanted to know what package he had exchanged with Hut in the driveway under cover of darkness—but Mr. Carver made it clear our conversation was over by tuning his guitar.

I turned for the door, then took one last chance. "Mr. Carver, can you tell me what Honeybelle and President Cornfelter argued about?"

Exasperated, he exclaimed, "Why are you so concerned about all this? It's over! Honeybelle is gone, and that's that. Now, run along, Sunny."

That was my cue to leave, but my gaze was suddenly riveted to something else besides the sheet music. A bottle of pills—an amber plastic pharmacy bottle. As if by accident, I knocked it sideways, and it clattered to the floor. I bent to pick it up.

"Sorry," I said, trying to read the label. I couldn't do so surreptitiously.

And Mr. Carver took the bottle from me anyway. He said, "My heart medicine."

"Better take good care of that," I said.

I went down the stairs with my mind churning with a totally new idea. If Honeybelle had been murdered and it looked like a heart attack, how had her death actually been accomplished? On the bottom step, I shook my head to get rid of the new theory that was pushing its way into my mind. Surely Mr. Carver hadn't given her some of his heart medication.

No, that was impossible. Why would he want to harm her?

I checked the back gate again for another communication. The original note had said I'd be contacted on Monday, today. I had assumed Posie would reach me the same way she had done the first time. But there was no flutter of paper in the gate or anywhere around it.

I put Fred on a leash and dragged him out onto the street. Fred thought I had exercise in mind, and he immediately objected. He planted his butt on the dusty driveway.

"C'mon, Fred." I tugged the leash. "Please?"

Across the street, the black car was back in position. Nobody waved from inside, though, I assumed they were laughing too hard.

Fred gave me his most woeful gaze and flopped down on his belly.

"Please, Fred." I glanced up and down the street, concerned that my fake Miss Ruffles was acting decidedly un-Miss-Ruffles-like. "C'mon. What do you say we go find a nice juicy bone on our trip to the grocery store?"

CHAPTER SIXTEEN

Don't squat on your spurs.
—DERN GOOD ADVICE

I was saved from arguing with a dog by the arrival of the U.S. Postal Service. The postman waved at me from behind the wheel of his truck, then braked with a squeak. He was wearing a straw cowboy hat that looked as if it had barely survived a stampede.

"Hey, there, missy," he said to me. "How's Miss Ruffles this morning?"

"Feeling lazy," I said.

He looked down at Fred, who remained crouched at my feet. "I saw her getting the royal treatment at the game on Saturday. She's getting used to getting drove around in a golf cart, ain't she?"

"Yes, she loves it. Do you have Honeybelle's mail?"

"Sure do. Here you go." He handed an armful over to me and waved. "'Bye, Miss Ruffles. See you at the next game!"

He drove off, and I stood there, flooded with relief. To the untrained eye, maybe the Fred masquerade was going to work. I flipped through the mail. In addition to the usual stack of gift catalogs and other junk, I sifted through some handwritten envelopes—most addressed to Honeybelle's

family, so I assumed they were more condolence notes—
and a couple of bills. A colorful brochure from a cruise
line gave me a pang.

At the bottom of the stack was an envelope addressed
to me. At least I assumed it was me.

Dog lady

That's all that the envelope said, with Honeybelle's address. Was there more blood on the envelope? I thought so.
The stamp looked a little raggedy, too. I tucked the other
mail under my elbow and tore open the envelope. Fred
watched from a prone position while I found some tufts
of brindle hair and a note hand-printed on the same kind
of notepaper the ransom note had been on. But this time
I could see the paper had been chewed—maybe wrestled
out of a dog's possession. Miss Ruffles still fighting her
captor?

*$10,000. I will contack you tonite with futher
instrutions. Wait by the stockyard at 9pm.*

Ten thousand dollars. An impossible sum.

I stared at the note, already thinking past the money issues. So far, all other signs had pointed to Posie as the
dognapper. Crazy Mary had heard Miss Ruffles yipping
in Posie's car. Gracie and I had seen Posie take one look
at me and roar out of town as if she had a crime to con-
ceal. And then the restraining order.

So why was this note as illiterate as the previous one?
Did Posie think she was throwing me off the track?

I crumpled the note in my hand and took another look
inside the envelope. Ten thousand dollars was bad enough,
but the envelope contained no proof that Miss Ruffles was

alive and well. And now I had a whole day of worrying ahead of me.

Not to mention trying to figure some way of finding the amount of money needed to get Miss Ruffles back. Maybe I'd have to use my powers of persuasion instead.

I paced around Fred, stewing. Monday was shaping up to be hot and miserable in more ways than one.

In the end, I took Fred up to my room and left him sleeping there while I drove to the Tejas.

Across the parking lot, Gracie Garcia was climbing out of her Volkswagen. I caught up with her at the door. She was dressed for business in a suit and heels. The suit might have come from Victoria's Secret Lawyer Collection, though. It had a tight-fitting jacket, a short skirt that showed off Gracie's legs, and a blouse that allowed for just a little jiggle.

"Hey, darlin'," she said. "I'm pickin' up coffee for the office. Since Mule Stop is the last place on earth not to have a Starbucks, here I am here. Can I buy you a cup?"

"Thanks, but I'm on an errand for Mae Mae."

She pulled a sympathetic face. "No lollygagging, I get it. How's your pup?"

"Still missing."

"Ready for me to join your posse? I used to practice with a lasso." She feigned twirling a lariat over her heat. "I can rope any bad guy you point me at. Or bad girl."

"Thanks, but I'm still thinking how to do this best."

She patted my arm. "You're better at thinking than me. Catch up with you later."

Gracie made a turn and headed for the in-store coffee counter, and I headed for the meat department at the back of the store. I asked the attendant for Mae Mae's sausage and waited while it was located and wrapped up.

Four minutes later, Gracie rushed up, balancing a

cardboard tray containing three jumbo cups of coffee. "Red alert! Posie's here."

At that moment, Posie Hensley turned the corner by the bakery, headed my way, pushing a grocery cart and giving a display of whole wheat bread a cursory study.

"Quick! We have to hide."

With a hasty thank-you, I grabbed the sausage off the top of the meat counter and ducked into the cereal aisle. Right behind me, Gracie seized the biggest box of Cheerios and handed it over. I grabbed the box and held it up in front of my face, pretending to study the nutritional information.

We needn't have worried. Posie pushed her cart past the meat counter and kept going. She was wearing workout clothes and sneakers. Her hair was in a perfect ponytail, very jaunty.

"Let's get out of here," Gracie muttered.

"Just a minute."

"What are you doing?"

I kept the Cheerios. "I don't know yet."

We edged out of the aisle and peeked to see where Posie was headed next. Looked like the deli counter.

Gracie said, "We ought to torture her, ask about Miss Ruffles. We could tie her up in the deli, maybe force her to eat some of that olive loaf stuff. That should make her confess in a heartbeat."

"I'm going to follow her out of the store, see where she goes next. If she's on a bunch of errands, I might have time to drive out to her house to look for Miss Ruffles."

"You won't know if she's coming back any minute. Wait, I've got an idea. Here, hold this." Gracie shoved her tray of coffee into my hands and grabbed a bag of dog food off the nearest shelf. She marched Posie's way.

"Gracie!"

She shushed me and kept going.

Posie appeared to be doing her weekly shopping. She

had a list and a small pencil that she used to efficiently check off the items she picked up. At the deli counter, she left her cart by the pickles and took a number. While she discussed sliced turkey with the attendant, Gracie dropped the dog food in her cart and kept going. Posie never noticed.

I lingered by the peanut butter, watching.

Gracie must have circled the aisle, because she came up behind me. "What happened?"

"Nothing yet."

Posie put the sliced turkey in her shopping cart and moved on.

"She didn't even notice!" Gracie hissed.

"Let's go to the checkout line. She'll show up there eventually."

At the checkout, I paid for the Cheerios and the sausage, and Gracie paid for her coffee order.

As she tucked her change into her wallet, she said, "I gotta go before this gets cold. Call me later. Tell me what happens with Posie."

She swished out the automatic doors. I hung around the locked cigarette case where I could keep an eye on the checkout lanes.

In ten minutes, Posie came along, ready to check out. The clerk got as far as the dog food when Posie stopped her.

"What's that?"

"Your dog food, ma'am."

"I didn't put that in my cart."

The clerk shrugged and put the food aside. "People put stuff in the wrong carts all the time. No problem."

Posie lost interest in the dog food and began going through her wallet. "I wouldn't have a dog in my house if you paid me. My son is allergic. Plus, dogs make an awful mess."

The clerk smiled as she scanned the rest of Posie's

items. "I love dogs. I have three. And our beagle just had puppies. Three boys, two girls. Beagles are the cutest puppies ever. You want one?"

"No, thank you." Posie remained polite and repeated, "My son is allergic. We can't have pets of any kind."

I went outside, more puzzled than ever. If Posie was so protective of her allergic son, why would she have Miss Ruffles in her possession? Or didn't she? And why would Posie need ten thousand dollars when she had a sizable inheritance, even if it wasn't all of Honeybelle's fortune? It didn't make sense. Was the misspelled ransom note a clue telling me Posie hadn't kidnapped the dog after all?

I decided to hang around Honeybelle's car to see what happened when she came out of the store.

In a couple of minutes, Posie came outside in the company of the young man who sometimes helped customers to their cars. He pushed the cart, and Posie followed, tucking her shopping list into her shoulder bag and making conversation. She wore her sunglasses. When the young man had loaded her shopping bags into her trunk, she tried to give him a tip, but he politely refused to accept it. Pretending to offer a tip in a parking lot where signs plainly said employees weren't allowed to accept was a routine exercise. Honeybelle had always offered tips and rarely succeeded in handing over any money. Posie was also unsuccessful. If she had grown up poor, at least she had learned how to behave in her new socioeconomic world. She must have said something nice to the employee, because he laughed. She smiled, too.

It was not the kind of exchange I expected of the bitchy Posie I knew.

She got into her car and pulled out of her parking space. As she drove by me, she finally noticed who was standing there in the sunshine. She looked beyond me and recognized Honeybelle's car.

She braked and rolled down her window. Tartly, she asked, "I see you've commandeered Honeybelle's car now."

"I'm doing my job," I said. "Running errands."

"I hope you don't leave Miss Ruffles in a hot vehicle. You wouldn't want to endanger her life, now, would you?"

With that, she rolled up her window and drove away.

I stood frowning, thinking. What the heck did that all mean?

I went home and spent the afternoon second-guessing myself.

At eight thirty that evening, I left Fred dozing on the warm pool deck. Mae Mae was sitting at the kitchen table tirelessly laboring with a pencil and a dime store notebook. Writing down recipes, I guessed. Mr. Carver was upstairs in his apartment with music playing.

The Blues Brothers had gone back to their hotel for the night. I let myself out the gate and walked quietly through the gathering gloom to the appointed place. As directed by the ransom note, I headed toward the stockyard where Miss Ruffles and I had visited the longhorn steers. Inside the houses that I passed, lights were coming on. Air conditioners hummed. Through the windows, I could see families settling down for the night—parents turning on televisions, children going off to bed. In one yard I heard a group of kids shrieking as they captured fireflies. I smelled cigarette smoke beside one house, the sweet hickory woodsmoke of a barbecue from another.

As I drew closer to the stockyard, I caught the whiff of manure on the steady breeze that constantly blew through Mule Stop. The wind never ceased, but I hadn't gotten used to it yet. It was one of the many signs that told me I wasn't in Ohio anymore.

A set of headlights caught me from behind, and I faltered to a stop at the spot where the sidewalk petered out.

The vehicle turned out to be a big pickup truck, heading out of town. It rattled past me and kept going. When my heart stopped pounding, I headed for the stockyard again.

As I reached the entrance to the stockyard, I saw a big sign for the upcoming Junior Rodeo. Underneath the sign, a car's engine started up. I could see two figures inside the vehicle. One was a girl who seemed to be straightening her shirt. The teenaged boy at the wheel lit up a cigarette and blew smoke at me through his open window as he drove by. I guessed that I had stumbled upon a teen hangout. No doubt the town's high school kids came here after dark.

The longhorns had already bedded themselves down for the night, unperturbed by the teenagers. By the light of a single streetlamp that glowed over the corral, two of the big steers stood quietly chewing their cud. The rest of them were still, dark shapes on the ground. I peered at them through the rails, but they paid me no attention. Beyond the corral stood a bunkhouse—a long, low building used for assorted municipal purposes, but empty and dark tonight.

I waited, counting the minutes. Nine o'clock came. I heard church bells announce it. I tried to stay calm, but my fears rose with every passing minute. Until I started to get mad. Where was the dognapper?

I paced by the fence. In the distance, I could hear the sounds of the town. The university's drum line practicing on a distant field. The buzz of a motorcycle. The church bells chimed again, a quarter past, and again at nine thirty.

The motorcycle sound grew closer, coming from the big emptiness beyond the town. A headlight jiggled into my view, and I realized it wasn't a motorcycle but some kind of all-terrain vehicle. A dark figure held the handlebar with one hand. He came closer and closer, the noise of the engine sounding like an angry hornet.

"Hey," I said, half to myself. The ATV was headed

straight at me. I moved aside, but the driver corrected his course and bore down on me.

In the nick of time I realized he really was aiming for me, and I barely dodged out of the way before he roared past in a cloud of dust. I glanced back and saw its dusty bumper sticker: I MAY GET LOST BUT I DON'T GET STUCK.

I tried to run toward the corral fence, thinking I could climb high to safety. Or maybe I could make it as far as the bunkhouse. But the driver had cut me off from the safety of the fence. He circled past, driving me farther out into the open space beyond the stockyard. The scrubland stretched to the horizon.

I could barely see the silhouette of a cowboy hat as he went by the second time, but didn't catch his face. He swung the machine in a circle around me, kicking up grit, then cut sharply and came back, accelerating fast. This time he stood on the pedals, and in his free hand I saw a rope swing overhead—a lasso.

Instinct kicked in. I turned and ran.

But he caught me. As the ATV blew past, I felt the rope cinch around my shoulders. It tightened with a snap, pinning my arms, and I fell flat in the dust, all air driven from my lungs. I barely managed to avoid going face-first, but ended up on my side and tasted dirt. The rope bit into me, taut and painful. I bounced on the ground, hit my head, scraped my knees. I panicked. If he intended to drag me out into the scrub, I'd bounce helplessly behind him and be torn to bits in a minute.

The rope stayed tight. But the ATV stopped dead, thank heaven. I felt like an animal—roped and too stunned to fight back. I tried to suck in some air as he strode toward me. But I couldn't make my lungs work.

Then he was standing over my body, yanking me up from the dirt by the rope. He turned me and flung me down on my belly and grabbed one of my feet. He yanked it up behind my thigh. I cried out in pain. In a second, he whipped the rope around my ankle, then did the same with my other foot. He straddled my shoulders, pinning my face into the dirt, squeezing my chest so hard I thought I'd smother. I lay stunned, unconsciously making a noise that didn't sound human.

He grabbed my ponytail and jerked my head up. His breath smelled of pizza and whiskey as he leaned close.

His voice was a rasp. "You leave this alone, you hear? Forget about the dog and stop asking questions."

I struggled against him, trying to wriggle him off.

He clouted my ear with a gloved hand. "Stop, or you'll get it worse than this."

He threw me back down into the dust, and my skull rang at the impact. With a jerk, he unwound the rope from my legs. Expertly, he lifted me up long enough to rip it from around my shoulders, then dumped me back on the ground.

A second later, he was gone.

I heard the ATV rev up again, and it buzzed off into the darkness.

I lay panting in the dirt.

I should have been crying, but I was too stunned. I tried to get up but got only as far as my hands and knees before I let out a gasp. I hurt all over. I stayed where I was, taking an inventory. No broken bones. Plenty of cuts and scrapes, though. I took a deep breath, then another. A few more to steady my nerves.

I was almost ready to clamber to my feet when something cold touched my face.

I yelped and scrambled backwards onto my butt. When I opened my eyes, Miss Ruffles stood smiling and panting at me from a few feet away.

Not Miss Ruffles. It was Fred. In my disoriented state, I had not recognized him. He had licked my face. His stump of a tail stirred, and he took a nervous pace forward. He dipped his head and stared at me with friendly concern clear in his brown eyes.

"I'm okay," I told him, reassuring myself at the same time. "How did you get here?"

His tail wagged a little more. He had followed me, obviously. But his slow pace had only just now allowed him to reach me. He came closer and nuzzled my arm.

That's when I did burst into tears. I hugged Fred, and he let me. His warm body comforted me, gave me the courage to gather my composure.

I took a deep breath and let it out. "Boy, I'm glad to see you."

He wiggled in my embrace, and I let him go. I petted his head, gave his ribs a pat, and climbed to my feet.

The ATV was long gone. All that remained was a haze of dust that hung in the air, glowing from the light of the streetlamp over the corral. The slight breeze was dissipating the dust fast.

To Fred, I said, "I hope you can walk home. Because I don't think I can carry you right now." I swiped my dirty forearm across my face to get rid of the tears. My cheeks felt gritty.

He gave an all-over body shake that said he didn't care how I looked, but he was happy to see me, too.

My heart filled. I was glad to have his company. "C'mon, then. Let's go home."

Fred waddled beside me, staying close. I wasn't going to set any land speed records. My whole body was stiffening up fast. My knees were cut and bleeding. I walked tentatively, pausing now and then for Fred to get his breath, too.

My mother's research advice included something about endurance. I struggled to remember it. When confronting difficulties, she said, a scientist had to develop endurance to keep going. Fred and I made slow progress. He stopped twice to lie down. His ribs were heaving, and I thought maybe mine were doing the same thing. I was still scared, still stunned by what had happened. Still not making sense of what my attacker had said. As I waited for Fred to recover enough to get going again, my imagination conjured up my attacker over and over. He might come back for me. And then what? I hadn't been able to fight him off before, and now I was in much worse shape.

"C'mon, Fred. We've got to keep moving."

We made it back to Honeybelle's house at last, and I saw that the back gate was open just a few inches. I must not have latched it tightly when I left, and Fred had nosed it open. Really stupid of me, considering what had happened to Miss Ruffles. When we got into the yard, I closed the gate firmly this time and latched it. I could hear Mr. Carver's music up in his apartment. Mae Mae's bedroom light was on.

I thought about taking off my clothes and slipping into the swimming pool. The water shimmered, and I could imagine how cool it might feel against my scraped skin and aching muscles. But I didn't want any splashing to bring Mr. Carver or Mae Mae outside. If they found me, I was going to have a hard time explaining my injuries. So I dusted myself off outside and prepared to sneak into the house.

Fred and I tiptoed to the back door and let ourselves into the darkened kitchen. Fred went straight to the water bowl and drank. Then he stretched out on the cool kitchen floor and heaved a sigh of exhaustion. He was asleep a moment later.

I kicked off my sneakers by the back door and headed for the kitchen sink. I didn't want to track dirt through the house. Cautiously, I turned on the water, glad I could see only a bad reflection of myself in the window over the sink. I didn't want a good look at what my face looked like.

Carefully, I filled my palms with cool water and gently splashed my cheeks. The water ran down my elbows, carrying dirt and sand into the sink. I leaned weakly there, holding my wet hands against my throbbing eyes. I fought down the urge to blubber again. I was home. Safe. In a few minutes, I would be upstairs in the tub, and then my bed. I longed for sleep.

But the light snapped on overhead, filling the kitchen with a bright glare.

I straightened up and whirled to see who had arrived.

Mae Mae stood in the doorway, wearing her bathrobe and boiling mad. "You're making a mess of my kitchen. Look at that floor! And—Lorda mercy! What happened to you?"

"I . . . I tripped and fell." My voice quavered. "Out walking Miss Ruffles."

Mae Mae's gaze grew more hostile. "Tripped over what? And fell down what canyon? You look terrible. Why—that's blood!"

She stared at my knees. Blood had indeed trickled down my shins and soaked into my shoes.

There was no way to hide my injuries, but I hugged myself, hands trying to cover the scrapes on my arms. Inadequately, I said, "I fell, that's all. I'll be okay in a minute."

"Whyn't you stop lying?" Mae Mae snapped. "You been lying since you set foot in this house."

"W-what?"

"I'm sick of your deceitful ways. You've been a shifty little sneak since you sashayed into town."

"I have not!"

She stormed into the kitchen, yanked open a drawer, and pulled out her rolling pin. She pointed it at my nose. "You bulldozed Honeybelle from the start. She was the kindest, best lady in this whole town, and you took advantage of her like everybody else!"

"I did no such thing!"

"I shoulda run you out of here a long time ago."

"Mae Mae—"

"You're a snake in the grass, and I have a mind to finally call the police and tell 'em exactly what you did."

"What do you think I did?"

"It was you." Mae Mae's eyes narrowed to slits, and her breathing was ragged. "You gave some of those dog pills to Honeybelle. That's how she had her heart attack and died—from you giving her dog pills when she wasn't looking!"

I barely made it to the kitchen table before my legs gave out. I plunked into a chair, stunned into silence.

★ ★ ★

CHAPTER SEVENTEEN

If the Good Lord's willing and the creek don't rise.
—TRADITIONAL

It's strange not being trusted when you're accustomed to being the most trustworthy person around. All my life, I'd taken care of my mother, taken care of her colleagues. I picked up their laundry, did their taxes, even house-sat for a few people and fed their tropical fish. So it was weird and hurtful to be the object of Mae Mae's obvious dislike.

Now, though, Mae Mae advanced on me, a towering figure with the rolling pin raised aloft. "Maybe I can't prove it, but Honeybelle didn't die of no natural causes. It was you!"

The pills I had been asked to give Miss Ruffles were only vitamins. Certainly nothing lethal. But Mae Mae didn't know that. More calmly than I felt, I said, "Why would you say such a thing?"

"You wanted her money, same as everybody. You're so smart, you figured a way to get it. Smiling, doing everything she asked, sweet as pie, talking to her day and night—you got her to change her will, to include you. And then you killed her."

It was so absurd, and yet I could see how it made perfect sense to her. But I was tired and shaken and in no shape to make sense, so I laughed. I hiccoughed and laughed and sputtered and finally clapped one hand over my mouth and just shook my head at her.

"What's so funny?" Mae Mae demanded.

"It's not," I said when I could finally speak. "It's not a bit funny. I thought the same thing, Mae Mae. Somebody must have poisoned her. I think somebody killed her, but it wasn't me. I swear it wasn't me."

Mae Mae stood for a full minute, working her jaw, staring into my face as if she could learn the truth by drilling into my brain with a laser. Finally she plopped into the chair opposite mine and spoke. "You really think somebody killed Honeybelle?"

I sobered up fast. "I don't think she died of an ordinary heart attack."

"Why not?"

"You know why. Because she was healthy. She didn't have any health problems at all. She was upset about the garden club thing and her disagreement with President Cornfelter and . . . and everything else, but she was getting over that."

Mae Mae still glared at me with suspicion. "It broke her heart, the garden club ladies turning their backs on her the way they did. Posie turned them all against her."

"But after a few days, she decided to put the garden club behind her and start doing new things. She was going to lunch in Dallas. She was thinking about travel."

"She was never sick for a day," Mae Mae said, more to herself than to me. "Not except a little cold now and then. She took good care of herself."

"There's no reason she should have had a heart attack," I agreed. With great relief at finally having someone to share my jumbled theories with, I said, "Honeybelle rewrote her will just in the last month or so—just before she died. And then how quickly the funeral happened—

that was even stranger, wasn't it? It was like everybody was hurrying through the process. And now Ten saying he can't find a death certificate. Why would her death certificate be missing if there wasn't something fishy going on?"

Mae Mae snapped her gaze up to mine again, mistrust back in place. "You're not thinking Mr. Ten had anything to do with Honeybelle's death?"

"I hardly know him—not the way you do."

She shook her head. "He's a good boy. Had his wild ways when he was younger, before he got himself banged up, but he'd never hurt a fly. Not even those bulls that near killed him. And anyway, what did he stand to get when Honeybelle died?"

"I don't know." I sighed, starting to feel exhausted in addition to my aches and pains. "All I'm thinking is that Honeybelle didn't die of a plain old heart attack." I took a deep breath to gather what was left of my courage. "I was down at the stockyard tonight. A man on an ATV came out of nowhere and lassoed me. He knocked me down and threatened me."

Mae Mae was shocked. "Lassoed you like a steer?"

"Yes, and when I was down in the dirt, he told me to stop asking questions."

"About Honeybelle?" She sucked in a shocked breath. "Are you sure? Stop asking questions or what? What did he say he'd do?"

"He said for me to forget about the dog and stop asking questions. I was flat on my face in the dirt at the time. I presume he meant he'd hurt me more than he had already."

For the first time, I considered the truth of what tonight's violent incident meant. Honeybelle's death hadn't been something accidental or natural. Somehow, too, the kidnapping of Miss Ruffles was tangled up in Honeybelle's death.

Mae Mae was staring at nothing, her mind going just

as fast as mine. She watched a lot of crime television, so maybe the leap from heart attack to murder wasn't such a great distance for her. Abruptly, she set the rolling pin on the table. "I knew it. I just knew it."

"You didn't mention it to me," I said tartly.

She shot back, " 'Cause I figured you were the one that done it."

"Well, it wasn't me. The man tonight convinced me she was murdered, though."

Mae Mae's stare narrowed. "You're thinking it was Ten who roped you."

"No," I said at once. "But he was a cowboy. Somebody good with a rope. I didn't see his face. It had to be somebody strong."

"He ain't as strong as he used to be, not since his accident. He's not supposed to be riding a horse, but he does, easy like. I don't know if he could ride one of those ATV things. Anyway, in this town, half the men rope and ride in competitions on the weekends. Coulda been anybody."

"I don't think it was Ten," I said softly. "It didn't—I don't know—it didn't feel like him."

Mae Mae's thoughts had already traveled back to Honeybelle. "Who else you been thinking could have murdered our Honeybelle?"

I liked the sound of "our Honeybelle." Still, I was reluctant to share all my suspicions with my newfound ally. "Well . . ."

"Go on and say it," she ordered.

I started to rub my forehead, but my skin hurt and I stopped. "Listen, this is all speculation. And maybe my imagination got carried away—"

"Who else?" Mae Mae asked again.

I gave up trying to hold back. "President Cornfelter. He wanted a new football stadium very badly. He wanted a big donation."

"And maybe figured he'd get it faster if she got herself killed."

"Yes. And he had an argument with her the morning she died. She was in the car, and he went over and had words with her."

Mae Mae shook her head. "He's too high class to kill somebody. Anybody else?"

I didn't agree, but I didn't argue either. I said, "Okay, this is going to sound crazy."

"I've seen plenty of crazy." Mae Mae leaned on her elbows. "Who else you thinking about?"

"Posie."

Mae Mae snorted like a horse. "Now, that's just foolish talk."

"Think about the wedding. How much Posie wanted to have it here, how adamant Honeybelle was about not hosting it."

"No way she'd kill her own mother-in-law. Not over a wedding."

"Even though she thought she'd inherit millions? She'd already humiliated Honeybelle in front of the garden club. She's ambitious, Mae Mae. And she seems pretty ruthless to me. Mr. Carver said there's been a long dispute between them. Over Hut Junior. And Honeybelle's rose garden."

"What?"

"The rose garden. Honeybelle stole a lot of the roses in her collection."

Mae Mae was scandalized. "That's a damn lie!"

"Is it?" I asked. "The Appleby family sold a rose to Honeybelle, but they're saying she didn't pay them what the rose was really worth. Or that she cheated them somehow. Anyway, something strange was going on between them. I just don't know what yet."

Mae Mae didn't answer, but I could see her chewing on my ideas. Finally, she said, "Anybody else?"

"Mr. Gamble. He's the only one who could have cremated Honeybelle without requesting an autopsy that would confirm her exact cause of death. And now he's mysteriously left town."

"He was over the moon for her! Why would he kill her?"

"Okay, if not him, there are dozens, maybe hundreds of people who borrowed money from Honeybelle, and probably some who couldn't pay her back. Shop owners, scholarship recipients—"

"She only loaned out small amounts to local people. Not enough to kill for."

"Maybe you're right. I met some of them at the church, and they all seemed nice. It only takes one of them who wasn't so nice, though." I tried to steady my racing pulse. "The big question is who had a reason to kill her and the opportunity to poison her or . . . or drug her or do whatever it took for Honeybelle to die. It had to be somebody close enough, somebody she trusted, don't you think?"

"She trusted a lot of folks."

"Yes, she did. But one of them must have slipped some medicine or poison to her without her knowledge."

"Who?"

But I had no time to say more. At that moment, Mr. Carver tapped on the back door and stepped inside.

"Sunny!" He gaped at me from the doorway. "What happened?"

I must have looked awful, because Mr. Carver's expression was horrified.

Before I could manufacture a plausible lie, Mae Mae said, "She fell. She was walking that dog, and she fell. That dog was always tripping up Miss Honeybelle, too, and now this. I was just going to help her get cleaned up."

Mr. Carver closed the door. "Dear girl, you need a doctor! You should go to the hospital!"

"I'm okay." Although I felt woozy all over again. "Just banged up and dirty."

Mae Mae got up from the table, her bulk shielding me from Mr. Carver's view. She sent me a look that ordered me to be careful. "I'll get a basin and some towels. Get her something to drink."

She bustled up the stairs as fast as she could and disappeared.

Mr. Carver came to the table. He had his car keys in one hand and wore his going-out clothes—loose trousers and an old shirt rolled at the sleeves. He said, "I saw the kitchen light and wondered if something was wrong. What can I get you to drink?"

"Anything." My strength was starting to drain away again. I closed my eyes and put my head down on the table.

Mae Mae came back down from her apartment and snapped, "What did you do to her?"

I sat up, and Mr. Carver stuttered, "I-I didn't do anything. I'm getting her a drink."

They bustled around, and in a moment Mr. Carver set a juice glass of something amber in front of me. It took a big effort for me to pick up the glass and sip from it. Honeybelle's Dubonnet. It burned in my throat, but felt warm going down. Only after I swallowed did I realize I shouldn't have done it. Mr. Carver could have tainted my drink.

But that was ridiculous.

With her basin, Mae Mae knocked over the glass, and its contents immediately spilled across the table. "So sorry," she said, without meaning it.

Her basin was filled with hastily gathered items. She handed me a kitchen towel to sop up the spill.

"My daddy was a Louisiana *traiteur*," she said as she worked at sponging my scraped knees with a clean, wet washcloth. "A kind of faith healer, you'd call him. Here, hold this leaf. Stay still, child. I'm gonna cut a snip of your hair."

"What—?" I finished wiping up the spill and obediently grabbed the small leaf between my fingers. It was dry and delicate.

She tossed the bloody washcloth aside. With a rough hand, she squared my shoulders. "Sit up straight and stay still, I'm telling you. Now put the leaf in the basin and hold out your hands." She trimmed a tiny lock of my hair with her scissors and dropped it into my cupped hands. "Drop that in the basin now, too."

Mr. Carver said, "Mae Mae, you're going to scare this young lady with your black magic country ways. Let me drive her to a proper doctor."

"You hush with your insults," she snapped. "Ain't nothing magic about it." From her deep pocket she withdrew a small cloth bag. She untied the strings and upended it, spilling a cascade of small items onto the table—an acorn, some bits of plant, a figurine, an animal tooth, and more. "It's all natural, from God's earth. Don't touch that," she said to me, pointing at the tooth. "It's for my rheumatism. It bites the pain. Don't pick up your hair neither." She hustled to a drawer and came back with kitchen matches.

"You say a prayer now," she said to me. "Don't matter what kind. *Now I lay me down to sleep* will do just fine. Just so you're talking to God."

I obeyed and started reciting the bedtime prayer in a shaky whisper. She struck a match. In the basin, she set the snippet of my hair on fire—a sharp smell, a puff of smoke. The leaf caught fire, too, and a bright flame flared up. The edges of the leaf burned fast, curling, then turning black.

The flame went out at the moment I finished the prayer. Mae Mae gathered up the burned black bits and stuffed them into the small bag. She clasped the bag between her

hands and bowed her head. "Stay still now, and let me pray."

"What nonsense," Mr. Carver said. "In Memphis, you'd be arrested for fraud."

She muttered her prayer and finished with a hasty "Amen. Now take this bag and put it next to your heart. Yes, right there in your bra."

She held wide the neck of my shirt so I could obey her command. Mr. Carver turned away, making an exasperated noise in his throat. Then Mae Mae passed her hands up and down on either side of my body, not quite touching me. Presumably not speaking to God, she said, "And you can hush your mouth about fraud, mister."

Mr. Carver shook his head.

"There," she said to me when she had finished moving her hands around me. "Tonight I will make you a tea to add to your bathwater. It will be healing and restful. Meantime, put this Band-Aid on your knee."

"Thank you, Mae Mae." I wasn't sure I felt any better, but I sat in wonder as she gathered up her little charms and stowed them in her pocket. The little bag was warm against my skin. I opened the Band-Aid and applied it to the worst cut on my knee.

"I hope you feel better," Mr. Carver said, edging for the door.

"Are you on your way out?" I asked.

"Me? No, of course not." But he slid a set of car keys into his pocket.

Mae Mae rolled her eyes at me, then began to rinse the basin at the sink. "We're just fine. You run along now, Mr. Carver. I'll take care of things here."

He hesitated, looking at me uncertainly. "If you say so."

"I just need a good night's rest," I said.

"Well, then. Good night."

Unwillingly, he went out the door, and we heard him

go down the porch steps. Mae Mae and I exchanged a glance. Then we hurried to the back door to watch out the window.

"Turn off the light," I whispered to her.

She flipped the switch, and we were in darkness. Together, we peered outside.

Mae Mae kept her voice low. "What's he doing?"

"Going into the garage. He's going out, isn't he?"

"He's been acting suspicious for a long time."

"You don't think he'd hurt Honeybelle, do you?"

"They had a big fight the morning she died. I heard 'em."

I had, too. And Mr. Carver had access to his own heart medication. It would have been an easy task to slip a few of his own pills into her morning coffee.

I asked, "Where does he go at this time of night? Out to get ice cream or something?"

"He won't tell. He goes on Mondays and Saturdays, and sometimes on Thursdays. He goes late—not always this late, but after dark."

I glanced over at the clock on the stove. A little after ten. "Does he have a girlfriend?"

"At his age? A man that old couldn't handle a woman with a pair of barbecue tongs."

"Then where does he go? Did he ever tell Honeybelle?"

Mae Mae said, "Maybe so."

We saw the light go on in the garage, indicating the garage door was opening. I hurried to the sink. "I'm going to follow him. He's probably taking the van. I'll take Honeybelle's car."

"Tonight? Looking the way you do?"

"My mother took me on a couple of her expeditions. After a while, you can convince yourself that cleaning up with a couple of baby wipes is just as good as a hot shower. But here. Help me get the rest of this grit washed off."

"You should stay here. Take a cool bath." Mae Mae ran

water into the sink and sponged at my arms with a dish-cloth. "It wouldn't take but ten minutes for me to make you up a tea."

"I feel much better already. Really, whatever you did, it helped."

"Of course it helped. But it needs more time to work." Maybe Mae Mae objected, but she handed me a kitchen towel to dry off my face, neck, and arms. "Hurry up. Wipe off your legs again, too. You don't want to go bleeding on Honeybelle's nice Lexus upholstery. I'd go with you, but all I've got on under this robe is my nightie."

"I can go alone." I had splashed water in all directions but managed to rinse most of the dust off my face and arms. My legs were another story. I needed more time to clean up properly—time I didn't have. In another few seconds I was pulling on my shoes. "Is he taking the van?"

Mae Mae risked another peek out the kitchen door window. "I can't tell yet, but—hang on, yes! I can see the lights. He's pulling out now."

"Where are the keys to Honeybelle's car? Darn! I left them upstairs—"

"There's another set here in the drawer." She opened a drawer and rummaged.

I finished with the towel. "How do I look?"

"You're not going to win any pageants, but you look less like a dead cat." Mae Mae clapped the keys into my hand and opened the back door for me. "Don't lose him!"

I hobbled down the porch stairs and hurried across the dark lawn.

"Be careful, Sunny!"

The first time Mae Mae had ever said my name. It made me smile. I turned around and waved to her, then ran for the garage.

★ ★ ★

CHAPTER EIGHTEEN

No dancing on the tables with spurs.
—ROADHOUSE SIGN

By the time I reached the gate, Mr. Carver had pulled out onto the street and was heading for town. I waited until he was halfway down the block, then dashed into the garage. A few seconds later, I was behind the wheel of Honeybelle's car. I backed out of the garage and followed the lights of the van, careful to hang back as far as I dared. The air-conditioning blew on my face, cooling but also calming me. My pulse steadied as I drove the dark streets of Mule Stop, keeping an eye on Carver's taillights.

Sedately, he drove through town, past the university and the Tejas store. He took the road past the animal shelter, and I started to think he was heading to Posie's house. There was nothing else out on this end of town.

But he went past the housing development and the water tower, heading out of Mule Stop on the long, flat road toward Lubbock. I glanced at my gas gauge. Less than a quarter of a tank—not enough to get me the hundred or so miles to Lubbock.

Behind me, another car's headlights suddenly swung into my rearview mirror. I slowed down automatically, and within a minute that car passed me, going fast. I took a furtive look at the car as it went by and nearly choked.

Hut Junior, traveling far above the speed limit. The co-conspirators were up to something.

I stayed back, following the two of them by keeping their lights in view. Within five miles, though, both the van and Hut's car pulled into a parking lot. I hadn't realized there was anything out this far from town. I didn't risk pulling in. Going by, I peered out my window and saw the building was some kind of roadside bar. Neon lights glowed over the doorway, and beer signs flickered in the windows. The parking lot was full of pickup trucks and SUVs. Both Mr. Carver and Hut parked in the lot.

I continued along the road for another half mile, trying to think what to do. With no cars coming from the opposite direction, I slowed and turned around. As I headed back toward the bar, I tried to come up with a plan.

Neither Hut nor Mr. Carver was in sight when I reached the parking lot. I found a spot on the opposite side of the building from where they had left their vehicles. I turned off the engine and checked the clock on the dash.

It was just a few minutes before eleven o'clock—hardly an hour when two men ought to be meeting for a drink without a nefarious reason.

Another truck pulled into the lot and parked a few slots down from me. I noticed the truck's bumper sported a parking sticker from Hensley Oil and Gas. A pass to get into an employee parking lot. Several other vehicles around me had the same sticker. Two young couples jumped out of the truck and ran, laughing, for the door. The women wore short, fluffy skirts and cowboy boots. The men were in jeans, boots, and crisp shirts. They looked ready to party.

I could hear music from inside the bar, so loud the whole building seemed to vibrate. My mother used to say that a scientist had to go looking in order to find something. You couldn't just wait for a discovery to fall into your lap. So I got out of the Lexus and headed for the door.

A neon sign mounted over the entrance said HARLEY'S ROADHOUSE. A paper notice fluttered on the door. It announced dancing on Monday nights, nine to midnight, no cover charge. Even out on the porch, the music was deafening.

More curious than ever, I let myself inside.

In my shorts and sneakers, I was dressed all wrong, but nobody noticed. Nor did anybody see my injuries, because the bodies were packed so tightly together. And I saw plenty of sunburned faces and Band-Aids in the crowd. A lot of people worked outdoors around Mule Stop, and nobody cared how you looked when you came out dancing.

The dance floor was crowded with couples doing the two-step to a rockabilly band that blasted from a makeshift stage. Through the crush of people, I could barely make out a bar on one end of the room. It was mobbed with men and women of all ages. Not just college students, but grown-ups out to have a good time. The two couples who arrived before me grabbed longneck beers and pushed through to find places to stand around the dance floor.

I saw a familiar face behind the bar and made my way through the jostling crowd.

It was Rico, Gracie's would-be boyfriend. He looked up from his work to see me on the other side of the bar, and his eyes widened. "Sunny!"

"Hi," I shouted over the noise around us, then couldn't come up with something to say. I had run out of the house without a nickel in my pocket, so I couldn't even buy a drink.

"What happened to you?" he asked, matching my volume. "Were you in an accident?"

"Nothing major," I yelled, wishing I could have taken

time to clean up better, but if I had paused to put on makeup, I might have missed Mr. Carver's destination. I hoped Mae Mae's Cajun cure had done its best. "I thought you worked at the saloon in town."

Rico grinned. "I do. But I pick up a few hours here. On Monday nights, this is the place to be. Did you find Miss Ruffles?"

I put one finger to my lips to keep the secret.

Just then, the band finished their song, and the young, tattooed singer bellowed "Good night" into the microphone. The dancers shouted and applauded. Whistles pierced the air. Onstage, an older man in a cowboy hat brushed past the members of the band as they unplugged their instruments, and he announced the next act—the Rootin' Tooters. Around me, the crowd roared with approval.

There was a rush to the bar for more beer, and I got swept away from Rico before I could ask him any more questions.

But I didn't need to ask. The next band was already climbing onto the stage and setting up to play. Four men and a beautiful young female singer in a red dress. I didn't recognize her, but I spotted Mr. Carver right away. He settled himself at the electric piano. One of the other men had a guitar in hand. Another man turned out to be not a man at all, but Crazy Mary in jeans, tuning a fiddle as she took her place.

Bringing up the rear came Hut Junior. Even with his oversized Stetson pulled low over his face, I recognized him. He held two instruments—a small mandolin in one hand and a bass by its neck. He handed the mandolin to someone else, and I wondered if it might have been in the package I'd seen him receive from Mr. Carver. Then he planted the big bass at his feet before thumping the strings a few times with his right hand. The wooden face of the instrument was worn as if by years of hard play. Hut's thick fingers were agile on the strings. I couldn't have been more surprised if he'd shown up with a trained pony and a couple of poodles wearing party hats. This was a side of Hut Junior I'd never imagined. Then I remembered the photo of the little boy with the guitar on Honeybelle's desk, and a lot of things began to make sense.

A minute later, the Rootin' Tooters burst into song. Everybody in the building applauded the opening notes of their honky-tonk tune. The singer had a throbbing voice that rose to the rafters, with a Mexican lilt to her accent. She sang her heart out and snapped her fingers to the beat of Hut Junior's bass. The enthusiastic mob of dancers swung into motion.

Rico appeared at my side. He was smiling. "How about it?"

I heard him over the music, but wasn't quite sure what he meant "How about what?"

"I get a break while the band plays. Let's dance!"

Before I could say no, he drew me into the sea of dancers and pulled me close. My legs still felt quivery, but I hung on to my partner, and he didn't seem to mind. I was terrified that Mr. Carver might see me. Or Mary or Hut Junior. But they were focused on their music, and it was pretty darn good. I couldn't have escaped Rico's embrace anyway. Expertly, he whirled me into the crowd that was all traveling the same direction with a polka-like step that was easy to follow. I tried to forget about my injuries and keep up.

Rico was just an inch or two taller than me, so we were evenly matched. He was a good dancer. Holding my hand, he gave me a flourishing spin, then pulled me back into his chest without missing a beat. I settled my hand on his strong shoulder and found myself laughing. Six months ago, I'd never have guessed I'd be in Mule Stop, Texas, dancing

to music played by a couple of possible murderers in cowboy hats. Except they didn't look like the murdering types
just then. They were rocking through a fast-paced country
song that was irresistible. The band could really swing.

Rico's arm was tight on my waist, and he guided me
smoothly around the dance floor.

"How do you like it?" he yelled in my ear.

"This is great! You're a terrific dancer."

"Thanks. I'm from Miami. Everybody dances in Miami. Did you find Miss Ruffles?"

I pretended I couldn't hear him. The music really was
too energetic for more talk, but when the song ended and
the musicians immediately began to play something
slower, Rico pulled me snug against his chest and spoke
into my ear. "It's nice to see you here."

His body felt tight and damp with sweat, but I was no
prize either. If Gracie learned I was dancing with the man
she'd set her sights on, though, she was going to be upset.
So I carefully considered what my response should be.

Finally, I said, "I work with one of the musicians in the
band. I wanted to hear him play."

Rico spun me around so he could see the stage as we
danced. "Which one?"

"Mr. Carver—the man at the piano."

"The old guy? I've seen him around, never met him.
Wait—he was some kind of friend of Honeybelle Hensley,
right?"

"You knew Honeybelle?"

"Everybody knew who she was. Me, not personally. I
saw her around town, that's all. You worked for her, right?
Taking care of Miss Ruffles. So he must have worked for
her, too?"

"Yes."

Surely Honeybelle had known Mr. Carver and Hut
Junior played together in a band. Or hadn't she? Mr. Carver

obviously kept it a secret from Mae Mae, so maybe he'd also been silent around Honeybelle. If so, why?

When Rico guided me around to the front of the stage, I took a longer, surreptitious look at Hut as he played the bass. He kept his hat down and focused on the strings. He was almost hiding behind his instrument. If he could have made himself invisible, he'd have done it.

Why play music in public if he preferred to be anonymous?

Rico spun me away from the stage, and I suddenly found myself looking straight into the startled face of Poppy Appleby. She was dancing—not with Ten, but with an older man who seemed to be just as expert a dancer as Rico. Poppy's smile of enjoyment evaporated as her wide eyes met mine. I could see a dozen thoughts crossing her mind. Then she looked at Rico and blinked.

In another second she was gone, whirled away by her partner. Of course she couldn't go dancing with Ten, I thought. He was still not recovered from his injuries.

Rico saw where I was staring. "Oh, that's Poppy, the television weather lady."

"Yes, I know."

"She's a really great dancer. She comes every week."

"Have you danced with her?"

"Nah, she's always got plenty of partners."

The music got loud again, and we danced in the heat, with other bodies bumping close, everybody having a good time.

When the music eased up, Rico said in my ear, "You should come more often."

I felt guilty. I wasn't looking for love, that's for sure, and even if I had been, Rico was off-limits. I didn't want to spoil my friendship with Gracie.

So I said, "It's getting late. I better go."

He was gracious about it, but I could see hurt feelings in his dark eyes.

So I smiled and said, "Thanks for the dance. You have terrific moves, Rico. I had fun."

"Sure." He danced me to the edge of the floor and released me. "See you around."

The band took a break, and Rico headed back to the bar. The dancers pushed past me in search of drinks. I tried to get lost in the crowd while I let various impressions settle in my mind. I found myself buffeted toward the back of the room. Suddenly a big man shouldered his way through the other people, on his way to the bathroom, maybe. When he got closer, I realized it was Hut Junior.

He didn't see me—didn't take the time—but moved swiftly past me and down the narrow hallway. He stopped where some coats and bags were hanging on hooks. Purposefully, he ran his hands through one jacket until he came up with an object. Before he palmed it, I saw it was a bottle of pills—in a small amber pharmacy container. He turned at once and came back toward me.

I turned my back so he wouldn't recognize who I was, but I needn't have worried. He was on his way back to the stage, pills in hand.

I watched from the doorway. He climbed back onstage, twisting open the pharmacy bottle. He shook a tablet into Mr. Carver's hand. Mr. Carver smiled gratefully and popped the pill into his mouth. Hut Junior dropped a comforting hand on Mr. Carver's shoulder. Despite the noise in the dance hall, Mr. Carver sat quietly for a few minutes, eyes closed, waiting for his pill to take effect.

With Hut there to look after him, I didn't need to stay. I had learned enough for one night anyway. I needed time to let the information simmer in my brain.

I went back to Honeybelle's house. I parked the Lexus

in the garage and hoped the engine would cool off before Mr. Carver returned from his nighttime outing. My whole body ached, but I knew it would be worse in the morning.

Mae Mae met me at the kitchen door, still in her bathrobe. The kitchen smelled of coffee and baking. She had kept herself busy while I was gone. "Well?"

For once it was nice not to see her glowering at me, expecting the worst. "Mr. Carver went to a roadhouse out past the interstate. He's a regular there, playing in a band."

I might as well have told her he had joined a nudist colony. "A band!"

"That's not all. Hut Junior is in the band, too. They play together."

Mae Mae's expression cleared. "Hut Junior? And Mr. Carver?"

"Do you know something about the two of them?" I kicked off my sneakers, stumbling in the process and catching my balance on the kitchen counter.

"I know a lot, but we can talk in the morning." With concern, Mae Mae said, "For now, you should get yourself a bath and go to bed. Here's a tea." She handed me a muslin bag, tied with a string. Inside, I could see bits of twigs and leaves. "Don't drink it. Put it in your bathwater."

"Thank you," I said. "I'm beat."

"Also in the morning," she said just as sternly, "you can explain what happened to Miss Ruffles."

Behind her on the floor, Fred snored. He had rolled over onto his back to get comfortable, and his anatomical differences from Miss Ruffles were on full display. With Mae Mae giving me a long frown, I picked him up and carried him upstairs.

★ ★ ★

CHAPTER NINETEEN

Remove boots and spurs before entering tub.
—BOARDINGHOUSE RULES

I took the bath in Mae Mae's concoction and nearly zonked out in the tub. Exhausted, I barely made it into the bed with Fred before falling into a coma. In the morning, I turned off my alarm when it went off and fell back to sleep for another two hours. It was past nine when I finally pulled Fred out of my bed and headed down the stairs to the kitchen.

By which time Mr. Carver was already seated at the table and fastidiously finishing his scrambled eggs with a generous slice of cinnamon coffee cake that Mae Mae must have baked while she waited for me to return last night. He had the angelic air of a man who'd slept well, with no guilt.

Mae Mae was back to freezing me out.

I fed Fred and let him outside into the backyard before returning to the kitchen and sliding into the chair opposite Mr. Carver.

"So, Mr. Carver, how long have you been playing music with Hut Junior?"

With a clatter, he dropped his coffee cup back into its saucer. He looked across the table at me with a wounded expression. I had betrayed him.

"Playing music," Mae Mae repeated.

"They're really good," I said. "They play at Harley's Roadhouse, right, Mr. Carver?"

"What kind of den of iniquity is a Harley roadhouse?"

"It's not a den. There's dancing." I reached for a slice of coffee cake. "What I want to know is how long Mr. Carver and Hut have played together. Well?"

"For many years," he replied at last, trying not to sneak a frightened look at Mae Mae. "I taught Hut his first piano lesson. And his introduction to the guitar. But he went for professional lessons after that. Guitar, mandolin, and the bass, of course. He's very good."

"He took lessons at the university?"

"Yes, at first. Honeybelle got him the best lessons money could buy."

To Mae Mae, I said. "They really swing. And the place was jammed. You and I will have to go some night, just to listen."

Mr. Carver looked imploringly at Mae Mae. "Hut didn't want anybody to know."

"I knew just fine he was musical," she said shortly. "I thought he stopped years ago. Honeybelle said so."

"Well, he kept on going. His mother wanted him to keep at it, but he wanted to go into the Hensley oil business, and thought it would be better if—"

"If his music was a secret from Honeybelle," I finished. "Neither you or Hut wanted her to know you moonlight at a roadhouse?"

"It wasn't a secret," he said. "Not exactly."

"I guess not," Mae Mae said. "Not if everybody in town goes out there to hear you play."

The doorbell rang at the front of the house. I got up quickly, my mouth full of heavenly coffee cake. "I'll get it. Then we'll talk more."

"No, no." Mr. Carver reached for his blue jacket. "It's my job to answer the door."

"Finish your breakfast," I said. "And talk to Mae Mae."

I pushed through the swinging door as Mr. Carver sank back into his chair with a nervous sigh.

I was startled to open the front door to Poppy Appleby. She stood on the porch in sky-high heels that showed off her pedicure and a pretty pink sundress printed with tiny turtles. On her arm, she carried a straw handbag—the perfect size to hold her peashooter. In her other hand, she twirled her sunglasses as she pretended to admire Honeybelle's roses.

"Good morning." She turned on me with a smile that looked stiff around the edges. "Your name's Bunny, isn't it? Am I too early to pay a call?"

"Sunny." Belatedly, I brushed crumbs from my mouth. "No, you're not too early."

"Oh, I'm so glad." Although I had not invited her inside, she squeezed past me and stepped into the foyer. "I'm a bit of an early bird myself. In television, you have to be. But I thought I'd take a chance and stop by after the morning news. I saw you at the roadhouse last night. Did you have a good time?"

"I only stayed a short while, but yes."

"Who was that you were dancing with?"

"Just a friend."

She wanted to ask more, but her manners were too good. She said, "He's a good dancer."

"He said the same about you."

"Really? How nice of him." In a rush, she said, "Poor Ten can't dance, you know. He's steady enough on a horse, but he hasn't quite got his balance and flexibility back yet. He doesn't mind if I go out dancing, because I love it so much. That was my uncle I was with when you saw me last night."

I realized that she had come to assure me she hadn't been cheating on her fiancé. Did she think I was going to tattle on her? That idea made me feel a little sorry for her. Maybe she wasn't as self-confident as she let on.

Mae Mae had once mentioned that the Appleby family came from humble beginnings. Maybe Poppy was a woman who overachieved to overcome her feeling of inadequacy? To my eye, she had everything. But perhaps that had not come easily.

Making an effort to be friendly, I said, "Your uncle was pretty agile."

"Yes. Yes, he is." She seemed at a loss about what to say next and finally asked, "Is Mae Mae at home?"

"Sure. Come in."

In the act of closing the door, I noticed another vehicle pull up in front of the house. It parked behind a small white convertible that must have been Poppy's ride. The newcomer was a large van with the Critter Control logo painted on its side.

To Poppy, I said, "Mae Mae's in the kitchen." I hooked my thumb at the arriving truck. "I should probably intercept this guy, show him the backyard, so could you find your way?"

Poppy blinked as if I had suggested she kick off her shoes, put her feet up on Honeybelle's furniture, and drink a beer directly from the can.

"You won't get lost." I shrugged off my lack of good southern manners and pointed. "If you've forgotten, kitchen's that way."

"I remember," she said, cool again.

We parted, and I hotfooted it out to the Critter Control truck.

The exterminator was a crusty, bandy-legged old man who stood maybe five-two, with a wispy gray beard and an enormous hat on a skinny body. He had the back of the van already open. The vehicle was full of traps, barrels of poison, and what looked like several guns in carrying cases padlocked into racks.

"Good morning," I said. "It might be easier if you pulled your vehicle around the back."

"Why, good morning there, little lady—whoa, not so little. You're high altitude, aren't you?" He stood so much shorter than me that he had to crane his neck to look up, but he made up for his lack of stature with a big smile that showed lots of empty spaces. With panache, he swept off his hat to show a pink scalp, bushy eyebrows, and large, permanently sunburned ears with plenty more gray hair sprouting out of them. He touched his hat to his chest. "I'm Rudolphus Barnstable, but you can call me Rudy, everybody does, even Miss Honeybelle, rest her soul. What a character she was. Hope you don't mind an old cuss like me saying you're as tall as a sunflower in a cotton field."

"Thanks, I think." I smiled and pointed. "This way. I'll show you."

He climbed back into his truck and followed me around the block to the back gate.

When he was out again and opening up his truck to show all his critter remedies, I couldn't help asking, "You're the one who helped Honeybelle get rid of prairie dogs once before, right?"

"Yes, ma'am, I am. She was a satisfied customer, too. I don't guarantee critters won't come back, though. You can't stop nature, if you know what I mean." He waggled his eyebrows.

I decided to ignore his implication. "I was wondering if you have a humane solution for getting rid of prairie dogs."

His flirtatious manner evaporated. "Humane for who?"

"The prairie dogs. Maybe you could trap them this time, and release them somewhere else?"

He looked at me sadly. "You're not from around here, are you, Sunflower?"

"No, sir, I'm not."

"I could tell," he said, turning morose. "Every now and then, I gotta put up with—that is, I have to go along with the wishes of a misguided client."

"So you'll try the trap idea?" I said firmly.

His voice took on a whine. "Depends on how big your infestation is. If you've got a few hundred prairie dogs, there's no way to keep up with them. They can make more prairie dogs faster than I can catch 'em. They tunnel underground, and that's how come you can never tell how many you got."

"We don't have hundreds."

"Not yet," he said darkly.

"Not yet," I agreed. "But maybe I could help you somehow."

His bushy eyebrows took an ornery angle. "It costs extra if you help."

"Now, look—"

"Oh, simmer down, Sunflower." He had a cackling laugh. "Let's have a look at your situation, then we'll chew the fat."

"Good plan. This way."

Fred looked up from his nap on the terrace and decided not to stir himself. This morning he looked physically exhausted, but I was glad to see him alert.

Rudy knew his way around Honeybelle's property, and he took a tour of the prairie dog town that was under construction around the gazebo. In a few minutes he completed his inspection and leaned on the swimming pool ladder. He pulled a plug of tobacco from the hip pocket of his jeans. With a pocketknife, he cut himself off a chunk and conveyed it into his mouth.

"Well now," he said. "You don't have more'n a handful

out there now. Good thing you called before they got outta hand. If you wanner try trappin' 'em, I could set up some traps and you could call me when we got something."

"I'm happy to do that."

"I got some oatmeal and peanut butter in the truck. There's nothing like oatmeal and peanut butter to tempt a prairie dog. But you gotta keep your own animal away from the traps." He pointed his knife at Fred.

"Okay," I said.

By that time, Mr. Carver was coming out the kitchen door while shrugging into his jacket.

Crowing, Rudy said, "Here comes the boss man. We'll see what he has to say. Or maybe he'll just sing us a tune."

"You know Mr. Carver? You've heard his music?"

"Shore. He's been playin' around these parts since almost before the railroad came through. Honeybelle tol' me he wanted to move back up to Nashville and work in the recording industry. Looks like that didn't happen yet. Hey, there, Mr. Carver. How you doing this fine morning?"

I left them to their discussion. I gave Fred a pat and went back inside, where Poppy was making her pitch to Mae Mae.

"I can't promise you a program of your own," Poppy was saying. "I thought I'd suggest to my boss that I produce three three-minute segments for our noon news program. We'll see how those go, what kind of viewer response we have."

Poppy was seated at the table, and Mae Mae was pouring hot coffee into one of Honeybelle's delicate china cups. She had set a slice of coffee cake in front of Poppy on a china plate, too. "What kind of segment?"

"Cooking, of course. Cajun cooking. That's your specialty, right? Ten told me so."

Today's apron said THIS KITCHEN IS SEASONED WITH LOVE, with a picture of a big red heart that seemed magnified by Mae Mae's enormous bosom. Mae Mae said, "I cook New Orleans style. That's not Cajun, no, ma'am. It's refined Creole cooking." She spoke with pride. "Fine dining."

"Then that's what we'll do," Poppy said promptly. "You can provide a little education, too. Explain the differences in the cuisines of your region, the way Paula Deen did. And Martha Stewart—you could talk about your family traditions like she does. How you came to Mule Stop, that sort of thing. Our viewers will love it."

Mae Mae glowered. "I don't see how no viewers are gonna want to hear about me wading out of the city through five feet of sewage."

"Mae Mae," I said gently, "don't play hard to get. Poppy's offering you a nice proposition. You could have fun with it."

Poppy looked surprised to hear me take her side. "It will be a lot of fun, yes. Also hard work."

"I'm used to hard work," Mae Mae shot back.

"Sit down," I said to her. "Listen to what Poppy has to say."

"I don't need another job," Mae Mae said as I guided her into one of the kitchen chairs. "I got plenty of work to do right here. I'm supposed to prepare meals every day. Just because Honeybelle isn't here don't mean I can shirk my duties. People depend on me."

"I'm sure yours is a very daunting job," Poppy said. "But we could work around your schedule. We'll tape the segments at your convenience."

Mae Mae continued to frown and finally said, "I don't know how to talk on television like Paula Deen or Martha Stewart."

Poppy smiled. "The same as you're talking right now."

"What about my recipes?"

"You can share only the ones you're willing to," I said. "They're not asking you to give away family secrets."

"No, no, nothing like that," Poppy assured her. "We'll start with something simple."

"Your beignets," I suggested. "They're delicious, and you could make them in your sleep."

Mae Mae said, "It's not like I can't make something complicated."

"Why don't we look through some of your recipes?" Poppy said. "We'll put our heads together and come up with three fun segments."

"You want to see 'em now?" Mae Mae asked. Without glancing at me, she went on, "I got 'em written down. They're upstairs."

Poppy smiled. "That sounds like a plan. Would you like me to go up . . . ?"

"I'll bring 'em down here."

Mae Mae puffed up the back staircase, and we could soon hear her heavy footsteps overhead.

Poppy sipped her coffee and eyed me over the rim of her cup. "Thank you for helping."

"Mae Mae just needs to be cajoled sometimes," I said. "She's going to love showing people how to cook the way she does."

"Does she show you how to cook?"

"No, I'm all thumbs in the kitchen."

We were silent for a moment, and then Poppy said, "I have an all-afternoon meeting with my boss. I want to show up with ideas of my own so he doesn't lose confidence in me. I've been working here for eight months, and this is my first chance to demonstrate that I can do something besides be the weather girl with the big smile. Okay, maybe my last chance." She couldn't meet my eye. "I don't want to be another former baton twirler with her sights set on the *Today* show. It's such a cliché." With another smile, this one more genuine than before, she said, "I'm all thumbs in the kitchen, too. But Ten loves anything Mae

Mae makes, so maybe I'll learn something useful along the way."

"If anyone can show you, it's Mae Mae. Are you really setting your sights on the *Today* show?"

She turned pink. "Who wouldn't like to go far? But I'm already thirty and working at the only television station in Mule Stop. They fired me in Tulsa. Don't tell Ten, okay? They found somebody prettier, with a degree in meteorology, so I got the boot. I'm probably better off in a small town anyway, but . . ."

"It's a very nice small town."

She nodded vigorously. "Yes, it is. I didn't appreciate it as much when I was growing up here, but now I see it's pretty great." Poppy took another sip of coffee, considering me. After a moment, she set her cup carefully into the saucer. "I think I owe you an apology. I had you figured all wrong. I thought you were here in Mule Stop to get your hands on whatever you could get away with. But you're helping Mae Mae, aren't you?"

I tried not to be offended. It was starting to look like I was being misunderstood by a lot of people. I thought the Texans were all hard to figure, but maybe I wasn't exactly transparent to them either. My silence had been interpreted as calculating. And maybe cold.

I said, "Mae Mae needs to do something now that Honeybelle's gone. Since nobody's hiring private cooks these days, and you needed a show idea, I thought the two of you could help each other out."

Poppy laughed a little. "Maybe I should hire Mae Mae myself. For after the wedding. Both Ten and I will be working, no time to cook."

Here was my chance to ask about the wedding, about her sister, about the yellow rose in Honeybelle's garden that might have set off a war between the families. But just as we were starting to be friendly, I thought bringing up her wedding to Ten might be misconstrued.

"Mae Mae's great," I said. We heard her coming down the stairs again, so I dropped my voice to a whisper and added, "It helps if you make everything sound as if it's her idea."

Poppy shot me a thumbs-up just as Mae Mae arrived, already shuffling through her notebook and giving her opinions.

They sorted through Mae Mae's recipes, both talking in overlapping sentences. While their creative juices flowed together, I cut myself another slice of coffee cake and ate it standing at the kitchen window. I felt much better than I had expected after my experience at the stockyard. Maybe Mae Mae's *traiteur* ritual worked better than I'd imagined it might, or maybe her bathtub tea was a miracle elixir. Whatever the reason, I was grateful not to be hobbling around and moaning with pain. I finished my breakfast, then went outside to check on Fred.

He saw me coming and responded by thumping his tail in the grass. Otherwise, he didn't move from his comfortable spot in the sunshine. I took my shovel and pickup bucket around the yard to clean up after him, then sat down to pet him while the Critter Control man and Mr. Carver explored the prairie dog town that was under construction in the back of the yard.

While they finished talking, I took Fred into the house.

Mae Mae was flipping her recipes at the table, and Poppy was gone.

I said, "Did you make some decisions?"

"We did. I'm going to the station tomorrow to practice for a tryout in the studio kitchen. What do you think of that?"

"I think it's fantastic. Do you want me to drive you?"

"Miss Appleby is going to pick me up."

"First-class treatment."

"Maybe so." Mae Mae closed the notebook on her recipes and turned to me. "It's high time we went to the police about Honeybelle."

"I know we should," I said, changing gears just as fast. "And believe me, I'd have done it before, but I can't, Mae Mae. Neither can you. Not until I get Miss Ruffles back."

"Get her back?"

I asked Mae Mae to sit down, and as I faced her across the table, I told her about Miss Ruffles disappearing. I did not tell her my prime suspect had been Posie. After my assault at the stockyard, not to mention our short exchange at the grocery store, I was beginning to doubt my assumptions about Posie anyway.

From my pocket I pulled the notes sent to me by the dognapper. I handed them over to Mae Mae and let her read them. "If we go to the police, there's a chance the dognapper might find out. And then something bad happens to Miss Ruffles. Also, the police squad includes Posie's brother, Bubba. With him on the force, we'd have to worry about information getting to . . . well, to someone who might want to harm Miss Ruffles."

Mae Mae took the notes from me and studied the paper. "This looks like blood. Is the kidnapper hurting her?"

"I hope it's the other way around."

Mae Mae allowed a grim smile. "Me, too. That dog had a temper."

"Don't say 'had,' please," I said. "She's still alive. I have to believe that. But we need help. I've run out of ideas, and I can't go to the police."

Mae Mae looked sharply into my face. "Who, then?"

"There's only one person I think could be helpful."

Mae Mae agreed. She pulled a Tupperware container of her étouffée from the freezer and handed it over. I took some time to cover up my scraped knees with jeans, and my skinned elbows with a shirt that reached my forearms. I put a Band-Aid on my cheek where a gash looked not too bad, but unattractive. Within the hour I was in Honeybelle's Lexus heading toward Ten Tennyson's office, with Fred sleeping on the passenger seat.

★ ★ ★

CHAPTER TWENTY

It has been coming on so gradually, that I hardly know when it began. But I believe I must date it from my first seeing his beautiful grounds at Pemberley.
—JANE AUSTEN, *PRIDE AND PREJUDICE*

At the Tennyson law office, I found Gracie Garcia sitting alone behind a big desk, frowning at a computer screen and typing very fast. Her desk was located in what had once been an alcove off the center hall of the old house. A reception desk sat in the middle of the center hall, but it was vacant today except for a telephone and a large Remington bronze of a cowboy on a horse. Around the desk, three doors stood ajar. In each of the rooms I could see a desk with a big swivel chair, bookcases, and a computer. All three offices were unoccupied.

Gracie looked up from her work when I came through the door from the vestibule, and she brightened when she recognized me.

"Sunny! You found Miss Ruffles!"

I eased Fred into an armchair in the deserted waiting area. The more I carried him around, the happier he seemed. He thumped his stub on the chair's upholstery. I decided to avoid lying to Gracie by changing the subject. "You look fantastic. New dress?"

Gracie was looking not exactly professional in a sleeveless black and white print dress with a low scoop neckline. A long chain with an elaborate hunk of metal nestled in the valley of her cleavage. The print on the dress seemed to exaggerate her curves—a fun-house version of the sexy secretary look.

She beamed at the compliment. "I figure with the big bosses still on vacation, and the little boss out at the ranch today, I could dress as I please. I'm all by my lonesome."

"Ten is out of the office today?"

"Yep. Today's Junior Rodeo practice out at the old Tennyson family ranch. He told me to call him if anything came up. But nothing comes up—not with his daddy and granddaddy on vacation. He even gave the secretary a couple of days off so she could get ready for her grandma's ninetieth birthday this weekend. So I'm holding the fort—catching up on some documents. Hey, I can use the paycheck."

"Sorry you're all alone. I was actually hoping to talk to Ten."

She pulled out her keyboard again and tapped it, studying her computer screen intently. "He's coming in tomorrow at nine to meet with one of his daddy's clients. That should only take an hour. Want me to put you on his calendar for ten?"

"Can I get back to you?"

"Sure." Her gaze met mine, suddenly curious. "Everything okay?"

"I just need to talk to him. Gracie, were you involved in Honeybelle's will at all?"

"I did most of the typing. But, darlin', I can't talk about that."

If she'd typed it, she knew every detail of the will. Still, she was right to keep client business to herself. "Sure, of course," I said. "Sorry to ask."

She checked the clock on the wall. "You could catch Ten out at the ranch. It's the old place where his granddaddy

grew up—about two miles past the stockyard, take Boone
Parkway past the Grotz family cotton fields and Miss
Patty's Pies. You can't miss it. There's a big pasture with
a mean ol' bull in it. On the right, past the dry creekbed.
Easy drive."

"Okay, thanks." Although she seemed eager to get back
to her work, I hesitated. "Hey, Sunday I met somebody I
wonder if you know."

She quit fiddling with her keyboard and glanced at the
clock again. "Who?"

"A local cop. Bubba Appleby."

"He's an Appleby?"

"Right. Posie and Poppy's younger brother."

She wrinkled her nose. "His name is really Bubba?"

"That's what his friends and family call him. He's kinda
cute. Okay, he's really cute. Have you met him?"

"I don't know any cops. Did he go to Alamo?"

I had forgotten that Gracie knew the university crowd
more than the townies. When I considered whether Appleby had the brains to attend the local college, I said, "I
doubt it."

She put her chin in her hand and sighed. "I saw Rico
this morning, going to the saloon. I think he might have
waved at me."

That made me feel even guiltier for dancing with her
would-be Romeo at the roadhouse, so I grabbed Fred up
into my arms and headed for the door. "Well, thanks for
the directions. I'll talk to you later!"

"Bye-bye!"

I hustled out the door and headed for the parking lot.
Fred licked my face and was happy to find us back in the
Lexus. He sat up in the passenger seat to watch the world
go by. I started the car and had put it into reverse to back
out of my parking space when another car whipped up behind me and pulled into the handicapped space right by

the door to the law office. I waited to see who was in such a rush to see a lawyer. And I couldn't help it—I wanted to see if the driver really deserved the handicapped space.

To my surprise, President Cornfelter got out of the car. He looked far from handicapped. He had another bunch of flowers in his hand—the kind from the supermarket checkout stand, wrapped in cellophane. Big spender. As I watched, he went into the office and disappeared.

Fred made a noise in his throat—not a whine or a growl, but a noise of puzzlement.

"I know," I said to him. "Who is President Cornfelter taking flowers to? There's nobody in the office but Gracie."

I thought of the way Gracie had been watching the clock.

Had she been expecting President Cornfelter?

To Fred, I said, "That's impossible."

He looked at me with his ears pricked up.

"There's no way Gracie is dating a man that age."

But that didn't mean President Cornfelter wasn't smitten with Gracie. Was he bothering her?

To Fred, I said, "I think I better go back inside. I'll leave the air conditioner running for you, okay?" I lowered the windows a few inches to be on the safe side.

A minute later, I let myself back inside the building and slammed the door to give Gracie some warning. From the vestibule, I called, "Gracie? Did I leave a dog leash in here?"

By the time I reached her desk, she was sitting at her keyboard, smoothing her hair and acting as if nothing was amiss. One of the office doors that had been standing open minutes earlier was now closed. I guessed President Cornfelter was hiding behind it. His flowers lay on the desk, still in their cellophane wrapping.

Gracie's voice was pitched just a tad too high. "I didn't notice a leash. Are you sure you left it?"

Her lipstick didn't look as precise as it had a couple of

minutes ago, and she didn't meet my eye. If she'd been afraid, she could have signaled me somehow, but she wasn't in distress. I could see that.

"My mistake." I said, "I must have left it in the car."

She gave me a fingertip wave. "Bye!"

A moment later, I was back in the car with Fred, stunned. "I don't believe it," I said to him.

He gave a dog snort and shook himself all over as if ridding himself of a distasteful idea.

"I know what you mean," I said. "Cornfelter is a creep. Is Gracie so desperate for a boyfriend, she'll date even him?"

I drove out of the parking lot, still trying to get my head around Gracie and President Cornfelter. What kind of horndog romanced Honeybelle Hensley and later took the same cheap flowers to a paralegal half his age?

According to Gracie, Ten's ranch lay out of town on the Boone Parkway—a glorious name for a dusty two-lane road that started out with a row of mobile homes planted in a cotton field. Then came a large garage surrounded by pickup trucks. I slowed down as I reached Miss Patty's pie shop—an old gas station converted to a picturesque bakery with cheery paint and a drive-up window. A hand-lettered sign stuck in the ground out front announced today's special—blueberry pie. After that, the wind blew dust sideways across the road, sending bolls of cotton skittering along in the wake of Honeybelle's Lexus.

At last I reached a pasture where a large, speckled, mostly Brahman bull grazed on thin grass. A painted sign hung on the fence, proclaiming his name.

HELLRAZOR
WORLD CHAMPION BUCKING BULL

As I turned, the bull looked up from eating and stared at me with menace. I was glad to put him in my rearview mirror. I bumped the car on a tar and chip road for several hundred yards.

The ranch buildings came into view. First I saw a low, faded clapboard one-story house that must have stood on the property for a hundred years. It had a long, crooked front porch that featured a picnic table and a wooden swing, painted blue, on chains. The roof was new—bright red tin. A single tree shaded the house but looked as if it had been struck by lightning a long time ago. Only a lopsided half remained—a magnificent curve of graceful branches that sheltered the house.

Stretching away from the house was the land as I had never really seen it before. Wide and sun baked, but not colorless. Far from it. The shades of gold seemed endless, punctuated by splashes of blue flowers—bluebonnets, I guessed. The vastness made me suddenly think of the native people who must have traveled this land for centuries. They must have dwelled in a place as long as it could sustain them, then moved on without inflicting change on the landscape. This endless prairie seemed untouched by anything but earth, wind, and very little water, which magically produced an astonishing beauty.

I had been determined to learn the town and the university to find how I might fit in, but here was the Texas I had not yet allowed myself to know. The horizon cut the vivid azure sky so distinctly I could have hung my heart on it.

I tried to think of something wise my mother might have said about land, but I couldn't. She had loved her butterflies and the adventure of discovery, but I had never heard her speak of any connection she felt to a special place. Maybe she had never been emotionally rooted to earth and sky the way I was suddenly aware of. Had she missed this feeling?

I saw a lone butterfly dancing over a flower by the edge

of the drive. It fluttered one moment but seemed to disappear the next. I watched carefully, but it did not reappear. Perhaps I had imagined it.

As beautiful as the scenery was, I had a hard time picturing someone like Poppy Appleby enjoying her newlywed status in such a wild and remote place.

Across the driveway were several corrals and a pole barn with a very old tractor sitting in its open doorway. In one corral, several horses swished their tails under the shade of another big tree. I recognized Hondo by his spots. Ten's Jeep was parked in the shadow of the barn.

Out in the pasture sat a livestock trailer with its gate down, as if awaiting an animal.

In another corral, Ten worked a young chestnut horse on a lunge line. The horse reared up on his hind legs and batted at the rope, trying to escape. Ten pulled him down and got him cantering again, but the horse bucked with every few strides and shook his head as if objecting to the exercise. Ten steadily held the line in one hand, and with the other he wielded a long, thin whip with a small flag on its tip, gently flicking it behind the horse to keep him moving. The young horse fought the line, occasionally throwing his weight against it, but Ten coaxed him back into a canter every time.

Ten looked happy to be doing battle with a large, angry animal.

Ten also looked good in his dusty jeans—a thought I tried to wash out of my head as soon as it arrived.

From the backseat, I grabbed the container of Mae Mae's frozen étouffée. I left the car door open on the off-chance Fred woke up and wanted to take a tour of the place. In the searing sunlight I went over to the fence. I balanced the container on the top of a fence post and climbed up to hang on the top rail to squint into the sun. The ranch smell was different from the smell of farms in

Ohio—drier, certainly. The angle of the sun was sharper in Texas, too. But the chirping of swallows in the barn sounded the same. Ten's voice—quietly reassuring as he talked nonsense to the horse—sounded like every other person who worked well with animals.

After about ten minutes, the chestnut was sweating and calmer. Ten eased up on the line, and the horse immediately slowed to a tired walk. Ten drew him nearer and gave his long neck a rub before unclipping the line and turning him loose. The horse swung his head to bite Ten, but he missed and trotted away to the other side of the corral.

Ten ambled over to me. Wearing those delicious jeans.

Unaware that my impure thoughts were roaming around his pockets, he tucked his sunglasses into his shirt and used his teeth to pull off his gloves. "When are you going to learn to wear a hat?"

I realized my skin was prickling as if more freckles were bursting out before his eyes. "I'll remember one of these days." I shaded my eyes with my hand. "You were having a good time out there. You must like animals that can break you into little pieces."

"I appreciate a challenge," he agreed with a grin. "Stick around. In a little while I'm going to lure my bull into a trailer." He pointed at the vehicle parked out in the pasture. "We've got the Junior Rodeo later this week, and he's the main attraction. Getting him loaded up is the ultimate test."

"You like the danger," I said.

"Don't start. I've heard all the lectures before."

"Who's lecturing?"

"My mom, my dad. Poppy."

"You look like you know what you're doing. Here, I brought you some dinner from Mae Mae."

His eyes lit up, and he reached for the container. He unscrewed the lid and took a peek. "Give Mae Mae a big kiss from me."

"I'm getting along with her better now, but we haven't reached that stage." I threw caution to the wind. "What are the chances Mae Mae could be your fiancée's next big television star?"

"She sure has the right cooking skills." Ten screwed the lid back on the container.

"And a big personality, too. Did you mention Mae Mae to her?"

"To Poppy? Not me. She said you brought up the idea. I might have chimed in, that's all."

"Well, thanks. Poppy dropped by this morning to propose an audition. I think Mae Mae's really excited about it."

"Mae Mae deserves something good."

"Thank Poppy for me."

"Thank her yourself."

Even though Poppy and I seemed to have reached a détente, I said, "It might be heard better, coming from you."

Ten glanced up at me on the fence, then focused on placing the container carefully back on top of the post. "Maybe you're right."

"Listen," I said after a strange second slipped by, "I appreciate the help on the restraining order thing. I should probably get another lawyer, though, considering you're already working for the Hensley family, right?"

"You're right again," he said. "I know all the lawyers in town. Let me think about who could help you. Somebody will be the right fit."

"Someone who can put me on a payment plan. I'm not exactly rolling in money."

"Not yet," he said, voice loaded.

I had a feeling my inheritance from Honeybelle was in big jeopardy, but I didn't say so. "I don't suppose you heard anything from your future in-laws at Sunday supper? About the order against me or Miss Ruffles, that is?"

"It didn't come up, and I didn't ask," Ten said. "There was a lot of wedding talk, which I tend to tune out."

I smiled. "That's how you end up wearing a powder blue tuxedo with a ruffled shirt, you know."

"I trust Poppy to make the right decisions."

"That's nice," I said. "Trust is . . . nice. You've known each other a long time?"

"Since kindergarten." Ten lifted a loop of rope from the gate and let himself out of the corral. "Junior high trip to Dallas, senior prom, all that. She went off to college out east, though, and I went to A&M, so it wasn't until these last couple of years that we got together again. She came around when I . . . when I needed somebody. She was great. Really helped improve my outlook on things so I could get back on my feet."

With a nod, he pointed out a field where a patch of grass had been blackened by a bonfire. It looked like the kind of spot where he dragged branches and scrap wood to burn; a brush pile was stacked there, ready for a match. The wood leaned against the frame of a wheelchair. Its seat was burned away, and the rubber wheels were long gone, but the structure of the chair had been left to hold the wood for fires. To me, it looked like an act of rage had first parked the wheelchair there, and someone took satisfaction in seeing it in the center of many bonfires thereafter.

It was a kind of monument to his recovery from whatever bull-riding accident had injured him so badly. I didn't say that, however.

Instead, I climbed down from the fence and faced him. "So you were friends first. That's supposed to be good for a marriage."

"We were never friends," he said in a tone that surprised me. "Maybe that will change once she moves out here."

"She's moving here?" I glanced at the ramshackle house, thinking back to when I overheard Posie talking to

Hut about her plans to move into Honeybelle's mansion and to pass her own home along to Poppy and her new husband.

"Sure she's coming here," Ten said. "After the wedding."

Over by the house, Fred jumped down from the car and stretched stiffly. Awake from his nap, he spotted us and waddled over to me with the slow gait of an old animal with a bad case of arthritis. I gave him a pat, and he stretched his neck to touch his nose to Ten's knee for a tentative sniff. I held my breath.

Ten bent to give him a reassuring stroke. "Where's Miss Ruffles? You could bring her out here to show her some cattle."

I had been waiting for him to recognize the dog in my company wasn't Miss Ruffles. I wasn't ready to explain my errand yet, though, so I said, "I don't see any cattle. Except the Brahman bull out front. Hellrazor, huh? Is he yours?"

Still smoothing Fred's coat, Ten shot a grin up at me. "He's my nemesis—the bull that near killed me. When he got to be too old for rodeoing, I bought him, gave him a place of honor in the front pasture. This fall, I'm going to use him for some breeding."

"Do you raise cattle?

"I keep a few to work the horses. They're out in a field." He waved vaguely past the corrals. "I thought I might try raising some rodeo stock, too. Bulls for riding, steers for roping, that kind of thing. I can't give up on rodeo yet." He gave Fred one last pat and stood tall again. More firmly than before, he said, "Where's Miss Ruffles?"

There wasn't any use putting it off any longer.

"That's why I'm here."

I tried to muster my courage, but my hands were suddenly shaking. Now that the time had come to tell the truth, I wasn't sure I wanted to.

Concerned, Ten reached out and pulled me by my elbow into the welcome shade of the tree. On the other side of the fence, the horses dozed, tails occasionally twitching. The air was blessedly cooler there, but it didn't make me feel any better.

"What's going on?" Ten asked. "You look . . . What's wrong?"

"I should have brought the notes so you could read them yourself."

"What notes?"

"I didn't tell you Sunday morning because the cop was there, and then your . . . Poppy, that is, was . . . Look, this is bad news, so I'm just going to blurt it out. Miss Ruffles has been kidnapped. On Saturday after the football game, after you came to Honeybelle's house, I went outside to get her and found a note—"

"Wait. What? Kidnapped?"

"Dognapped. Whatever you want to call it. It happened late Saturday afternoon. You came over, remember? To check on us. But Miss Ruffles must have—"

His voice cut sharper still. "You mean she's actually been taken? By who?"

"I don't know who. The note said—"

"Are you sure?"

"Of course I'm sure."

"Who would kidnap a dog? Let alone Miss Ruffles? Everybody in town knows Miss Ruffles."

"I don't know who did it exactly. The notes weren't signed. For all I know, it could have been you. You were the last visitor at the house that afternoon, but—"

"Why would I take Miss Ruffles? Why would anybody?" He shook his head as if couldn't get his brain to register what I was telling him. "This doesn't make any sense. What did the note say?"

"The first one said they had taken Miss Ruffles, and she would be safe until Monday when they'd communicate their demands."

"What kind of demands? How do you know she's safe?"

"I don't. They sent me some of her hair in the envelope. They want ten thousand dollars."

"Do you think she's still alive?"

I couldn't answer the question. Couldn't find my voice. Something big and horrible welled up inside me, and my vision blurred.

He put his hand on the back of my neck and squeezed. He calmed himself down, too. "Okay, sorry. Take it easy."

It took almost a minute for me to pull myself together. Finally I said, "She's got to be alive."

"I'm sorry I said that. Don't be upset. They can't exchange her for money if she's dead."

I let out a hiccough that maybe sounded like a sob, and I clapped one hand over my mouth to stop more from coming out. He squeezed me again, and I steadied myself. I said, "I've got to figure a way for them to show me she's alive. A picture with the newspaper or something. That's what they do on TV."

"We'll figure it out." His voice was calm and steady again. "Don't worry about that now. Can you tell me everything? Start at the beginning."

"Okay." I took a deep breath and let it out. "Okay."

As if suddenly aware of what he was doing, he took his hand away from my neck. More coherently than I thought possible, I told Ten the whole story from the moment I realized Miss Ruffles was gone—hoping like crazy she had been kidnapped as a college prank after the football game, looking for her with Gracie, being followed home by the police Saturday night. I left out only a few details, like the one about Posie's car. I got as far as telling him about Monday morning when the mailman delivered the letter about meeting at the stockyard. At that, I stopped.

"Did you go to the stockyard last night?"

"Yes," I said. "It didn't go well. A man rode up on an ATV and—"

"An ATV? Like a four-wheeler?"

"Yes. I didn't know him. He . . . he chased me, lassoed me, and knocked me down. He threatened me. But he didn't give Miss Ruffles back."

Stone-voiced, Ten said, "He hurt you? Are you all right?"

Unconsciously, I touched the Band-Aid on my cheek. "I'm okay now. Mae Mae helped me. I was . . . it was scary, that's all."

"Okay, back up." Ten took a closer look at my Band-Aid and made a visible effort to control his temper. He asked, "Why didn't you tell Bubba that Miss Ruffles was missing when he went to Honeybelle's house on Sunday morning? If you had told the police then, you wouldn't have been knocked around by some stupid cowboy on a—"

"The first note told me not to contact the police," I reminded him, "or they'd kill Miss Ruffles. I couldn't risk telling any policeman."

"I'll do it," Ten said. "I'll talk to him now, get the cops working on this while—"

"Hang on. There's more," I said. "A lot more."

He scanned my face and saw I hadn't gotten to the tough part yet. He waited.

I pulled myself together and said, "When the man on the ATV knocked me down, he told me to stop asking questions."

"What kind of questions?"

"I assumed he meant about Honeybelle. About her

death. I've been . . . Okay, I might have asked around town about the circumstances of her death."

The breeze whispered between us, and Fred sat down in the dust.

"Ten," I said, "I don't think Honeybelle died of a heart attack."

Ten said nothing and didn't move, but he was very much alert and listening.

"I think something happened to her. Something terrible. And whoever did it took Miss Ruffles, too."

Still Ten didn't speak. But he watched my face, listening to the tone of my voice as well as my words.

I said, "When Honeybelle died, her nurse drove her straight to Mr. Gamble, who declared her dead and cremated her body right away—in the blink of an eye, really. The family had a quick, private funeral, and that would have been it until the garden club decided they wanted to have a public memorial service. Honeybelle was gone so fast—it was crazy how fast all of it happened. But since then, I've remembered several strange things—things Honeybelle said before she died, about people and her money and her family. And things people said to me. In the crowd outside the church, someone made a remark—a crack, really, that some folks wanted to . . . to bump her off. It just all jumbled around in my head, so I started getting curious."

"And?"

"For one thing, I wonder about Honeybelle's will. In it, she specified we should take care of Miss Ruffles for a year, and you said during that time all the people who hoped to get money or whatever from Honeybelle had to wait. If Miss Ruffles was out of the way, though, they'd have their money right away."

"You mentioned this before. You think Miss Ruffles was taken because . . . ?"

"Because everybody gets what they want if she's gone. I know you don't believe that. But I . . . I think somebody killed Honeybelle, then grabbed Miss Ruffles when they realized they wouldn't get their share of her money for a year."

"Like who?"

"Like the university, for one thing. President Cornfelter was trying to get Honeybelle to pay for a new stadium."

"Every college in Texas wants a new stadium."

"But she didn't want to pay for this one. She only wanted to pay naming rights on the old one. Unless her will . . . What does her will say about funding the stadium?"

Automatically, he said, "I can't tell you what the will says."

"Okay, don't tell me. But think about it for yourself. Does the possibility of a new stadium make a motive for murder?"

Grimly, Ten looked off into the scrub. At last, he said, "In Texas? A new football stadium makes a motive for just about anything."

"Okay, then. Maybe lots of other people want their share now, too. Not just business people around town, but . . . well, Hut Junior for one."

"Hold on." Ten stared at me, incredulous. "You think Hut killed his own mother? Then kidnapped Miss Ruffles to get what's coming to him?"

"Makes sense, right?"

"No, it doesn't make sense. No sense at all. Hut's a nice guy. I've known him all my life. He loved his mother. He was broken up about her death."

"He's also angry that he isn't going to run Hensley Oil and Gas."

Ten didn't argue with me. He looked away again, though, and took off his hat and ran his hand across his short hair.

I said, "What doesn't make sense is how Honeybelle died. She couldn't have had a heart attack, but she might have been poisoned or . . . or medicated somehow. And afterward—you said yourself you couldn't get a death certificate. It's unusual not to find the death certificate, isn't it?"

"Yes, but maybe I don't know what I'm doing. I stopped at Gamble's again today, but his nephew didn't know where to find it either. Come to think of it, Honeybelle's will pays off the mortgage on his funeral home." He caught himself. "You didn't hear that from me, got it?"

"Got it."

Ten let out a sigh of exasperation. "This is all . . . I hate not knowing how everything works. If my dad was here—if he would at least answer his phone messages— things would be different."

"He doesn't answer his phone?"

"They're in Greece. My mom booked a cruise, and they're spending a week on some island. I got a postcard from them," he said with a twinge of bitterness, "but they don't answer any of my calls. And my grandfather is somewhere in Mexico where there aren't any phones."

"Are you worried about them?"

"Worried? No. Exasperated? Yes. My parents do this every couple of years, take a trip, radio silence. They have a ball together." Ten frowned for a while and said, "But Gramps—he doesn't usually go away at the same time Mom and Dad do. And none of them leave town during football season. They're all crazy Alamo football fans. I can't remember them ever missing a game."

"They left you here to mind the store."

"Yes," he said uneasily.

"They must trust you."

"That could be misplaced trust."

"I'm not saying they were part of something nefarious—"

"Good," he snapped.

"—but doesn't it seem strange that all these odd circumstances are happening around Honeybelle's sudden death?"

At our feet, Fred suddenly let out a woof. He scrambled upright and glared into the distance. Ten and I followed his stare and saw Hellrazor ambling across the front pasture. The bull stopped and sniffed the wind. Then he started plodding toward a bucket placed on the ground beside the trailer. As he walked, he bobbed his head like a tired plow horse.

Ten and I watched the bull approach, both of us silent and thinking until Ten said, "I put some corn in the bucket to lure him in. That's what he smells."

Suddenly Fred took off like a rocket.

"Fred!"

"What's he . . . ? That bull will stomp him into little pieces! Call him back!"

"Fred! Fred!"

We ran after him, but Fred bolted under the fence and raced toward the bull, barking with wild delight. I started to duck between the fence rails to chase him, but Ten grabbed me around the waist and pulled me back. "Don't! He might be old, but that bull will kill you."

"Fred!" I cried.

Fred zoomed in a tight circle around the bull. Hellrazor stopped dead and jerked up his head as if amazed that any creature dared disrupt his afternoon stroll. As Fred went roaring around him a second time, the bull lowered his head and snorted. He dug threateningly at the dirt with his fore hoof. Fred was undaunted. He darted close and snapped at Hellrazor's hind leg. The bull let out a bellow and swung a kick at Fred, but missed. He spun laboriously around, but by the time he was ready to face the dog, Fred had already dashed around again and nipped the bull's

other hind leg. Hellrazor finally gathered his energy and
let out an enraged roar. With more speed than I thought
possible, he charged at Fred. Except Fred wasn't there anymore. The dog ran around and around the bull until Hellrazor was dizzily flummoxed.

The bull planted his feet and let out another furious
bawl as if demanding Fred stop and face him head-on.
Fred barked a taunt back. Hellrazor finally blew a snort
and began reluctantly moving in our direction. Not fast
enough for Fred, though. Fred leaped and nipped at Hellrazor's heels until the bull picked up speed. He was soon
trotting toward us with the inexorable momentum of a
freight train.

"Fred! Stop that!"

My shout only seemed to strengthen Fred's determina-
tion to drive the bull toward us.

Ten cursed and pulled me back from the fence just in
case Hellrazor decided to smash through it.

But as he chased Hellrazor toward us, Fred realized his
mistake, and with renewed joy he herded the bull back out
into the pasture. He romped, barking with delight while
Hellrazor's mood went from rage through resentful to sur-
render and back again. But the bull kept moving, going
exactly where Fred wanted him to go.

"Stay here," Ten said, already with one leg clumsily up
on the fence.

"Where are you going?"

"If that dog can do it, I'm going to help him get Hellrazor into the trailer."

"Stop! Please, you'll get hurt."

"There's no time to put a saddle on a horse. Let me go
while he's on the run."

I realized I had been clutching Ten's arm. I released
him, and Ten vaulted over the fence. He tried to run across
the pasture, but immediately I could see he wasn't going

to be fast enough to make it to the trailer before the bull caught sight of him. He was too stiff, one leg not quite strong enough.

I went over the fence, too.

"Fred!" I waved my arms and gave a whistle.

I had no idea what I was doing, but Fred understood. He zipped between Ten and the bull, drawing Hellrazor's attention long enough for Ten to grab the rails of the livestock trailer and climb up to safety. I took off across the pasture and soon clambered up beside him.

"Now what?" I panted.

Ten was grinning. "You're something. See if you can get Fred to herd him into the trailer. As soon as he's inside, I'll close the gate."

"Okay, but—"

Ten grabbed me again. "Just don't get close to the bull. Make sure you can jump up here if he decides to chase you."

He climbed down, and I cautiously followed his lead. I waved to Fred, and his keen gaze took in the open trailer gate. He grasped the situation and quickly began to complete the task.

The dog darted close to nip Hellrazor again, and the bull bellowed. But he moved again, kicking up dust, and Fred chased him toward the trailer. Hellrazor missed the entrance the first time, so Ten and I scrambled up onto the safety of the trailer while Fred circled him around again and made another attempt. This time, Hellrazor figured out that the best place to get away from the dog was the trailer. So he thundered up the ramp, neat as you please.

Ten heaved the gate closed and bolted it shut. Hellrazor gave a pathetic groan, declaring himself defeated.

Fred raced jubilantly around the trailer once more, then ran to me and barked.

Ten was laughing, and so was I. The adrenaline was like lightning inside me—bright and exciting.

Fred barked again, then wobbled unsteadily. His legs trembled. His eyes widened. He gave a little wheeze and dropped at my feet as if every bone in his body suddenly had melted.

★ ★ ★

CHAPTER TWENTY-ONE

One riot, one ranger.
—MOTTO OF THE TEXAS RANGERS

"Heart attack," I said, down on my knees in an instant. "Fred—Fred!"

Fred's eyes glazed over. His breath came in labored gasps, and foam gathered at his mouth. His ribs heaved with the effort to take in air.

And he stopped breathing.

"No!"

I rolled Fred onto his side and put my hand against his chest. I could feel no flutter of his heart, no breath in his lungs. I started doing compressions on his chest, pushing hard, up and down, up and down.

Ten hunkered down beside me. He cupped Fred's muzzle between his hands and bent to blow air into Fred's mouth. I pushed and pushed on Fred's chest; Ten blew. We kept it up for a minute, two minutes, three minutes. I knew I was crying and couldn't stop. Sweat ran down my arms, tears down my face.

"Switch places," Ten said when I started to weaken.

We traded. I blew into Fred's lungs, and Ten thumped on his chest. I don't know how long we worked.

It was up to me to decide when to stop. I slowed down

and finally sat back on my heels. I swiped my face with
my arm. "It's okay," I said in a small voice. "He's gone.
You can stop."

Ten gave Fred a few more compressions, then gave up.

We looked down at the motionless dog. Brave Fred.
Sweet-tempered Fred. He had been a smart, hardworking
dog with a lot of heart. He reminded me of somebody, but
in that moment I couldn't think who.

Then I thought about Miss Ruffles. In her, there was the
same tenacious courage and loyalty Fred had shown to me.
She was every bit as tough and intelligent as he had been,
only she was untrained. She needed help and guidance and
discipline, that's all, to be just as dependable and brave as
Fred had been.

I needed to find her. I needed to give her the chance to
grow up into a great dog just like Fred.

"He's a little Texas Ranger." Ten wiped sweat from his
brow with the back of his hand. "One riot, one ranger."

"What?"

"Texas Rangers—so tough you only need one to settle
a riot."

At those words, Fred gave a shuddering gasp and
opened his eyes. He cast his eyes up at me and started to
pant. He was smiling, too.

"You little sneak!" I cried.

Fred tried to struggle to stand up.

"Not yet, buddy," Ten murmured. He pressed Fred back
down onto the ground. "Take it easy for a minute."

"I can't believe it," I said. "He's alive!"

Ten was grinning. "I reckon it's just not his time yet.
But it sure looked that way."

Fred sat up as suddenly as he had collapsed. With a
whine, he licked my face. I laughed unsteadily and hugged
him close.

Ten sat back on his heels, shaking his head. "That's one

tough little herder. I've never seen Hellrazor so confounded by a cur before."

I wiped my nose. "It would be a shame for him to die after that performance."

"Short of a trophy, he needs a beer and a girl," Ten said with a grin.

"Is that rodeo talk?"

"Yes, ma'am, that's rodeo talk for winning big."

I picked up Fred and carried him out of the pasture. Ten helped me get him through the gate and into the shade. Fred sprawled manfully on the ground, panting in the heat and taking his ease after a hard day's work.

Ten and I didn't have time for more conversation. A pickup truck turned into the lane and came barreling toward us, sending clouds of dust up into the sky. Fred swung his head to look, but I grabbed his collar.

Ten put his hat on, tipped back from his face. When he recognized the approaching truck, his expression turned worried. "I lost track of time. You shouldn't be here."

"Why not?"

I saw why. In the passenger seat of the pickup truck was Trey Hensley. His little brother, Travis Joe, sat beside him. Another boy drove. When the truck stopped, two other boys came piling out of the jump seat of the vehicle, revealing a large Confederate flag sticker in the back window. Trey opened the passenger door and up-ended a bag of potato chips into his mouth before climbing down to the ground.

To me, Ten said, "The boys are here for rodeo practice. They show up every week when their mom has her appointment at the beauty shop."

Travis Joe saw us and came running over. He had clearly not been informed of his mother's restraining order against me, because he had a big grin on his face and barely managed to stop himself before crashing straight into me.

"Hey!" he said. "Are you here to watch us ride? Hi, Miss Ruffles!"

He threw himself in the dirt and rubbed Fred between the ears. Fred accepted the attention without objection.

To Travis Joe, Ten said, "Go catch yourself a horse. Saddles are in the barn. You know what to do."

"We're going to round up some steers," Travis Joe said to me. He got to his feet. He wore a pair of cowboy boots with grubby jeans and a faded T-shirt that advertised the University of the Alamo. He had come to get dirty. Without his mother around, he seemed braver. He said, "I'm really good on a horse. I'm not bad with a rope either."

"You're terrible with a rope," Ten said on a laugh. "You ride Hondo because he makes you look good."

"We're a good team," Travis Joe said with delight.

The other boys were already sliding through the rails of the horse corral, and Travis Joe scrambled to catch up with them. The sleepy horses woke, and some of them tried to amble away, but the boys soon had halters in hand and were taking their animals into the barn for saddling.

If the older Hensley boy, Trey, knew anything about the restraining order, he wasn't letting it show. He had taken a long look at Fred but ignored me. He had a big gray horse in hand, and he led it directly into the barn without a glance in my direction. Maybe a little too obviously.

The other boys all gawked at me.

"I gotta go," Ten said apologetically to me. "These boys will get away with anything if I don't keep an eye on them."

"Even Travis Joe?"

"That one's liable to hurt himself. It's the other four who are future delinquents. I need to stay alert—and make sure they're on horses that'll keep their minds off making trouble."

I couldn't help but smile. "Were you a delinquent at their age?"

He laughed. "Maybe a little. Look, I don't want you to lie, but it might work out best for you if you don't mention this to anyone unless you're asked. These boys come out here against their mother's wishes."

I took a guess. "Posie's afraid they'll get hurt?"

"I can't blame her," Ten said. "Travis Joe got real sick when he was little. But Hut Junior and I thought this would be good for him—for all of them. The kid's illness was a long time ago, and you have to live a life, you know? But Posie's still easily worried."

I withheld my views on Posie. After all, Ten was marrying her sister.

He was distracted and already moving toward the barn. "Have you told anybody else about your theory? About Honeybelle? You should keep it quiet, too, okay? Let me think about what to do, and we'll talk about it. For now, go home, stay safe."

"Okay, thanks. When can we talk?"

"I can't come tonight. Tomorrow I've got to haul livestock for the Junior Rodeo. The whole week is Junior Rodeo. It's a big deal here. But I'll stop by after, for sure. We have to figure out a plan. We need to get Miss Ruffles back. Can you hang on a little longer?"

"Yes," I said, relieved to have an ally at last. "Thank you."

"And then you can explain why you have a dog that looks so much like Miss Ruffles."

I swallowed hard and nodded.

I gathered up Fred and carried him to the car. He was back to being lazy and flopped on the seat as if exhausted by his run with the bull, but he smiled at me.

"You're a delinquent, too," I said to him as I started the car.

I pulled around and drove past the house, the corrals, and finally the barn. As I went by, I looked into the barn and was startled to find Trey Hensley staring sullenly back at me.

In front of him in the barn sat an all-terrain vehicle. I could see the dusty bumper sticker on it. I MAY GET LOST BUT I DON'T GET STUCK.

★ ★ ★

CHAPTER TWENTY-TWO

Sometimes the best cowboy for the job is a cowgirl.
—FLAT-OUT TRUTH

So Ten owned the ATV that my attacker had used.

Before I left his ranch, he had asked if I'd told anybody about my theory that Honeybelle had been murdered. He had said, "You should keep it quiet."

My head reeled so hard that I had to stop the car at the end of his driveway to regain my wits. I put my forehead down onto the steering wheel and tried not to think what it all meant. The car's air-conditioning blew across my neck, drying the sweat but not clearing my head enough to make thinking straight possible.

Everybody knew everybody in this small town—everybody except me. I had Mae Mae on my side, and that was about it. And what kind of help could she be? Even Gracie was suspect now. She was having a fling with President Cornfelter. And she had typed up all the legal documents, so she knew the terms of Honeybelle's will and who knew what else.

And Ten . . . maybe I had decided to trust him too soon.

"I found my own adventure, Mom," I said aloud. "But I don't like it much."

Again I thought maybe it was time to bug out of Mule

Stop. Just leave everything and go. Find a new place to live, a new job, new friends, a new life. I had been broke before, and leaving behind Honeybelle's money wasn't a big sacrifice. Inheriting a boatload of money had felt like a bizarre kind of miracle anyway—like winning the lottery when I hadn't bought a ticket. The kind of thing that ruined a person's luck for good.

Fred nudged my arm with his nose, and I turned my head to look at him. "You're thinking about Miss Ruffles, aren't you?"

His steady gaze met mine. He woofed softly.

"I can't abandon her," I said. "Wherever she is, she needs help."

Fred put one dirty paw up on my arm.

"You wouldn't give up, would you?"

He didn't answer, but held my eyes with his.

"One riot, one ranger. I guess that's me now."

Someone rapped on the car window beside me, and I couldn't help myself. I screamed.

A friendly Blues Brother was bending down to look at me through the window, smiling. "Sorry to scare you. How you doing, Stretch? You okay in there?"

It was Mr. Costello. I realized that his rental car was parked a hundred yards down the road, engine running. His partner waved through the windshield. They must have followed me out of town and parked to wait for my exit from the ranch. Today he had finally taken off his suit coat and stood in the sunshine with the sleeves of his shirt rolled up.

I rolled the window down. "What are you doing here?"

"We took a drive to see the scenery. A lotta flat land around here, right? And not nearly enough trees."

"You scared the hell out of me."

"Now, now, don't get all mad, Stretch. You don't look

so good. You feeling sick?" In a more belligerent tone, he demanded, "What's the bandage on your face for?"

"Does it strike you as ironic that you're asking after my health? Last I heard, you were threatening me."

"Hey, nothing personal."

I couldn't help myself. I laughed. Maybe too unsteadily to seem entirely rational.

He frowned. "What's going on here? You in some kind of trouble?"

Fred climbed onto my lap and poked his nose out of the car to sniff Costello. I got a good grip on his collar. "One kind of trouble I'm in is that you two are shaking me down for money I don't have and never owed to begin with."

"What's the other kind of trouble?" He glanced down toward Ten's ranch. The tallest tree and the barn roof were just barely visible over the small rise. "Is there something you want us to take care of for you? 'Cause we've been a little itchy for some action."

I found myself smiling and my spirits lifting. "That's the best offer I've had in a long time. But no, thank you."

"You sure?"

"Yes, I'm sure. I'm going back to the house now. I'm probably going to stay there, if you want to take the night off."

"You're a good kid," Costello said. "But we're getting a paycheck, you know? So we'll follow you back, if that's okay."

It felt strange to smile at Mr. Costello, considering he had been trying to intimidate me just a short time ago, but I did. I waved good-bye and rolled up the window and headed back to Honeybelle's house. Mr. Costello followed and pulled to the curb beside Honeybelle's driveway, his usual surveillance position. Parked across the street was the other black car.

I parked and put the garage door down and took Fred with me through the back gate. Mr. Carver and Mae Mae were standing on the back porch, looking out past the swimming pool.

Mae Mae pointed. "There's a prairie dog caught in one of those traps back there."

My mood lifted again. Finally, some success. "Great! Let's call Rudy and tell him to come get it."

"We already called, and he said he can't come until morning. He's busy with termites out at the Bum Steer."

"The barbecue joint? Fine. Let's load the cage into the trunk of the car, and I'll drive it out there to him."

For all the disasters I'd encountered lately, it felt good to save a prairie dog from certain death. I had a feeling it was the beginning of many traps filling up soon. "I'll even spring for dinner. Brisket or ribs?"

Mr. Carver had been looking dismayed until I brought up dinner. His expression turned hopeful. "I haven't had ribs in a long time."

Mae Mae said, "I have fresh sausage. I was going to stuff it in an eggplant with rice and peppers. It's a dish my uncle used to make. I want to try it out."

Mr. Carver winced. "That sausage of yours gives me indigestion."

"Everything gives you indigestion! How am I going to be the next Paula Deen or Martha Stewart if I don't practice my recipes?"

"Maybe this is a good time to take a night off," I said to Mae Mae. "If you're going to audition for Poppy's boss tomorrow, you should maybe make some notes about things to talk about. Family traditions and whatnot."

Mae Mae frowned. "My family traditions aren't worth talking about."

"Martha Stewart's probably weren't either, but she made a good story out of what she had."

With a grumble, Mae Mae said, "Okay, I'll think it over."

"Mr. Carver, you can help me with the animal trap."

Fred had already gone out to investigate the hissing and scrabbling going on in the small cage out by the gazebo. He sniffed it cautiously. As we got closer, I realized the prairie dog had upset the cage and was now trying to tear it apart from the inside. With short legs, a short tail, and a pudgy body, it looked like a smallish Ohio groundhog, but it had a lot more energy. It was using its front teeth to try biting through the wire bars of the trap.

Mr. Carver looked dubiously at the frantic animal. "How are we going to get it out of there?"

"I think we leave it in the trap. We just have to carry the trap to the garage and put it into the car."

"How do we carry it without getting bitten?" On top of the trap were two folding handles, but they were perilously close to the animal's sharp teeth. For such a little guy, he was looking very vicious.

I mulled over the problem for a moment and went into the house for the kitchen broom. When I returned, I threaded the broomstick through the wire of the trap. I held one end of the broom, and Mr. Carver took the other. Between us, we managed to carry the trap across the lawn and into the garage—not an easy task with the prairie dog flinging itself around inside. Fred trotted around us, as if supervising. We put Fred's towel in the backseat and let him ride along. Out of breath, Mr. Carver sat in the passenger seat. I drove.

As we pulled out of the driveway, I spotted the Blues Brothers parked on the street. I rolled my window down and pulled up beside them.

Mr. Costello had been reading a newspaper, but he amiably rolled down his window, too. "Where are you off to?"

"We're going for some barbecue. Can we pick you up some ribs? My treat."

"Aw, you're such a nice girl. No, thanks, we'll just follow along. Maybe we'll get some for ourselves."

"What about your friends? Shall we ask them?"

"Friends?"

I pointed at the other black car that had remained parked on the other side of the street.

Mr. Costello shook his head. "They're not with us. Those are the feds, see the license plate? You don't want to go talking to them. They're just gonna make life difficult."

"What kind of feds?" I asked, trying to read the license plate on the other car. At the top of the plate, it did indeed say U.S. GOVERNMENT.

Mr. Costello shrugged. "They aren't real friendly with us. Just so's it's not the IRS, I don't care who they are."

I was feeling punchy, so I waved, he waved, and we rolled up our windows.

As I pulled away, Mr. Carver said, "Who was that?"

I had no idea what to tell him, so I said, "An uncle of mine. So, ribs? Or something else? They have good barbecued chicken at the Bum Steer, right?"

We drove across town to the barbecue joint and found it bustling with dinnertime patrons picking up food at the takeout window. Out front, smoke billowed enticingly from the great black smokers. A sweating attendant wearing a cowboy hat and a splattered apron used a large mop to spread something wet on the charred hunks of meat.

I parked and went inside to ask after the Critter Control man.

"Oh, Rudy left about an hour ago," the cashier told me. She weighed about eighty pounds and had a raspy voice—probably from breathing smoke all day "He's coming back tomorrow. Unfortunately, we're going to have to close for a few days while he treats the termites. You're lucky you got here today while we still have some meat."

Mr. Carver was overwhelmed by the menu and couldn't decide what to order, so we asked for brisket and ribs *and* chicken—enough to last us for lunches the next few days. Along with the meat came a container of coleslaw and another of beans. The cashier gave us half a loaf of sliced white bread, too, and three small containers of different sauces with increasing degrees of heat.

Mr. Costello came in behind us and ordered ribs. He asked the cashier's advice about sauces and ended up taking the trio, too. He asked for extra napkins and a six-pack of beer. She recommended Shiner Bock. We waited until his food and drink were packaged, discussing the Texas heat.

"But it's dry heat," Mr. Carver said.

"It's still stinkin' hot," Mr. Costello replied.

We all left together.

While I drove home, Mr. Carver kept the tantalizing bags of food on his lap. Fred leaned over the seat, sniffing. The Blues Brothers followed in their car.

Mr. Carver watched the rearview mirror and finally said, "How long will your uncle be visiting?"

"I'm not sure," I said before seizing on a diversionary topic. "Mr. Carver, when you get your million dollars, will you go to Nashville?"

"What?" He finally gave up staring at the car behind us. "Nashville."

"Well, I suppose I could go there. I hear there are lots of places to play," he said. "Even for an amateur like me. But maybe I'm getting to be too old."

"You won't know until you try, right? You ought to do what makes you happy. You've worked hard all your life. Maybe now it's time to do what you really enjoy."

"I'd really enjoy knowing what all those cars and trucks are doing on our street."

I slowed down before Honeybelle's driveway to gawk at all the vehicles that had joined the single black car with the federal license plate. There were large SUVs and pickup trucks, their doors all emblazoned with a federal seal. A handful of people milled around in the middle of the street, but nobody stopped me, so I pulled into the garage.

Mystified, Mr. Carver and I stood looking at the crowd on the street for a moment. Nobody paid us any attention, so we took the prairie dog out of the trunk. We left him in the garage with a wet rag dripping through the wire so he'd be cool and have something to drink. Feeling sorry for him, I gave him the rest of the peanut butter and oatmeal Rudy had left to bait the trap again. While he settled in for a big meal, we closed the garage door on him.

Mr. Carver stared at all the extra vehicles and the uniformed officers. "What are all these people doing here? Is there something going on in the neighborhood?"

I was pretty sure I didn't want to know. My hope was that some law enforcement entity had come to arrest the Blues Brothers. But I said, "Let's go eat before our dinner gets cold."

Mr. Carver willingly headed for the house with me. Fred followed.

Mae Mae came out of the house and charged across the backyard toward us, arms flailing. "The police are here! I had to let them in, Mr. Carver! They wouldn't take no for an answer! They barged right in!"

"What police?" I asked. "Bubba Appleby?"

"No, it's people in black vests and wearing badges, and one man carrying a really big gun!"

"Mr. Carver, hold the dog. I'll go check." I was already running for the house, hoping this turn of events had something good to do with Miss Ruffles.

But Mae Mae called after me, "They're out in Honey-belle's rose garden!"

The rose garden?

In the slanting afternoon sunlight, I changed course and ran for the front yard, where I found half a dozen officers poking through Honeybelle's bushes. A man wearing sunglasses and holding a rifle of some kind stood apart from the rest, as if standing guard over the others. I went to him first. "Can I help you? I work here."

He gave me a glance up and down to confirm I wasn't dangerous and gestured with his free hand. "Talk to Miss Simpkins over there."

Miss Simpkins turned out to be a square-shaped, no-nonsense, middle-aged lady in khaki green shirtsleeves and a matching baseball cap. She showed me her badge in a leather wallet. "U.S. Department of Agriculture, ma'am. We're here about the roses."

"I see that." I saw other officers with gardening shears and one with a shovel. "I'm Sunny McKillip. I used to be Honeybelle Hensley's assistant. Is there a problem?"

"We think so, ma'am. We've been waiting for a warrant, and now that we have it, we're taking a close look at Mrs. Hensley's roses."

That explained the second car hanging around the neighborhood for the last several days. It had held federal agriculture agents, not more wiseguys from New Jersey.

"Can I ask why you're disturbing the roses?"

"About ten days ago, officials at the Dallas–Fort Worth airport stopped an illegal shipment of a rosebush from Germany. You know, it's illegal to falsify shipping labels when moving agricultural products internationally, and this one was particularly sloppy. Apparently, your Mrs. Hensley tried to send home a rosebush without any of the proper permits or documentation. We can't risk bringing disease or parasites into this country, so we need to check all of her plants for foreign organisms. Right now there's a particularly virulent form of bacteria that—"

"The shipment can't have come from Mrs. Hensley. She died. And before that, she didn't travel. She never left Texas in her whole life. Her roses all came from here in Texas. She must have purchased one, had it sent from Germany. The lack of permits is hardly her fault."

Miss Simpkins blinked at me.

One of her assistants came over with a rose cutting in a bag. He was a gawky young man with a brand-new uniform. "We mark 'em like this, Maggie?"

Miss Simpkins checked his scribbles on the bag and gave him a nod. "Just like that, Caleb." To me, she said, "We're going to have to catalog what we find here. It may take a couple of days. We'll have to dig soil samples and take some roots as well as cuttings. This is a big garden. And we're probably going to quarantine the area."

"The garden was her pride and joy," I said. "The family plans to hold a big wedding here soon."

"Yeah, well, it may look real pretty right now, but we can't have citizens bringing bad stuff into Texas. Think about pythons taking over Florida. You wouldn't want a wedding with pythons."

"There aren't any pythons here. Just look—it's beautiful."

"You can't always see what might be very harmful. Insects, bacteria, diseases. Who knows what else? We're going to have to check everything out." She gave me a stern yet motherly look. "If you get in our way, Miss McKillip, I have the power to ban you from the property. You and the rest of your merry band."

She gestured to indicate anxious Mr. Carver and bullishly aggressive Mae Mae, who were standing on the front porch. Mae Mae was wearing one of her frilly aprons, one that said HOT AND SPICY. Beside her and looking half her size, Mr. Carver looked dejected as he watched the workers dig in Honeybelle's garden. He clutched our barbecue dinner to his chest as if it might save his life. Fred sat on the porch between them.

"We won't get in your way," I said.

In front of the house, a police car stopped, and Bubba Appleby got out. He came through the front gate and spoke to the armed guard. Then he strode over toward Miss Simpkins.

He noticed me and made a detour in my direction with a big smile appearing on his face. "Hey, there, Miss McKillip. Y'all've got quite a hubbub going here. The neighbors are complaining. How you doing today?"

"Not so great." I indicated the mess in the garden. "These people are destroying Honeybelle's roses."

He assembled a solemn expression. "My sisters aren't going to be happy about this. Their hearts are set on having the wedding here."

"Is there anything you can do to help us?"

Bubba straightened his shoulders as if I'd asked him to untie me from the railroad tracks. "Let me see."

It turned out the handsome assistant deputy couldn't do much of anything but listen. Miss Simpkins took Bubba by his elbow and steered him out into the lawn, where she explained her mission. He almost saluted her.

I joined Mr. Carver, Fred, and Mae Mae on the porch, and together we watched the slow destruction of Honeybelle's rose garden.

Finally Bubba returned to the porch and addressed us. "I'm gonna have to call my sergeant to find out who's got jurisdiction here, but it doesn't look good for the roses."

I was sure the feds had plenty of jurisdiction, so I said, "Sorry the neighbors brought you out like this. We'll try to make it up to them."

A radio pinned to Bubba's shoulder suddenly squawked.

He lifted it closer to his ear to listen. When the communication finished, he looked energized. "I gotta go. They need me for backup over at the university."

"What's wrong over there?" I asked.

"They went to arrest President Cornfelter. I guess he's putting up a fuss."

Bubba hadn't learned the discretion aspect of police work, I guessed. I took advantage of his rookie mistake and said, "They're arresting him for what?"

"I heard the guys talking about it down at the station while they waited for the warrant. A couple of ladies over at the university say he's been threatening them."

Hannibal the Animal, someone had called him. I asked, "What kind of threats?"

Bubba shrugged. "Started out as workplace harassment, I heard. Then he got real nasty. Not a very nice boss, if you ask me. A big shot in public, but a jerk when the door closed." He hooked his thumb over his shoulder in the direction of his car. "Look, I gotta run along. Y'all will apologize to the neighbors?"

Mae Mae said, "I'll bake something. Cinnamon always makes people happy. I'll make extra for you, too, young man."

"Yes, ma'am. Thank you, ma'am. I'm real partial to cinnamon rolls." With a big, boyish smile, Bubba tipped his hat and hurried back to his cruiser.

To Mr. Carver and Mae Mae, I said, "Cornfelter arrested! What would Honeybelle say?"

"She'd say it's about time," Mr. Carver muttered. "That man was always throwing his weight around. The only person who stood up to him was Honeybelle herself."

Unable to watch the ravaging of the garden any longer, I herded him and Mae Mae into the house for dinner. Fred followed. At the kitchen table, I explained what Miss

Simpkins had told me about digging up the garden and checking all the roses for diseases.

Despite wearing quite a bit of barbecue sauce on his chin, Mr. Carver was outraged. "They can't do that! Honeybelle would never break any laws!"

"They're going to have egg on their faces," Mae Mae predicted. "This is all a big mistake."

"Why did the FBI decide to pick on Honeybelle?" Mr. Carver asked me. "Did somebody report her?"

"It's not the FBI. It's the Department of Agriculture," I soothed. "And it was a shipment of a rosebush from Germany, caught by customs, that alerted them to the potential problem. There's no—"

"From Germany?"

"Maybe Honeybelle ordered a rose from a catalog before she died," I said. "There has to be some logical explanation."

"Well, they shouldn't dig up her garden without . . . without—"

"Without asking her?" I said. "You know that's impossible, Mr. Carver. We'll just have to wait until the agriculture people complete their investigation."

We picked at our barbecue while listening to the local news on the television.

When Poppy Appleby came on to talk about the weather, Mae Mae turned to watch the screen and said, "She looks real nice in pink. And I like her hair that way, too." She put a hand to her own hair, wrenched back into her usual tight bun, not very becoming. "I wonder if Poppy has a beautician in the studio?"

She did look nice in pink, and she did a good job. She was perky, but concise and informative. Tonight, though, I was more interested in the weather report than in the reporter. For the first time since I'd come to Mule Stop,

Poppy's map pictured something other than a big, smiling sun. I squinted at the television. "What's that thing on the map?"

Unhappily, Mr. Carver said, "It's a haboob."

I had heard the word before but didn't expect to hear it in Texas. "One of those really big dust storms like they get on the Sahara? I've never seen one." With a thought for Mr. Gamble's twister obsession, I asked, "Is it like a tornado?"

"No, not a tornado. Tornados spin and are much more destructive. When a haboob comes, the wind kicks up and gathers all the grit into a big cloud in the air and blows it basically in a straight line. It's a blinding dust storm. The dust gets everywhere."

With distaste, Mae Mae said, "It's like a hurricane, but with dirt, not water."

"It's over fast," Mr. Carver went on, "but there'll be dust in your hair for weeks afterward. Last time, we had to re-paint one whole side of the house. The sand in the air blasted the paint right off."

"Are we getting one? Do we have enough water?" Alarmed, I tried to hear what Poppy was saying on the air, but Mae Mae had gotten up from the table and was noisily running dishwater into the sink.

"We have plenty of water. And maybe we won't get the storm," Mr. Carver said. "Depends on heat and weather patterns and which way the wind is blowing."

The video Poppy was playing on her screen showed a massive red cloud of dust bearing down on Phoenix.

"That's all we need right now," Mae Mae grumbled. "A natural disaster."

The agriculture people said they planned on working all night, so when Mr. Carver and Mae Mae retired, I took Honeybelle's rose notebook out of her office and up to my bed. Fred came along and snored while I read. Outside, the Department of Agriculture set up bright lights and continued to dig while I carefully read every page of the notebook and looked at all the pictures.

About midnight, I decided I had a good idea who had Miss Ruffles.

And I was willing to bet my million-dollar inheritance she was still very much alive.

★ ★ ★

CHAPTER TWENTY-THREE

Always drink upstream from the herd.
—COWBOY WISDOM

In the morning, the Department of Agriculture team continued their meticulous labors in the rose garden while munching Egg McMuffins. I noticed some of them had upgraded to hazmat suits.

I tried to put their work out of my mind. With my new theory in mind, I started making phone calls. I used Honeybelle's computer, too.

At ten, Poppy stopped by to pick up Mae Mae for her day in the television studio. I answered the door.

"What's going on here?" Poppy asked, aghast at the devastation already apparent in the front yard. She clapped one pretty hand to her lipsticked mouth in horror.

"Just a little inspection," I assured her. "Nothing to worry about. It'll all be cleaned up very soon." At least, I hoped so.

There wasn't time for Poppy to get more upset, because Mae Mae bustled into view. She was already huffing and puffing, a stormy look on her face.

"Break a leg," I said to her at the door.

Mae Mae couldn't summon any reply. She looked like a walking case of stage fight.

Poppy diagnosed the situation instantly. Warmly, she said, "Mae Mae will be great."

I had noticed Mae Mae hadn't been able to eat her breakfast, but she put her Sunday church hat firmly on her head and went out to Poppy's car with her new recipe notebook clutched in one hand.

Mr. Carver joined me, looking more mournful than ever. "Those people are still making a terrible mess of the garden. What are we going to do when they're finished?"

"We'll have to try putting things back the way they were, I guess."

"Do you know anything about gardening?"

"Not much," I admitted. "But I have Honeybelle's map and notebook. We'll manage somehow."

As if the morning couldn't get any worse, he said, "There are more prairie dogs in those traps out back. Maybe three or four."

I checked the clock on the wall. "Where's Critter Control? Rudy said he'd come back this morning."

"I already called him." Mr. Carver grew even more glum. "He said after he finishes the termites at the Bum Steer, he has to go over to the stockyard. There's a snake in the men's Porta-Potti toilet, and the rodeo people want it out of there right away."

"I can't blame them."

"That leaves us with all these prairie dogs, and I don't mind telling you they make me nervous. Once the sun gets high enough, they're going to cook in those traps."

I went outside and draped wet kitchen towels over the traps. Then I went out to the street to speak with the Blues Brothers.

"Could you give me a hand?" I asked.

They were not happy, but they helped move all the prairie dogs into Honeybelle's car.

"Where you taking them?" Mr. Costello asked.

"Over to the stockyard to give them to Critter Control. I hear there's a rodeo today, if you want to come watch."

He was using his handkerchief to rub his hands clean. "This is enough animal stuff for me for one day."

"Me, too," said his partner. "I don't even like cats much. My first wife had a cat, and that animal hated me. It used to sit in my shoes."

"Just so long as it was just sitting," Costello said, "and not doing something else."

"Okay," I said, "thanks, fellas. I'm going over to the stockyard."

"It's awful hot," Costello said. "Maybe we'll go grab some lunch somewhere air-conditioned. We'll meet you back here later."

"Fine by me."

"Take your time, Stretch."

First I made a quick stop at the Tennyson law office. Gracie was nowhere to be seen.

I spoke with the receptionist, back from her days off, who reported Ten had been in the office all morning but had already left for the day.

"He's delivering livestock over to the stockyard. Today's the first day of the rodeo. School even lets out early so the kids can go." Her face was alight with anticipation. "Are you going? It's always a lot of fun. My son Isaac is bull riding."

"How old is Isaac?" I asked, thinking the receptionist wasn't much older than I was. Her child surely couldn't be old enough to ride the likes of Hellrazor.

She had a dimple when she smiled. "He's four. His life's dream is to be a cowboy."

I found it hard to believe a four-year-old already had a life's dream, let alone one about being crushed by a massive animal, but she looked convinced. I thanked her and told her I'd catch up with Ten at the rodeo.

When I got to the stockyard, I found it transformed. No longer a sleepy outpost at the end of town, it was now crowded with people, vehicles, and animals. Not just horses and cattle of all sizes, but ponies and sheep and goats and dogs. Fred sat up in the passenger seat and looked keenly around.

I parked at the end of a row of cars and got out. Fred scrambled after me. "I don't think this is a good idea," I told him.

But he woofed a promise to stick close to me, so we set off together. I opened the trunk to give the prairie dogs some air. The trunk lid provided some shade, and there was just enough breeze to keep the heat down. The prairie dogs hissed at me. I went looking for Rudy's Critter Control truck.

The parking area was full of cars, but also small family groups setting up chairs and umbrellas and coolers packed with food. Picnics were breaking out all over. I headed past them toward the corral where the longhorns were kept. In the shadow of a large trailer on my way, I ran across a farrier putting new shoes on an enormous pinto horse. While he worked, the placid animal's lead rope was held by a smiling pixie in a cowboy hat—no older than the four-year-old bull rider I had already heard about.

Next to the farrier was a portable fence enclosing a dozen black-faced sheep. They were nestled down in fresh straw, awaiting some kind of action I couldn't guess. A grandmother in a plaid shirt and jeans sat in a folding chair. She had her hat tilted down over her face and seemed to be dozing, too.

From there, the stockyard took on a carnival atmosphere. A local Girl Scout troop was already selling sandwiches and sweet tea from a table set up in front of an RV. The Rotary Club had a dunking booth almost ready to go, with a blushing middle-aged man in a bathing suit nervously waiting to get wet in the tank. The ladies of the League of Women Voters were decked out in bright square-dancing dresses to distribute information about a coming election. The Sorghum Society had samples of sorghum molasses to give away while they sold 50/50 raffle tickets to benefit a local project.

Somewhere in the distance, I could hear a banjo and assumed Crazy Mary was at work in the crowd.

No sign of Critter Control.

In front of the corral, a school bus pulled up and disgorged a crowd of kids, all in jeans and wearing hats. They dashed off in different directions. I saw Travis Joe Hensley among them and tried to follow him, but I lost him in the crowd.

As every minute passed, the throng grew. I spotted my friend Cody from the university alumni office. He stood holding a clipboard in a milling group of students, but he saw me waving and came over to greet me.

"Hey, there, ma'am, it's nice to see you again." He tucked the clipboard under his arm, took off his hat, and shook my hand. "Hey, there, Miss Ruffles."

Fred sat down beside me, perfectly obedient.

"Looks like you're in charge of something today, Cody."

"Incoming freshmen," he reported. "We take small groups out to show them the town. The students from outside Texas think this is a real rodeo."

"It isn't?"

"Oh, no, ma'am, this is just fun for kids. But the freshmen think it's cool. We bring a lot of Alamo students and faculty here. President Cornfelter's even with us today. He's singing with a barbershop group later." Cody pointed.

I turned to see Hannibal Cornfelter standing in a cluster of men wearing striped vests and straw hats. He did not look as if he'd been recently arrested. If he saw me, he avoided my eye.

Cody said, "I think they're going to start the mutton busting in a minute. Want to watch with us?"

"Mutton what?"

He laughed. "C'mon, you'll see."

I went back to the car to check on the prairie dogs first, and they seemed perfectly fine. The trunk must have felt like their cozy den. I hurried back to find Cody. The temporary bleachers were already full, but we squeezed into a spot at the far end of the corral fence and climbed up to watch. The longhorns had been herded elsewhere, and the corral was set up like an arena with wooden chutes at one end. A group of young fathers milled around there, talking to kids and sorting out numbered cards to pin on the backs of their shirts. The rodeo clown seemed to be in charge. He organized the kids into a line and the fathers around the openings of the chutes. I heard some animals making noise in the chutes but couldn't see what they were.

The man who'd been the master of ceremonies out at Harley's Roadhouse climbed up on a small grandstand with a microphone and announced the first contestants in the mutton busting. The next thing I knew, a chute burst open and a sheep came barreling into the arena with a shrieking little boy on its back. The boy wore a helmet on his head and cowboy boots on his feet, and he had dug his hands deep into the sheep's woolly neck. He hung on for dear life. The sheep galloped straight out into the dusty space, and with every leap, the little boy slipped farther sideways until he was practically upside down. He plopped off into the dust, and the happy sheep scampered for our end of the corral. The boy popped up with a big smile on his face, dusting his jeans off, and the crowd cheered. The rodeo clown guided the boy back to the chutes. Two of the fathers ran after the rollicking sheep, caught it, and sent it back to its friends.

The next little boys fell off their sheep right away to

more cheers, and then came two little girls who had better success. One hung on until the sheep gave up and lay down, to roars of laughter from the crowd. When the chute flew open the next time, I saw the Tennyson receptionist yelling encouragement from the top of the fence. Her little boy survived his bucking sheep only a few seconds before he landed flat on his back in the dust, but he got up grinning, and the clown laughingly lifted him up into his mother's arms.

Behind me I heard the toot of a horn and turned to see a couple of big pickup trucks entering the rodeo area. One was the same pickup that had brought Trey Hensley to Ten's ranch just yesterday. I looked through the windshield and saw Trey lounging in the passenger seat, one booted foot on the dashboard, while his buddy drove. Trey was either chewing on a hunk of straw or smoking a cigarette, I couldn't be sure. Both pickups were full of teenage boys in full rodeo gear. They drove on toward the parking area and disappeared.

I asked Cody a few questions, and he explained.

"Yeah, they do the events for the elementary kids first. Next there's the junior high kids. The high schoolers have football practice after school, so their events are tonight. But the rodeo lasts right through to the weekend, so you'll have to come back for the events you like best."

"What do you like best?"

He smiled. "Well, my sisters all did barrel racing, so that's always fun for me, but really, it's the bronc riding and bull riding that's the most exciting."

"Because people get hurt," I guessed.

He laughed. "Nobody gets hurt too bad, not at this level."

I thought of Ten and his wheelchair, but I didn't argue.

After the mutton busting, the fathers turned a bunch of young calves loose in the corral, each with a ribbon tied to its tail. A mob of little kids jumped into the corral and chased the calves around, trying to grab a ribbon. It was a way of teaching ranch children not to be afraid of cattle, I could see. They all ran around yelling with delight. One child got knocked down and cried about it, but the rodeo clown appeared and plucked him up out of the dust to cheer him up.

I realized the rodeo clown looked familiar.

The junior high event turned out to be pole bending—girls on very fast horses looping in and out of a series of tall-standing poles, then galloping for the finish line. The horses were quick and feisty. All the contestants seemed to be best friends, and they took turns fixing each other's hair or holding each other's horses between runs.

There was a break in the action after that, and I went back to look in on the prairie dogs. They still looked comfy, snuggled in their cages. I returned to the arena just as the barbershop singers climbed up on the little stage to sing. President Cornfelter fit right in, I noted bitterly, except he was the youngest performer by about twenty years. He managed to look perfectly innocent as they sang their hearts out. I wanted to throw a rock at him.

While the music carried over the whole stockyard, parents gathered up their young children and herded them out to the parking lot to take them home for dinner. I figured I'd better follow their example. As I headed back to the car, I had to be careful of the traffic; there were lots of vehicles going out and coming in. As the afternoon slipped away, a different crowd seemed to be filling up the parking lot—parents and their older kids. Lights had been strung from some of the trailers, and they lit up all at once, making the crowd applaud.

Still listening to the barbershop harmonies, I made another circuit around the parking lot, looking one more time for Critter Control. No luck.

I saw Cody again, and he pointed, showing me that his platoon of college freshmen was going to tour the area behind the chutes where more animals were waiting for later events. I waved Cody off, intending to go home, but then I saw a sign for Hellrazor. I stood in the long line to get a look at him in a reinforced stall made of steel pipe. Fred seemed especially happy to see his friend. Hellrazor lowered his head and shook his horns at Fred.

A pair of mischievous little boys toyed slyly with the latch on the gate to Hellrazor's pen.

The rodeo clown was leaning against Hellrazor's fence, making sure the latch stayed bolted. It was Ten. He wore shorts and a colorful T-shirt with sneakers and red knee socks. His hat was rainbow colored, and he wore a red ball on the end of his nose.

"Hey," he said to me with a smile.

People jostled around us, but I said, "Hey, yourself."

He heard my tone, and his gaze sharpened. "You okay?"

No, I wasn't okay. I was definitely on the edge of figuring out everything about Honeybelle's death and the disappearance of Miss Ruffles and all the evil that lurked behind the polite sweet talk of some of the smiling Texans I had met, and that made me brave. I decided not to beat around the bush. I said, "The four-wheeler in your barn. The one with the 'don't get lost' bumper sticker?"

His face registered surprise. "What about it?"

"When was the last time you used it?"

"Me?" Baffled, he said, "Years ago. I can't . . . my leg. Why do you want to know?"

"Just tell me, Ten. Was it you? Monday night?"

"What are you talking about? I told you I can't . . . Monday? Aw, Sunny." He snatched off his red nose, expression shocked. "The guy who hurt you? He was riding my ATV?"

I knew at once he couldn't fake the concern he showed.

It hadn't been Ten who lassoed me and threw me to the ground. Someone must have stolen his four-wheeler, and I could guess who. I was so relieved that I found myself smiling shakily. "It's okay. I'm okay. I'm glad it wasn't you."

I had a lot more to discuss with Ten, but not in public.

He said, "Have you heard anything more about Miss Ruffles?"

"Not yet."

"Okay, we'll talk later." He stuck his red nose back on. "You just missed Poppy. She had to run back to the station for some weather thing, but she was looking for you."

"How was her day with Mae Mae?"

"They can tell you about it. Thing is, Poppy got a phone call this afternoon. From a television station in Atlanta."

My heart skipped. "Oh?"

"Seems like they advertised for an on-air weather forecaster. Somebody sent them an e-mail about Poppy, and they called her for an interview right away."

"Imagine that," I said. "Is she interested?"

"She's over the moon." Ten was watching my face with the same acute attention as when I told him my concern that Honeybelle had been murdered. Behind his silly nose, I couldn't tell if he was angry or something else.

"I hope she gets what she wants," I said with all honesty. "She's a nice person. She deserves a lot of happiness."

At my heel, Fred, who had been keeping an eye on Hellrazor, suddenly gave an impatient bark. Hellrazor responded by kicking up some dirt and shaking his horns. The little boys playing with the gate giggled in anticipation of a bullfight.

I said, "I'm going to take Fred out of here before he gets himself in trouble."

"You going to stick around?" Then he asked. "Or should I come by Honeybelle's place when this is over?"

"I'll be here," I said, as the crowd carried me away from Hellrazor's pen.

I'd taken a big risk contacting the Atlanta television station that morning. Now that the deed was done, I'd have to wait to see how things played out. Poppy and Ten would make their own decisions. I'd keep my nose out of it. But part of me suddenly felt exhilarated.

Travis Joe was at the end of the exhibition area, sitting on Hondo and holding a lariat. The saddle's stirrups had been shortened, and he looked steady up there. He spotted me and grinned. "Hey, Miss McKillip!"

"Hey, Travis Joe. You look good. Hondo won't buck you off, will he?" I pretended to be concerned as I looked up at the boy in the saddle. Already he seemed to have lots more confidence than when I'd first seen him in Honeybelle's swimming pool. The big Appaloosa paid attention to the crowd as if ready to protect Travis Joe if the need arose.

With a cocksure grin, Travis Joe said, "I can handle Hondo."

The barbershop singers had stopped at last. The smell of hot popcorn filled the air, and somewhere nearby a fiddle played a lively tune. The happy voices of the crowd rose. It was a good night in a small town.

The next person I bumped into—literally—was Gracie Garcia. For once, she looked dreadful. Her mascara was halfway down her cheeks, and her hair was a mess. She ricocheted off me and then turned and stared.

"Sunny!"

I suddenly wondered if she'd been drinking. "You okay, Gracie?"

Tears pooled in her dark eyes. "Sunny, I'm so sorry."

I reached for her arms and held her upright. "Take it easy. What's wrong?"

"Everything." She sagged in my grasp. "I blew it. I'm an idiot."

"Calm down. Is there somewhere we can sit? I've got Honeybelle's car if you want to go somewhere quiet and—"

She shook her head, hair flying untidily. "I've been really stupid. And I got fired for it."

"Fired! For what?"

The tears started to flow then, and I guided her by the shoulders out of the crowd and over to stand by the farrier's trailer, which was empty and quiet. She started talking, but I only understood every other word.

I said, "Take a deep breath, Gracie. Calm down. You're too upset to—"

She snuffled up her tears. "I'll be okay. I'll land on my feet, get another job somehow. I just feel so dumb. I shouldn't have said anything to anybody. I knew that from the start, but I . . . I couldn't stop myself."

"Couldn't stop yourself from what?"

"I told Han about Honeybelle's will."

"Han?"

"Hannibal. President Cornfelter. I told him last week. Even with the words coming out of my mouth, I knew it was unprofessional. But he was so nice to me! He wanted to know all about Honeybelle's will, and he . . . he said he was getting a divorce and needed a girlfriend. And . . . and pretty soon everybody was talking about . . . about you and Mr. Carver and Mae Mae getting Honeybelle's money and . . . and Miss Ruffles and everything! It's my fault. I'm so sorry!" She collapsed against my shoulder and began to cry in earnest. "Mr. Tennyson was right to fire me. I just . . . I feel like such a dope!"

The lights strung overhead started to feel like a kaleidoscope, spinning around us, glaringly, painfully bright. I couldn't think it all through. I felt sorry for Gracie, but a spark of anger spurted up inside me, too. My friend had betrayed me. I wanted to forgive her. I felt sorry for her emotional state, but at the same time I wanted to shake some sense into her. It could have been because of her that Miss Ruffles had been kidnapped. If Gracie had kept her mouth shut like she was supposed to, nobody would know about Miss Ruffles inheriting everything for a year.

"I'm so sorry," she moaned. "I'm really sorry I made this hard for you."

I gathered my wits and said, "It's okay. You'll be all right." I patted her shoulder. "Gracie, I need to know about President Cornfelter. He's in trouble at the university, right? He was harassing employees?"

She shook her head. "It wasn't a sex thing. He just . . . he needs to have people on his team, to get things done, to . . . to . . . I don't know . . . make everything good for the university. Sometimes he pushes too hard. It's all for a good cause, that's what he says."

"But he threatened someone? How?"

"He told them he'd fire them if they didn't work harder."

"And Honeybelle? Did he threaten Honeybelle?"

"I guess so," she said miserably. "He said if she didn't pay for the new stadium, he'd set fire to her car, with her in it. But he didn't mean that—not really. It's just the way he gets sometimes." She shuddered on a big sigh and stood straight, trying to wipe her eyes. "He bullied me, too, I guess. I'm such a loser."

I managed to say, "You're not a loser."

She tried to laugh. "Thanks, but you're wrong. Tonight I'm a big, big loser."

I felt sorry for Gracie. There was no use making her feel worse about herself. "How about if I buy you a drink somewhere?"

She shook her head. "I've already had too much. I came here to . . . to meet Han, but he blew me off. He was using me, Sunny. He doesn't want me for a girlfriend. So I'm going back to my place. I need to be alone to figure out what comes next."

I put my arm through hers. "I'll give you a ride."

She shook her head. "Thanks, but the walk will clear my head."

"I'll bring you some coffee in the morning."

"Okay, that'd be great. You're great. Thanks." Gracie gave me a hasty hug, then turned and disappeared into the rodeo crowd.

I looked beyond the spot where she'd slipped into the throng and saw Hondo again—this time with Hut Junior and Posie standing beside him, Travis Joe still in the saddle. Posie's expression was one of shock and fear, but Hut Junior had his arm around his wife. There was no mistaking the pleasure in Travis Joe's face. He was happier than I'd ever seen him. Posie surely had to see that, too.

I watched Hut Junior comforting his wife. He looked so normal. A nice man, a supportive husband, a thoughtful father. Did he have it in his soul to kill his own mother? He knew about Mr. Carver's heart medication and where to find it. Had he come for breakfast with his mother on the morning of her death and slipped the pills to her? If so, what was his motive? The sole leadership of Hensley Oil and Gas? Or had Posie done it to give her husband what he wanted?

If it wasn't Hut Junior or Posie who killed Honeybelle, it had to have been President Cornfelter, who could have given Honeybelle some kind of poison in a doughnut outside the bakery while she waited in her car. He must have assumed he'd get his stadium when she died. Only after he pumped Gracie for information about Honeybelle's will would he have learned Honeybelle outsmarted him.

Then there was Mr. Gamble, the only one who could have concealed Honeybelle's true cause of death. Because he inflicted it himself?

Either way, it was an ugly mess. I still couldn't get my

head around the idea of anyone wanting to kill Honeybelle—that outrageous but lovable woman who despite her flaws had made a big difference to many people.

I still had to find Rudy to unload the prairie dogs, so I made an about-face and headed in the other direction. Fred came with me. By sheer luck, I saw Rudy standing by a trash can, eating a chili dog. He spilled on his shirt and used one finger to scoop up the dribble and put it into his mouth. Half of it slid back down onto his beard. His hat looked more mashed than ever.

A bunch of kids stood in a circle around him, listening to the old-timer tell a tall tale.

"Shore," he drawled, in answer to a piped-up question, "I yanked open the door and grabbed that rattler by its tail and threw it in this here sack, and tomorry I'll take it out somewhere and turn it loose so it can sneak back and into your house to bite you!" He jabbed one boy in the chest with a bony finger to imitate a snake's bite.

The kids screamed and laughed.

In midchortle, Rudy caught sight of me. "Well, if it ain't the president of the Be Kind to Prairie Dogs Society! You serving tea and crumpets to those critters yet, Sunflower?"

"I have four in the trunk of my car for you," I said. "I presume you're going to give us a discount for doing half your job."

"You presume, huh? You gotta be the smartest dern customer I ever had." He polished off his hot dog in a single gulp and used a paper napkin to inadequately wipe his beard. "What do you say, kids? You want to come help ol' Rudy wrassle some prairie dogs?"

I decided I didn't want to watch, certainly not if he truly had a snake in his sack. I pointed. "The car's parked up that way, just past the farrier. A white car with the trunk open, and four traps in plain sight. You can't miss it.

"Right you are, Sunflower." He saluted. "C'mon, kids. Who wants to help ol' Rudy?"

The kids all jumped up and down and turned to follow him. He was the Pied Piper with a writhing sack on his shoulder. More kids joined the parade until there was a whole mob of them headed toward Honeybelle's car.

I blew a sigh, and Fred gave me a commiserating look. He didn't want to watch either. We walked away from the parking lot, back into the stockyard.

I soon found myself behind the bleachers, between the corral and the abandoned bunkhouse. People surrounded us, but here the crowd wasn't moving so fast. People were standing in groups, waiting for the rodeo to start again. Small children darted through the crowd, laughing.

I stopped still, looking at the bunkhouse.

I remembered the teenagers I'd interrupted when I came to the stockyard to meet the person who'd stolen Miss Ruffles. At the time, I thought it had been a place where the local kids came to socialize.

Tonight on the bunkhouse steps, a trio of teenage boys sat passing a brown paper bag back and forth. Two of them were boys who had been at Ten's ranch to practice their rodeo skills. In the middle sat Trey Hensley.

He was smiling loosely, a little drunk, maybe. Enjoying his friends. Looking relaxed and confident as they waited for their rodeo events. Two of his fingers were bandaged. So was one wrist.

He saw me staring and stopped smiling. His gaze dropped to Fred. Then he glanced over his shoulder at the bunkhouse.

"C'mon, Fred," I said, heading for the bunkhouse.

At the same instant, screams erupted from the parking lot.

"Snake! Snake!"

Whether because of the screams or the look on my face, Trey suddenly scrambled to his feet and dropped the brown paper bag. His friends shouted at him, but he turned and ran into the darkened bunkhouse.

Fred and I went in right after him.

★ ★ ★

CHAPTER TWENTY-FOUR

Pony Express Riders Wanted. Young, skinny,
wiry fellows not over 18. Must be expert riders,
willing to risk death daily. Orphans preferred.
—PONY EXPRESS EMPLOYMENT AD

It was dark inside the bunkhouse, but not so gloomy that Fred and I couldn't make our way across the large, empty room toward a door. Underfoot, the warped floor was uneven, but I went straight after Trey. Fred shot ahead of me, in hot pursuit, barking. His bark almost drowned out the screaming outside.

Trey plunged through the door and tried to slam it behind himself, but the door bounced on its hinges and flew open far enough for me to shoulder my way into a tiny room. Trey spun around to face me, trapped, the look on his face frightened, then turning angry.

"You can't hurt me," he snapped.

"Where is she?" I demanded. "Where's Miss Ruffles?"

"It's not my fault. None of it."

"Where is she?"

"This isn't your business," he insisted. "It's family business, and you don't belong here."

"Where's the dog? Is she alive? What have you done with her?"

"I didn't hurt her!"

"Where is she?"

Fred was already under the remains of a bunk bed, digging at the floorboards and barking.

"She doesn't belong to you," Trey said.

"She's my responsibility. Your grandmother wanted me to take care of her."

"My grandmother was a mean old bat."

"Mean!"

"She shoulda promoted my dad, given him what he wanted, not made him wait. Now we have to move away, and it's all her fault."

"So you took Miss Ruffles? So your dad could have Hensley Oil and Gas?"

"All my friends are here. My mom doesn't want to leave. None of us do. But my dad—it's not fair!"

"It was Honeybelle's property, her decision—"

"This is none of your business." Trey's jaw was set. "You should go back where you came from."

"Where's Miss Ruffles?"

Fred had already made it very clear where Miss Ruffles was. He dug frantically at the floor under the bunk. My heart was a heavy lump in my chest, though, because I didn't hear any responding sounds from under the floor—not a whine, not a scratch.

Trey tried to dodge past me, but I blocked his path. I was exactly his height. Maybe I wasn't as strong as he was—he had proved that when he lassoed me and knocked me down—but tonight I was more determined. In a hard voice, I said, "Get her out of there. I want to see her."

"She bit me." Trey displayed his bandages. "I had to tie her up."

I pointed under the bunk. "Get her out."

"Call off the other dog."

"Fred," I said, and Fred came to me at once. He dashed in a circle around me, though, crazy with excitement.

Trey gave up playing tough. Sullen again, he got down

on his hands and knees and shoved himself under the bunk. He pulled up two of the floorboards and struggled to reach both hands underneath. He cursed and heaved, and a moment later out came a furry bundle. He threw it down on the floor at my feet.

I went down on my knees beside Miss Ruffles. For a horrible instant I thought she was dead.

But she was only muzzled and bound into submission—all four legs trapped together by a stout rope. She rolled her eyes at me. She was breathing in harsh, shallow pants, and when she saw me, she began to struggle against her bonds. Her whine was desperate. I heard myself talking to her, soothing her, as I strained to untie the rope.

"I only got her tied up an hour ago. Don't let her loose." Trey backed up against the bunk. "She'll bite me again."

My fingers hurt as I tore at the rope, but I managed to loosen it and pull it off her legs. I went to work on the muzzle next. The rope was fastened tight at the back of her head.

"Go get some water for her," I said. "Right now."

Trey didn't need to be told twice. He rushed past me, and I could hear his boots as he ran across the floor of the bunkhouse behind me. I heard the crowd outside, too, shouting and screaming—clearly declaring some kind of emergency.

But I had one of my own. Miss Ruffles was free but couldn't stand. Was she weak from hunger? In shock? I didn't know, but it was something bad.

Fred crouched close beside her, poking her with his nose, licking her face. Miss Ruffles looked from me to Fred and back up at me again, and I saw the spark of life grow in her eyes. A second later, she scrambled up, swaying just a little. Panting, she climbed into my lap and began frantically licking my chin. I held her tight, glad to feel her strong, squirming body.

"Oh, honey," I said to her. "I'm sorry it took me so long. It's so good to have you back!"

I got to my feet with Miss Ruffles in my arms. She let me carry her. Fred dashed in circles around us as we made our way out of the bunkhouse to the porch.

From that vantage point, I could see most of the stockyard. People were running in all directions, and I realized most of them were trying to find their children in the melee. The crowd that thronged the space between the corral and the bunkhouse parted suddenly, and I saw two prairie dogs go racing down the open path.

It all made sense. Rudy had been showing off for the kids, and now my prairie dogs were loose.

Directly in the path of the two escaping prairie dogs were the barbershop singers. They scattered like bowling pins, straw hats flying—all except for President Cornfelter. He stood rooted to his spot, staring, and in another second one of the prairie dogs was running up his leg as if seeking shelter in an especially colorful tree. Cornfelter shrieked and danced, and the prairie dog flew off him and ran away.

From the exhibition area, another swarm of people came bursting out, shouting. Parents picked up their kids and ran. Men jumped up onto the tall fences for safety. Some of the women ran up on the bunkhouse porch with me, gathering their children around them.

"What happened?" I asked.

"It's Hellrazor," one of them shouted. "He's loose!"

The bull suddenly appeared at the opening of the fence. He wasn't just loose in the arena, he was loose in the public area. Hundreds of people were in his path.

The only thing between Hellrazor and mass destruction was Travis Joe, sitting on Hondo. The old horse stood very still, eyes on the bull, but in his saddle Travis Joe looked frozen with fear. His lariat slipped from his hand and landed in the dust at Hondo's feet.

Hellrazor bellowed and put his head down. He charged Hondo.

"Fred!" I cried.

Fred was already racing down the porch steps. He took a flying leap and landed running, straight as a bullet toward the bull.

Hondo knew cattle, and he made a neat escape, dodging sideways. But Travis Joe had only one hand on the saddle horn, and that grip wasn't enough. As the horse went one way, he went another. In midair, he tried to grab the fence for safety, but he didn't quite make it. He hung for an instant, then fell to the dust and sprawled there.

I heard a scream and saw it was Posie. Hut Junior shoved her out of the way and stepped into Hellrazor's path. The crowd saw what was happening before it actually occurred, and their chorused shout distracted the bull just enough that he caught Hut Junior with his head, not his horns. Hut Junior went airborne and made a crash landing against the fence. Hellrazor turned to charge him again, but Fred was there, barking bravely. Hellrazor hesitated.

I don't know how it happened, but I was suddenly in the mix, grabbing up Travis Joe and boosting him up onto the corral fence. I climbed up beside him and pinned him there, safe. I felt rather than saw someone rush past us—then realized it was Ten in his clown clothes. He vaulted into Hondo's saddle and reined him around to face Hellrazor.

I had dropped Miss Ruffles. But she appeared, side by side with Fred, both of them with their forepaws splayed, their stumpy tails high as they faced their adversary. Together, they barked, then Fred dove in to nip the bull and get him moving. Miss Ruffles took her cue from Fred and did the same—barely escaping when the bull thundered forward to gore her. Fred led her around the bull, moving so fast he was a blur. Hut spurred his horse forward, waving his hat, and together the three of them forced Hellrazor to step back away from the people still on the ground.

It was Trey who swung the corral gate wide. With that opening in sight, the dogs and Ten rounded Hellrazor up and chased him into the big arena. Trey slammed the gate shut behind them, trapping Ten and Hondo with the bull. Fred and Miss Ruffles raced around Hellrazor, herding him to the back of the corral. Once he was pinned there, Ten spurred Hondo to the gate, and Trey let them out.

I let go of Travis Joe and climbed higher on the fence. "Fred! Miss Ruffles!"

Happily, the dogs gave up on the bull and streaked across the corral to me. I clambered down, and they ducked under the fence and came up, leaping against my legs with delight. I was laughing—and maybe crying, too—as I roughed them up.

Ten jumped down from Hondo and gathered me into his arms "Are you okay? Not hurt?"

"Scared silly," I gasped. "You?"

"I heard the screaming, went to help. While my back was turned, somebody must have opened Hellrazor's gate. Next thing I knew, he was out." Ten's hands were all over me, as if making sure I was still in one piece. "I knew you were here. I was afraid—"

"I'm okay," I said on a shaky laugh, holding him, too. "We're all okay."

"You found Miss Ruffles!"

It was hard to ignore the dogs. Both of them cavorted around us in celebration.

The crowd settled down as families were reunited, parents finding their children safe and accounted for after the mayhem. We heard laughter again, and everyone moved to the fence to get a look at Hellrazor. He snorted around the corral, flashing his horns menacingly, pleased to be the center of attention.

Trey appeared beside me, the picture of teenage remorse. "Here's the water." He handed over a plastic bottle. He kept his head low. "I'm sorry about Miss Ruffles."

He looked genuinely contrite. I wasn't sure if he was sorry for his actions or sorry he'd been caught, but I accepted the bottle from him.

Hut Junior and Posie rushed over to gather up Travis Joe. Weeping, Posie clutched her younger child. Hut Junior put his arm across Trey's shoulders and drew his older son close, too. They were a family unit again.

I stood still in the shelter of Ten's arm, still trembling with adrenaline. Or maybe something else.

The rodeo announcer got up on his platform and, using the microphone, he made an announcement.

"Folks," he said, "the Weather Service says we're going to get some rough weather soon. We're going to postpone the rest of tonight's events until another day. There's time for everybody to get home safe, if we take our time and don't panic. See y'all here tomorrow night, now, hear?"

The crowd took his message seriously and moved toward the parking lot. Ten pulled me to one side where we wouldn't be jostled. I saw two police cars arrive, and the officers got out of their vehicles to direct traffic. The third cop to pull up was Bubba Appleby.

"Hey, there, Ten," he said out the window of his cruiser. "Poppy says the sky's looking bad. Y'all best get on home."

"Thanks, Bubba. We're on our way."

"Bubba," I said, "I thought you were going to arrest President Cornfelter."

"We did. He's out on bail, awaiting a hearing."

"I see. Listen, a friend of mine decided to walk home

from here. She lives in town." I was worried about Gracie. "Do you think she'll be okay on foot?"

He frowned. "When did she leave?"

"About ten minutes ago. She was . . . she wasn't feeling well. I'm worried about her. Her name's Gracie. Long dark hair."

He nodded shortly. "I'll go have a look for her."

When the cruiser had turned around and departed, Ten looked at me. "I had to fire Gracie today. Are you really worried about her? Or are you matchmaking?"

I laughed, feeling dizzy. "Both, I guess. I bet Bubba finds her." And Gracie would love being rescued by a handsome prince. "I better take these dogs home. Miss Ruffles needs some TLC."

"C'mon," Ten said. "I'll load up Hondo, and we'll take my Jeep."

"What about Hellrazor?"

"He's been through tornados and worse. He'll be fine here. I'll come back and check on him later."

I ran back to Honeybelle's car to make sure the trunk was closed. It wasn't—it was wide open, with no sign of prairie dogs, or traps either. Probably Rudy had taken them. I wasn't going to worry about that now.

The wind had kicked up, so I put both dogs in the backseat of the car. They were happy to be together, sniffing and nosing at each other. The parking lot had emptied fast, so I drove the Lexus over to where I saw Ten's Jeep. He was just finishing loading Hondo into his trailer along with three young steers.

He turned to me and leaned down to speak through the car's window. "I'll follow you to Honeybelle's, okay?"

"Is there going to be a tornado?"

"Nah," he said confidently. "Just some wind."

I wasn't sure I believed him.

There was traffic all through Mule Stop for once, but

everyone moved with purpose, and I got to Honeybelle's in good time. I let the dogs into the backyard and went out to the street to help Ten. He was opening the back of the trailer. Above us, thunder rolled in a long, threatening rumble.

"What do you say we put Hondo and these steers in Honeybelle's garage?" he asked. "I don't want to leave them in the trailer, and I don't think there's time to get them out to the ranch."

A flash of lightning made his point. The usual Mule Stop breeze had definitely moved beyond brisk to a high wind. Honeybelle's trees were hissing with it, branches waving wildly. More than the usual amount of dust stung my cheeks. I could taste the grit in my mouth, too.

I moved Honeybelle's convertible out into the street while Ten led Hondo down the ramp of the trailer.

"Tell me how to help," I said.

"Hold Hondo." He handed over the reins. The horse was still saddled, and he stood calmly for me while Ten used a lariat to wave the steers into the garage. The steers were half tame and cantered inside willingly. Hondo went with them and didn't mind the noise of the garage door going down. A final click of the door reaching the floor was punctuated by a jagged snap of lightning.

"Is this the haboob?" I cried.

"I think so. Keep your mouth closed. We better run!"

Ten took my hand, and we hurried across the dark backyard just as grit filled the air. Fred and Miss Ruffles met us on the porch, and we were soon in the kitchen, slamming the door behind us.

Mae Mae was there, staring at the television, where Poppy was delivering the weather report with a red flashing line crawling across the bottom of the screen. I couldn't hear what Poppy was saying for the noise outside. Mae Mae had candles ready in case the electricity went out. Mr. Carver sat at the table, looking ill. I patted his shoulder.

"How bad is it?" Ten asked Mae Mae, taking off his hat and shaking the raindrops from it.

"Pretty bad," she reported.

I filled a water bowl and set it on the floor for Miss Ruffles. She shared with Fred.

Mae Mae didn't question why Ten was in the house. I said to her, "Should we go to Honeybelle's storm shelter?"

Ten was grinning. "Would that make you feel better?"

No, probably not.

Mae Mae finally took a look at him and said, "What are you wearing? If you're going to meet your maker tonight, you don't want to do it looking like a clown, do you?"

"I've been a fool before," he said amiably.

Outside, the wind kicked up another notch. With it came a knock at the door that made the dogs renew their barking.

I went to open the door and found the Blues Brothers standing on the porch, looking unnerved. I hadn't noticed their car out on the street when we moved the animals into the garage, but I had been distracted. Nor had I noticed if any of the federal officers were still outside, but I assumed they had taken off before the storm started.

"Mr. Costello!" I grabbed his arm. "Come in before you drown."

"It's raining mud out there!" he cried. "How is that possible?"

"All the dust in our air," Ten said. "When it rains, we get mud."

"Mind if we come inside for a while?" Costello asked plaintively. "This weather's making us nervous."

"Welcome to Texas," I said. "Would you like a cup of coffee? Mae Mae, there's coffee, isn't there?"

A thunderous crack of lightning made her answer impossible to hear. The dogs began to bark again and dashed around our feet. The lights flickered. Mae Mae said a prayer.

In the chaos, Mr. Carver went to the window and peered out. "Looks like one of the big tree limbs came down in the pool."

Another crack followed the first, and the rain beat hard against the window. The lights flickered again and then went out. The television died with a loud pop, and the dogs dove under the kitchen table. I must have let out a frightened yelp, because a moment later I found myself enveloped in Ten's warm arms. I held on tight. If everything was big in Texas, I could only imagine how bad a Texas storm could get.

Around the house, the noise grew even louder. Lightning flashed. Thunder roared. Fred began to howl. I heard Mr. Costello reel off a string of curses, and Mae Mae's prayer got faster.

Lightning flashed against the window, filling the kitchen with a wild, blazing jolt of light that blinded us all. The tremendous crash of thunder that followed made me think the whole roof was coming down on us.

The door burst open, and the storm blew inside. Another blast of lightning flashed, illuminating a human figure in the doorway.

Honeybelle Hensley said, "What a night to come home!"

Nobody moved. Nobody spoke. The roar of the storm filled my ears. Or maybe it was my head exploding.

★ ★ ★

CHAPTER TWENTY-FIVE

Manure happens.
UNIVERSAL OBSERVATION

My mother used to say that the scientific method is the logical and rational order of steps by which scientists come to conclusions about the world around them. I had used some of her method, and I thought I had just about everything figured out. But obviously I was wrong about one big thing.

Honeybelle was alive.

Honeybelle slammed the door and unwound a big scarf from around her shoulders and threw it at the nearest chair. "A party! Mae Mae, you know I love champagne during a storm. Get us a bottle from the icebox."

The electricity came on at that instant, and the lights nearly blinded us all over again. When we blinked, it was definitely Honeybelle standing in our midst. She looked suntanned and exhilarated. She set down her travel bag and smiled. "Champagne for everybody!"

Miss Ruffles was the first to react. She yelped from under the table and burst out, barking and throwing herself at Honeybelle, who bent down and cooed into the dog's face. "My darling girl! Aren't you a sight for sore eyes! I missed you so much!"

I found my voice at last. "It's you. You're alive!"

"Yes, it's me, and yes, of course I'm alive. More alive than I've ever been! I brought you a scarf, Sunny. And presents for everyone! I love Europe! I can't wait to go back!"

Mae Mae collected herself next. She grabbed her black skillet from the stove and raised it over her head. Her face was furious. "What in the name of Sam Hill did you do to us?" she shouted. "We thought you was dead!"

"What? But I . . . Mae Mae, what are you saying?"

"You was dead and buried! They had a funeral for you! *Two* funerals!"

"Well, I . . . that's almost what I had in mind for everyone else in town, but surely . . ." She looked prettily astonished. "Surely you read my letters?"

"What letters?" I asked.

"I left them on the desk! One for Hut Junior, and one for the three of you. And—oh, hello, Ten. My goodness, what are you wearing?" She gave his colorful clown outfit a startled glance.

He spoke with surprising calm. "Where's my dad?"

"On vacation, of course. Your grandfather decided it would be best if they were all out of town while I . . . well, he said I was faking my death, but I wasn't really, not if I told y'all where I was going to be. I tried to pay for their trips, too, but Max said he was probably going to be disbarred for helping me, but he didn't want to make things too easy, so he paid for his own. Who are these attractive gentlemen? Hello, I'm Honeybelle Hensley."

The Blues Brothers stepped forward to shake her extended hand. Ten caught Mae Mae before she could clobber Honeybelle with her frying pan. "Take it easy, now, Mae Mae. Don't do anything you might regret."

"Regret!" Mae Mae shouted, fighting against him. "There's somebody here who'd better regret! We thought you were *dead*! How could you *do* such a thing?"

"Well, I *wrote* you." Honeybelle's voice rose, too. "I told you everything. Told you I'd be back in two weeks! Okay, we decided to stay a few extra days, but—here I am! Isn't anybody happy for me?"

Happy wasn't my first thought. I couldn't get my brain to accept all the emotions I was feeling. Stunned, amazed, and dumbfounded all qualified. Mae Mae had a lock on furious.

"Miss Ruffles chewed up the letters," I said to Honeybelle. "We never got them."

At that moment, Mr. Gamble walked in the back door, carrying Honeybelle's suitcases.

I said to her, "You had Mr. Gamble pretend you were dead?"

"It was the best idea!" She was alight with pleasure. "After that awful Hannibal Cornfelter marched up to my car that day and practically said he was going to light a stick of dynamite and throw it at me for declining to fund his ridiculous stadium, what was I supposed to do? Stay here in Mule Stop and put my life on the line? I thought if I died right on the spot, he'd feel terrible, and that's when I had my stroke of genius. Mr. Gamble and I had been talking about going on a vacation, so Shelby Ann drove me over to his funeral home, and we decided on the spot, the three of us, to seize the day, take a trip. It was your idea, Sunny."

"Mine?" I cried.

"Yes, you urged me to see the world. So I did! Shelby Ann and I went first, and Mr. Gamble caught up with us the next week. I thought everybody in Mule Stop needed to see what life would be like without Honeybelle around." Two spots of pink bloomed on her otherwise suntanned cheekbones as she grasped how little we seemed to enjoy her story. She was quite wounded that we weren't delighted by her plan. "Besides," she added, "I got a rather unsettling communication from the government. Why they get worried about flower gardens when there are so many problems in the world, I don't know, but they wanted to come investigate me, if you can imagine. So I thought it might be a good time to, well, get out of Dodge and let things cool down a bit. Nobody has come knocking, have they?"

"About that," I began.

Mr. Carver put an end to my explanation by fainting dead away. He fell over like a sack of potatoes, and Ten barely caught him. It took a while to get him up off the floor and into the living room, but the Blues Brothers helped. Ten called for an ambulance; I patted Mr. Carver's wrists and talked quietly while he came around again. Then we all helped the paramedics make poor Mr. Carver comfortable. The storm eased as if Honeybelle's homecoming had placated the gods. I tried to calm down Mae Mae, who had begun to pace up and down the dining room, swinging her skillet. Mr. Costello made more coffee, and Ten went out to check on his animals, and Fred took a nap under the table while the tumult raged around him. Miss Ruffles dashed between me and Honeybelle, not sure where she wanted to be.

"Somebody has to break the good news to Hut Junior," I said to Ten. "He doesn't know his mother is alive."

"I guess that's my job," he replied, looking grim. "I'm going to have to talk with my dad, too."

Ten took the phone outside to the porch, where the storm had settled down to a light, muddy rain. Fred followed him.

The Blues Brothers came over and shook my hand with obvious regret. Mr. Costello said, "I guess all the excitement of your boss lady coming home means you're not coming into money anytime soon?"

"That's right. You'll have to tell your boss he's out of luck. I'm sorry you came all this way for nothing."

Mr. Costello smiled. "It's okay. This trip was a change of scenery for us. We're thinking we might come back sometime for a vacation. Maybe catch a rodeo. We already like the barbecued ribs."

"Thank you for your help," I said. "Just knowing you were around was sometimes a nice comfort."

He finally released my hand. "You're a good kid, Stretch."

"Yeah," said his partner. "It's been a pleasure watching you."

Costello elbowed him. "Be nice to her. She's had a hard day."

I showed them out, and they waved cheerfully at a somewhat startled Ten as they walked across the backyard, heading for their car.

I went back inside, and Miss Ruffles jumped up on my leg. She wagged her stub and nuzzled my hand, then successfully herded me out of the kitchen to the staircase. We sat on the bottom step together, listening to various battles raging around the house. Miss Ruffles nudged me until I pulled her close and hugged her. I was ridiculously happy to have her back.

"Well, Honeybelle, darling," Mr. Gamble was saying in the living room, "I thought I'd move in here with you now that we . . . that we're—"

"Good heavens, what exactly do you think we are?" Honeybelle demanded. "I wanted a *fling,* not a husband!"

When the doorbell rang, I got up and opened the door to Hut Junior and Posie, both of them white-faced with anger. Their sons were not with them.

Hut Junior stepped close to me, jaw thrust forward. "Did you know about this?"

"I had no idea."

"Because if I find out you knew my mother was alive and didn't tell us—"

"Hut!" Posie grabbed his arm and pulled him back. "Look at her face. Of course she didn't know."

He brushed past me, heading toward the sound of his mother's voice.

Posie looked as if she'd been crying hard. Her makeup was gone; her eyes were red and swollen. To me, she said, "I'm very sorry about all of this. We had no idea Honeybelle was alive. None of us knew."

I didn't say a word but met her gaze steadily.

"All right," she admitted. "Maybe Trey knew. He and his grandmother thought this was a great idea—a big joke, he tells me. But when her plan backfired for him—when his father said we were moving to Dallas—Trey took the dog."

"Why?"

"With the dog gone, Trey thought Hut would get the company and we'd stay here in Mule Stop."

"But—"

Posie knew my question before I could ask it. "Honeybelle has never understood Hut. She wanted him to follow his dream, become a musician—but that was her dream, not his. He really wants to run the company, build it into something great. Music is his hobby, not his passion. Trey thought he was helping his father get what he wants." Posie looked down at Miss Ruffles with distaste. "I had just learned Trey took the dog when I saw you downtown last Saturday night. You were already searching for her then, weren't you? You looked frantic."

"She was in the car with you." I couldn't keep the accusation from my voice.

"Y-yes, I had just picked them up. Trey was dragging her into his friend's truck when I . . . well, I took them in my car and . . . and I insisted he return her to you immediately."

"But he didn't," I said. "You could have driven over here right away and dropped her off, but you didn't do that."

"No, I said he'd have to do it himself—return the dog and apologize. I thought he did so the next day—that's what he told me. He's just a boy. He wasn't thinking things through. He was impulsive, and it backfired. When I saw you with a dog later in the week, I assumed it was Miss Ruffles—that is, I assumed he had obeyed me and brought her back here. Only tonight, he tells me he didn't do that."

"So Trey knew all along? That Honeybelle was alive?"

Posie closed her eyes and nodded. "She swore him to secrecy, but that's no excuse. It was a vile, horrible dirty trick for her to pull on her family. I don't care if she wrote a hundred letters that were accidentally destroyed. She put her son through hell. And making Trey a part of her lie was just as bad—maybe worse. Hut was in terrible grief. We all were."

"You, too?" I asked tartly.

She had the grace to blush. "I felt sorry for my husband. She's his mother, after all."

"For you, it was all about the roses, wasn't it? The yellow rose that came from your family."

"She stole it," Posie snapped. "Honeybelle stole it from my grandparents' property, and when they found out and confronted her, she paid them a pittance for it. They took the money because they were poor people. But Honeybelle had no right to take it in the first place. She had the audacity to enter it in the flower show last year—and claim it was her very own. But I knew where that rose came from. She refused to discuss it with me. She didn't deserve to be president of the garden club." Posie stopped herself and finally said, "What she did—taking my grandmother's precious rose—was wrong. It showed she was capable of taking whatever she wanted. Running away like this—surely it shows she has no care for the feelings of other people."

"I think she'll soon understand what she did was wrong, and she's going to be punished in a big way," I said, thinking of Miss Simpkins and her band of helpers who were dismantling the rose garden and testing every leaf and kernel of soil. Honeybelle was going to have to explain where all her precious roses came from—and maybe she'd have to explain herself to a court, too. But I didn't say so to Posie. She had her own issues to untangle.

I said, "What about the restraining order?"

She looked embarrassed all over again. "After Trey took the dog, I thought . . . well, I didn't want you coming around our home, making trouble. I thought he'd returned the dog by then, truly, I did. But—"

"I get it," I said. "Look, we have Miss Ruffles back now, and that's what I care about tonight. What you decide to do about your son, that's up to you."

Posie straightened her shoulders. "Thank you," she said. "Now, if you'll excuse me, I need to join my husband."

At that moment, her husband was yelling at his mother, but I didn't stand in Posie's way. She went into the living room and pulled the doors closed behind herself.

I was dizzy with exhaustion. Or maybe lack of food. Miss Ruffles followed me as I went into Honeybelle's office and grabbed a lollipop. Lime. I tore off the wrapper and stuck it into my mouth. The sweetness started melting on my tongue right away, very soothing. Miss Ruffles wagged her stub.

I took her out of the office—the scene of her crime of chewing up the letters that would have explained to us all that Honeybelle was alive and only leaving town because she felt threatened—and we sat down on the staircase again. Miss Ruffles sat in front of me while I scratched her ears. "Everything will all sort itself out," I told her. "It might take a while, that's all."

She woofed very softly.

"I know," I said to her. "I'm not letting you out of my sight, either."

Fred waddled out of the kitchen and came to us at the other end of the foyer. He sprawled down on the cool floor and heaved an exhausted sigh. He rolled his eyes and me, and his stubby tail thumped.

To Miss Ruffles, I said, "You're going to like him."

Honeybelle was back, my surrogate mother. Surprisingly, though, I didn't care about the mother part of it. I still missed my own mom, of course, but somehow I felt as if I didn't need either of them anymore. I had come to Texas looking for a way to be a daughter again, maybe, but now that felt like needing a crutch or a safety harness. I had found a place I loved—with heat and dust and endless horizons and wild flowers and dogs with hearts as big as my own. And people, too. People I wanted to be with. I didn't need a mother's hand to guide me anymore. Instead I found myself thinking of having kids of my own—kids I could turn loose in a corral of calves with ribbons on their tails to help them learn to be brave on their own. I could teach them that falling down wasn't the end of the world. That flying on a zip line could be exciting, not scary.

I finished my lollipop while listening to the Hensleys shout at each other.

After a while, Ten found us and came to sit with me on the step. He put his arm around me, pulled me briefly close, and kissed my temple—a light, brushing kiss that felt right between us.

He said, "You don't look so good. I mean, you look great to me." He smiled, but his eyes were full of concern. "Just upset."

"Upset, yes. Stunned, even. I'm relieved, too, but . . . do I understand it all yet? No."

"I finally got through to my dad. They're in the Atlanta airport, should be home tomorrow. I told him what I know so far. He's furious. Didn't know a thing about Honeybelle's disappearance. He talked to my grandfather, then called me back. Gramps sent them on a vacation because he knew all about Honeybelle's plan."

"Your grandfather really knew?" I was shocked. "And let us all believe she was dead?"

"Apparently, Honeybelle made him an offer he couldn't refuse. Plus she promised she'd leave letters for everyone important. Except I didn't know anything about all this, so I read her will because the estate file gave those directions. Anyway, Gramps is hiding out in Mexico, under the belief that he's going to be disbarred for helping her cook up her disappearance. He's probably right."

"So she really faked her own death?"

"She tried," Ten said, sounding tired. "Looks like Gamble was in on it, too. They took a river cruise in Germany. Had a wonderful time, he tells me. He says they've reached a new stage in their relationship. He's deliriously in love. I almost slugged him."

I said, "He's going to lose his business, too, isn't he? He surely committed some kind of fraud."

"Yes, ma'am, he did."

"What about you?" I asked. "You're not going to get into trouble for any of this, are you?"

"My first client pretending to be dead? I hope not." He ran the palm of his hand across the bristle of his hair and shook his head. "I can't imagine doing something like this to the people you love."

I thought about it. Thought about Honeybelle and how she'd been so insulted by her friends in the garden club not leaping to her defense. How she'd been the most important person in the whole town and kept things that way by lending money to anyone who asked. But then she was humiliated by her own daughter-in-law in front of the garden club. I thought about how she had asked me to help her think up a prank to retaliate against her former friends. She had wanted to punish everybody who'd done her wrong. Most especially President Cornfelter. She came up with a plan, all right, but it punished all the wrong people.

I said, "She willed all her property to Miss Ruffles."

"I think that was intended to be temporary," Ten said. "She probably figured if she gave all her possessions to the dog, it would be easier to get them back when she returned. My bet is, my grandfather helped cook up that scheme, too. It has his sense of humor all over it."

I looked at Ten and wished I could clear the frown from his brow with a touch. A kiss, maybe. But I refrained.

He caught my look and got serious. He took my hand in his. "I made a commitment to Poppy, you know."

I let out an unsteady breath. "And you're not going to break that commitment, are you?"

"Poppy wants to go to Atlanta. If she gets the job, she's going."

"What about you? Are you moving to Atlanta with her?"

Ten met my gaze. "My place is here. I was born and raised here, and I'm making my life here. And Poppy knows that."

I found myself smiling. "So what are you saying, Ten?"

His smile started to dawn, too. "I'm saying this situation has made Poppy and me both think we've made a mistake. She thought she wanted to get married, have a family, but . . . well, turns out she'd really like to have a glamorous career."

"She could go far. She just needed a little nudge in the right direction."

He laughed. "Is that what you call it? A nudge?" He shook his head wryly. "Doesn't matter. We're going to talk tomorrow. This probably means there's going be a producer's job opening up at the television station. They need somebody smart. Somebody who has good ideas and can make things happen."

I was feeling happily dizzy again. "Sounds interesting.

Especially since I don't think I can work for Honeybelle anymore. Miss Ruffles and Fred and I—we might have to find a new home."

"I might be able to help you with that." Ten's grin was steady. "Want to have supper with me tomorrow night? Out at the ranch, after the rodeo? I bet Mae Mae will make us something good to eat."

"Are you breaking things off with your fiancée tomorrow, and asking me to dinner the same day?"

"Yes, ma'am," he said. "And after supper, we're going to take a walk under the stars, and I'm going to kiss you. Think you could arrange not to have a funny color on your mouth?"

"Yes, I can arrange that," I said.